THE CRIME OF PUNISHMENT

OTHER BOOKS BY KARL MENNINGER, M.D.

The Human Mind / *Man Against Himself* / *Love Against Hate*

Theory of Psychoanalytic Technique / *A Psychiatrist's World*

Manual for Psychiatric Case Study / *A Guide to Psychiatric Books*

The Vital Balance (with Martin Mayman, Ph.D., and Paul Pruyser, Ph.D.)

THE ISAAC RAY AWARD BOOK

THE CRIME

OF PUNISHMENT

by Karl Menninger, M.D.

NEW YORK | THE VIKING PRESS

First published in 1968 by The Viking Press, Inc.

625 Madison Avenue, New York, N.Y. 10022

Published simultaneously in Canada by
The Macmillan Company of Canada Limited

Library of Congress catalog card number: 66-15905

Printed in U.S.A. by Vail-Ballou Press / Fifth printing March 1969

The quoted material in this volume originally appeared in the publications listed below and in the footnotes and Reference Notes.

The American Correctional Association; *American Journal of Correction; American Journal of Psychiatry* ("Psychiatry and Law: Use and Abuse of Psychiatry in a Murder Case" by Frederick Wiseman, Copyright 1961, American Psychiatric Association); "That Other Helping Profession" by Henry A. Davidson, Copyright 1965, the American Psychiatric Association; American Psychological Association; Atherton Press ("Self and Society" by Nevitt Sanford, reprinted by permission of the publishers, Atherton Press, Copyright © 1966, Atherton Press, New York, all rights reserved); *The Atlantian; The British Journal of Psychiatry; Chicago Sun-Times;* Chicago Tribune-New York News Syndicate; Farrar, Straus & Giroux, Inc.; Fellowship Publications; Fortress Press; Harcourt, Brace & World, Inc.; Holt, Rinehart and Winston, Inc. (from "fraulein reads instructive rhymes" from *Halfway* by Maxine W. Kumin, Copyright © 1961 by Maxine W. Kumin, originally published in *The New Yorker,* reprinted by permission of Holt, Rinehart and Winston, Inc.); *The Hutchinson News;* International Association of Chiefs of Police, Inc. (*The Police Yearbook,* 1958); International Universities Press, Inc. (*Psychoanalytic Study of the Child*); *Issues in Criminology; Journal of the American Medical Association; Journal of Criminal Law, Criminology and Police Science* ("Criminal Justice, Legal Values and the Rehabilitative Ideal," by Dean Francis A. Allen, reprinted with special permission from the *Journal of Criminal Law, Criminology and Police Science,* Copyright © 1959 by the Northwestern University School of Law, Volume 50, Number 3); *The Kansas City Star; Key Issues* (published by St. Leonard's House); Little, Brown and Company; The Macmillan Company (*Children Who Hate* by Fritz Redl and David Wineman, Copyright 1951 by The Free Press, a Corporation, reprinted by permission of The Macmillan Company); *The Miami Herald; The Nation;* National Council on Crime and Delinquency; The National Jail Association, Inc.; National Prison Association; *The New Republic* (Charles Curran's review reprinted by permission of *The New Republic,* © 1957, Harrison-Blaine of New Jersey, Inc., and "No Room in the Jail," by Ronald Goldfarb); *The New York Herald Tribune; The New York Times;* The Osborne Association, Inc.; Pageant Press, Inc.; *The Philadelphia Evening and Sunday Bulletin; The Pioneer News; Police;* Prentice-Hall, Inc.; *Quarterly Journal of Speech;* Random House, Inc. (*The Idiot* by Feodor Dostoevski); *Redwood City Tribune; Rocky Mountain News; Saturday Evening Post; Saturday Review;* Sweet & Maxwell, Ltd.; *Time;* poem by Alan Ward, Copyright 1962 by *The Oakland Tribune; The Yale Law Journal* ("Police Discretion Not to Invoke the Criminal Process: Low-Visibility Decisions in the Administration of Justice," by Joseph Goldstein, reprinted by permission of The Yale Law Journal Company and Fred B. Rothman & Company from *The Yale Law Journal,* Vol. 69, pp. 543-594).

Preface

In 1924 two well-born Chicago boys conspired to kill an unoffending younger friend for no obvious reason. Partly just because the crime seemed so senseless, and partly because the families could afford to pay for their services, many prominent American psychiatrists were brought into the limelight of the trial to explain the state of mind of the offenders. These colleagues were arraigned against one another; the opinions sworn to by some were flatly contradicted and denied by others.

This awkward and inconclusive exhibition gave rise to widespread public comment. It came at a time when in fields other than the law, psychiatry was leaping into a new prominence and promise of usefulness. The outpatient clinic had been created, neoarsphenamine had been discovered, psychological tests were being developed, the child guidance clinic had been born, and psychoanalysis and other forms of psychiatric treatment were inspiring new hope in a field long characterized by cheerlessness and despair. It seemed appropriate, therefore, to William Alanson White, then president of the American Psychiatric Association, to appoint a special committee of that organization to study the relations of psychiatry and psychiatrists to the law and lawyers, to crime control, and to court procedure. To my great surprise, Dr. White appointed me chairman of that committee, and from my experience with its studies I grew increasingly interested in the fields of criminology, penology, and jurisprudence, especially as they involved the discipline of psychiatry. In theory, there would seem to be an intimate connection; in practice, the gulf is very wide.

Many distinguished colleagues joined and succeeded me on this committee over the years to follow. Two of the most active were my friends Dr. Gregory Zilboorg and Dr. Winfred Overholser, and it was largely through their efforts that special funds were obtained from an anonymous giver, since identified as the Aquinas Foundation, for an annual prize entitled the Isaac Ray Award. This was to be given to a psychiatrist or jurist of some attainments in his field who would undertake a series of lectures on the subject of medical-legal relationships at a university where there was both a law school and a medical school. The first award was given in 1952 to Dr. Overholser, and subsequent awards were given to Gregory Zilboorg, John Biggs, Henry Weihofen, Philip Q. Roche, Manfred S. Guttmacher, Alister W. MacLeod, Maxwell Jones, David Bazelon, and Sheldon Glueck.

In 1962, when I received the Isaac Ray Award, Columbia University was selected for two of the lectures, which I gave on December 5, 1963, and April 14, 1964. The third lecture was given at the University of Kansas on April 14, 1966, as a part of its Centennial Anniversary. This book is an expansion of those presentations.

When it came time to select a theme for these lectures, I found myself with an embarrassment of riches from which to choose. I reflected long and hard on the question: Just what *is* the problem that we are concerned with? Is it that so many crimes are committed in spite of our increasing degree of civilization? But is the incidence of crime actually or even relatively increasing? Is the problem the fact that relatively few offenders are caught? Or that they are not convicted? Or that we don't know what to do with them when found guilty? Is it that lawyers and psychiatrists don't get along or come to any agreement regarding the psychology of crime? Luck, today, seems to decide whether an offender goes to a doctor or to a prosecutor; is this proper? Is it possible to call crime a sickness when we know that most crimes are not committed by criminals but by ordinary citizens who lift goods off supermarket shelves?

What, then, really is the crime problem? Each one of us wants the highest possible degree of physical safety. We all want freedom of action, but since some people abuse this privilege and impair our freedom we have had to set up some rules to keep the King's Peace. Long ago this was done; the King set them up, and we have accepted them and restated them in our terms. In substance it was agreed that we shall each have our freedom under God and the King and the law; BUT

> *Certain people,* ideas, beliefs, conceptions, and social customs must not be treated with disrespect. (Others may be.)
>
> *Certain persons* must not be killed or injured. (Others may be.)
>
> *Certain persons* must not be taken as sexual partners, and certain methods of sexual gratification must not be indulged in. (Again there are exceptions.)
>
> *Certain objects* must not be used or removed by others than the owners because they are someone else's property. (But one may borrow, and if one is powerful enough, one may take.)
>
> *Certain services* must not be demanded from servants, employees, or subordinates.

These ambiguous stipulations and prohibitions were all tied up with penalties and sanctions for violation with intent (*mens rea*). A minor transgression is usually considered to be a private affair between the offender and the offended, and is regulated mainly by civil law. But a major crime injures not only the offended individual but the whole community; the social order itself is affected. The offender's management therefore becomes a public ritual of theatrical character. In a kind of medieval morality play, a villain is suspected, captured, exhibited, subjected to trial by ordeal, and duly executed or sent to the dungeons. This is to show the truth of the scripture that the wages of sin are death, and for centuries this was the wage commonly paid.

It is a well-known fact that relatively few offenders are caught, and most of those arrested are released. But society makes a fetish of wreaking "punishment," as it is called, on an occasional captured and convicted one. This is supposed to "control crime" by deterrence. The more valid and obvious conclusion—that getting caught is thus made the unthinkable thing—is overlooked by all but the offenders. We shut our eyes likewise to the fact that the control performance is frightfully expensive and inefficient. Enough scapegoats must go through the mill to keep the legend of punitive "justice" alive and to keep our jails and prisons, however futile and expensive, crowded and wretched.

All this we have observed for years. Many of us have participated in this dumb show many times. Now that I was about to become a public oracle, a spokesman for liaison between law and psychiatry, what should I declare about this social monstrosity? What should I emphasize or demand, remembering that I am not a political scientist or a criminologist but only a psychiatrist?

Now, a cat may look at a queen, they say, and even a psychiatrist can see that the King's Peace system no longer works. Nor need one be a psychiatrist to know that our justice is anything but just for most of the people it is "applied" to, and anything but efficient in protecting the rest of us from the rule-breakers. And since I have been watching all this for a good many years, I decided to talk about what I had seen and felt as a psychiatrist and citizen.

What is the crime problem as I perceive it? What can be done to improve the safety of the average citizen's life? What is wrong with the present system? What, in the light of modern science, would be a more rational and efficient way of dealing with the transgressing nonconformists?

Acknowledgments

I have had so much assistance in putting this book together that I tremble lest my long list of wise and helpful friends still omits names which have slipped my mind in these final, hurried moments before going to press. But well I remember how much I owe to the Honorable James V. Bennett, formerly Director of Federal

Prisons, with and for whom I have worked these many years trying to make the best use of the system we have. Since his retirement
from the prison service, he has worked assiduously toward securing
legislation to regulate the sale and possession of killing machines.
He has also been chairman of the legal advisory committee to the
American Bar Foundation's program on "Mental Illness and the
Law." The members of this committee included Judges Biggs and
Bazelon (see below), Stephen Chandler and John W. Oliver; Hon-
orable J. Frank Coakley, Professor Norval Morris, Edmond F. De-
Vine, Oliver Schrader, Jr., and the project's director, Arthur R.
Matthews. To all of these gentlemen and to my colleagues on
the affiliated Psychiatric Advisory Committee (A. E. Bennett, Karl
Bowman, W. P. Camp, Robert Felix, Francis Gerty, Alan Stone,
Gene Usdin, and Raymond Waggoner) I am indebted for many
stimulating ideas arising from our long and fervent discussions on
problems relating to mental disability and the criminal law.

In addition to these leaders, many other judges, lawyers, and
penologists have helped me both in learning what is and in visu-
alizing what might be. From former Commissioner of Correction
Anna Kross, whose consultant I was during her years of directing
the prisons of New York City, I derived more benefit than I could
possibly have given her. The same is true of her friend, the Reverend E. Frederick Proelss, who besides being a prison chaplain
(at Riker's Island) is a philosopher, a lawyer, and a wise and
good man. To many friends on the bench I am indebted for inspiration, information and friendly counsel—especially Federal Judges
David Bazelon, Alfred Murrah, Irving Ben Cooper, George Edwards, and John Biggs, Jr.—and in my own parish, Judges Mal-
colm Copeland, Newton Vickers, and David Prager. To these add
attorneys-at-law Robert Anderson of Ottawa, Kansas, and Willard
King of Chicago, to mention only two of many counselors. The
Reverend Dr. Seward Hiltner of Princeton Seminary and The
Menninger Foundation's Division of Religion and Psychiatry
was—as often before in my writing—a most constructive and helpful critic.

The help of Richard McGee of California was in his friendship and example. Captain Fred Feaker and other good friends on the Topeka Police Force gave assistance by discussing police problems with me, as did (on several occasions) my friend of many years, Superintendent O. W. Wilson, a model of the perfect policeman and a disciple of the great Gus Vollmer who also inspired me. The late Colonel Guy C. Rexroad of western Kansas dedicated the last few years of his useful life to setting up the Kansas Reception and Diagnostic Center where I have since consulted with the clinical director, Dr. Karl Targownik, and his staff on many cases and many problems.

Dr. Lewis Wheelock, my associate in Chicago, and our mutual friend there, Mrs. Edward H. Weiss, read the manuscript critically from beginning to end. Professor Joseph Goldstein of the Yale Law School and Professor Hans Zeisel of the University of Chicago read several chapters from their backgrounds of legal and sociological scholarship. Joseph R. Rowan, executive director of the John Howard Association of Chicago with which I am associated, and my wife's nephew, David Lyle of Connecticut, were very helpful. Finally, no legal and penological authority perused my manuscript with greater conscientiousness than that great public servant and social idealist, Austin MacCormick, who crossed out many things that he felt I was wrong about but underlined others that he wanted me to put in capital letters.

Among my professional colleagues I would list first the late Manfred Guttmacher, who was chairman of the committee that selected me as a recipient of the Isaac Ray Award and personally presided at my first two lectures. He and another committee member, the late Philip Roche of Philadelphia, were dear friends and colleagues of mine; by their writings, their commendations, and their unflagging friendship they encouraged me to say again what they, themselves, in life and letters had often eloquently proclaimed. My long-time friend, Dr. Frederick Hacker of The Hacker Clinic and Foundation in Los Angeles, himself the author of a book on the present subject, supplied me with several of my most dramatic illustrative cases. Dr. G. K. Stürup of Copenhagen joined us in seminars in Chicago and Topeka and demonstrated to me in Denmark his magnificent example of progressive penology. My former student and now outstanding colleague, Seymour Halleck of the University of Wisconsin, not only read my manuscript but published a book himself, *Psychiatry and the Dilemmas of Crime,* from which I have quoted copiously herein. To Dr. Joseph Satten, Dr. Russell Settle, Dr. Ralph Slovenko, and Dr. Sydney Smith of the Department of Law and Psychiatry at The Menninger Foundation, with whom I have worked for many years, I am especially grateful. They all read the manuscript and talked with me about it many times. Dr. Slovenko was especially kind in supplying legal references and commentaries, and Dr. Smith read and reread the galleys with painstaking care, making valuable amendments.

Mrs. Virginia Eicholtz, assistant editor of the *Bulletin of the Menninger Clinic,* spent many hours of creative labor first in putting the manuscript in proper shape, then in obtaining the necessary permissions and correcting and editing the proof. Our librarian, Vesta Walker, checked the references and looked up many sources and quotations. Berenice Brinker, Hilda Donnelly, Marie Douglas, Dorothy Rosebrough, Lillabelle Stahl—all of Topeka— and Helen Hogen and Joyce White of Chicago typed and retyped the fifteen or twenty drafts of the manuscript with thousands of alterations, patiently and painstakingly.

To all these people I am indebted—to them and to many others whom I would like to mention except that soon this preface would resemble the genealogical lists in the Bible—long and important but very hard to read and remember. These many unmentioned people include patients and professors, prisoners and policemen, wardens and ward-heelers, and not a few whose views about crime are widely divergent from my own.

But one of these anonymous helpers I must name. Her many years as editor of the *Bulletin of the Menninger Clinic* and her long association with psychiatry and psychiatrists qualify my wife to be my best critic. Her loyalty, inspiration, and counsel have so blessed all that I do, that it is only fitting that I dedicate this, the completed book, to Jeanetta Lyle Menninger.

K. A. M.

Topeka, Kansas
Chicago, Illinois
June 1, 1968

Contents

THE CRIME OF PUNISHMENT

CHAPTER I

The Injustice of Justice

Few words in our language arrest our attention as do "crime," "violence," "revenge," and "injustice."

We abhor crime; we adore justice; we boast that we live by the rule of law. Violence and vengefulness we repudiate as unworthy of our civilization, and we assume this sentiment to be unanimous among all human beings.

Yet crime continues to be a national disgrace and a world-wide problem. It is threatening, alarming, wasteful, expensive, abundant, and apparently increasing! It seems to increase faster than the growth of population, faster than the spread of civilization.

Included among the crimes that make up the total are those which *we* commit, we noncriminals. These are not in the tabulations. They are not listed in the statistics and are not described in the President's Crime Commission studies. But *our* crimes help to make the recorded crimes possible, even necessary; and the worst of it is we do not even know we are guilty.

Perhaps our *worst* crime is our ignorance about crime; our easy satisfaction with headlines and the accounts of lurid cases; and our smug assumption that it is all a matter of some tough "bad guys" whom the tough "good guys" will soon capture. And even the assassination of one of our most beloved Presidents has not really changed public thinking—or nonthinking—about crime. The public still thinks of it as Lee Harvey Oswald's crime (with or without accomplice). Respected and dignified authorities solemnly accumulate volumes of evidence to prove that he, and he alone, did this foul deed. Our part in it is rarely, if ever, mentioned.

By our part, I mean the encouragement we give to criminal acts and criminal careers, including Oswald's, our neglect of preventive steps such as had been recommended for Oswald long before he killed President Kennedy, and our quickly subsiding hysterical reactions to sensational cases. I mean our love of vindictive "justice," our generally smug detachment, and our prevailing public apathy.

Only a few weeks before President Kennedy's death, another brave young leader, who *also* had a young wife and children, was *also* shot from ambush by a man who *also* used a telescope-sighted rifle. It was soon forgotten. How many people today even remember the name of Medgar Evers?

And who even knows or remembers the names of any of the thousands of other people in the United States who have been murdered, maimed, raped, robbed, and beaten during every hour since? Who heeds the cries of alarm from scientific authorities, police authorities, governmental authorities, and even from the President? Commissions are appointed; books are written; research is approved. But the basic public attitude remains unchanged.

What is wrong with this picture?

Why don't we care? And if we *do* care, some of us, why not more intelligently and effectively?

The Scientific Position

I propose in this book to examine this strange paradox of social danger, social error, and social indifference. I shall do so from the standpoint of one whose life has been spent in scientific work.

Scientists are not illusion-proof. We are not always or altogether objective. We are not oracles. But we have been trained in a way of observing and interpreting things that has produced rich harvests for the civilized world. This is the systematic collection of certain facts, the orderly arrangement of those facts, and the drawing of tentative conclusions from them to be submitted to further investigation for proof or disproof. These conclusions often contradict and revise "commonsense" solutions which were the best we could do—until we learned better. People no longer have to rely upon common sense for traveling. The commonsense way is to walk, or to ride an animal. Science has discovered better ways by the use of *uncommon* sense. The commonsense time to go to bed is when it gets dark; the uncommon sense of artificial illumination has changed all that. Crime problems have been dealt with too long with only the aid of common sense. Catch criminals and lock them up; if they hit you, hit them back. This is common sense, but it does not work.

Now there *is* a science of criminology and there is a broader spectrum of social sciences. Psychiatry is only one of these. But sciences are all related, and social scientists all share a faith in the scientific method as contrasted to obsolete methods based on tradition, precedent, and common sense.

I am a psychiatrist. But do not think of me as one of those "alienists" called to the witness stand to prove some culprit "insane" and "irresponsible" and hence "not guilty." I abhor such performances worse than you, dear reader, possibly can.

Think of me as a doctor to whom people come to talk about their troubles, and talk very frankly. They may spend most of their time talking about the acts and attitudes of other people, people with whom they interact.

Think of me as a doctor who has worked for years with fellow scientists—physicians, neurologists, surgeons, psychiatrists, psychoanalysts, sociologists, anthropologists, psychiatric social workers, nurses, therapists—to try to alleviate painful situations. Our common objective has been to obtain a better understanding of why some people do certain things that hurt themselves or other people. We have tried to use this understanding to improve situations— sometimes by changing the particular subject of our study or getting him to change himself, and sometimes by trying to effect changes in his surroundings. Frequently, not always, we have been successful; the undesirable behavior ceased; the patient "got well," and he and his family and neighbors gave thanks. We rejoiced then, not merely in the pride of successful achievement and in human sympathy, but in the satisfaction of having our basic scientific working hypotheses confirmed as "true." This is the crowning reward of the scientist.

When, therefore, we turn our eyes or ears toward the great cry for help arising from the crime situation (better called the social safety problem), we tend to think in terms of the basic postulates and procedures that have guided us in responding to these other forms of human distress. But when we do, one great difficulty immediately arises:

Who is the patient we are to treat?

We should not jump to the assumption that the *criminal* is the obvious subject upon whom to concentrate our attention. For who *is* he? Do we mean, really, the *convicted* criminal? Knowing that most offenders are never convicted, do we perhaps mean to say the accused offender? But do we want to exclude the potential offender, whose crime might be or may have been prevented? And if we are seeking all the potential offenders, we surely must include ourselves.

Crime is *everybody's* temptation. It is easy to look with proud disdain upon "those people" who get caught—the stupid ones, the unlucky ones, the blatant ones. But who does not get nervous when a police car follows closely? We squirm over our income tax statements and make some "adjustments." We tell the customs officials that we have nothing to declare—well, practically nothing. Some of us who have never been convicted of any crime picked up over two billion dollars' worth of merchandise last year from the stores we patronize. Over a billion dollars was embezzled by employees last year. One hotel in New York lost over seventy-five thousand finger bowls, demitasse spoons, and other objects in its first ten months of operation. The Claims Bureau of the American Insurance Association estimates that seventy-five per cent of all claims are dishonest in some respect and the amount of overpayment more than $350,000,000 a year! [1]

These facts disturb us, or should. They give us an uneasy feeling that we are all indicted. "Let him who is without sin cast the first stone."

But, we say, even if it be true that many of us *are* guilty of committing these petty crimes, they are at least "semi-respectable crimes." Everybody does it! What about those villains, thugs in the park, drug pushers, car thieves, rapists, killers? *We* do not do *those* terrible things. It is "those people" that the police are too easy with, *those* who prey upon society and do terrible, violent things. What with sentimentalists who give no thought to the plight of the victims, and psychiatrists who get criminals "off" by calling them "insane," and Supreme Court rulings that protect the "so-called rights" of villains who resist the police, is it any wonder crime is increasing in our country?

We cannot escape our responsibilities with vehement denials or with rhetoric and oratory, nor can we assume that offenders have no "rights." We *do* commit our crimes, too. Most crimes go undetected, including ours. And even those of us who have "forgotten" our offenses, hoping they will have been forgiven by God if not officially by man, will not deny the casual experience of criminal wishes or fantasies of criminal acts. "The moral man," said Freud, "is not he who is never tempted, but he who can resist his temptations."

It was a brave and honest writer who, in reviewing the dreary Truman Capote record of one spectacular crime episode, began his article thus:

> When I was 14 I committed a series of crimes that were apparently motiveless. Technically, they were acts of vandalism. Once at night I climbed into an unlocked car, found some camera equipment and broke it. Four times, during broad daylight, I broke into homes, wandered around the emptiness, searched through desks and bureaus, made a few messes and left. Once I found a bottle of whiskey in a drawer and emptied it onto a bed. I did other things I can't bring myself to mention even now, after 20 years. I was seen twice, once only a few seconds after I had entered the house. The woman had

not answered the door because she didn't feel like it, but right after I had expertly pried open a window and dropped to the hall floor, she came out and stared at me. I told her I had heard sounds and thought she might be in trouble. More talk, more lies, and I got away. I was not frightened for hours.

This, of course, is the point of my confession: I was not scared. Normally I was a cowardly little boy and when I went out on these obviously sexual episodes, I felt nothing. I did not even feel like a master criminal. I did not attempt to justify myself to myself. I just did them. Something came over me, and out I would go. But this calmness was a form of emotion, it was an excitement beyond excitement, a feeling so powerful that it keyed all my reactions to their peak, gave me the ability to act, to escape when necessary, without panic or even fear.

But my mind. Where was my mind? Lost, I think, in the aura of madness, returning only later, when I would enter a frenzied hangover of terror and guilt. Only then would I realize, with increasing panic, that only dumb luck kept me from being caught. But the next time the feeling would come over me I would forget the guilt and the terror and go out again. My criminal career lasted only a few weeks, and then went away.

The point of all this belated confession is that I think it gives me a particular sense of empathy with the two men Capote writes about in *In Cold Blood*. When I put the book down all I could think was that a little more hate, an ounce less stability, and I might have been a murderer. That woman who caught me: mightn't I have decided it was too risky to let her live? What if she hadn't believed (or appeared to have believed) my story? At a moment like that, ethics or fear of any sort simply do not exist: the beast is in charge.[2]

This startling confession does not surprise any psychiatrist. We hear such recollections and "confessions" daily. Most people, however, do not report the derelictions of which they are consciously guilty. We repress the memory of them, if and as soon as possible. Then they never happened! " 'I *did* that,' says my memory. 'I *could not have done that,*' says my pride, and remains inexorable. Eventually—the memory yields." [3]

But I have no wish to make the reader feel uneasy or vaguely guilty about his past derelictions. We all do the best we can and, if we have made mistakes we deplore, we repent. We make such restitution or propitiation as we can. We will try to do better, but we must go on. But we should not displace our guilt feelings to official scapegoats in blind vindictiveness.

And there is one crime we all keep committing, over and over. I accuse the reader of this—and myself, too—and all the nonreaders. We commit the crime of damning some of our fellow citizens with the label "criminal." And having done this, we force them through an experience that is soul-searing and dehumanizing. In this way we exculpate ourselves from the guilt *we* feel and tell ourselves that we do it to "correct" the "criminal" and make us all safer from crime. We commit this crime every day that we retain our present stupid, futile, abominable practices against detected offenders.

Let us deal here with the unpleasant rhetorical ploy which some radio and television speakers have passed around for use in public attacks on the Supreme Court because of its recent definitions of the limitations of police authority.* "Doesn't anybody care about the victims?" cry some demagogues, with melodramatic flourishes. "Why should all this attention be given to the criminals and none to those they have beaten or robbed?"

This childish outcry has an appeal for the unthinking. Of course no victim should be neglected. But the *individual* victim has no more right to be protected than those of us *who may become victims*. We all want to be better protected. And we are not being protected by a system that attacks "criminals" as if they were the embodiment of all evil. That is what this book is about.

* "The Supreme Court's *Miranda* decision has dismayed some policemen, embittered some prosecutors, and baffled some judges. But United States television is taking it in stride. In Denver last week, a meeting of 500 district attorneys from across the country was visited by actor Ben Alexander, burly, laconic co-star with Jack Webb in the popular *Dragnet* series of the 1950s. Puffing his *Felony Squad* show, Alexander said: 'The Supreme Court says we can't interrogate crooks any more. So what choice do we have?' His answer: 'We shoot 'em. On our show the viewers will see the crime committed, so they know the guy's guilty. That way, nobody gets upset when we shoot him.' " (*Time,* August 26, 1966.)

"The defendant has 'a constitution,'" says a sprightly lawyer and lecturer in an article for *Police* magazine.[4] This constitution is "the one the nine men in Washington are always talking about." The author throughout his article refers to the Constitution of the United States as "the criminal's constitution" and implies that the person robbed or raped does not have this constitution. Why the victim of a crime would cease to be an American citizen is not made clear, but this young man is very angry because he feels that victims are not protected by the Constitution and implies that, therefore, offenders should not be protected by the Constitution either. He suggests that the victims "form some kind of a constitutional convention with delegates and platforms and banners and all that stuff and then they could draft some kind of a constitution for themselves."

This lawyer, no doubt, means well in this oration. He did not mean to sneer at the Constitution of his country. He really believes that the law is so occupied trying to do something fierce but legal to the offender that it neglects the person offended. In this, I think, he is right. The law neglects all of us. The more fiercely, the more ruthlessly, the more inhumanely the offender is treated—however legally—the more certain we are to have *more* victims. *Of course* victims should not be forgotten in the hubbub of capturing and dealing with their victimizers, but neither should the next victim be forgotten—the one who is going to get hurt next so long as the vicious cycle of evil for evil and vengeance for vengeance perpetuates the revolving-door principle of penal justice.

"Justice"

We justify the perpetuation of this social anachronism by reference to the holy principle of justice. I am told that Justice Oliver Wendell Holmes was always outraged when a lawyer before the Supreme Court used the word "justice." He said it showed he was shirking his job. The problem in every case is what should be done in *this* situation. It does not advance a solution to use the word *justice*. It is a subjective emotional word. Every litigant thinks that justice demands a decision in his favor.

I propose to demonstrate the paradox that much of the laborious effort made in the noble name of justice results in its very opposite. The concept is so vague, so distorted in its applications, so hypocritical, and usually so irrelevant that it offers no help in the solution of the crime problem which it exists to combat but results in its exact opposite—injustice, injustice to everybody. Socrates defined justice as the awarding to each that which is due him. But Plato perceived the sophistry of this and admitted that justice basically means power, "the interest of the stronger," a clear note that has been repeated by Machiavelli, Hobbs, Spinoza, Marx, Kalsem, on down to Justice Holmes.*

Contrast the two ways in which the word is commonly used. On the one hand, we want to obtain justice for the unfairly treated; we render justice to an oppressed people, we deal justly with our neighbor. (Cf. Micah.) We think of justice in terms of fair dealing and the rescue of the exploited and we associate it with freedom and social progress and democracy.

On the other hand, when justice is "meted out," justice is "served," justice is "satisfied" or "paid." It is something terrible which somebody "sees to it" that somebody else gets; not something good, helpful, or valuable, but something that hurts. It is the whiplash of retribution about to descend on the naked back of transgressors. The end of justice is thus to give help to some, pain to others.

What is it that defeats and twists the idea of justice in its legal

---

* Historically, justice has been conceived of in the most diverse terms. *The Great Ideas: A Syntopicon of Great Books of the Western World,* Vol. I (Chicago: Encyclopedia Britannica, 1952) lists and discusses many of these, citing over a thousand supporting references. Some of these authorities all of us have read, some of them few of us. But any word that can elude precise usage by metamorphosis into scores of shades of meaning is apt to be more inspirational and rhetorical than scientifically useful (see especially pages 859–878).

applications? Is it our trial court system? We would like to think of our courts as reflections of our civilization, bulwarks of public safety, tribunals for the insurance of fair and objective judgment. Should we revert to some earlier process of investigation of the alleged offender? Or is it that people confuse justice with the elimination of dangerousness from human misbehavior? Is protection from violence something obtained with the *aid* of justice or *in spite* of it?

A few years ago Dr. Frederick Hacker and Mrs. Menninger and I were in a European city on tour. We had parked our car in front of our hotel for the night. As we came out in the morning after a pleasant night's rest, prepared to take our leave, the concierge came running toward us from the hotel. "Was there some mistake in the bill?" we inquired. Oh, no, everything was in order. But would we please go immediately to the police station?

"What for?" we asked indignantly. "What have we done?"

"Oh, nothing, nothing." The concierge was most apologetic. "Not at all. But there has been an attempted crime."

"By us?" we asked, in astonishment.

"No, no, no. But, please, the police will explain. Please go."

So to the police station we went. When we arrived, annoyed, mystified, and apprehensive, one clerk after another, in what seemed to be ascending echelons of authority, queried us. Where did we park our car last night? Had we missed anything? Had we seen the molesters?

"No, no," we all said.

"Was the car door pried open?"

Again, "No."

"Was anything taken?"

"No."

Where did we come from? Where were we going? Why were we there?

We explained in laborious French and Italian, and rose to take our leave. But no, we must remain.

"How long?"

"Perhaps for several days."

"But why? What for?"

"To testify at the trial! "

"*What* trial? *Whose* trial?"

Why, the trial of some prisoners now languishing in jail—"*in vinculo.*" The officer illustrated this state of detention by clutching his own wrists with his opposing hands.

We began to be desperate. We said we knew no prisoner, we had seen no molester, we had suffered no damage, we had made no charge. So far as we knew, nothing had happened. Again we painfully "explained" and sought to leave.

Ah, but if the alert and clever police had not *seen* the marauder *about to open the Americans' car* and pounced upon him instantly, the Americans would have indeed suffered loss. But bravo! the *police!*

All right. Fine! Alert policemen, crime prevented. No crime. No trial. So, now, let's go!

Unfortunately not possible.

But why?

"Ah" (solemnly), *"Giustizia! Giustizia!"* (Justice! Justice!)

So for the sake of "justice" we must remain! And remain we did, continuing to argue and gesture. We looked angry and we looked sad. More police officials were called from upstairs offices. We identified ourselves again thoroughly and painstakingly. We laid before them our passports and identification. I certified that I was an American citizen, a physician, a psychiatrist, a member of the American Medical Association and of the American Psychiatric Association, the Masonic Lodge and the American Contract Bridge League. I even submitted a letter from my friend Commissioner Bennett of the United States Department of Justice.

None of this information seemed to have the slightest influence. *"Giustizia!"* they would murmur to one another and to us, shaking their heads significantly and remaining motionless. As good citizens surely we desired to see the law upheld. Would we have the prisoner languish in jail untried? Is it not the right of the accused to confront his accusers and to cross-examine? (But we had not accused.)

The abstract concept of justice never seemed to me so ridiculous. And I must confess that at the moment it was not the unjust plight of the prisoner that concerned me but the unjust plight of the innocent nonvictims!

Dr. Hacker suddenly recalled that he was carrying with him a large, bronze, deputy sheriff's badge from a southern California county where he was a consultant to the county court. With a magnificent flourish he tossed this badge, face up, upon the police desk and pointed.

The effect of this gesture was electric. The chief of police and his assistants leaped to their feet and saluted. The chief grasped both my friend's hands, then seized him and kissed him on both cheeks. All officers smiled broadly and bowed to each of us. With gestures of respect and friendliness they pointed to the door. As colleagues in the enforcement of the law we could be granted a special favor.

Justice (!) had prevailed.

Of course this ludicrous incident does not do justice to justice. One might well ask what would have happened if we actually had lost some property. What would have happened if we had been less insistent, less self-assured, less prosperous than we seemed to these simple but officious men? It might have been we who invoked the principle of justice for a better disposition of the matter.

But the paradox is that we all extol justice as a principle when it is working against someone we do not like. Justice was not invented, as we think, to protect the weak but to protect the King's Peace; it was belatedly applied—in a measure—to the protection of (some of) the King's subjects.

Edmond Cahn made this brilliantly clear in various essays which he had intended to publish in a book entitled *The Meaning of Justice*. In it he intended to demonstrate that "Justice is not a collection of principles or criteria. . . . Justice is the active process of the preventing or repairing of injustice."

"Why is it," he asked, "that able minds of some two centuries have turned against the concept of justice and denigrated it? How account for the wide gap between justice according to the philosophers (a superfluous if not entirely irrelevant term) and justice according to the people (a vital necessity of their lives)? Surely the authors we have mentioned have not been callous to ideal values, nor have they been preaching the kind of academic cynicism that certain professors affect in every generation in order to impress unsophisticated students. If men of the caliber of Hume, Bentham, and Marx shock us by disparaging justice it is not because they are engaged in striking classroom poses. It is rather because the conceptions of justice which they find about them are genuinely inadequate." [5]

Unhappily, then, we must recognize that, in practice, justice does not mean fairness to all parties. To some people the law is an inexorable, inscrutable Sinai—the highest virtue is to submit unquestioningly. But to others, law and the principle of justice should, as Cahn wrote, "embody the plasticity and reasonableness that Aristotle praised in his famous description of equity. He said: 'Equity bids us be merciful to the weakness of human nature; to think less about the laws than about the man who framed them, and less about what he said than about what he meant; not to consider the actions of the accused so much as his intentions, nor this or that detail so much as the whole story; to ask not what a man is now but what he has always or usually been. It bids us remember benefits rather than injuries, and benefits received rather than benefits conferred; to be patient when we are wronged; to settle a dispute by negotiation and not by force.' " [6]

CHAPTER 2

Who Is to Blame?

The trend of the preceding chapter was the uncertainty of where to begin in solving the crime problem. Upon whom or what should we focus our diagnostic lenses? In theory it is public safety we want, and justice—whatever that is. In theory it is crime that we don't want. But crime we have and injustice we have, and where shall we look for the remedy? Whom shall we blame for the injustice of practical justice? Who is responsible for our continuing crimes against criminals? Who "lets" public safety deteriorate as civilization and scientific discovery increase?

All of us in approaching problems of daily living, problems in our families or our occupations, try to find the most expedient, the most effective, the most sensible thing to do about these problems. We sit and ponder them, we confer, we consult. We put our heads together in little quarterback huddles—or big ones—a dozen times a day. We try to decide what can be done and how best to do it. Families do it; engineers, doctors, hospital staffs, plumbers, businessmen, and salesmen do it. So do schoolteachers, bankers, merchants, railroad officials, and government officials. *Everybody* does it. Everybody, that is, except our representatives in the juridical system.

In juridical thinking one does not ask what will work, or what will be useful, or what will be the most economical or the most effective. All "principles" but one are disregarded; one asks only, "What is legal?" What will comply with the fantastic, distorted, historic notion of abstract justice as expressed in precedent? How shocking this principle of changelessness is to those who look constantly for improvements through change in a dynamic world! Justice Oliver Wendell Holmes once said, "It is revolting to have no better reason for a rule of law than that it was so laid down in the time of Henry IV. It is still more revolting if the grounds upon which it was laid down have vanished long since, and the rule simply persists from blind imitation of the past." [1] How can I describe the reaction of scientists to the principle that there must be no change in a procedure no matter how ineffective and obsolete it has become?

Behavior, both orderly and disorderly, *can* be scientifically studied and appraised. The disciplines of psychology, psychiatry, sociology, ethnology, genetics, anthropology, and ekistics can be and are constantly being applied to the behavior of human beings. There really *is* such a thing as behavioral science.

But if the public scarcely believes this, the courts believe it not at all. Research studies in the field go on daily in a thousand places. Many facts and principles have been discovered; more are constantly being discovered. But the findings are of little interest to the legal establishment; no question of justice is involved.

Justice in Science

The very word *justice* irritates scientists. No surgeon expects to be asked if an operation for cancer is just or not. No doctor will be reproached on the grounds that the dose of penicillin he has prescribed is less or more than *justice* would stipulate.

Behavioral scientists regard it as equally absurd to invoke the question of justice in deciding what to do with a woman who cannot resist her propensity to shoplift, or with a man who cannot repress an impulse to assault somebody. This sort of behavior has to be controlled; it has to be discouraged; it has to be *stopped*. This (to the scientist) is a matter of public safety and amicable coexistence, not of justice.

I do not mean that science discards value systems. Doctors do not like to be beaten up or robbed or cheated any more than lawyers do. But the question doctors might ask is not what would be *just* to do to this dangerous fellow, this dishonest woman, but, as in the case of a patient with compulsions, what would be effective in deterring them! That he or she has broken the law gives us a technical reason for acting on behalf of society to try to do something that will lead him to react more acceptably, and which will protect the environment in the meantime. And this is exactly what the present system based on the concepts of justice and precedent *fails* to do.

What *is* this system of justice that does its job so poorly, after all these years of trial and error? (No pun intended.) Who is responsible for the continuation of an ineffective, expensive, "unjust," and barbarous method of dealing with delinquency that produces only more delinquency? Where are our lawyers? They know how wretched it is. Where are our judges? They wrestle with its creaking machinery daily. Where are our scientists, who ought to be offering some remedies? Are they really trying to help the lawyers or do they disdainfully ignore them as hopelessly argumentative or scholastic? And the responsible, intelligent press—is it really indifferent to the abuses and failures of the system? Or has it become cynical about the possibility of any constructive change?

The lawyers, the judges, the scientists, the editors—all of these are honorable men. All are intelligent men. They know the system is rotten and they know it is not working. Many of them want to see it change. Many of them are working to bring this about. But they encounter great difficulty, on the one hand, from rigidities in state constitutions, and even greater rigidities in the attitude of the public.

In a way, everyone desires a peaceful community. We want the social order preserved, bad actors locked up, violence curbed, and safety insured in our streets and parks and homes. But are we getting it? Are we demanding improvement? And why not?

We cannot blame it all on the lawyers, judges, and policemen. Perhaps they deserve a little of the blame; likewise the press. We really cannot blame the public for not joining in a crusade if people do not know rather definitely what the issue is. Everybody knows a little about crime, the police, the trial court, the jury system, the prison, the parole board. But most people actually do not know much about crime—only about what they glean from the newspapers and crime stories. And the fact is that many newspapermen do not know very much about it either.

People in the communication businesses want a better world; they also want to please the public. And the public loves drama. It loves a fight. Can we make the fight against an ineffective penology as exciting as television dramatizations of the manhunt?

Take this newspaper clipping, which happens to be one at hand from the *Kansas City Star* for August 21, 1961, entitled "Brushes with the Law."

Note first of all the headline: "Brushes."

Some readers might call them that. Perhaps some lawyers would. But certainly social scientists could not accept this metaphor. These "brushes" are dreary, repetitious crises in the dismal, dreary life of one of the miserable ones. They are signals of distress, signals of failure, signals of crises which society sees primarily in terms of *its* annoyance, *its* irritation, *its* injury. They are the spasms and struggles and convulsions of a submarginal human being trying to make it in our complex society with inadequate equipment and inadequate preparation.

Please read it—even though it is a *dull* case. You may be bored before you finish. Nothing exciting happens, just "brushes with the law." Brushes that cost the city and the state a good deal of money; brushes that kept a good many people busy doing the prescribed but futile things that the law calls for; brushes that spelled agony and despair and failure for one guy—a worthless guy maybe—but a human being.

Read it and weep:

SERIES OF BRUSHES WITH THE LAW LAUNCHED AT AGE II
BY RICHARD J. OLIVE

Policemen knew him as "Crow." Any friends he had called him "Pookie." Last Thursday night, Talmadge Woodson, 25 years old, staggered from the Paseo market with a bullet hole in his stomach and another in his back. He had exchanged shots with Kenneth Spring, 37, of 4140 The Paseo, after taking about $50 from the cash register and a money bag containing about $150. Spring, who was wounded in the stomach, had been caring for the store, owned by Mrs. Anthony T. Mangiaracina.

Woodson fell into the street but whichever expression was on his face was hidden by a Halloween mask he wore. Ironically the mask bore a ghoulish face with a contorted look of agony.

Less than a half hour later he died at the General Hospital. . . .

At the age of 25 Woodson left behind a police file an inch and a half thick that documented years of violence and criminal activity. Since the age of 11, "Little Crow," as he was first called, compiled more than 100 arrests. . . .

Detective Harold Kirchoff, who has been working in the Sheffield station eight years, said, "Ever since I've been out here 'Crow' was a name you always heard. He was always up to something."

The police here were introduced to "Crow" in August, 1950, shortly after the boy's 11th birthday. He had been turned over to juvenile authorities for larceny and destruction.

Woodson's name crossed the desks of juvenile authorities eight months later. He was being investigated for larceny.

A statement signed by Woodson, his older brother, and a friend reads: "(We) broke the window to a parked truck in front of 801 Admiral Boulevard, and stole a hydraulic jack and took it down to a garage at Eighth and Charlotte and sold it to a man for $3.50 . . . we then took this money and split it between us."

Woodson's inauspicious career had been launched. In 1952 it was bicycle theft. In 1953 (at the age of 13), it was burglary. In 1954, he was declared "incorrigible." In 1955, he was under investigation for purse snatches and armed robbery.

In January, 1956, Woodson, still a juvenile, was under investigation for homicide. A man whom Woodson said was in the area of Eighth and Charlotte streets looking for a girl had been fatally stabbed. Police felt "Crow" was the killer.

In March, he appeared in a juvenile court hearing on the charges and was cleared. In April, 1957, he was sentenced to the Kansas State Industrial Reformatory in Hutchinson, for one to five years. While he was in the reformatory, his 17 juvenile arrests gave way to a clean slate. He was an adult in June, 1957.

On October 15, 1958, he was released on parole: to the amazement of police, once again he returned to the streets. Before May, 1963 —when he was tried under the habitual criminal act and sentenced to three years at Jefferson City for stealing—Woodson had been arrested 81 times.

He served half his term at the penitentiary, and was released on parole January 21, of this year.

On January 22, he was under arrest. He was charged with stealing under $50, and sentenced to one year at the Jackson County jail.

Less than two weeks ago, Woodson was arrested for holding up a Yellow Cab in the rear of the Queen of the World Hospital. The driver, 64-year-old Daniel L. Williams, positively identified "Crow" as the man who held a pistol on him, while an accomplice took his billfold.

The city charged Woodson with first-degree robbery. Magistrate Robert Berrey III set his bond at $4,000, which Woodson made. The hearing was to have been last Thursday.

Crow did not appear at magistrate court and a warrant was issued for his arrest. Thursday night he was killed.

This newspaper reporter was unusually thorough. Telling his story carefully, he resisted the temptation to make anything sensational out of it. He described a fellow who seemed to have spent his life going from one difficulty into another, into the jail and out of it, only to get back in again, like one caught in a revolving door. It ended in death. The story reflects no credit to *us*, no credit to Kansas City, no credit to the system. The grinding mills of the law did nothing for Crow; they cost Kansas City a lot of money, mostly wasted. It gave a score of people something to do, mostly useless. One might wonder what could have been done early in this chap's life to have protected his victims better.

Surely there ought to be a better way to deal with this kind of incompetence and irresponsibility and dangerousness. Arrest him, sentence him, lock him up a while, and then loose him into the current again and let him try to swim. If he "keeps out of trouble" we lose sight of him. If he flounders into "crime" again, he reappears in the limelight for a brief moment.

Criminals are rarely viewed in the long perspective. Neither is our system, nor our philosophy. News is news when it happens. The hearing on the trial of the accused culprit is a local one-time show.

Now look at another newspaper report of some "brushes with the law." I cite it exactly as it appeared (except for some minor deletions) in the Denver *Rocky Mountain News* of January 27, 1965:

> A 21-year-old Denver man with 12 previous traffic violations was granted probation after an accident in which two teenage girls were killed.
>
> Superior Court Judge Paul V. Hodges placed Dennis Ruben Vigil of 525 Grape St. on probation, setting aside a $300 fine and 90-day jail sentence imposed in Municipal Court.
>
> Vigil's driver's license had been suspended twice before his car hurled off the Valley Highway overpass at Santa Fe Dr. July 22, 1962, plunging 35 feet to the road below.
>
> One of the girls who died, Jean Roybal, 17, of 750 Irving St. pleaded for Vigil when she regained consciousness briefly in Denver General Hospital. "Don't blame Dennis for what happened," she told her grief stricken mother. "It wasn't his fault. He wasn't going fast."
>
> Witnesses told police Vigil was driving 80 to 85 miles an hour in the rain. Vigil claimed he was traveling 55 miles an hour, the maximum limit, when his car hit a slick spot and went out of control, ripping out 62 feet of guard rail as it went over the side.
>
> It took police and firemen 20 minutes to remove Jean, Vigil, and

the body of Jean's sister, Dolores, 19, from the wreckage. Vigil suffered only minor injuries.

Judge Hodges said he granted probation because "the accident apparently wasn't his fault" and because it was recommended by the Denver Probation Department.

Vigil is a nephew of Probation Officer Sam Passarelli. . . .

Vigil carried no auto insurance. His traffic record shows one previous accident involving an injury for which he was not charged.

Previous traffic violations include: Speeding 38 miles an hour in a 25-mile zone, running a red light, careless driving, speeding 38 miles an hour in a 30-mile zone, running a stop light and three citations for driving with his license suspended. Vigil was ticketed once for driving without signal lights, and three times for muffler violations. He received probation from Municipal Judge James C. Flanigan last Sept. 26 after pleading guilty to driving while his license was suspended following a 2-death accident.

Vigil's father was killed in a one-car accident Nov. 15, 1961, when his auto skidded out of control on U.S. Highway 87 a half mile north of E. Hampden Ave.

Another case—this time only *one* "brush with the law":

In 1925, Stephen Dennison, 16, a boy from a broken home, swiped $5 worth of candy from a roadside candy stand near Salem, N.Y. For that one act, the boy drew a ten-year burglary sentence—and was later buried alive for 34 years by an avalanche of injustice that matches the nightmare novels of Franz Kafka.

"Through a tragic error," ruled Judge Richard S. Heller for the New York Court of Claims last week, Prisoner Dennison was wrongly classified as a *low-grade moron* in 1927, declared *criminally insane* in 1936, and illegally confined without judicial review in a state asylum until 1960, when his half brother finally managed to win his release on a writ of habeas corpus. "Society labeled him as subhuman," declared Judge Heller, "placed him in a cage with genuine subhumans, drove him insane, and then used insanity as an excuse for holding him indefinitely in an institution with few, if any, facilities for genuine treatment and rehabilitation of the mentally ill."

After having stolen 24 years of Dennison's life, New York obeyed the letter of the law on his release in 1960. The state duly returned his sole possession: the two pennies taken from him when he entered prison. Now a gray-haired, unemployed man of 57, Dennison understandably sued New York for $500,000 in damages. Last week the Court of Claims awarded him $115,000—freely admitting, in Judge Heller's words, that "no sum of money would be adequate to compensate the claimant for the injuries he suffered and the scars which he obviously bears." [2]

These three cases illustrating "brushes with the law" suggest something of the range of failure in the legal process. In a sense, these are three faces of justice: in the first, a cat and mouse game leading to repetitive arrests and incarcerations, but with no constructive response to the personality disturbance that must underlie such an accumulation of transgressions; in the second, a minimizing of a serious threat to the safety of the innocent; and in the third, an example of inflating to unbelievable proportions a minor piece of delinquency. Each case contains its own tragedy, and probably all were avoidable.

Most criminal cases are not very dramatic, and most offenders, if they are caught, convicted, and labeled "criminal," pretty clearly demonstrate thereby their incompetence. The smart fellows are more apt to "get away with it." But the great mass of offenders are nobodies. Their lives are dull; their escapades are dull; their trials are dull. Even their crimes do not get them much attention from anybody except the police, the judges, and the jailers. Most offenders commit their offenses and slip into anonymity, in or out of jail. Most of them are not detected. They are not tried. They are not "punished."

This item appeared in the *Athens* (Greece) *Daily,* June 13, 1966:

Sydney, July 12 (Reuters): A 19-year-old youth, accused of attempting to murder Australian labour opposition leader Arthur Calwell, allegedly told police: "I realised that unless I did something out of the ordinary I would remain a nobody all my life."

The reader is almost certainly not a Mr. or Mrs. Anonymous and may find it hard to realize how it feels to be a nobody, to have to expect to remain all one's life with few friends, few pleasures, hemmed in by circumstances, and feeling ignored or despised by everyone.

"Half of the harm that is done in this world," said the psychiatrist in T. S. Eliot's *The Cocktail Party,*

> Is due to people who want to feel important.
> They don't mean to do harm—but the harm does not interest them.
> Or they do not see it, or they justify it
> Because they are absorbed in the endless struggle
> To think well of themselves.[3]

It is not likely to occur to the average peaceable citizen to relieve his self-deprecatory opinions by a crime. In his social class that is not the usual thing, even if one sometimes feels like doing it. Problems one has, yes, indeed—economic, marital, political, physiological, psychological—but not overwhelming criminal temptations.

Oh, he might stoop to accepting a small and subtle bribe, or making a mild, temporary embezzlement, or doing a little fudging on the expense account, or indulging in a little private slander or intrigue or blackmail. But crime with a capital "C"—no. No temptation for him at all. One does not need to go around shooting people, although this was once socially condoned, providing the people were Indians. One can charge forth on a campaign of shooting animals, which is still condoned by many, but some money and equipment are required. Hunting is not violent enough to satisfy the internal yearnings of some; vandalism, fighting, bullying women or children, and outright lawbreaking of one kind or another may be necessary. Yes, necessary; necessary to the psychological economy of some people.

Of course, these methods entail the risk of trouble, but if it comes this will be *external* trouble; *internal* troubles will have been assuaged. The individual will no longer go unnoticed, unexpressed, ignored, and even despised. He will have made *cou.**

In the eyes of the law all of these acts are of a kind, with but one motive—the wish to break the law. Why the wish to do so becomes so powerful as to elude all the existing controls, internal and external, is of no interest to the law or the representatives of the law. What various forces combine to determine a particular antisocial, illegal act—this is no concern of the law. What internal pressures and external events led up to the criminal act as a logical link in a continuing chain of behavior and adaptation—this is not a legal question nor a legal concern. The law is concerned only with the fact that its stipulations were *broken,* and the one who breached them—provided he can be convicted—must pay the penalty. Having erred, he must be officially and socially hurt—"punished." Then everything will be all right again. "Justice" will have been done.

On the other hand, science, represented by psychiatry, looks at all such instances of lawbreaking as pieces in a total pattern of behavior. It asks, Why? What was behind the discovered act which brought the matter to our attention? What pain would drive a man to such a reaction, such a desperate outbreak, and such a deliberate gamble?

Could not a better way be found for dealing with despair and ignominy and poverty and frustration and bitterness than to let pressures mount until they result in social aggression and irreversible tragedy?

Interruption

At almost this exact point, I was interrupted in the preparation of the first draft of this manuscript. Over the radio came the announcement that one of the anonymous, ignominious, embit-

---

* The Sioux Indians and some other tribes used to make *cou* by a dash into the most dangerous combat areas, sometimes getting out with a lock of hair or a piece of legging or a button (not necessarily a scalp) as proof of the possessor's courage, bigness, importance. Such an act wiped out all suspicion that one was an insignificant, impotent, incompetent, merely tolerated member of the group.

tered, disorganized attention-seekers described earlier had burst into the limelight, fluttered like a moth for a few seconds in the incandescence of horrified world attention, and vanished from sight, leaving behind him a hundred million shocked, grief-stricken mourners for a fallen President.

Thwarted in repeated efforts to have someone pay attention to his puffed-up insignificance, this nonentity had concealed himself in a warehouse whence he could overlook thousands of his despised fellow citizens. Far below him they were singing hosannas to their radiant, beloved young leader who, despite sneers and smears from a few *other* envious nonentities, had ridden smilingly in an open car through happy throngs of admirers. From his point of vantage far above, the insignificant but ambitious misfit watched intently through a telescope until the right moment.

The little man in the warehouse was no longer anonymous.

CHAPTER 3

Crimes against Criminals

"The laws are like cobwebs: where the
small flies are caught, and the great
break through."   —*Anacharsis*

What *is* our system for the prevention of crime and for the
protection of the public from evildoers?

How does it work? And how or where does it fail? Why, in
spite of it, does the incidence of crime seem to increase?

Is the system something good in theory but increasingly inadequate in practice in spite of continued efforts these past forty-odd
years by the United States Supreme Court (and others) to repair
and improve it?

Or is it being incorrectly applied through ignorance of the law
regarding scientific discoveries of the past fifty years?

Or is it inherently defective, obsolete, deserving only to be discarded?

*I suspect that all the crimes committed by all the jailed criminals
do not equal in total social damage that of the crimes committed
against them.* In our vengeful ferocity toward this miserable minority of offenders, we overlook the major contributors to crime who
operate openly, successfully, and undeterred. We are busy pursuing
and persecuting thousands of failures and blunderers in order to
capture, confine, or execute a few conspicuous monsters who set the
pace for a code that has to do mainly with petty thieves, bungling
burglars, pill peddlers, and mugs. We neglect intelligent, scientific

methods of effective law enforcement that would protect us from them and from the much larger group of professionals.

A scientific adviser employed by President Lyndon Johnson's Commission on Law Enforcement and the Administration of Justice was recently quoted as saying in substance that our system of crime control is an unplanned product of history, and shows this fact plainly.[1] Year after year the nation's police forces and criminal courts have steamed ahead, never knowing whether the measures they take against crime are effective and meaningful or a total waste of time, or worse. Said the executive director of the Commission, James Vorenberg, "We lack even the most essential knowledge about crime. . . . We know very little—much less than most people think and newspaper stories would suggest—about the volume, kinds, and effects of crime and who the perpetrators and the victims are."[2]

I propose that we examine the whole juridical system in its functioning from the time a man is arrested to the time he is released from prison. Let us look at the actual process rather than merely at the philosophy of the police, the lawyer, the judge, or the psychiatrist. For these men do what they have to do within the limits of their assigned roles according to their best lights.

In the course of examining the "system," I shall cite observations and opinions and cases both from my own experience and from that of generous colleagues. Some of these will seem shocking—at least they do to me. But they are cited not to indict or to reflect upon any particular judge or lawyer or colleague. They are just vivid illustrations of things that seem to keep happening which I do not think ought to happen this way.

This book is not intended to be an answer, but a question—and an invitation to discussion and research and mutual decision. Even those involved somewhere in our system of dealing with offenders are rarely acquainted with what goes on in other parts of the system. Few judges ever visit prisons. Few wardens ever work with attorneys. Few jurymen know much about the internal difficulties of the police force. Few policemen see the reports of the prison psychiatrists.

Grist for the "System"

Before attempting to describe the operations of the system in some detail, let us examine for a minute the kind of material the system deals with. It's not what the average newspaper reader thinks. The chaps who keep the police busy and the jails full and the judges occupied are not glamour boys. They are not, as a rule, sinister-looking hoods or shrewd, wily slickers. The run-of-the-mill offender is an ordinary-looking fellow, usually poor and poorly dressed, almost always friendless, very frequently a Negro. He is *probably not* a first offender.

But let us take a first offender as a sample. Of course he *could* be all sorts of persons. But because he *is* a "first time" man we assume that his life until now has been smooth, dull, uneventful—an "average" citizen not unlike the rest of us; perhaps less comfortable, with more exposure to hard work and rough weather and less need to pay income taxes and buy theater tickets, and possibly less supported in morale by family or social groups, and likewise less restricted by them; some responsibilities, most likely—wife, children, dependent relatives—but not always; just the ups-and-downs and give-and-take of the average, lower-class American citizen, floundering along trying to make the best decisions he can—like the rest of us—at each of the daily forks in the road. Now and then—like the rest of us—he feels under pressure and takes a short cut. It is a risk; but it seems at the moment to be a justified or necessary one. He exceeds his bank balance. He runs a red light. He "borrows" a car. Nine times out of ten he escapes detection.

But every once in a while—in fact, *every minute or two*—somewhere in this country one of these unimportant people does one of these forbidden things and *does not* get away with it. He may have been careless or impulsive or greedy; he may have been drunk, or only very angry; he may have been jealous, embittered, frightened, or just plain hungry. He may have been head-over-heels in an insoluble complication of commitments, indebtedness, and despair. He gets caught. He becomes involved with the "system."

Most crime surveys come up with some statistics to the effect that only about one law violation in a dozen is detected and, of course, most detected offenders are not arrested. Some who are arrested immediately plead guilty; others are tried. But when a crime is observed or suspected by the police, and when they are able to make an arrest and bring a man into the police station, he is booked. I shall pass over the many conditions of pursuit, struggle, surrender, transportation, and the like. I shall also pass over the delicate matter of police station confessions.

The motives for the committing of a crime are usually taken for granted. People think they know exactly "why" it was done. But even the most obvious cases are apt to be wrongly appraised. The looting that is done in street violence has far more meaning than the mere wish to acquire a television set or a bottle of whisky—for instance: vengeful retaliation, peer approval, coup making, masculinity assertion. But the law doesn't ask the motive; it assumes it. When Jean Valjean broke the window of a bakery to take a loaf of bread for a starving sister and her cold, hungry children, was this motive taken into consideration by the court? Why, no; theft is theft and a ruffian of that sort must pay the penalty of his impertinence and public violence with five years in the galleys. Victor Hugo's sense of outrage at the tyrannical injustice of the law to "the miserable ones" produced his great masterpiece, which in one sense is as true today as when it was written. Many men are driven to criminal acts, without any doubt, not by hunger and fear but by an emptiness in their lives that is perceived as sheer boredom and purposelessness.*

I have known individuals who broke into bakeries not because

* See Arthur Miller's sensitive review of *All the Way Down* by Vincent Riccio and Bill Slocum in the November 1962 *Harper's*.

they had nephews and nieces who were starving, not because they were hungry or poverty stricken, not even because they were penniless or frightened or desperate. I could tell you what their motives were and, being a very intelligent reader, you *might* believe me.

The offenders I see in my office are rarely written up in the newspapers; they rarely go to court. They have some money and friends and the matter is "taken care of." I do not imply bribery, corruption, or anything sinister. But *there are ways*—much better ways, as everyone knows—and we are glad there are. But it is different in lower levels of our society.

In quiet, uneventful lives, wrote Samuel Butler, changes internal and external are often so small that the process of fusion and accommodation between changed and unchanged surroundings produces little evidence of strain. In some lives there is great strain, but also great power of adaptation. And in some lives there is great strain with less accommodation power, fewer resources, greater fragility.

The strain resulting from attempted adaptation with inadequate powers may reach the point where it is a choice of breaking or being broken. For some persons the former seems the lesser evil. Is not self-preservation the first law of life? Sometimes something must yield and a "crime" is committed to prevent a crash. For some people an aggression is less evidence of weakness than is depression. An internal balance is thus and thereby reestablished.

But now another imbalance has been created—the reaction of the social environment. "We" do not like crimes. We do not like these offenses against us and our rules. They frighten us; they anger us; they hurt us. If we can *catch* these poor fellows, who may only be trying to save themselves, we are not likely to go very easy on them. And so, caught, they come before the bar of justice.

Arrest

The problem of arrest, including detection, suspicion, and police science generally, is a phase of the process that is probably the most important part of the system.[3] I have worked with the police for years; I am working with them at present; I hope to learn more of this obscure, confusing area.

Booking and charging are for the police a daily work-routine, but for the man arrested they are usually a crisis. If he has any friends, now is when he wants them. Will they come? Can they do anything? Will anybody lend money to help out in this emergency, or is his credit overextended? Such questions mean one thing to well-connected people like our presumptive readers, and they mean quite another thing to a confused, unlettered, frightened, friendless man in handcuffs, standing in a police station surrounded by "cops." The cops may be tired, sweaty men, irritated by the difficulties the offender has caused them and far from tactful or gentle or, to tell the truth, even civil.

Arrested individuals are usually not very prepossessing, scarcely likely to arouse pity or sympathy in the observer. Rough, tough, belligerent, or sleazy, evasive exteriors are the common façades. In many offenders, this ugliness extends deep beneath the surface of the personality; they are surly, cruel, defiant, ill-mannered, ruthless, "vicious." If aggression has become the necessary mode of achieving a balance, why should anyone present *or expect* a pleasant manner? War has been declared, and usually there is no hypocrisy about it. Fear and hate fuse with guilt and despair.

One study [4] of a municipal police force in the United States concluded that "the illegal use of violence by the police is a consequence of their occupational experience and that the policeman's colleague group sanctions such usage." Policemen see this use of violence as morally acceptable and legitimate in terms of the ends sought.* They see these ends "as constituting a legitimation for violence which is equal to or superior to the legitimation derived from the law." Violence becomes a personal property to be used at

---

* A Florida police chief announced he was equipping every officer with a shotgun, and if the term "cruelty" was applied to them, that's a price they would gladly pay. (CBS Radio news broadcast, December 27, 1967.)

the policeman's discretion.* This is a distortion of the policeman's task; his job is to enforce the law, not to punish or oppress the citizenry.

This is only one study, and it related to only one sample of policemen. But we all know that *some* police *sometimes* act illegally. Whether from fear or from temperament, some are tough and crude. We who are economically secure can *endure* this, when it affects us, but the more defenseless individuals can suffer grievously from it.

I have no general charges to make against the police as individuals. They do their jobs as they have learned them. They are not themselves criminals any more (or any less) than the rest of us. I consider them just as good as I am, and I know many of them to be truly superior individuals, as I shall document later. What I would point out is that they are trying to do an impossibly difficult job. They are caught in an obsolete, ineffective, crime-breeding—rather than crime-preventing—system, which we have inherited. My

---

* The March–April 1967 issue of *Police* contains intelligent articles on the role of the laboratory in a law enforcement agency, conflict of criminal jurisdictions, the narcotics problem, and other topics. It also contains (on page 72) this advertisement, with a picture of a club:

FIT FOR ACTION . . . ALL-WAYS!
Monadnock's 31–30 Mob Control Stick . . . the most efficient length and weight

The 31–30 Stick is designed to fit both its use *and its user*. Its length—31—places the grips close enough to each end for stick control, yet keeps the officer's arms aligned at shoulder width for maximum use of strength.

The 31–30 Stick weighs 30 ounces. It is precision-made of our solid, scar-resistant "M-Pact" plastic. It cannot dry out and is guaranteed to give a lifetime of normal service.

Steel balls anchored in each end give pin-point jab action for defense or offense.

Violence can flare up tomorrow. Be certain that *your* department's equipment is always fit for action. Specify Monadnock Lifetime 31–30 Mob Control Stick . . . stocked by leading dealers everywhere.

Illustrated folder on request.

charges are against the system, not the people in it. The system is ours as much as theirs.

Preliminary Hearing

There are few pretrial discovery devices in the criminal law. The preliminary hearing is a procedure that allows the defendant to have a prima-facie hearing of the prosecutor's case against him. In practice, when he urges the right to a preliminary hearing, he does so for the purpose of working up evidence of an alibi. The defendant is not entitled to a preliminary hearing when a formal charge has been brought against him, and for that reason the procedure is rarely used. Rather than disclose its case, the state will quickly file a charge.

The state does not have a right to discover the evidence that a defendant may have. As you know, the defendant may be a mere bystander at his trial, and the privilege against self-incrimination allows him to remain silent. The state in exceptional cases may resort to a preliminary examination to have the support of the judge that the case has some merit in proceeding to trial.

This is the practice. Theoretically, the right for preliminary examination is considered to be an important protection against high-handed police procedures and third-degree methods. It provides an opportunity to bring defense counsel into the picture.

Awaiting Trial—On Bail

With or without episodes of violence and voluntary or involuntary confession, a person charged with committing a crime may be jailed, or he may be released on promise to return for a hearing for a trial if he makes bail. About fourteen million Americans do this each year. A person on bail can go about his ordinary way of life until his trial. But if he does not make bail, as about one and one-half million people each year in this country cannot, he goes to jail until his trial, which may be months or years in the future! Most city jails are overcrowded for this reason.

The defendant without bail enters the court in the company of a guard, a fact not lost on jurors. If found guilty, he is unable to point to recent employment or good conduct as grounds for probation; if found not guilty, he has needlessly suffered the degradation of jail. His family thus has been unjustly punished as well. There are good grounds for suspecting that the outcome of an accused's case, as to both judgment and sentence, is materially influenced by whether he is in jail or on bail.[5]

A research project on the administration of the bail system in New York City revealed that most defendants unable to obtain bail are severely handicapped in preparing defenses. They cannot afford a lawyer, pay for investigation, or help locate witnesses. They must consult often indifferent and inexperienced court-appointed counsel, and not in the privacy or convenience of an office but in the jail. The project began in 1961, when, in cooperation with the New York University Law School, the Vera Foundation set up the Manhattan Bail Project on a trial basis in Manhattan Criminal Court. Each morning after the newly arrested prisoners were herded into the detention pen to await pretrial hearings, a team of Vera staffers, who by night are New York University law students, conducted interviews through the bars and verified statements by telephoning friends and employers. Then they rushed a one-page recommendation to the judge, asking that the prisoner be "released on his own recognizance"—freed on his own promise to return to trial.

In the project's early months, Vera staffers cautiously recommended the release of only 30 per cent of the prisoners interviewed; now they intercede for 60 per cent. At first the judges followed the Foundation's advice in only half of the cases, but now they turn loose 70 per cent of the prisoners for whom Vera vouches. This remarkable trend is based on equally remarkable results. Of the 2,300 prisoners—ranging from muggers to embezzlers—that Vera has recommended for release, less than 1 per cent have failed to show up for trial *v.* a 3 per cent no-show rate in Manhattan for defendants who were free on regular bail.

Even Vera's most enthusiastic supporters do not claim that the new system will work in all cases, and Vera itself avoids homicide, sex and narcotics offenses as too risky to handle. But the success of the project strongly suggests that many indigent defendants can be turned loose by sidestepping the old concept of money bail and substituting character checks and supervision (Vera sends special letters and makes telephone calls to remind the defendants to show up for trial). The Vera system would not only greatly reduce the cost of jailing pretrial prisoners—$10 million annually in New York City alone—but would also give defendants a better chance to prepare their defense, allow them to continue to work and support their families while awaiting trial, and avoid placing on the unconvicted the onus of serving time.

New York City in January [1964] decided to adopt Vera procedures for all its criminal courts. Experiments with the system have also been started in eight other major cities, including Chicago, Los Angeles and San Francisco, and Attorney General Robert Kennedy is encouraging federal courts to release more prisoners without bail.[6]

I am sure the average citizen does not know what goes on in regard to the bail bond business. I have long kept my eyes open to crime news but, until I read Ronald Goldfarb's book, *Ransom: A Critique of the American Bail System,*[7] I did not know how far the bail racket went, how lucrative bail bonding was for a few who make payoffs to officials or infiltrate bonding companies and politics.[8] Some judges use the bail business sadistically—e.g., an Episcopal rector of Chester, Pennsylvania, was arrested for protest actions against segregation in the schools and was put in jail because he was unable to meet bail set at $26,500! Other clergymen in a number of places in the U.S. have been kept in prison because of bail set at $10,000, $12,000, and $20,000! These are not bank robbers, remember, but religious idealists protesting what they believe to be unrighteousness. Many persons innocent of any crime are kept in jail because they cannot afford to hire a bondsman to make bail for them. This cost and the ability to meet this cost have no relation whatsoever to the protection of society. As Goldfarb says, many of the worst and most dangerous criminals can easily afford bail, if, indeed, they are not actually bondsmen themselves.

Awaiting Trial—In Jail

For the great majority of offenders, bail is out of the question. The accused usually goes to jail, hears the lock click behind him, sits down, and waits. It is one of the proudest tenets of American law that any accused person is innocent until proved guilty. Yet each year thousands of Americans who have been charged with a crime but not yet brought to trial spend weeks and sometimes months in jail.

Would the reader please imagine himself in the embarrassing and distressing situation of having been arrested, accused of the commission of a crime, and placed in jail. Let us assume that the circumstances are such that he cannot make bail, he cannot go home and discuss it with his family and friends and obtain the best possible lawyer. He is detained in prison, surrounded by uncouth, unprepossessing strangers who are in similar trouble. He knows or he is told that he will shortly be brought to trial and it would be well for him to get a lawyer. He learns from other prisoners or from the jailer that certain lawyers are available and this one or that is particularly "keen."

On February 24, 1964, Commissioner Anna M. Kross of New York City announced that the number of prisoners in the city jails had reached an all-time high. Unbelievable overcrowding prevailed throughout, with two or even three people living and sleeping in one cell five feet by nine feet in area. "Prison sewing areas, maintenance, carpentry and machine shops (have) been reduced so the areas could be used for sleeping facilities." A shoe-repair shop had been converted to a one-hundred-bed dormitory. What was formerly used as a gymnasium in the Riker's Island Prison had been converted into a two-hundred-and-fifty-bed dormitory. "We shouldn't treat cattle the way we have to house our inmates," Mrs. Kross said.[9]

Or read another description of a modern American jail, a structure in full-blown use in 1966—the jail of the District of Columbia, where several presidential assassins and over a hundred other prisoners have been executed. Built to house about seven hundred prisoners, it today houses an average of twelve hundred with an annual turnover of thirty-eight thousand! Of these about a third are *charged* with (not yet convicted of) felonies. Two-thirds are charged with misdemeanors.

On most days the prisoner population of 1,200 breaks down as follows: about 100 are sentenced but awaiting further court action; about 300 are sentenced but awaiting assignment; about 100 are awaiting some administrative action for special reasons (medical, psychological examinations, solitary confinement, escapees, etc.). *But about 700 have been convicted of nothing; they are simply awaiting trial* [italics mine]. . . .

To house men charged only with misdemeanors, dormitories are used. There are two dormitories—180 by 120 feet—the size of three tennis courts. Into each are herded about 500 prisoners. There is a narrow aisle for passage up the middle of the room teeming with double-decked beds and men. There is nothing else in the room. It is like a human stockyard. One prison official, ashamed and offended, referred to the dormitories as "the Black Hole of Calcutta." The few windows are barred. Some mattresses are crammed into places where the windows are broken.

Mattresses without beds have been placed on the floor in an adjoining recreation room (an old chapel) to hold some of the overflow from these dormitories. There is one guard for each 350 prisoners. In these dorms the prisoners sleep, play cards, lie or mill about with nothing to do—nothing is required, nothing is provided, little is allowed. The men cannot work (some clean or do chores); they get no exercise; they do not go outside the building.

The tiers of cells for those charged with the more serious crimes look like every 1940 James Cagney movie verison of a prison. Two men are closeted in each six-by-eight-by-nine-foot cell (the size of the surface of a pool table). Each cell has (besides two men) double-decked beds, an open toilet, a small narrow table and a chair, three steel walls, no windows. Electrically operated bars lock the entry.

There is no room to pace. The men lie and sit around in their prison trousers (few wear shirts, it is so hot), fester, corrupt each other.

I stopped at a cell and asked one man if he cared to talk. He rolled off his bed and ambled up to the bars. He said that he had been there over a year *waiting to be tried.* . . .

Recently the chief assistant U. S. Attorney in the District was shocked to discover that two men were in jail almost a year *and had not been indicted*. He got them out. . . .

Cramming two young people of the same sex into a jammed cell for long periods with nothing to do has obvious degrading effects. According to Commissioner of Corrections Thomas Sard, these conditions lead to concealed private acts of homosexuality, occasional acts of forced sodomy, as well as blatant open affairs between inveterate "queers" and inmates who compete for their favors. Lesbianism is a big problem in the women's wing, too, prison officials say.[10]

A few weeks after the manuscript of this book was sent to the publisher, I visited the Cook County (Chicago) jail with Joseph Rowan, executive director of the John Howard Association, and talked with the jail superintendent, Jack Johnson. Johnson conceded publicly "that deviate sex practices, beating of inmates by other inmates, smuggling of contraband and other vicious practices were routine in the jail." But he contended that many of his underpaid (and I might add largely underqualified and undertrained) staff members were doing the best they could under virtually untolerable conditions. The John Howard Association had recommended that Civil Service be introduced to elevate and standardize the positions of the prison guards. The jail superintendent strongly favored this change but the politicians had consistently opposed it.

I was taken through the jail and, from long experience, I knew where to look and what to look for. I was shocked and frightened. Less than a week later the scandal broke and a grand jury was summoned. The terrible conditions in this great steel and concrete machine for grinding up human beings was in the headlines of all the papers. Bear in mind that a large portion of the men and women, boys and girls who were crowded into this institution had

not been convicted of *any* crime. (See "The Worst I've Seen" by
Bill Davidson *).

The people of Chicago were particularly impressed by the volun-
teered testimony of a businesswoman from Evanston, a widow
with nine children, a university graduate who was voted the most
popular woman at the University of Illinois during her senior year.
She and her late husband operated a games manufacturing company. One of the card games which she herself invented, based on
the Constitution of the United States, won an award from the
Freedoms Foundation. She had had a quarrel with the local court
in connection with a complicated inheritance suit of nearly thirty
years standing and when she refused to allow the representatives of
a bank to come and assess her home, as ordered, she was cited for
contempt of court and sentenced to the Cook County Jail for a
week.

According to her account, she was constantly horrified and
often terrified by the inhumanity on the part of both the staff and
the inmates. It began with the physical examination when the matron searched seven women for concealed narcotics, using a vaginal
tool without sterilizing it between the examinations. When Mrs.
X. protested, the matron made her the last of the women to be
examined. The doctor who examined her took away her prescription medicine for a heart condition and never returned it, although he had promised to do so.

In the female prisoners' open room, she was shocked to see
women, nude from the waist up, walking around in view of male
guards. She was turned over to a stout Negro woman, a prisoner
accused of murder, who was in charge of that section of the jail.
This woman provided her with unclean clothes and dirty linen and
showed her to her bedbug-ridden and odorous cell. For sixty-eight
women on her tier she found only three workable toilets, but she
was warned by the other prisoners not to report this because the
empty shut-off pipes were used to transport candy and narcotics,
pulled up by strings from the first floor.

* Saturday Evening Post, July 13, 1968.

The shower room, she said, was used for acts of perversion, and new women were often attacked there. But sexual molestation was also carried on in the open on the eating tables, and Mrs. X. was threatened but managed to buy herself off with cigarettes and candy.

There was a catwalk running all around the section, she said. At night the guards would walk around to make sure everybody was accounted for. But during the day the prisoners were left to themselves. . . . Everybody was at the mercy of the strong and violent ones.

There was nothing to do, nothing to read, and you couldn't go outside—not even in the summer. Dope was the only thing. Dope and perversions. . . .

What really hurt me was hearing about the young boys who were molested. The male prisoners forced them into homosexual acts under threat of stabbing, beating, starving. The boys were frightened and defenseless. The guards just pretended not to hear, or were not around.[11]

She told of narcotic addicts going through withdrawal. "These unfortunate persons had no help, no pity. Sometimes they were preyed upon by other prisoners who would sexually assault them even while they were in their terrible agony. They rolled around on the concrete floor trying to keep cool during the worst of it, and then afterward they would have a great craving for sugar, which they would steal or fight for.

"A prisoner named Shirley was mentally ill. She thought she had killed her husband after catching him in an affair with her maid. Two women in the next cell started to torment her. The woman was reeling, and the more she reacted, the more they tortured her. She begged and pleaded with them to stop. She hit her head against the wall, and they said, 'That's good. Do it once more—once for your maid.' Finally she put her head in the bowl of the toilet and tried to drown herself, flushing the toilet over and over again while the animal women screamed and laughed."

I'd been warned never to call a guard under any circumstances, unless I wanted a beating. But I called now. I screamed for a guard.

Nobody came. I grabbed a broom and shoved it through the bars. I pushed her away from the toilet. And then I kept pushing with the broom to keep her away. Finally somebody came. The guards strapped her to her bed and then left. As soon as they were gone the women started again, redoubling their efforts. Shirley thrashed and cried out. She broke the springs in her bed, and they were cutting her back. That day Shirley was given no food. She cried that she would do anything the women wanted . . . if they would leave her alone. But of course they wouldn't and didn't. What finally happened to her I don't know. . . .

One day in the compound two women got into a fight, and one of them threw a large container of scalding water. It spilled over me and burned me. But none of the prisoners tried to get any help, and nobody came for 10 minutes. Then they smeared Vaseline on the burns, and that was all. I never saw a doctor. . . .

On the sixth day I was nursed by a woman named Helen, in her 70s, who was in jail for bad checks. She brought me cold towels for relief, and she brought me water. But I couldn't eat, and I couldn't sleep.

Then my daughter came to the jail to visit me, and she begged me to obey the court order . . . and I left the jail. After seven days.

I saw what happens there. And I don't see how any person who has the slightest connection with the jail can be ignorant about all the hate, torture and terror there.[12]

This woman was in the jail for seven days—not seven weeks, not seven months, not seven years. She speaks with restraint when she says that she does not see how any person "who has the slightest connection with the jail" can be ignorant about its horror. It is the people who have no connection with the jails who are ignorant about them and who fancy that things are getting better.

A place where idle, frustrated, unkempt, frightened, resentful men are pushed into physical and psychological intimacy and left to await someone else's pleasure and convenience is a prime breeding place of evil and violence. And remember, please, they may not have done anything wrong! *

* After this chapter was set in type, the Grand Jury returned a report on the

We have been speaking of jails, which are to be distinguished from prisons, of which we shall speak later. Both are wretched, abominable institutions of evil, but generally the jails are by far the worse.* Theoretically they are for brief, temporary confinement and in no sense for punishment. They exist to protect threatened individuals, and these individuals may be the ones incarcerated.

As I sit here and write, or as you sit and read these words, these horrible institutions are operating in every city, every state in our union. Some of us think of ourselves as the most civilized nation on earth. Social scientists from Denmark, Mexico, and other countries where far more enlightened systems are in operation are shocked at what they see here. They go to see what most American citizens spare themselves the pain of looking at.

Certainly jails *should* be pleasant *and* comfortable. They should also be secure. But security does not require austerity and physical discomfort. The city, the county, the law—none of them has been authorized or commissioned to force citizens to endure privation and discomfort without a trial, and without conviction of offense. But it is done even today in thousands of communities—*only* to

---

basis of which a new, scientifically trained warden was appointed, who has instituted many reforms in the prison and has made plans for a Diagnostic Center.

* Of course, there are those rare, bright, shining exceptions:

Madison, Wis.—Early in the morning the front door at the Dane County jail looks like the check-in counter at many factories.

Prisoners line up, sign out, pick up their lunch buckets—"only three sandwiches, sorry, no choice," reads a sign—and leave by foot, bus or car for their jobs.

One prisoner, serving a year for statutory rape, works a 48-hour week at a factory, to which he drives in his own car, then goes to his tobacco patch to work it before he returns to the jail.

"They even let me go to union meetings," the thin, nervous, apparently penitent man said. "If a young man wants to be straightened out, he can save a lot of money and support his family here. It's what you make it here."

For many men, alcoholics or vagrants, being sentenced to the Dane County jail means getting the first job in their lives. (*Kansas City Star,* September 12, 1965.)

people too poor, too ignorant, or too intimidated to escape it "legally." All this in the name of justice.

Readers may be thinking that our miserable, overcrowded, crime-and-disease-breeding lockups are just anachronistic residuals in the onrush of civilization. Along with improved hotels, transportation, housing, and streets, the jail-building profession, whatever that is, has also gone a little modern and made some improvements. Here and there the city fathers may have slighted the needs urged by the chief of police and the sheriff, but in general things are probably improving.

"Things" are improving but conditions are not. The architects who get the contract for designing the new jail are apt to be pretty far down on the list—but even so, they know *something*. They know where to get stronger steel and harder concrete than was used in the old days. They know about some improved abuse-proof toilets. Some very "nice looking" jails emerge here and there.*

The jail *idea* does not change. It is still the lockup, the place of ill repute, the place the town is ashamed of (or should be). It is apt to be one of the lesser political areas for the employment of men of nondescript skills, or of difficult assignment. No jail in the country—so far as I know—has been dignified and elevated to being the cornerstone of community security and justice. Why shouldn't it be?

Once the hospital was despised and rejected as a pesthouse, a place to die in, a stinking horror, taboo in the civilized community. Today towns and cities alike are proud of their beautiful, efficient hospitals and rely on them as protectors of health. But the jails remain where they have been for centuries, and where the hospitals

---

* "Why this gratuitous slap at architects?" asks a pre-publication reader. Not at "architects" but at *the* architects who take these political plums and "please the people" when they—the architects—know better. They know these wretched lockups are a failure, no matter how beautiful. An elite class, they have the brains, the training, and the vision to look ahead and see the possibilities for improvement. As cultural leaders, they must assume the responsibilities of their prerogative position. And they *do* know better, and should hold out for their principles. Many do.

once were. What kind of justice is served by this designation?

Who is to blame for the persistence of this medieval institution, the jail? Lawyers will tell you that it is no child of theirs. The chiefs of police long for better quarters and civilized facilities for dealing with the frightened, angry, desperate, crafty, intoxicated subjects in their charge. But who are we, they say, to demand such frills when we need so sorely better salaries, better equipment, more personnel? Dare we suggest an addition to the taxpayer's burdens that will only arouse the wrath and denunciation of political demagogues? No. The police—like everyone else—feel they must play it cool. Their "customers" have no votes, and the public might get the wrong idea.

The public has no idea of what jail conditions are like. It took a score of books to convince even a fraction of the public that state (and city) mental hospitals were snake pits! Many more than a dozen books [13] have been written since John Howard's classic about jail conditions.[14] Still the public doesn't quite believe it. A few defensive words from some annoyed or threatened old-timer, a few cracks about "do-gooders," "meddling," "pampering these bums," "socialists and social workers," "sentimental slobberers," and the sensible citizen heaves a sigh and turns his attention to other problems.

Trial Preparations

Most offenders do not get a fair trial; they do not get a trial at all! Ninety per cent of the defendants in American cases plead guilty and are promptly sentenced without a trial. This means, of course, that most of them have been "convicted by the police—not by judges and juries. And because most police insist that interrogation must be secret, the courts have no way of knowing just what led up to the confession. Without tapes, films, or neutral witnesses, judges have no way of determining whether a suspect really talked freely or was tricked or bullied into 'waiving' his right to silence, or even into confession falsely—a not unknown reaction to the sinister air of the police station." [15]

More and more the trial is becoming mandatory in most jurisdictions for serious crimes, even when the accused has announced an intention to plead guilty. This means that a lawyer must be had either by employment or appointment. And who shall this lawyer be? Even in our large cities, only a handful of lawyers engage in the practice of criminal law. Most attorneys seem to prefer civil practice, some frankly giving the reason that they do not want to associate even professionally with criminals—or with criminal lawyers. Some decline because they feel that they serve no useful function in the criminal law process.*

The criminal lawyer seems almost to be the black sheep of the legal profession. There are, of course, notable exceptions. Frank Hogan, former president of the American Bar Association, was a leading criminal lawyer in Washington. Several others have become prominent recently, but there is a general impression that many lawyers who seek criminal cases are second rate in ability.

A Hypothetical Interrogation

Although judges are sometimes very pained to see the awkward mismanagement of the defense, it is difficult for them to interfere without prejudice. One judge assures me that ignorance and indifference play far greater roles than mendacity and greed in the poor defenses tendered. But what sometimes happens can be portrayed by the following sketch, which is an occurrence personally known to me.

JUDGE: Who is your lawyer?

PRISONER: I have no lawyer; I cannot afford to pay a lawyer.

JUDGE: Then I will appoint a lawyer. Bailiff, who is next on the list?

BAILIFF: Mr. Walter Jones, sir.

JUDGE: Prisoner, Mr. Jones will be your lawyer and will defend your case.

* See, "A New Approach to Criminal Law," by Professor B. J. George, Jr., of the Michigan Law School in the April 1964 *Harper's,* Vol. 228, pp. 183–188.

(A few days later in the prisoner's cell, or an anteroom):

MR. JONES: Well, what have you got to say?

PRISONER: I didn't kill anybody, sir. I was with two other fellows and we were in a car and this guy stopped us and asked for a ride and we said we couldn't take him because the car was full, and he stepped back and I guess another car hit him.

MR. JONES: What did *you* boys do?

PRISONER: We went off as fast as we could.

MR. JONES: Well, then, you were leaving the scene of an accident and that is a crime. But they say you also ran over the fellow purposely.

PRISONER: I didn't see him.

MR. JONES: Why not?

PRISONER: I don't know.

MR. JONES: Well, I'm afraid the evidence is going to show you saw him and didn't try to miss him, and they are going to get you for second degree murder. So I think we'd better take a plea.

PRISONER: What is that?

MR. JONES: You'll plead guilty to manslaughter. That will get you a shorter sentence.

PRISONER: But I didn't do any murder and I didn't do any manslaughter!

MR. JONES: Now look, fellow, I'm defending you and I know the best thing to do. Don't get smart here or you'll pull thirty years to life.

PRISONER: But, listen, sir. I'm just not guilty of a thing like manslaughter. All I did was—

MR. JONES: Shut up! *You* listen. You're in deep trouble, whether you know it or not, and I'm trying to make it easy on you. I don't get rich doing this, you know, and I'm not going to fool around with you. Will you sign a confession to manslaughter and let's get this thing over with? Or do you want to go back to the cooler?

I will tell you something else. You turn down this plea if I can get it for you and do you know what is gonna happen? The County Attorney will pour it on you to make it hard for you and he is gonna try to get the stiffest penalty he can. He doesn't like to have you boys get smart with him. Take my advice now, and plead guilty.

Bargaining with the district attorney is called "copping a plea." In some places, as many as ninety-three per cent of defendants are convicted on pleas of guilty.[16] An examination of the records in Boone and Callaway Counties, Missouri, for example, revealed that for the year from May 1963 to May 1964, 178 felony cases were filed and, of this number, ten were tried! There were 125 guilty pleas, 22 dismissals, and the remainder were still pending.

Usually judges will give a defendant pleading guilty a less severe sentence than one who has actually gone to trial and been found guilty of the same offense. It saves the time of the court, and it is often considered that by pleading guilty the defendant is repenting and therefore deserves mercy.

What about the prosecuting attorney?

If a prosecuting attorney can make a good record of successful convictions, he can step out of the system into the private practice of law (or into politics) with the acclaim of the community and ultimately graduate into the upper stratum of "No criminal cases, please." He usually serves in the office for a few years, hoping to advance himself politically. He is often mainly interested in prosecuting cases in such a way that it will get his name in the papers. Many district attorney offices throughout the country have bulletin boards with won-lost records indicating the "batting averages" of the members of the staff. And why not? Don't insurance agencies and automobile sales departments use such incentive devices? It is called "motivation" and indicates man's healthy striving to surpass.

But consider the circumstances. What *is* success for the prosecutor? Not the best disposition of the prisoner. Not protection of society. Not *justice*. None of these. Once a charge is accepted, his goal is *conviction* and any other outcome is a loss. To get his name in the paper as a winner is a coup for him.

Under the adversary system, the prosecutor is unable to interview the defendant. He proceeds on the basis of a complaint made by the policeman; or, less frequently, by the victim or witnesses who are interested enough to want to see the case prosecuted. When there is no guilty plea and the case goes to trial, both prosecuting attorney and defense counsel usually proceed on very little study of the facts of the case. Witnesses are often interviewed in the courtroom a few minutes before trial. The witnesses are apt to be policemen, and often they are not called in off the beat to be interviewed prior to trial because this is costly; the community needs their services on the street.

The recent Gideon case decision has brought the defense ritual forcibly to public attention. The public gathers, or at least I do, that many judges have thought it unnecessary for anyone to present a defense for the prisoners.[17] With this philosophy so widely prevailing, it is not surprising that many judges feel that it is not very important which lawyer they appoint or how skillful he is or how well he does his job.

We physicians know that in the early days of medical training, when internships were first established, it was thought that young physicians needed a place to try their wings, to get a little experience with patients who were not paying for it anyway and therefore should not expect too much. Later, strict supervision of interns was instituted, but there is no doubt that many indigent patients have suffered from inexperienced and unsupervised physicians. (Fifty years ago it was quite the fashion for young doctors, and even older ones, to go to Vienna where for a fee they could be permitted to learn the trick of removing tonsils by the trial and error method, supervised theoretically by the professor-doctor who, however, was very apt to have far more students than he could personally supervise.)

Certainly young attorneys need experience, and because they are legally permitted to practice, they should get their experience on the cases that matter least in the long run, so that, if they are poorly handled, there will not be a scandal. But why is not such a young defense lawyer required to have professional supervision in the same way that the young physician is supervised and recognized in his virginal experiences of practice as an intern in a public hospital?

As a consultant in numerous prisons and a visitor to many others, I have frequently heard case reports that indicated that the lawyer appointed to defend the accused did not have the slightest idea of how to proceed, or what defenses were available, or what help he could actually give to his client other than the traditional bargain-making with the county attorney or challenging some of the evidence of the prosecution witnesses. Nor did he have any senior attorney to counsel him. I am told by legal colleagues, and especially by law school faculty members, that the law schools until recently have not spent much time in this area. Very few of their students would have much use for such training, inasmuch as the brief experiences during a lawyer's first year or two in practice are not likely to continue as a main interest.

One case of which I have personal knowledge was taken care of in the following way: After drinking with a companion rather late one Saturday night, a young soldier with no previous police record "borrowed" a car that stood in front of the tavern and drove home in it, a distance of about three miles. At most, this constitutes the misdemeanor of having borrowed a car without permission and "making unauthorized use of a motor vehicle." There was no conceivable way of proving intent to steal. Nevertheless, the attorney appointed to *defend* the soldier actually *assisted the prosecuting attorney in obtaining a conviction of car theft* with a sentence of one to ten years in prison! Obtaining this magnificent help from his defense attorney cost the young man, or rather his relatives, some $1,500. He is at the present moment behind bars serving that sentence.*

* Some legal colleagues have asked me why the judge, who must have been dismayed at the turn of events, did not declare a mistrial or give the offender a bench parole. As a matter of fact, the judge did that very (latter)

The action of this attorney for the defense is not uncommon. Many prisoners have exhausted their funds to retain lawyers who exist by preying on miserable, ignorant persons caught by the law. The lawyer may induce them to plead guilty, promising to get them off by his influence or by a private "deal" with the judge or the prosecutor. But even a poor or inexperienced lawyer may be better than none. The Gideon decision assumes this. So do some spot checks such as the following:

About two-thirds of all defendants represented by lawyers in trials in Miami Municipal Court last fall went free, while more than three-fourths of those not represented served jail terms, according to a report sent to city commissioners this week by Howard Dixon, director of the legal services program of the Dade Economic Opportunity Program, Inc.

The fact that only five per cent of all defendants employed lawyers "suggests that the instrumentalities of justice of the City of Miami are primarily concerned with control of the lowest strata of society and not the middle and upper strata," the report says.

It questions whether the behavior of various social groups merits such an "enormous differential in treatment" before the bar of justice. . . .

Although Florida courts have ruled that misdemeanor defendants are not entitled to counsel, the staff report says, "a poor person in the City of Miami Municipal Court may face as serious a penalty as someone who is charged with a felony."

It says there is a "substantial difference in the quality of justice meted out" to persons accused of municipal offenses who are represented by lawyers and those who are not.

For example, in Municipal Court cases last October, November and December, more than 75 per cent of all defendants with attorneys

thing. One of the conditions of the parole was, however, that the parolee not leave the county. Whatever it may show about his character structure, the man turned up some months later in a beer spot in "the big town" just across the county line. Inasmuch as this constituted parole violation, the original sentence was invoked and to prison he went.

pleaded not guilty, while only about 39 per cent of those without attorneys did so.

Nearly 13 per cent of those with attorneys obtained a dismissal of charges, compared to 4.5 per cent of those without attorneys.

And, when their cases came to trial, a third of those with lawyers—compared to more than three-fourths of those without lawyers—were found guilty.

Sentences were suspended for 23.6 per cent of the defendants who were represented by counsel, but only 12.5 per cent of those who were not represented.[18]

The Trial and the Adversary System

For some—perhaps for one offender in a hundred—there comes at last the trial. Much or little preparation may have been done on both sides, but a charge has been made and a defense of some sort is to be offered before a laboriously selected jury. Evidence will be introduced by lawyers representing the prosecution, and this evidence will be attacked or possibly refuted by the defense. The judge will umpire the game. Ultimately, the jury will decide who won the debate.

The questioning, the testifying, the countertestifying, the cross-questioning, and all the rest of the pro and con investigation proceed according to long-established and accumulated rules. These rules and their interpretation seem to the casual observer to be far more important than the content of the evidence to which they relate. Some important information that would help to solve the problem can be inadmissible for technical reasons. The admissibility of some evidence seems to be moot, and the judge has to make many decisions; he may make an error, which in turn may impair the validity of the decision.

This dramatic public ritual, this climax in the pursuit and capture of an offender, his arraignment, his indictment, his accusation, and his defense—this age-old *mise en scène* is the stylized symbol of the whole process of legal justice. The spectacular accouterments have greatly diminished since the days of the British Assizes, when robed, bewigged judges sat far above the prisoner and intoned their comments. Even though we distrust such pageantry, it still intrigues us.

To a scientist, the whole thing is monstrous strange, and more than a little absurd. The noisy public exposure of the details of certain disapproved behavior, for example, is in startling contrast with the quiet, private, sensitive but searching examination made of an individual who is a patient rather than a criminal. The patient may have exhibited exactly the same behavior as the criminal, but he has had the wit or the friends or the good luck to land him in a clinic instead of a court.

In both instances there is a search for truth. But there are many kinds of "truth," and many ways to search for it. The grim jailers of the Middle Ages were also after the truth when they put people through frightful ordeals. The officials of the Spanish Inquisition were searchers after the truth, they said. Torture still goes on in the search for truth from military prisoners, according to the newspapers. The jury * and the adversarial combat are not so cruel as the rack and the thumbscrew, but they are only a little less clumsy, outworn, and inquisitional.

This, our persistent mode of trial, is based on what the late Judge Jerome Frank called the "fight" theory, a theory that derives from the origin of trials as substitutes for private out-of-court brawls. The adversary system assumes that the best way for a court to discover the facts about *any* matter is to have each of two opposing sides strive as hard as it can, in a keenly partisan spirit, to bring to the court's attention the evidence favorable to its side. But this system also assumes that both sides will be represented with equal skill, and have equal amounts of luck. Is it justifiable to put

---

* "Lord Justice Devlin recently said at Chicago, 'Trial by jury is not an instrument for getting at the truth; it is a process designed to make it as sure as humanly possible that no innocent man is convicted.' " (Kalven, Harry, Jr., and Zeisel, Hans: "Law, Science and Humanism." In *The Humanist Frame,* Julian Huxley, ed. New York: Harper & Row, 1962, p. 337.)

men on trial for their lives under a system in which skill and luck
so vitally influence the outcome? *

Judge Frank comments, "I suggest that the fighting theory of
justice is not unrelated to, and not uninfluenced by, extreme laissez
faire in the economic field. The 'fight' theory of justice is a sort of
legal laissez faire. . . . Legal laissez-faire theory assumes that government can safely rely on the 'individual enterprise' of individual
litigants to insure that court orders will be grounded on all the
practical, attainable, relevant facts." He quotes Professor John Wigmore as saying that this theory "has contributed to lowering the
system of administering justice, and in particular of ascertaining
truth in litigation, to the level of a mere game of skill or chance,"
in which lawyers use evidence "as one plays a trump card, or draws
to three aces, or holds back a good horse until the home stretch." [19]

Following the Norman conquest, combat became a recognized
method of trial. Trials by battle were more often used to settle civil
disputes, but a man accused of felony might also establish his innocence by challenging his accuser to a judicial duel. Knights fought
with swords and lances, and commoners fought with staves with
iron heads. In time, both parties were represented by counsel whose
duties, according to a procedure laid down for trials of treason,
were to teach them "all manner of fightings and subtleties of arms
that belong to a battle sworn." It was counsel's duty to engage
three priests for the contestants and to see that these priests each
sang a mass on the day of the trial.

Primitive trials such as these were still held in the fourteenth
century, but while they have now been abolished, the contentious
trial method in court has survived. How is this survival explained? Professor Wigmore, following a suggestion made by Jer-
emy Bentham, suggested that "the common law, originating in a

---

* Kalven and Zeisel's study (*The American Jury*) seems to show that defense
counsel and prosecutor are both surprisingly powerless (relatively) to influence the outcome of the verdict. For a defense of the adversary system,
see the contribution of Dean Francis A. Allen of the University of Michigan
Law School in *Community Psychiatry,* edited by L. M. Roberts, S. L. Halleck,
and M. B. Loeb (Madison: University of Wisconsin Press, 1966, p. 183).

community of sports and games, was permeated by the instinct of sportsmanship," which led to a "sporting theory of justice," a theory of "legalized gambling."

It seems to me, and I have seen the idea expressed by others, that the prevalent trial procedure has in it a large element of the recently explored concept of "game theory." What move should A make to anticipate B's making a move that would require A to make a different move, etc.? One colleague has written an amusing and popular book, showing to what extent game theory applies to many social operations and activities.[20] In the crime prevention field, there are several such games, not so far as one might think, in principle, from the childhood games of cops and robbers and button, button, who's got the button—and forfeits. The finer mathematics of this have been extensively studied by Anatol Rapoport.[21]

Closely related to this game theory of searching for truth by public verbal duels is the question of ethics. Professor Monroe Freedman of George Washington University Law School recently submitted three "ethical riddles" for lawyers:

> "Is it proper to cross-examine for the purpose of discrediting the reliability or the credibility of an adverse witness whom you know to be telling the truth?"
>
> "Is it proper to put on the stand a witness who you know will commit perjury?"
>
> "Is it proper to give your client legal advice when you have reason to believe that the knowledge will tempt him to commit perjury?"

The answer to all of these questions, said Freedman, is yes, and by so declaring he has brought himself into the limelight of professional discussion. Was Freedman prescribing perjury? No, he says; he was merely discussing conflicts in the United States adversarial system.

In theory, that system produces truth and justice by pitting lawyers in a contest before neutral judges and juries. The defense lawyer is torn between his role as a truth-seeking officer of the court and his duty to fight as hard as possible for his client. . . .

The law professor suggests a hypothetical case: "The accused has admitted to you, in response to your assurance of confidentiality, that he is guilty. However, he insists upon taking the stand to protest his innocence." Should the lawyer permit such perjury? Yes, says Freedman. Despite the presumption of innocence, most jurors tend to presume guilt in a defendant who shuns the stand. To keep him off "will most seriously prejudice his case." The lawyer may quit the case, of course, but he may also have to tell the judge his reason—in effect, declare his client guilty. Thus, says Freedman, morality may sometimes require perjury.

Even worse is the dilemma of whether to give sound legal advice that may well tempt the defendant to give false testimony. When the accused confides his guilt in the 1959 bestseller *Anatomy of a Murder,* for example, his lawyer replies: "If the facts are as you have stated them so far, you have no defense, and you will be most likely electrocuted. On the other hand, if you acted in a blind rage, there is a possibility of saving your life. Think it over, and we will talk about it tomorrow." Is this unethical? Even though perjury may result, says Freedman, "the client is entitled to know this information and to make his own decision as to whether to act upon it." [22]

Psychology has long questioned the naïve acceptance by courts of the law of testimony by eyewitnesses. The old experiment, common in college psychology classes, of staging an unexpected incident and asking students to describe afterward what they saw happen, convinces anyone who has ever participated in it that no witness tells the whole truth and that most witnesses in all good faith tell many untruths regarding what happened right in front of their eyes. This has been studied many times in the psychological laboratory without the slightest impact upon the rules and procedure of the courtroom. Recently the distinguished James Marshall of New York combined his legal, psychological, and administrative expertise in a study of this conflict of law and science illustrated especially in regard to eyewitness testimony.[23] Some of the tragic errors of false identification have been dramatically rehearsed in the press and in numerous books.[24] But still the same old procedures proceed, and the same old problems remain.

We clinicians think we have access to much better methods of ascertaining truth. But how can a public court find out the truth, or at least the facts? Obviously they cannot use our methods. But then what *is* possible?

My esteemed friend and scientific legal scholar, Hans Zeisel, on reading these pages, has commented in the following thoughtful words:

> The adversary system has admitted shortcomings. The question is, is there a better one? The European continental one, the so-called inquisitorial system, makes the judge a more powerful director of the proceedings because he decides the order of proof and he does the bulk of the questioning. The English judge, though more like the American than the continental judge, is somewhat more active than the American trial judge. The question is: Which is the better system and how is one to decide which is the better one? It would not be easy to say, for instance, where miscarriages of justice are more likely.
>
> As to the many restrictive rules of evidence that characterize the Anglo-American trial system, do not forget that almost all have been designed to protect the defendant, not to strengthen the prosecution.
>
> All the shortcomings of evidence depending on perception, memory, etc., are indeed well established. The important question is: What consequences do you draw from it? No trial? No effort to find out the truth? Here, if anywhere, the problem is: What better solution can we offer? [25]

Cross-Examination

Cross-examination of a witness is called "one of the principal and most efficacious tests which the law has devised for the discovery of truth," but, in practice, cross-examination tends to confuse rather than to further the inquiry for truth. Trial tactics are determinative factors in the outcome of the case. In a recent book on cross-examination,[26] John Allen Appleman has innocently prepared a sad commentary on trial practice. Some of his revealing chapter titles are "Break Your Witness," "Witness on the Run," "Setting Traps for Opposing Counsel," "The Kill," "Use of Humor," "Rephrasing for Dramatic Impact," "Flattery Technique," and "Reducing the Testimony of a Physician." Truth? Justice? Search? *

The Jury

Most Americans do not realize that trial by jury is a relative rarity, not only throughout the world but even in this country. In many nations no one gets a jury trial. In Connecticut, there are only three jury trials per year per one hundred thousand people; in Georgia, jury trials are forty times more frequent relatively. The idea of a jury was certainly most useful and democratic at the time it was initiated, but it has long been a moot question as to whether

---

* Witnesses do not wish to testify at a trial because on cross-examination their credibility may be attacked by reference to their "character." Consider the following: A woman fifty-five years of age testified as a witness for the state in a murder case, and she was asked, among other things, on cross-examination, whether she used narcotics. The record, as made by the official court reporter, discloses the following questions and answers:

"Q. As much as I hate to I am going to have to ask you a personal question, Mrs. Irwin. Do you use narcotics? A. No, sir, not now.

"Q. You don't use any at all? A. I was ill for ten years and the doctor gave me morphine at the time I had operations.

"Q. You don't use them at all any more? A. No."

During the argument of the defense counsel to the jury he made the following statement of and concerning this witness: "Did you watch her? Did you see how she acted? The mind of a dope fiend, she was full of it, she was full of it when she testified; she showed she was an addict; why, she's a lunatic; she's a crazy lunatic, she's a dope fiend; how nervous she was all through her testimony; she's a hop head; her whole testimony is imagination and delusion from taking dope; all through, her testimony showed it; that she testified she had taken dope for ten years, and you may well know that she is still taking it; that you know when a person has taken dope for ten years, that they never stop it; she's a dope fiend; that she is lower than a rattlesnake; that a rattlesnake gives you warning before it strikes, but this woman gives no warning; that she is under a delusion from taking narcotics as long as she has; that she has a delusion; that all the testimony made regarding the accused is only in her mind; that on account of her being an addict, that I wouldn't believe a word she said; that for this reason her testimony is out of the case." (Reported in *Irwin* v. *Ashurst*, 158 Ore. 61, 74 P.2d 1127 [1938], where the woman unsuccessfully brought suit for defamation. Judge and lawyer have immunity from liability for defamatory words spoken in the course of trial.)

it is an asset. In the monumental and definitive study made by Kalven and Zeisel of the jury system in America, a "sampling" of the formidably long list of articles praising or blaming the jury system is given.[27] They quote the Dean of the Harvard Law School as having recommended in 1963, among other measures for improving the administration of justice, the abolition of the jury in civil cases.

Dean Griswold argued: "The jury trial at best is the apotheosis of the amateur. Why should anyone think that 12 persons brought in from the street, selected in various ways, for their lack of general ability, should have any special capacity for deciding controversies between persons?"

The more exasperated form of criticism . . . from an article in the *American Bar Association Journal* in 1924: "Too long has the effete and sterile jury system been permitted to tug at the throat of the nation's judiciary as it sinks under the smothering deluge of the obloquy of those it was designed to serve. Too long has ignorance been permitted to sit ensconced in the places of judicial administration where knowledge is so sorely needed. Too long has the lament of the Shakespearean character been echoed, 'Justice has fled to brutish beasts and men have lost their reason.' "

. . . The distinguished English scholar Glanville Williams, in the Seventh Series of Hamlyn Lectures in 1955 had, among other things, this to say of the jury: "If one proceeds by the light of reason, there seems to be a formidable weight of argument against the jury system. To begin with, the twelve men and women are chosen haphazard. There is a slight property qualification—too slight to be used as an index of ability, if indeed the mere possession of property can ever be so used; on the other hand, exemption is given to some professional people who would seem to be among the best qualified to serve—clergymen, ministers of religion, lawyers, doctors, dentists, chemists, justices of the peace (as well as all ranks of the armed forces). The subtraction of relatively intelligent classes means that it is an understatement to describe a jury, with Herbert Spencer, as a group of twelve people of average ignorance. There is no guarantee that members of a particular jury may not be quite unusually ignorant, credulous, slowwitted, narrow-minded, biased or temperamental. The danger of this happening is not one that can be removed by some minor procedural adjustment; it is inherent in the English notion of a jury as a body chosen from the general population at random." [28]

The jury also has its friends and defendants, and the findings of Kalven and Zeisel were to the effect that the jury usually does at least temper the sentence and act as a moderating influence. Nevertheless, to most psychiatrists, or at least to this one, the rigmarole of installing and instructing a mixed assembly of strangers, then presenting them with intricate problems, is an appalling anachronism. As Robert Lindner has well said, the weary and bewildered jurors are very apt to be "prejudiced for or against the defendant by irrational and preconceived factors having nothing to do with the matter at hand, and anxious only to put a swift termination to an uncomfortable episode and go home." [29] *

In the interest of fairness, I want to quote these dignified, sound concluding sentences of Kalven and Zeisel:

> Whether the jury is a desirable institution depends in no small measure on what we think about the judge. We have given a candid and rounded picture of the jury, but we treated the judge as an abstract, a baseline representing the law. We know, of course, that on the side of the judge too, discretion, freedom, and sentiment will be at work, and that the judge too is human. Until an equally full and candid story of the judge is available, we have only half the knowledge needed.
>
> And there is another point which goes to the time limitations of our study. We have noted that at this moment in history the jury's quarrel with the law is a slight one. But there have been times when the difference was larger and such times may come again.
>
> But no additional facts can decide the policy issue; they can only make it more precise. In the end, evaluation must turn on one's jurisprudence, on how, given the limitations of human foresight, experience, and character, one hopes to achieve the ideal of the rule of law. Whether or not one comes to admire the jury system as much as we

* See, for example, the magnificent portrayal of the group decision in the play, *Twelve Angry Men,* by Reginald Rose (*6 Television Plays.* New York: Simon and Schuster, 1956).

have, it must rank as a daring effort in human arrangement to work out a solution to the tensions between law and equity and anarchy.[30]

Sentencing

If the prisoner is found "not guilty," the judge dismisses the case and presumably all is over. Of course a man's reputation may have been ruined by the very trial. Moreover, he may have been found "not guilty" when there was every presumption that he did commit the alleged offense but for technical reasons could not be proved to have done so. I have often wondered what becomes of individuals like this who must carry with them the rest of their lives the private necessity of dealing with the injustice and untruth of a public exoneration.

If the jury returns a verdict of guilty, the prosecution can be considered to have won the debate and it then becomes the duty of the judge to pronounce a sentence. Perhaps nothing that we could say about this step in the process can be more damning than the implications of that very expression—"pronouncing a sentence." In the days of oracles, a sentence could be "pronounced" that would throw a whole nation into panic. Throughout ancient history and the Middle Ages, one "sentence" or even a few curt words from a king or overlord decided the fate of thousands.

What sentencing means in practice is simply that a judge tries to correlate a state and degree of guiltiness, which have been proved before his eyes, with the prescribed formula for dealing with such state and degree AND with the facilities and personnel available to carry out the formula. This—properly effected—takes some doing. Since the eighteenth century the punishment of an offender proved guilty is supposed to fit (in some metaphysical way) the crime that has been proved. This notion was introduced into the process of justice by Beccaria (not Hammurabi or Solon or any of the others so often cited). The archaic code arbitrarily assembled on this principle was "modernized" by a state legislature over a hundred years ago and variously copied and amended without material improvement in the succeeding decades.

There has been a gradual reduction over the past few centuries in the severity of the "punishment" which particular crimes are believed to "deserve." The varieties of official legal punishment have been narrowed from a long list of horrendous tortures, deprivals, and penalties until theoretically only two are left, detention and financial assessment. Hard labor is often specified in theory, but in fact most prisoners suffer from forced idleness. Nothing is said in the statutes about humiliation, sexual deprivation, regimentation, and many other punitive features of detention as it is actually carried out. No distinction is made in the degree of punishment for the dangerous, the docile, the stupid, the shrewd, the wistful, the confused, or the desperate on the basis of these characteristics. The man who has broken his baby's bones with a club, the man who has forced the door of a warehouse, the woman who has collected two hundred pairs of stockings from the department store, and the adolescent who has set fire to an outhouse—all receive the same treatment, the same "punishment," varying only in duration.

The prisoner is apt to think of himself as being at the mercy of the judge; actually it is the judge who is at the mercy of forces over which he has little control—tradition, precedent, and lack of information, especially the last. On the basis of what someone has written years ago and on the basis of what somebody—a lot of somebodies—has said in court, the poor judge must decide— within limits—where the prisoner goes next on his roundabout route back to society. All this the judge is obliged to decide with a minimal amount of scientific information as to what kind of a man he is dealing with.

Is any serious effort made by the state (for example, by an agent of the court) to investigate the unhealthy neighborhood in which the crime committed by the offender may seem to be endemic? Usually not. The judge is not a sociologist, a policeman, or a welfare worker. He is a judge, his jurisdiction limited to a sanction for the accused and convicted individual. He confirms the finding of guilt and he pronounces the sentence according to the book.

In sentencing an offender, will the court feel inclined to institute preventive measures? Has the judge any powers to prevent the repetition of the crime? Surely no judge seriously believes that a prison sentence acts in the direction of averting repetition of the offense; he knows that almost every penitentiary in America contains a preponderant number of individuals who have been there before.

The judge undoubtedly hopes that the prisoner whom he is sentencing will undergo a change in his personality. But from what influences? No judge wants him changed in the direction of the features of prison life. How will the character structure of the offender, his particular strengths and weaknesses, be ascertained? And were this possible, let us say by some diagnostic setup, to what agencies will the judge refer the man for carrying out a program of induced change?

Some judges do strive to accomplish these things in spite of the lack of facilities, the lack of time available to them, the lack of precedent in many jurisdictions. The judge may stipulate the maximum specified duration of the ordeal, or the minimum. In some jurisdictions he is permitted to give immediate parole on probation, prescribing a check on the offender's subsequent behavior. And in some enlightened states he may give an indeterminate sentence, leaving the duration of detention to those in charge of the prisons and the parole system.

The plight of the judge is worthy of special reflection. He is usually the most intelligent individual in the system but he gets too little opportunity to use this intelligence. He must sit passively during the delivery of all sorts of mumbo jumbo, striving to get some idea of the situation from poorly organized, tendentious stories. His observations are interrupted repeatedly by ritualistic trivialities, and he comes at last to the chore of selecting archaic medieval remedies for the treatment of an acute social and personal problem. Often he may not do what he knows or suspects might be the wisest thing to do; he must follow precedent and continue the merry-go-round.* Many of our best suggestions for juridical and penal reform have come from frustrated, morally outraged judges who yearn to see intelligence replace traditional routine. Some judges are, to be sure, sadistic and power loving; some are stupid; many are overworked and discouraged. But there is an insurgent minority that is demanding a change.

Judge Theodore Knudson, a member of the Advisory Council of Judges of the National Probation and Parole Association, was quoted in the *Saturday Evening Post* as saying:

> In all too many courts, sentences must be meted out hurriedly, without adequate prior investigation, on the basis of little more infor- mation than the type of offense committed and the impression the offender happens to make on the judge. My fellow judges and I are currently sentencing offenders at the rate of more than a million a year. Our problem—and it's a crushing one—is how to sentence wisely in each of these million cases.[31]

Another judge summed up sentencing with these words:

> When determining guilt or innocence, our courts are scrupulous in the extreme. A judge may spend a week or more hearing the case of one person. If he errs in the slightest particular, his ruling may be appealed to a higher court. But when the moment of sentencing comes, most safeguards vanish. Men who have pleaded guilty may parade past the bench to have their fates determined at the rate of forty or fifty a day, during what time the judge can spare from the trying of cases and other pressing duties. The judge may be guided by hunch or influenced by his mood at the moment, yet there is no appeal from his sentence on the ground that it is too harsh or too lenient.[32]

* In G. K. Chesterton's *The Club of Queer Trades* (London: Finlayson, 1960), a judge must pass sentence on a prisoner at the bar: "I sentence you to three year's penal servitude, in the firm and God-given conviction that what you really require is three weeks at the sea-side." Chesterton meant to jolt the reader a bit and to suggest the irrationality of the whole system the judge is called upon to administer.

"As a method of decision-making, the process by which offenders are sentenced must surely be almost without parallel," wrote Lady Wootton. She continued:

All its peculiarities are indeed well enough known, but even so it may perhaps be worth briefly listing them, so as to bring the whole picture into view.

In the first place, these decisions are always of importance—often of overwhelming importance—to the individuals concerned, and in the aggregate highly important also to the whole community: yet they are frequently made in a very few moments, often in magistrates' courts or quarter sessions after a brief whispered discussion between the chairman and his colleagues. Second, although in many cases the court has a very wide discretion in its choice of sentence, there are no explicit rules as to how this discretion should be exercised nor indeed any explicit principles determining the object of the whole exercise. Third, in many cases decisions as to sentence fall to be made by wholly untrained amateurs—indeed it might be said that all such decisions are amateurishly made, inasmuch as the subject of penology has no place in the training of a judge or stipendiary magistrate. Fourth, sentences may be passed by persons who have no first-hand knowledge of what they imply—who have for instance no clear idea as to just how the regime prescribed by a sentence of corrective training differs from that followed in ordinary imprisonment. Fifth, the more serious the decision, the more likely it is to be made by one man alone, rather than by a group in consultation. Sixth, whatever the objective aimed at, no machinery exists by which the success or failure of particular decisions in reaching that objective may be assessed. In consequence it is impossible for anyone who passes sentences either to test his own performances or to learn from experience, and equally impossible to test the relevance of any information provided with the object of assisting the court to arrive at its decisions.

Is it then surprising that the choice between the one sentence and another often seems to have remarkably little concrete effect?

One has only to glance . . . at the maximum penalties which the law attaches to various offences to realise how profoundly attitudes change in course of time. Life imprisonment, for example, is not only the obligatory sentence for non-capital murder and the maximum permissible for manslaughter. It may also be imposed for blasphemy or for the destruction of registers of births or baptisms. Again, the crime of abducting an heiress carries a potential sentence of fourteen years, while that for the abduction of a child under fourteen years is only half as long. For administering a drug to a female with a view to carnal knowledge a maximum of two years is provided, but for damage to cattle you are liable to fourteen years' imprisonment. For using unlawful oaths the maximum is seven years, but for keeping a child in a brothel it is a mere six months. Such sentences strike us today as quite fantastic; but they cannot have seemed fantastic to those who devised them.[33]

Disparities of sentences plague the courts. The State Director of Corrections in Kansas, Charles McAtee, has spoken out strongly on this problem: "Many sentences are too long, others too short. They are simply out of focus when compared in so many cases."[34] When a defendant is convicted on multiple counts, the judge arbitrarily decides whether the sentences for each count will run concurrently or consecutively. And if the court reserves the order of pronouncing the same sentences, prisoners' eligibility for parole consideration is greatly affected. Prisoner resentment at this type of procedure has led to bloody riots and rebellions.

Even more serious than the disparity of sentences is their futility, in many instances. Over and over some men and women overdraw their bank accounts or forge a signature or draw on a nonexistent account. Usually this is overlooked for a few times if the amount is made up quickly. In Europe it is not even considered a crime unless an intent to defraud is clearly evident and proved. Most banks, hotels, and business agencies take reasonable precautions to avoid letting this happen. But there are many filling stations, lunch counters, and beer halls where the amount involved is not large enough to arouse suspicion or the contact is too brief to permit identification of the person who pays with a check. It is easier to gamble on making a few dollars than to risk losing a customer.

That some individuals exploit this situation, there can be no doubt. But they are usually not villains, dangerous men (or women), or vicious crooks, but simply economic children (sometimes very defiant, disobedient, or spoiled children). The profundities of the monetary system and the machinery of the law are beyond their comprehension or their interest.

Does anyone really believe that a prison sentence has the slightest influence in developing maturity in such individuals, in teaching them that although one can legitimately gamble in many ways, such as on the stock market or the horse races, taking a chance on unsupported check passing is not a permitted way? The recidivism rate for such cases is almost a hundred per cent, and every state prison, especially the women's prison, has scores of these offenders. Small shopkeepers (and sometimes big ones) take checks on a chance. When checks bounce, merchants get mad and prefer charges, and lawyers can easily convict because the fraud is in writing. So the judges keep on sentencing and the prisons keep on receiving the offenders and a little later discharging them after the state has thrown good money after bad. The total amount of money actually involved is rarely more than a few hundred dollars, usually much less, and the cost of this incessant arresting, jailing, prosecuting, convicting, transporting, imprisoning, supervising, and finally releasing of these individuals runs into hundreds of thousands of dollars. Can anyone imagine a more absurd, wasteful, expensive routine?

If common sense were allowed to prevail, why could not the whole matter be settled simply by supervised restitution (with a penalty, of course)? But offenders of all kinds are rarely obliged to make restitution in kind. They are not even given the opportunity to earn money with which to do this (ten cents a day, which some prisons allow, cannot seriously be regarded as earned money), and the whole thing could be avoided by imposing a few regulations on the people who accept checks.

Leading judges have been worried about sentencing problems for many years, and many of them have been working to do some-

thing about them. In 1963, after many years of hard work, collec-
tively and individually, a Model Sentencing Act was brought out
by the Advisory Council of Judges of the National Council on
Crime and Delinquency. * It may be considered a definite break-

* In my opinion the members of this Council make up an honor roll of
leadership and progress. They are:

Chairman, Alfred P. Murrah, Chief Judge, United States Court of Appeals,
Oklahoma City, Okla.

Chairman, Juvenile and Family Courts Section, Leo B. Blessing, Judge,
Juvenile Court, Parish of Orleans, New Orleans, La.

Chairman, Criminal Courts Section, Irving Ben Cooper, Judge, United
States District Court, New York, N.Y.

Paul W. Alexander, Judge, Division of Domestic Relations and Juvenile
Court, Court of Common Pleas, Toledo, Ohio

Charles O. Betts, Judge, Ninety-Eighth District Court, Austin, Texas.

William J. Brennan, Jr., Justice, Supreme Court of the United States,
Washington, D.C.

James M. Carter, Judge, United States District Court, San Diego, Calif.

Alfred J. Chretien, Justice, Manchester Municipal Court, Manchester, N.H.

Paul K. Connolly, Judge, Second District Court of Eastern Middlesex, Wal-
tham, Mass.

Byron B. Conway, Judge, County Court of Wood County, Wisconsin Rapids,
Wis.

William E. Doyle, Judge, United States District Court, Denver, Colo.

George Edwards, Judge, United States Court of Appeals, Detroit, Mich.

Harold N. Fields, Judge, Marion County Juvenile Court, Indianapolis, Ind.

William S. Fort, Judge, Circuit Court, Eugene, Ore.

W. Turney Fox, Judge, District Court of Appeals, Los Angeles, Calif.

Thomas D. Gill, Judge, Juvenile Court for the State of Connecticut, Hart-
ford, Conn.

William A. Grimes, Associate Justice, Supreme Court, Dover, N.H.

Edward S. Heefner, Jr., Judge, Forsythe County Domestic Relations Court,
Winston-Salem, N.C.

Thomas Herlihy, Jr., Chief Judge, Municipal Court, Wilmington, Del.

Robert M. Hill, Circuit Judge, Eleventh Judicial Circuit Court, Florence,
Ala.

Ivan Lee Holt, Jr., Circuit Judge, Twenty-Second Judicial Circuit, St. Louis,
Mo.

Laurance M. Hyde, Chief Justice, Supreme Court of Missouri, Jefferson
City, Mo.

Bertil E. Johnson, Judge of the Juvenile Court, Superior Court, Tacoma,
Wash.

Florence M. Kelley, Administrative Judge, Family Court of the City of
New York, New York, N.Y.

through in correctional treatment and sentencing. The Model Act states in its first article that it "shall be liberally construed to the end that persons convicted of crime shall be dealt with in accordance with their individual characteristics, circumstances, needs, and potentialities as revealed by case studies; that dangerous offenders shall be correctively treated in custody for long terms as

---

Orman W. Ketcham, Judge, Juvenile Court, Washington, D.C.

Theodore B. Knudson, Judge, District Court of Minnesota, Minneapolis, Minn.

Arthur S. Lane, Judge, United States District Court, Trenton, N.J.

Donald E. Long, Judge, Retired, Portland, Ore.

Luther W. Maples, Judge, County Court, Gulfport, Miss.

John E. Mullen, Associate Justice, Superior Court of Rhode Island, Providence, R.I.

J. Donald Murphy, Judge, Sixteenth Judicial Circuit, Kansas City, Mo.

Frank W. Nicholas, Judge, Family Court Center, Dayton, Ohio.

Alfred D. Noyes, Judge, People's Court for Juvenile Causes of Montgomery County, Rockville, Md.

Donald A. Odell, Presiding Judge, Superior Court, Los Angeles, Calif.

James C. Otis, Judge, Supreme Court, St. Paul, Minn.

Claude M. Owens, Judge, Municipal Court, Anaheim-Fullerton Judicial District, Anaheim, Calif.

Clinton Budd Palmer, Judge, Third Judicial District Court, Easton, Pa.

Monroe J. Paxman, Judge, Third Juvenile District Court, Provo, Utah.

George H. Revelle, Judge, Superior Court, Seattle, Wash.

Henry A. Riederer, Judge, Circuit Court, Kansas City, Mo.

Clayton W. Rose, Judge, Division of Domestic Relations, Court of Common Pleas of Franklin County, Columbus, Ohio.

Joe W. Sanders, Associate Justice, Supreme Court of Louisiana, New Orleans, La.

Simon E. Sobeloff, Chief Judge, United States Court of Appeals, Baltimore, Md.

Herbert J. Steffes, Judge, Milwaukee County Municipal Court, Milwaukee, Wis.

Thomas Tallakson, Judge, Minneapolis, Minn.

G. Joseph Tauro, Chief Justice, Commonwealth of Massachusetts, The Superior Court, Boston, Mass.

William J. Thompson, Judge, Intermediate Court of Kanawha County, Charleston, W. Va.

Dorothy Young, Judge, Juvenile Court of Tulsa County, Tulsa, Okla.

Luther W. Youngdahl, Judge, United States District Court, Washington, D.C.

needed; and that other offenders shall be dealt with by probation, suspended sentence, or fine whenever such disposition appears practicable and not detrimental to the needs of public safety and the welfare of the offender, or shall be committed for a limited period." [35]

Imprisonment

The idea of punishment as the law interprets it seems to be that inasmuch as a man has offended society, society must officially offend him. It must deliver him a tit for the tat that he committed. This tit must not be impulsive retaliation; not mob action. It must be done dispassionately, by agency, by stipulation, and by statute. It must be something that will make the offender sorry (or sorrier) for what he did and resolve to do it no more.

Let no one deceive himself about the intention of the prison to be a terrible place. When the Maine State Prison was opened, its first warden proclaimed:

> Prisons should be so constructed that even their aspect might be terrific and appear like what they should be—dark and comfortless abodes of guilt and wretchedness. No more of degree of punishment . . . is in its nature so well adapted to purposes of preventing crime or reforming a criminal as close confinement in a solitary cell, in which, cut off from all hope of relief, the convict shall be furnished a hammock on which he may sleep, a block of wood on which he may sit, and with such coarse and wholesome food as may best be suited to a person in a situation designed for grief and penitence, and shall be favored with so much light from the firmament as may enable him to read the New Testament which will be given him as his sole companion and guide to a better life. There his vices and crimes shall become personified, and appear to his frightened imagination as co-tenants of his dark and dismal cell. They will surround him as so many hideous spectres and overwhelm him with horror and remorse.[36]

The Constitutional prohibition against "cruel and unusual" punishment implies that in some way or other the hurting done by the state must be a familiar garden variety and not something unexpected. For inexplicable reasons, to deprive a man of decent social relationships, palatable food, normal friendships and sexual relations, and constructive communication is not—in the eyes of the law—cruel or unusual. Imprisonment, it will be recalled, was not originally considered punishment; it was only a method of detention prior to sentence, banishment, or execution. Hard labor extracted from the individual, presumably disagreeable, monotonous, menial, and often pointless, was the other type of punishment available.

And so, on the basis of this philosophy, the convicted prisoner, now officially a "criminal," is remanded to the local jail after sentence until the sheriff or his deputy can get around to making the trip to the state prison. Sometimes this is done with the sheriff's car; more often the prisoner is handcuffed and loaded with his several fellows into a locked van and they are carted off like a load of trussed hogs.

At the prison he is unloaded into the reception division and there stripped, bathed, fingerprinted, and photographed with a large black and white serial number placarded across his neck. The mugging process is reminiscent of calf branding: when the hot iron is withdrawn, the calf struggles to his feet and staggers off in the direction indicated by his stony-faced handlers. The new prisoner goes to a cell block in which a large number of steel cages, built or fastened together and piled on top of each other in several tiers, provides for clapping one, two, or three individuals into each. A long iron bar, operated by remote control, closes a long tier of cages, and part of the typical music in any prison is the resounding clang of various bars on the various tiers being shot or ground into a state of closure.

In each cage is a small triangular wall basin, an open toilet bowl, a shelf, a chair or stool, and a cot or a double-decker. Visitors may pass by and gaze into each. Prisoners can be seen huddled on their chairs, lying on their cots, combing their hair at the wash basins. They are gazed at by passers-by with much the same sensation of mild curiosity that one has in walking past cages at the zoo.

These cages are opened early each morning with the same noisy mechanism that closed them. The prisoners emerge and march to breakfast and sometimes to thirty minutes of exercise, which means walking around in a paved enclosure. In a few institutions some of them go next to the prison industries—auto-repair shops, tailor shops, shoemaking, basketmaking, and occasionally a manufacturing plant of some kind. For some prisoners there may be a farm or a mine or a quarry. For some who elect it, there are educational classes. But the offender is in prison to be punished—not educated or amused.

In quarters such as these, the recipient of official punishment languishes in the cheerless company of others equally miserable, hopeless, and resentful. He is herded about by men half afraid and half contemptuous of him, toward whom all offenders early learn to present a steadfast attitude of hostility. An atmosphere of monotony, futility, hate, loneliness, and sexual frustration pervades the dank dungeons and cold hangars like a miasma, while time grinds out weary months and years. (Not every prison is like this, but too many are.)

When General Grant entered Richmond he found in operation a prison that had been opened in 1797; the prison is still in use (1967). According to former Federal Commissioner James V. Bennett, more than one hundred prisons still in operation were built before Grant took Richmond. In 1798—please do a little mental arithmetic—the state of New Jersey opened its Trenton prison "now standing as a disgrace to American penology and periodically erupting in violence, bloodshed and escape plots. . . . In 1956 I had heartfelt hopes that an era of infamy in American penology had closed. A New Jersey Governor had the funds to replace the Trenton penitentiary which had long shamed the consciences of professional penologists. An effort was made to patch it up, so I am told, and worry along with it under the delusion it can be modernized." [37]

If a doctor sends a man to a hospital to be treated, he goes to see whether the treatment is being carried on; but judges do not seem to believe in this principle. Judges rarely visit the institutions to which they are constantly committing their wards to be "treated." Whenever I have taken judges with me to visit prisons or closely examine prisoners, they have been far more shocked than I.

> Judges spend their lives in consigning their fellow creatures to prison; and when some whisper reaches them that prisons are horribly cruel and destructive places, and that no creature fit to live should be sent there, they only remark calmly that prisons are not meant to be comfortable, which is no doubt the consideration that reconciled Pontius Pilate to the practice of crucifixion. (Barnes [38])

But it is not only judges who rarely visit prisons. Who (except a few relatives) does visit prisons? Like the old-fashioned state mental hospitals, prisons have never welcomed visitors, and most people, even kindly, charitable-minded ones, feel they have no business there. George Bernard Shaw commented that one of the main evils of the prison system was the possibility of performing these inhumanities secretly, treatment which the public would never tolerate if they could see it.

The short, nonscientific term that best describes most adult penal institutions is *evil,* declared the director of the District of Columbia Department of Corrections.[39] Evil influences pervade jails. Perverse sexual behavior is commonplace; indeed the prison is excellently designed to promote this and along with it many other evidences of psychological and emotional imbalance, the very things which society wants psychiatrists to cure.

To describe what it means to be a prisoner, how it feels to be confined, the agonies of the "long moment of suffering," is impossible for one who has not, in the words of Fallada, "eaten out of the tin plate." [40] The psychological state of complete passivity and "dependence on the decisions of guards and officers must be included among the pains of imprisonment along with restrictions of physical liberty, the possession of goods and services and heterosexual relations. The frustration of the prisoner's ability to make choices and the frequent refusals to provide an explanation for the regulations and commands descending from the bureaucratic staff involve a profound threat to the prisoner's self-image because they reduce the prisoner to the weak, helpless, dependent status of childhood. . . . The imprisoned criminal finds his picture of himself as a self-determining individual being destroyed by the regime of the custodians." [41] *

Bill Sands in his book, *My Shadow Ran Fast,* describes some vivid scenes of daily horror recalled by him from his prison stay. But then he adds:

> If this sounds exciting, it is misleading. These things happen, but they happen quietly, furtively, sullenly. The men do their time with very little comment or conversation. Fighting makes a man lose his time off for good behavior (wherein he can serve as little as three years and nine months on a 5-year sentence). So there are no curses or insults—such as would lead to fistfights on the outside. There are no fistfights. If the issue is worth beefing about, it is done silently and quickly with a knife or a length of pipe. There is a small scuffle, a man lies bleeding; there is the clatter of a shiv or pipe being kicked away. If the weapon is ever found, it is not "on" anyone. There are no fingerprints. That is all.
>
> Everywhere, every minute—like the air you breathe—there is the threat of violence lurking beneath the surface. Unlike the air, it is heavy, massive, as oppressive as molasses. It permeates every second of everyone's existence—the potential threat of sudden, ferocious annihilation. It is as grey and swift and unpredictable as a shark and just as unvocal. There is no letup from it—ever. [42]

I have just come from interviewing another victim of the system. He is twenty years old. His crimes had not been so aggressive—

---

* The reader is referred to a study made by a very sensitive and very well-informed investigator, James A. Gittings, reported in the Presbyterian journal *Crossroads: Studies for Adults in Christian Faith and Life* (January–March 1966). Mr. Gittings' article is introduced and followed by articles written by former warden Wade Markley of the federal prison at Terre Haute. This study has been highly commended for its accuracy and fairness by prison officers and prisoners.

some minor stealing, reckless driving, and belligerent behavior, especially toward police officers—but he had served three years in a reformatory where the principle of management was "treat 'em rough." Most of the time he had spent in solitary confinement, chiefly as punishment for impudent and angry replies to the guards.

True, this lad was undoubtedly a "spoiled boy" to begin with, in the sense that he was indulged by his mother and either ignored or beaten by his father, but given no consistent love or home discipline by either. He was very much in need of "correction" of the right sort; he never got it. In that sense he was spoiled.

But what he received at the reformatory did not reform him; it did not correct him. It *ruined* him. The bitterness, the distrust, and the hate of older human beings which the "correction" in that institution produced became chronic, and irrational in degree. In spite of the fact that he thanked me after a brief interview (which began with sullen monosyllabic answers), and in spite of my temperamental optimism, I tended to agree with the staff consensus. Nobody wants him, and he wants nobody; he wants nobody's help. Probably only violent aggressive outbreaks will permit him to retain his "sanity." And violent aggression the police or the prison guards will certainly not tolerate. So in prison he will remain and deteriorate.

I remember vividly a prisoner I saw at the Kansas Diagnostic Center who had become what is variously labeled in prison slang "the barn boss" or "the whore master." These are the prisoners who rule the cell block or some part of the prison by force. They often have more power than the guards, maintained by bullying and brutality. They control the dispersal of new prisoners to various homosexual wolves, handle the narcotics that are smuggled into the prison, corner the cash supplies of the prisoners, and do other illegal things. This particular man was a small, wiry, athletic Negro who had confessed to many chokings and rapings of young women. He related his propensity for ruthless assaults to the chokings and beatings he used to receive from his grandmother, his mother having abandoned him completely to the former's care. He loved to play baseball on the school team, and his beatings would occur when he didn't arrive home promptly after school to do unpleasant chores for his grandmother.

Another prisoner referred to the Diagnostic Center is now twenty-four. When he was eighteen, he was sentenced to ten years in prison for statutory rape. He violated his parole last year and was taken back to prison. He was "combative" and hence was transferred to another "more secure" prison. Here he was so explosive, so violent, so given to attacks of rage and self-injury that he was transferred again, this time to a state hospital. But the doctors and nurses in the state hospital, accustomed to "maniacs" and "mad men," were afraid of him, so he was returned to prison for custody. However, the prison people still did not want him and he was sent to the Diagnostic Center to be referred—*where?*

"I can't control myself," he admitted, "but still I want to be turned loose. Yet I don't dare go back on the street. I'd kill or get killed. But I can't stand it in here either. My God, this is awful! Can you do something? I have half killed myself a dozen times; I will succeed one of these days—me or one of you. You better keep me locked up. But it ain't doing any good."

If this man were moaning with pain from a mangled hand, any of us would have pity on him because we could see blood and tendon. But because his pain is internal and because he has injured others, he gets little pity. He needs treatment; he begs for it. But where shall we treat him?

Thus, hidden from public gaze, with citizens enjoying a pleasant sense of security in thinking that they are being protected from the lawless by modern, civilized methods, the terrible, dreadful prison regimes grind on, an endless contest between caged animals—

that want to get out and regain their freedom and a prison staff which is consecrated to seeing to it that they do not realize this ceaseless and overpowering ambition. Prison life and administration is a perpetual cold war, which at times warms up notably, especially in the case of rioting. Prison industry, prison education, and even the rehabilitative efforts of the treatment staffs which have been set up in the better prisons of today, are all incidental to this perpetual cold war between restive inmates and their apprehensive and restraining captors. There are lesser conditions and issues which make it difficult to achieve the rehabilitation of inmates of prisons but the caging compulsion and the jailing psychosis lie at the basis of the failure of the prison system. (Barnes [43])

Many wardens live in dread of a riot. Uprisings of prisoners, for whatever cause, frighten the public and greatly alarm the politicians. A riot is taken to be prima-facie evidence that the system has broken down. And because the warden is probably a political appointee, to say nothing of scores of his employees, the party in power is nervous about this public exhibition of incompetent management. The warden is afraid he will lose his job, and the governor worries about his reputation for good management; the public worries about the demonstration of loss of control.

This is not the place to go into the details of why most of these riots develop; a more sensible question is why there are not many more of them. The maximum-security policy advocated by the old-time penologists has the effect of increasing frantic, desperate, and furious reactions. Anyone who, like the author, has been on prison commissions and survey teams has become familiar with the deep, hoarse cry for "maximum security" that characterizes the philosophy of certain prison people—fortunately a diminishing but still too influential group.

Prison riots might be—*sub specie aeternitatis*—blessings in disguise. They call attention to some aspects of the rottenness of prisons. The only trouble is that they do not keep the attention of the right people long enough nor do they call attention to the real things in the system that provoke the riot. The maximum-security people raise their strident voices of alarm again, and we renew the search for stronger steel and heavier bars and more restrictive regimes.

Monuments to stupidity are these institutions we have built—stupidity not so much of the inmates as of free citizens! What a mockery of science are our prison discipline, our amassing of social iniquity in prisons, the good and the bad together in one stupendous *potpourri*. How silly of us to think that we can prepare men for social life by reversing the ordinary process of socialization—silence for the only animal with speech; repressive regimentation of men who are in prison because they need to learn how to exercise their activities in constructive ways; outward conformity to rules which repress all efforts at constructive expression; work without the operation of economic motives; motivation by fear of punishment rather than hope of reward or appeal to their higher motives; cringing rather than growth in manliness; rewards secured by the betrayal of a fellow rather than the development of a larger loyalty. (John Gillin, 1931.[44])

In the *Chicago Tribune* (January 17, 1967) appeared this report of terror in an Arkansas prison:

Governor Winthrop Rockefeller released today a confidential report of beatings, torture, and extortion in the Tucker prison farm and called for creation of a blue-ribbon commission to study the state's prison system. The governor told a news conference that the 67-page report was shocking and that he hoped it would "shock the legislature and the people of this state into action." The report was prepared by the criminal investigation division of the Arkansas state police after its investigation last August of conditions at Tucker, one of two prison farms in the state. . . .

In the report, inmates told of being wired to a ring-type of telephone attached to two dry cell batteries with which they were "rung up," or given an electrical charge, for punishment. They called the instrument the "Tucker telephone." Investigators said they found in the main prison building other instruments of torture, whisky bottles, keys to open all cell doors, gambling equipment in the form of playing cards and loaded dice, illegal drugs and narcotics, and recording equipment and places for their concealment. . . .

One investigator said he was told that the inmates received meat only on visiting Sunday each month, one egg a year on Christmas morning, and never any milk. He said that each man he observed in a long line of field workers as they were brought to the kitchen to be fed appeared to be 40 to 60 pounds underweight. He said the prisoners' clothing was filthy and ragged. He added that inmates had no shoes and were required to wear rubber boots or go barefooted.

One inmate testified that he and a fellow prisoner were tortured for several hours with wirepliers applied to their fingers, toes, ears, noses, and other parts of their body. He said needles were stuck under their fingernails at least an inch deep.

Governor Rockefeller was surprised to learn of these terrible things. Governor Lester G. Maddox of Georgia—apparently also very naïve—was surprised when four Negro prisoners walked into the executive office on April 16, 1967, and told of the brutality with which they and their fellow prisoners were being treated. "If they're telling the truth, this camp ought to be shut down," said the Governor. "I believe there is a lot of truth in their statement." But the warden's quoted comment was: "A Nigger will tell a lie. Let 'em investigate." [45]

In 1963, Dr. Sol Rubin reported that

At least twenty-six prisons employed corporal punishment. Whipping with a strap was common. The Virginia "spread eagle," similar to the medieval rack, stretched the body by ropes and pulleys. Men died or came close to death in Florida's sweat box, an unventilated cell built around a fireplace. In Michigan and Ohio prisoners were kept in a standing position and unable to move; in Wisconsin they were gagged; in West Virginia they were subjected to frigid baths. . . . A leading authority on correctional work more recently wrote: "In a Southern state whose prison system I have recently surveyed, the prison system is under the Highway Department, and 85 per cent of the 8,500 prisoners are engaged in hard work. Misdemeanants as well as felons, boys of seventeen and men of seventy are sentenced 'to the roads.' They work under the gun, are shot down like rabbits if they attempt to escape, are chased with bloodhounds if they get away, and are punished by confinement in dark cells 3½ feet wide, or by handcuffing to the bars, or in some cases by flogging." [46]

There has been some improvement in many prisons, as we shall describe later. But in general prisons are still evil places—evil in conception, evil in operation. They are operated for the wrong purpose and in the wrong spirit, often (not always) by the wrong people.

The Exit from Prison

The time comes for some of those thus incarcerated to begin an upward climb, a status-restoration process in theory. Even in the face of the most terrible experiences, as we know from the dramatic letters published from the death cells of the German concentration camps,[47] the human spirit finds ways of survival. It seizes upon the cobweb strands of hope.

The majority of prisoners are given a minimum prescribed time, after serving which they may go before the parole board for consideration for supervised release. Most of them, it can be assumed, live the last twelve months of these periods in a state of mixed fear, uncertainty, and wistful hope.

This is the way status restoration proceeds: On the day appointed, the prisoner dresses in his best overalls. He may be allowed to have his shabby, old, out-of-style coat brought from the locker room and draped over his shoulders. Wistful, frightened, suspicious, sometimes sullen, but always apprehensive, he is called into the warden's office or conference room. He sits at or stands before the long table around which the solemn members of the parole board are seated. His name and number are read off; his record is produced; abstracts of his case lie before each member of the board.

The case load at a parole-board meeting may run from fifty to several hundred cases. This allows only a few minutes per prisoner.

"Do you think you have learned your lesson?"

"Do you intend to go straight now?"

"Will you behave yourself? Can you keep out of trouble?"

"Are you sorry for what you did?"

"Do you pray?"

"Do you have a job?"

Random questions are fired at a tense, frightened fellow who would answer almost any question in the world in whatever way he thought might get him out of the torture of his imprisonment, or safely past this critical inquisition. I am sure most members of most parole boards ask mostly intelligent questions, but they all should realize that the answers given under such circumstances are not very credible or revealing.

The real fault is that the board has so little data to go by. There will be at hand usually a history of the offense, a record of the prisoner's performance in the prison, a file of correspondence about him, work reports from some of his supervisors, and sometimes a physical examination report. In the vast majority of instances there is no psychiatric examination, clinical case study, personality inventory, or social-work investigation of the family and neighborhood from which he comes or the environment to which he goes. There is sometimes, alas and alack, a so-called "score" from psychological testing by means of the Minnesota Multiphasic Personality Inventory. In my opinion this and similar paper-and-pencil tests are limited in value, particularly when used in isolation and given by people who have little knowledge of the nature of human behavior. In fact, such tests offer information as limited as the other fragments of personal data at the disposal of the parole board.

One of my colleagues, Dr. Russell Settle, who as the warden of a federal prison has sat through many federal parole board meetings, feels that my judgment of state parole boards is too severe. He is certainly correct in reminding me that I have not sat with all or even many state boards and am extrapolating my conclusions. Surely the federal system and some states (including Kansas) have parole boards that do a better job than my description implies.

> Most boards have extensive information about parole applicants. Many have their offices in conjunction with the central office of the correctional system and use common case files with the director of corrections which contain all known information, test reports, and progress reports on the individual applicants. . . . It is the function

of parole boards, with the assistance of institutional staff, to make a social prognosis and to act upon it. Where board members are experienced persons out of the correctional field, as is often the case, astute decisions can often be made even in the absence of much clinical data.[48]

Thus, whether the parole board is as perspicacious and conscientious as I know some are, or as stupid and unscrupulous as I have known others to have been, the fate of the prisoner is a toss-up. He may be remanded to prison for a little more penitence and reflection—at state expense, of course. Or he may be dumped back upon society to sink or swim, blessed only with the expensive education he has had in concealing bitterness and fury. In some states, such as my own, he will not be released, no matter how good his record or how long his service, until he or someone else has obtained for him some sort of employment prospect. Many are kept waiting in a "postgraduate term" in prison because the available jobs are snapped up by outsiders. But if there are any jobs that no one wants, the "jailbirds" (ex-prisoners) may have a chance at them.

Some years ago (1959) the following chart by Roy A. Lartigue was published in *The Atlantian,* the prisoners' excellent magazine at the Federal Penitentiary in Atlanta. In terse but eloquent words it describes the futility of our system, step by step.

Our Wheel of Misfortune

ARRIVAL . . . we come into Quarantine . . . strangeness surrounds us —and then comes the inevitable reaction . . . a dreadful place—with its high walls, steel bars, watchful guards, and most difficult of all . . . LONELINESS!

ROUTINE . . . but life goes on—even in a penitentiary—and we become accustomed to clanging bells, bugle calls, regimentation, lack of privacy, loss of initiative, deprivation of individuality, menial work . . . but, soon, there comes the sign of ADJUSTMENT.

PROGRAM PARTICIPATION . . . despite our high average age, 40% of us become active in some phase of the Recreation Program; 23% of us become involved in some phase of the Education Program; 20% of us become aware of the Religious Program; and 12% of us take advantage of the Trade Training Program . . . we seek something to keep us occupied—and some of us even admit to ourselves that we would like to better ourselves . . . and we all become aware that we are coming close to completing ⅛ of our sentence and with it, the chance for Parole! At night, alone with our thoughts in the darkened cell, some of us vow that if we are granted Parole, we'll make good!

PAROLE DENIAL . . . 85% of us are turned down by the U.S. Board of parole—and no one seems surprised by their decision! . . . our institutional record has been good, our program participation has been excellent and sincere . . . and the numbing feeling, after denial, soon dims and is succeeded by action . . . we decide that there is another way to serve this sentence . . . so we decide to go into . . . MILL WORK . . . 45% of us ask to get assigned to Federal Prison Industries to do hard, menial work—a granted privilege—for we are paid money and also the chance to earn extra "good time" . . . we reason that we will, at least, get to save some money and also be able to make the rest of the sentence more tolerable . . . but being in the Mill has its disadvantages, too . . . and, soon, there comes a noticeable . . .

DECLINE OF ACTIVITY . . . working in the Mill prevents us from getting passes to take part in a show rehearsal, baseball practice, school debate or even browsing in the Library . . . the tight institutional schedule is further upset by the even tighter Mill schedule—and it soon wears down our desire to participate . . . we simply work, read, listen to our earphones and sleep . . . but, after a while, we become restless with this monotonous existence and we acquire a . . . .

HOBBY INTEREST . . . we start to search for some private rather than communal relaxational activity . . . we write, we draw, we carve and sometimes, in desperation, we buy yarn with which to crochet! . . . and the time passes until—suddenly!—we realize that the day we "gotta go" is approaching! . . . so we begin our. . . .

RELEASE PLANNING . . . we begin writing letters to friends outside, seeking help—and their replies are vague and not too encouraging . . . so many of us start searching for "connections" from some of the "conning convicts" . . . and, of course, in the quiet of our bunks, we get grandiose ideas of what we can do with the few hundred dollars we saved from our Mill Work . . . and, finally, we decide to take advantage of the . . .

ADMINISTRATIVE HELP . . . the institutional routine has us meet our Parole Officer who tells us that, under the rules, we will have to return to our officially listed residence—even after we protest that we have not lived there in years! He is sympathetic, but adamant as he explains that he is merely following the set rules . . . and we also get to fill out an employment form for a possible job secured by an agency which insists that the prospective employer will have to know about our past . . . and we are fitted out with clothes and a bus ticket to the place we often don't wish to ever see again . . . and the day comes for . . .

CONDITIONAL RELEASE . . . we have now served ⅔ of the Judge's sentence and it is mandatory that we be released because we have earned the "good time" by our behavior here—but now, we are told that even though we were denied Parole, so long ago, we must abide by the same rules outside as the Parolees . . . but we are so happy to leave that we sign the contract willingly—and we go out in the world to encounter . . .

PUBLIC REACTION . . . yes, we soon find that the "Old Timers" told us the truth! . . . we encounter apathy . . . and prejudice, and indifference, and ostracism, and futile sympathy—"I'd like to help you get started, but . . ." and we react: first there is discouragement . . . then resentment —and sometimes, with it, comes anger . . . and then, in some cases despair . . . and even panic . . . and, finally desperation . . . and it begins . . .

DETERIORATION & RECIDIVISM . . . our resistance is lowered by discouragement—and there is less and less resistance to temptation . . . and we still hang on while we watch how "normal people" are permitted to live . . . a good job . . . and friends . . . and family . . . and simple luxuries, like decent clothes and a car . . . and, inevitably, because we are human, envy arrives to haunt us . . . and, meanwhile, even those of us with families become aware of the burden we have become to them—hiding our past, explaining our presence after such a long absence—and we finally decide we're going to get some money for independence . . . and we commit another crime—and, of course, we get caught!

And back to Atlanta we come . . . and it begins again . . . and our WHEEL OF MISFORTUNE spins around and around . . . and those about to depart keep hoping that they'll adjust to "THE FIXED WHEEL."

The Reentry into the Outside World

Unfortunately our crimes against criminals do not cease when, having served his sentence, the offender is released from prison. He reenters a world utterly unlike the one he has been living in and also unlike the one he left some years before. In the new world, aside from a few uneasy relatives and uncertain friends, he is surrounded by hostility, suspicion, distrust, and dislike. He is a marked man—an ex-convict. Complex social and economic situations that proved too much for him before he went to prison have grown no simpler. The unequal tussle with smarter, "nicer," and more successful people begins again. Proscribed for employment by most concerns, and usually unable to find new friends or ways of earning a living, he tries to survive.

His chief occupation for a time will be the search for a means of livelihood, accompanied by innumerable rebuffs, suspicious glances, discouragements and hostile encounters and, of course, inevitably, temptations. Aside from his parole officer, toward whom he may not always feel kindly, the first friendly face that such an individual is likely to see is that of some crony of the old days who has been waiting for a little help to do a little job.

Remember, we are talking about a human being, a handicapped one at that, one who needs all the things that the rest of us do and a little bit more! You and I can get along without committing crimes (most of the time); but obviously the criminal cannot, or at least he did not, and often *does not*. The fellow who has been in prison is worse off; he suffers not only from whatever made him commit a crime in the first place, but he now has what the prison did to him and, in addition, what society gives to *former* victims. He has a heavy burden.

Do the churches reach out to take him in? Do business firms recruit him? Do the labor unions quickly take him in and help find him a job? Does the country club give him a locker? Does any but the lowest-class restaurant and rooming house welcome so unprepossessing, shabbily-dressed, and often ill-favored an individual? Does anyone know or care if he is lonely, depressed, desperate, deluded, or just plain hungry? Does anyone ask what might have been done to deter him from continuing the way he was obviously going? Does anyone ask what might be done to redirect him?

No, certainly not. That is not in the book. The law says nothing about "helping" criminals, or "ex-cons." (That is what they are called even after their guilt has been officially atoned for. We used to talk about ex-lunatics in the same way.)

Parole and Probation

Because I shall deal with it later in the book, I am passing over too swiftly the sustaining, supporting, and controlling functions performed by thousands of earnest and capable but overworked probation and parole officers. What they do cannot be praised too highly. Few citizens sufficiently appreciate either the contribution they are making or the contribution they could make if they were adequately provided for. This best part of the system has been tacked on to it in recent years (probation began in the United States in the 1840s, parole in the 1870s).

But despite the excellence of these concepts, the concrete procedures have been subjected to their own misuses, have become encrusted with their own inflexible rules, and have in many places become cogs of the creaking machinery of the whole correctional system. The truth is we have not given the idea of probation a fair shake. The underlying philosophy is based on our recognition of the offender's need for help, and we have developed a certain professional skill in giving such help. But in this area, as in others, "we have allowed our knowledge to run foolishly ahead of its application. . . . And haven't we, in addition, crippled the probation officer with case loads so heavy he cannot even become acquainted with the probationers in his own district, and further demoralized him through inadequate salary, lack of recognition, and incredible demands on his personal tolerance for frustration? . . . Where we can appeal to research results, we find that those communities willing to experiment with providing the probation staff with the time and the money to do the best possible job they know how to do—invoking drastically lowered case loads and engaging in one-to-one case work . . . the results have been startlingly successful. As one example, the Saginaw Probation Demonstration Project of the Michigan Council on Crime and Delinquency showed that less than 20 per cent of previously confined probationers were returned to the institution." [49]

There are also clear research indications that adequate probation cuts down on the rate of law violations and, of course, on welfare costs when the husbands and fathers of families are earning their own support. These and many other benefits of probation and parole work are examined in Volume 10 of the President's Crime Commission Report.

Recapitulation

This is the system. This is the way we do it. A handful of men, relatively, have been caught and convicted and consigned to prison, while most offenders remain at large. How can we change the public image of all this, from the handicapped police through the clumsy trial procedure, to the great lockup where wickedness is confined and penitent souls are beating their breasts? The prisons, whether new, shiny steel and concrete warehouses or old, gloomy, grimy lockups are full of people—not, for the most part, vicious, violent men who have done dreadful things, nor yet penitent, hand-wringing, breast-beating men who wish they had not robbed the bank. They are full of men labeled *criminal* because they got caught at something and convicted of something forbidden. But they are mostly poor, inadequate, incompetent, frustrated misfits—young failures, or lifelong failures, offenders who could not even make a success of crime!

And while an army of men across the country tries to serve our

interests and safety by turning the wheels of this infernal machine
for the grinding up of a minority of the easily-caught offenders and
administering to them the futile ritual of punishment, a horde of
known but immune predatory professional criminals grows fat and
famous in front of our eyes.

My hope in presenting this review is that the reader will become
concerned enough and *angry* enough to investigate for himself.
It is a creaking, groaning monster through whose heartless jaws
hundreds of American citizens grind daily, to be maimed and embittered so that they emerge implacable enemies of the social order
and confirmed in their "criminality."

> Many men on their release carry their prison about with them into
> the air, hide it as a secret disgrace in their hearts, and at length like
> poor poisoned things, creep into some hole and die. It is wretched
> that they should have to do so. . . . Society takes upon itself the right
> to inflict appalling punishment on the individual, but it also has the
> supreme vice of shallowness, and fails to realize what it has done.
> When a man's punishment is over, it leaves him to himself; that is to
> say, it abandons him at the very moment when its highest duty to-
> ward him begins. It is really ashamed of its own actions, and shuns
> those whom it has punished, as people shun a creditor whose debt
> they cannot pay, or one on whom they have inflicted an irreparable,
> an irredeemable wrong. (Quoted from Goldstein.[50])

CHAPTER 4

The Cold War between

Lawyers and Psychiatrists

For the festering sore, the chronic social self-destruction described in the preceding chapter, what do our helping professions offer us? The sad fact is that a chronic misunderstanding and even antagonism exists between lawyers and social scientists, including psychiatrists, which is in the nature of a cold war. This is sad because it is from the members of these two professions that society expects the most help in a solution of its crime problems.

The dilemma of the psychiatrists is whether to maintain a dignified classical pose of standing ready to treat those with enough good sense (and hard cash) to come to us, or to assault the complex engine of the legal machine at the risk of tripping over our own arrogance and self-righteousness. The dilemma of the lawyers is whether to renounce an age-old tradition and allegiance for which they have no affection for the promise of a new philosophy of which they have no intimate knowledge.

Both psychiatrists and lawyers may be sharing the illusion that they might be forcing an issue, advancing a new viewpoint to the public's awareness, when all they are doing is finding words and explanations in their own frames of reference to identify the subtle changes taking place in the confluent consciousness of the common citizenry regarding better ways of dealing with one another.

Medicine and law are both represented by intelligent, learned men and women. Both professions have ancient traditions and high ideals. Both are concerned with and feel a sense of responsibility for public safety. Both deal constantly with the tendency of people to get out of line, to deviate or threaten to deviate from the accepable code of behavior. This common theoretical interest should be a keystone bringing together their skills and knowledge in a cooperative effort.

But it does not work that way. Their understanding of human behavior, the "thing" they both have to deal with, is miles apart. And instead of cooperating they seem to view each other with suspicion, distrust, and sometimes disdain.

> There has always been this conflict in the courts between medicine and the law. . . . Judges and advocates tend to regard medical witnesses with suspicion, and to find them irritating. Psychiatrists are particularly liable to attract wrath and contumely upon themselves from the bench. Partly, no doubt, because their evidence is necessarily imprecise, they talk in terms of concepts rather than hard facts. They submit opinions rather than findings. And if there is one thing the judicial appetite demands, it is facts. (Donald Gould [1])

Psychiatrists aspire to facts; they spend their lives trying to more accurately describe and understand misbehavior of all kinds. They believe in the rules and laws related to their procedures with just as much conviction as the jurist believes in *his* laws. But these two sets of laws just do not gibe. And *which* "law" is it that is, as Pindar declared, "the king of all"?

The juridical system seems to the doctor to be an unscientific jumble based on clumsy and often self-defeating precedents.* Psy-

---

* One of my colleagues who has tried to understand and help this legal blindspot, as we see it, has written thus:

"The law finds that the older the precedent, the more firm the rule. A psychiatrist who treated agitation with bromides [as was often done one hundred years ago, but never today] could hardly justify it by appeal to precedent. The lawyer reasons deductively—he lays down a general principle. . . . Then from this principle, he determines the ruling on a specific case. The psychiatrist, as a medical scientist, must reason inductively—starting with observations, then drawing conclusions. The doctor confesses that there

chiatrists cannot understand why the legal profession continues to lend its support to such a system after the scientific discoveries of the past century have become common knowledge. That this knowledge is coolly ignored and flouted by the system is not so much an affront to the scientists as it is a denial of what was once mystery and is now common sense.

The discoveries of Sigmund Freud and other scientists near the turn of the century led to new understandings of human behavior that made a tremendous impact on almost all aspects of human life—all except law. The law assumes that when a person, regardless of his earlier experiences, reaches the age of discretion, he sees the wisdom—as it were—of being discreet, and so exercises appropriate control of his behavior except when overcome by passion or temptation. He and all other men are "equal" in the eyes of the law. But Freud showed that men are extremely unequal in respect to endowment, discretion, equlibrium, self-control, aspiration, and intelligence—differences depending not only on inherited genes and brain-cell configurations but also on childhood conditioning. Freud's discoveries made the ideals of the French Revolution confused in meaning and limited in application. Nothing could be more unfair than a "fair trial" operating on the assumption that in respect to behavior control "all men are created equal." The *corrective* purposes of the French Revolution slogan are clear enough now; we all applaud a *more nearly equitable* treatment of all individuals than then existed. But to set up a machine that presumes

are some questions to which he has no answers and acknowledges that some matters must be left open to await scientific proof. But no trial court can do that. Eventually, right or wrong, some judge will [have to] say: 'This is the answer; this is the end of the litigation.' The physician can say with honesty: 'I just don't know.' The judge can never say that." (Davidson, Henry A.: "That Other Helping Profession." *Amer. J. Psychiat.*, 122:691–692, December 1965.)

See also the epochal study of Judith Shklar entitled *Legalism* (Cambridge: Harvard University Press, 1964), and the significant comments of Dean Harold Reuschlein, Professor Samuel Shuman, Professor John Coons, and Professor Ernest Jones, as well as Dr. Shklar, in the *Journal of Legal Education*, 19:59–77, 1966.

that they are alike is to make a caricature of the ideal of justice.

The army woke up to the relevance of some of these discoveries about behavior control as far back as World War I, when military medical procedure was revolutionized. The disabilities of some soldiers, which were neither quite medical in the older sense nor yet strictly surgical, were no longer charged off as prima-facie evidence of malingering, "soldiering," and cowardice. These "shell-shocked" cases were made the subject of medical study and treatment, treatment directed not to the symptom nor to the "cowardice" but to the underlying psychological complex. And when it had been demonstrated that this type of treatment often resulted in returning the supposedly demoralized soldier to the battle lines—sometimes even to become a hero—even the tough old military was impressed. It had to abandon the old-fashioned idea that a man who tried to play sick because he was afraid needed only a sharp slap in the face, a kick in the rear, or a threat of court-martial. A different kind of treatment was introduced.

A famous telegram went from General Pershing to Washington in 1918 begging for the immediate dispatch of more of those "psychiatrists" who understood human behavior in a new way; they were urgently needed at the front where these demoralization casualties often exceeded in number the casualties from wounds.

But, while army medical procedure was thus radically revised by these discoveries fifty years ago, to this day they are, for the most part, unknown and unused in the police station, the courtroom, or the prison. Nearly every state and city in the nation is enlarging its custodial prison facilities at the very moment that mental hospitals are being reduced in size and number. While three-fourths of these hospital patients are now discharged within a few months after admission, seventy per cent of prisoners receiving penological "treatment" in jails are doing so for a second or third or fourth time.

And beyond all the thousands who are locked up and re-locked up, released and re-arrested, re-tried and re-sentenced (at great wasteful expense to the body politic) are the much larger number of offenders who are never detected, never convicted, never "treated" in any way. Our juridical-penal system remains incredibly backward, and the legal scientists and lawyers and judges must bear some blame for this.

Numerous distinguished lawyers and judges whom I know personally are much distressed by the situation and believe that some kind of revolutionary reform is necessary. In an article well entitled "Where Are The Lawyers? A Charge of Truancy," Arthur Selwyn Miller, professor of constitutional law at George Washington University, wrote:

> In a world characterized by rapid change, lawyerdom is not moving with the alacrity or celerity necessary to keep up. Lawyers still fly backwards and seek to answer the problems of today with the solutions of yesteryear—when simple existence of the problems means that the answers of yesteryear are suspect or in need of reexamination. The legal profession has no institutionalized method of self-analysis, which would enable it to determine whether it is adequately meeting the tasks presented by society. Chaos lies all about us: delay in the courts, politicalization of the administrative process, breakdown of respect for law, rise in crime, to name but a few examples. The old order is changing, and lawyers seem fated to be spectators.[2]

The Lawyers' Bias

How much of this estrangement may we lay at the feet of the lawyers? One of them, Neil W. Ross, wrote recently:

> Basically, the lawyer is interested in formulating correct rules of behavior—through the reasoning of the "reasonable man"—and is not interested in explaining how such reasoning and behavior operate. One might say that one of the greatest dilemmas for the law and the lawyer has been the reasoning of the *unreasonable man:* Since the entire system of the law, and in some cases the system of logic supported by the law, is based on the *reasonable man* and is by definition prescriptive, we find that the premises of the criminal law do not pertain as such to the irrational or unreasonable. Eluding the descriptive nature of the subject matter of psychiatry and maintaining its

prescriptive elements, the law has complemented this premise with the development of a rule capable of handling, though not describing or understanding, the exceptions.

The law assumes men responsible and sane. It could not be "recognized binding by supreme authority or made obligatory by sanction" unless this assumption was made; the structure of the law is founded on this assumption. The insane and the lunatic are not compatible with the law of reasonable men. We acknowledge the behavioral scientist as one who attempts to put the world of thought and action in some logical system of order. He does so through observation, description, experimentation, and replication. However, there seldom has taken place such an attempt to logically order the world in terms of the prescriptive "ought," "should," "must," and "must not" than has taken place in the law. Might then lawyers and psychiatrists use their logic differently? [3]

Lawyers, like psychiatrists, are a part of an organization, a system within the great social system. They study and work and talk together on the basis of a philosophy, partly tacit, partly proclaimed. They do not all agree, of course, but they develop characteristic ways of looking at things. They develop value systems based in part on the nature of their work.

In addition, lawyers acquire or inherit certain traditions and beliefs, practices, and prejudices that help determine their identity and character. Doctors do this just as much as lawyers, but there is a profound difference in the nature of these inheritances. The dogmas of science are always changing. The basic and subsidiary assumptions are always being questioned, revised, rejected, and reaffirmed. But this is not the case with law—or at least changes take place at a very slow rate. No one questions the truth spoken by Roscoe Pound: "The law must be stable, but it cannot stand still," but sometimes it almost *seems* to.

"The Law not only stands still but is proud and determined to stand still . . ." declares Professor Fred Rodell of Yale in his controversial but very lively book, *Woe Unto You, Lawyers!* "It just sits—aloof and practically motionless. Constitutions do not affect it and statutes do not change it. Lawyers talk wise about it and judges purport to 'apply' it when they lay down rules for men to follow, but actually The Law—with a capital L—has no real relation to the affairs of men. It is permanent and changeless—which means that it is not of this earth. It is a mass of vague abstract principles—which means that it is a lot of words. It is a brooding omnipresence in the sky—which means that it is a big balloon which has thus far escaped the lethal pin." [4]

Lawyers are concerned with placing or rebutting *blame* for specific acts of deviant, prohibited behavior; psychiatrists are interested in correcting total patterns of behavior. Instead of seeking for the *blame* or the exculpation of an accused, doctors seek the etiology, the explanation, the underlying motives, and contributing facts in the commission of certain undesirable acts. Lawyers and psychiatrists speak two different languages in regard to professional matters, and hence their common English tongue is of little help in meaningful communication with one another. To quote Ross again:

> Despite contrary appearances, lawyers and psychiatrists are incapable of communication on some issues because the two disciplines, although of common philosophical origin, have in terms of method and symbols taken the diverse paths of pragmatic versus semantic, subjectivistic versus objectivistic, and prescriptive versus descriptive. The logic, language, and orientation of each discipline are in many ways incompatible; some common ground does exist but both disciplines have to redefine their assumptions and methods if successful communication is to be made possible. [5]

For example, the word *justice,* which is so dear to lawyers, is one which the doctor *qua* scientist simply does not use or readily understand. No one thinks of justice as applying to the phenomena of physics. There is no "justice" in chemical reactions, in illness, or in behavior disorder.

Free will—to a lawyer—is not a philosophical theory or a religious concept or a scientific hypothesis. It is a "given," a *basic* assumption in legal theory and practice. To the psychiatrist, this position is preposterous; he seeks clear operational definitions of *free* and of *will*. On the other hand, the psychiatrist's assumption that motivation and mentation can go on *unconsciously* is preposterous to lawyers, constituting a veritable self-contradiction in terms.

Responsibility, to take another controversial word, is to a psychiatrist something one voluntarily assumes or has assigned to him. To a lawyer it is something which one "naturally" possesses until in some unnatural way he loses it. Truth to the lawyer is something one *tells* or *does not tell;* to the psychiatrist it is something that we—or at least some—strive wistfully and perpetually to discover and which others have no interest in.

Some Cases Illustrating Legal-Psychiatric Conflict and Confusion

Most criminal cases, including even the relatively small number that come to trial, are deadly dull. The dreary details of how some adolescents, in trying to outdo a rival gang, made off with somebody's automobile form a pattern of socio-legal difficulty that is repeated over and over with different names. Hundreds of bogus checks are tendered daily by improvident and immature boys and women to hundreds of careless or greedy shopkeepers, and some of these cases come to trial. All very dull.

One cannot blame newspaper reporters for picking up the occasionally sensational or dramatic case and playing it up disproportionately. The trouble is that often the wrong aspects of the case are stressed, and they tend to influence the prosecuting attorney, and even the defense attorney, to proceed in ways contrary to the best interests of the case or of the public. Scientific principles become lost in the drama.

I would like to cite some case illustrations of our present courtroom dilemmas. What *I* shall emphasize are not the lurid details of the crimes committed *by* the offenders, but the lurid details of the crimes committed *against* the offenders and the injustice resulting from conflicting efforts to serve justice. I call them "crimes" in a somewhat poetic sense, inasmuch as there is no law against conscientiously making absurd decisions and going through ridiculous procedures. But I submit that what you are about to read is a demonstration of wasted public funds, confused procedure, and total mismanagement of difficult, disturbed, and disturbing individuals, a process that thus wrongs the offender, the state, and the public, i.e., *us*. And in all of this, the total lack of mutual understanding between psychiatrists and lawyers will be evident.

This first case was a sensational one that attracted much newspaper attention.* It involved many lawyers, judges, and psychiatrists:

Attempting to disguise the identity of the man is of little use, for many readers and courtroom buffs will remember the second trial of one James Merkouris of California a few years ago. He had behaved in such a violent, threatening, belligerent manner in the courtroom, constantly interrupting speakers, shouting, and threatening various people in the room, that the judge finally felt obliged to order him chained and gagged. This, his lawyers correctly argued, constituted cruel and unusual punishment. But because the defendant had a constitutional right to be present at all proceedings against him, something had to be done. So at considerable expense a peculiar contraption was erected in the center of the courtroom, resembling the then fashionable television quiz-show isolation booths. It also somewhat resembled a gas execution chamber! Placed within it, Merkouris could hear everything that was going on but could not be heard in the courtroom when he shouted and roared. He could communicate with his defense counsel through a telephone line, but otherwise, while hearing everything, he could not be heard.

Now, what issue was being tried? The question was whether the prisoner was sane enough to be tried *again!* In other words, a trial was being held to determine whether it was possible for a man, already once tried, to have another trial—a *third* trial.

* The data pertaining to this case were kindly supplied to me by Dr. Frederick Hacker. I also had access to the commutation order and the report of the Attorney General to the Governor.

Merkouris had originally been charged with the murder of his former wife and her husband. He had vehemently denied the deed and refused to go along with the plea entered by his lawyers on his behalf, "Not Guilty by Reason of Insanity." He was indeed found guilty, and because he refused to allow this plea of "insanity" to be made, the trial judge informed him that this would mean he would have to be sentenced to death, according to law.

In California, sanity is "tried" separately, and Merkouris' lawyers again urged him strenuously to "plead insanity," and even filed such a plea for him, but he remained adamant and ordered his lawyers fired! The judge then permitted him to withdraw the plea of insanity and sentenced him to death.

California provides for an automatic review of every death sentence, and when this case came before the Supreme Court for review, the court scathingly revised the lower court's judgment. It was patently absurd, the Supreme Court said, to permit a person whose mental soundness was in doubt to prevent the investigation of just that alleged or suspected condition. Is it not common knowledge that the belief that *others* are mentally ill rather than oneself is one of the commonest signs of mental illness?

So the case went back to the lower court. But the original trial judge was now almost as adamant as the defendant. He declared that he himself had no doubt about the defendant's sanity, although there had been quite a bit of testimony impugning it. Having disqualified himself by thus expressing his views, the judge set a date for a new trial to be presided over by another judge. In this trial the glass booth was used.

Psychiatrists called at this trial expressed doubts of Merkouris' sanity, and after five days of trial and long deliberation by the jury, he was found incapable of standing trial! So there could be no third trial. Instead, he was sent to a state hospital for the criminally insane, where he remained for about a year.

He was returned to court from the hospital at the end of this period, not because he was considered to have recovered from his illness but because, the doctors alleged, he had become an intolerable burden to the hospital! Something had to be done, they stated, to have the question of guilt decided one way or the other.

And so *another* trial was arranged—this time to discover whether Merkouris was *now* able to "stand trial"!

The same witnesses who appeared in the first trial gave essentially the same testimony. The defendant in almost identical words denied his guilt. However, because in California the question of insanity is raised *after* the guilt has been *decided,* he was first found guilty (again), and then, over his objection, *another* trial was held before the same jury. This time he was found sane and competent, leaving the conviction of guilt unimpaired.

The next step would be to carry out the execution as originally ordered. But first the case had to go *again* for review by the Supreme Court, with special reference to the man's competence to be executed! This time the Supreme Court, after reviewing all the evidence and history of the case, found no evidence of a mental condition that would preclude an execution. Everything was cleared at last for the big day!

At this juncture, to his everlasting credit, the Governor of the state, Edmund G. Brown, stepped in. He expressed doubt as to the existence of "mental capacity" in the defendant at the time of the commission of the crime, and on this basis commuted the sentence to life imprisonment.

Thus, over a period of four years, with five public trials, two Supreme Court hearings, and long observation by psychiatrists and their associates in and out of a large psychiatric institution, the following scholastic questions were dealt with:

Did this obviously disturbed, disorganized, and dangerous man have the "it" that would prevent him from standing trial for a crime?

Did he have the "it" that would prevent him from being punished for the crime were he to be found able to be tried and then found guilty?

The answers arrived at, with the aid of perhaps $200,000 of taxpayers' money spent on the inquiry, were as follows:

Yes and *no.* He did and he didn't. He had "it," and again he didn't have "it."

Meanwhile, as this lawyer-psychiatrist controversy went on, the man was locked up, as he certainly should have been, detained in permanent custody with such care, treatment, and surveillance as the state medical service could provide. Some regard this as punishment, others as pampering; some as treatment, others as prophylaxis.

And this *occurred in a state that is far ahead of most of the other forty-nine in its progressive penal (correctional) system!*

For our purposes, the question is "What is wrong with this picture?" These were intelligent professional men—legal and scientific. They were men of integrity and good will who were trying to get a job done. They were not just "fooling." But they were completely enmeshed and trapped in a system where lawyers and psychiatrists cannot really cooperate to do the best thing for society or the individual.

I am also indebted to Dr. Frederick Hacker for another magnificent illustration of the breakdown of communication between psychiatrists and judges:

In the early morning hours of January 4, 1948, a forty-three-year-old man in tattered clothes appeared at the Long Beach police station, mumbling something about having killed his wife. He seemed confused and rambled on incoherently about Communists, the need to be a man, and other ill-sorted topics. The police sergeant assumed that he was drunk and sent him home to sleep it off. But an hour later he was back again, this time accompanied by his frail old mother, to whom he had gone as he had all his life when he was in trouble, the only person whom he always could trust. She had come with him while he explained again about his "crime."

The still skeptical police investigated what he tried to tell them and, indeed, found the mutilated body of his wife in a hotel room. He had apparently strangled her the night before, then cut her up with the ragged edges of a broken bottle, slashing her some forty times so that her body became a dreadful, bloody pulp, hardly recognizable as a human figure. He had (he said) then attempted intercourse with the corpse several times, despite its mutilation. After that he had left the hotel quietly in order to drive his car to the police and turn himself in. He knew what he had done and he knew it would be considered wrong by some, but he *had* to do it because his wife was a Communist agent betraying him and his country.

Now this case might seem to be obvious enough to any intelligent person with more than a modicum of experience with life. Many people are proud of being able to discover secret Communist plots, and many people who are quite mistaken about it suspect such plots and suspect other people of being Communists. But it is one thing to have a suspicion or even a delusion about subversive Communism and another thing to take the law into one's own hands and kill the suspect. Finally, there was in this instance not only the matter of killing but the gruesome complication of bloody slashing and mutilation and necrophilia. Most people would agree that these are prima-facie evidences of a state of extreme personality disorganization.

What should be done about it? Should we waive the time-honored formula of punishing people for their crimes and try to get the man treated? Or should we waste time and money trying to prove his guiltiness for a crime that he publicly confessed?

And whether we treat him or try him, let us give a little thought to the question of prevention. A man as disturbed as this did not become that way suddenly. Why had not somebody—perhaps his wife, or more to the point, his mother—taken some steps to prevent this tragedy?

As a matter of fact, this man *had* signed a voluntary application for admission to a state hospital *five weeks prior to the crime*. At that time he said he had not done anything wrong but feared that he might; he had felt "it" coming on again. He had once had psychiatric treatment long prior to this, and he was well aware there was something wrong with him at times; he could not stay the dreadful impulses that seemed to seize him every seven or eight years. Since his psychiatric treatment, however, he could at least recognize the first signs of his recurrent disorder before he was driven into open violence.

This is what he wanted to do, he said, when he went to the doctors at the state hospital and told them about this apprehension that he would lose control again. He told them that he had previously been treated in a psychiatric hospital. Afraid again of what might happen, he wanted to be confined and restrained.

He was admitted, but the hospital doctors were busy. Nobody—it seemed—could listen to him long enough to disentangle his confused statements. They could not find any overt evidence of masked irrationality (what some still call "psychosis"). So after a week he was discharged.

But his condition had evidently worsened. He became more confused, worried, and frightened. His mother and his wife took him to a private psychiatrist who gave him shock treatments in the office. He did not seem to improve. The psychiatrist was quite conscientious; he recognized he was not helping his patient and urged immediate hospitalization again.

But by now the patient had lost all insight and had no inclination to go to a hospital. On the last day of 1947, the doctor called the patient's mother and wife and informed them that he could no longer carry the responsibility, that the patient was dangerously mentally ill, and ought to be committed without delay. The women did not know exactly how to go about it and, what with New Year's Day coming, they postponed their decision. After all, he had not done anything or hurt anybody over the years; they would act on the plan immediately after the holidays.

On January 4th, the homicide occurred.

Now comes the still more incredible part. He was arraigned and charged, the case was taken to trial, and the man was prosecuted as if he were really a Communist killer who had gone too far! The prosecution urged that he could not possibly have been mentally ill,

or not very much so, because he said that he knew what he was doing; he knew it was wrong. To be sure, he was afraid of the Communists, but shouldn't one be? What is abnormal about that? And
most incriminating of all, after the deed was done, he had left the
hotel clandestinely to avoid capture! Sneaking! Clever! Crazy like
a fox!

The defense lawyer put on the stand the doctor who had administered the shock treatment prior to the commission of any criminal
deed, and who had advised hospitalization and commitment. But
the state hospital doctors were defensive. How could they run their
large hospital if they believed every crazy applicant who thought
he should be admitted? It was unfortunate that the man's previous
hospital record was not studied because the record did show that on
four previous occasions the patient *had* had to be hospitalized for periods of several months. The picture had always been the same: violent impulses that he could not control, thinking confused and suspicious, actions vehement. He had never done anything violent or
seriously criminal, but sometimes this had been prevented only at
the last moment. For example, seven years ago he had attempted to
strangle his beloved old mother, who recognized immediately that
it was a sign of illness and sought hospitalization for him.

How does the reader feel by this time? Here is a "mad man," a
man who had recovered from previous episodes but knew that he
was going mad again, and who *tried* to get himself taken into custody as had been done several times before. Here is a man in such
a frenzy of ill-restrained violence that he fears he will do dreadful
things. He asks for treatment; he *begs* for it. He is admitted to a
hospital, then discharged. He is seen by a doctor who agrees with
him that he should return to a hospital, and who urges the wife to
make him go immediately. There is a delay and before he gets there
the explosion occurs.

But then—even after the terrible outburst—he is *still* denied the
medical treatment he begged for. The lawyers, acting for the state
whose doctors would not give him the treatment he asked for and
needed, now charge him with "first degree murder with premedi-

tation, *the result of a malignant and abandoned heart"* (as the jury instruction in California reads), and the jury found for murder in the second degree. He was sentenced to prison, where he now is. But he is eligible for discharge just about the time when, according to his lifelong pattern, another cycle of attacks is due to appear!

Will the reader please tell us what is wrong with this picture? Good psychiatrists, good lawyers, good judges, all trying to do their duty—but do any of them involved in this mishmash actually believe that this poor, demoralized, murderous wretch ought to have been handled in this way?

When the lawyers get themselves into an absurd, awkward, preposterous situation, such as that of solemnly invoking government punishment for a man who had *tried* to get himself restrained and prevented from crime, they appeal to the psychiatrists for help. And then the psychiatrists, instead of saving the situation, may make it worse through their own uncertainties and controversies, controversies having to do for the most part with words, not with ideas. The doctors apparently knew that this man ought to be confined somewhere; the argument had to do with what label they were going to use to justify that confinement. The commonsense citizen might suppose that self-recognized dangerousness was enough. Evidently not. He had to have a "psychosis." He had to be "insane." He had to be "irresponsible." And as soon as these words are mentioned, babel sets in. The doctors cannot agree among themselves or with the lawyers what these words are supposed to mean, or do mean.

I can remember when I was an adolescent, a small group decided to mystify and possibly intimidate others in our school by inventing a private language. With much practice we were able to use this gibberish when others who did not understand it were listening, which, of course, greatly impressed them with our skillful powers of intercommunication. Just this sort of thing goes on in scientific circles as well as legal circles. The doctors who participate in it are actually not always aware of the hocus-pocus they are indulging in. I wonder if the public is? Pirandello scorched us for it in *Henry IV*, as did Molière, Dickens, and many others. But we keep it up.

One more blot on the record of constructive legal-psychiatric co-operation:

A few years ago some colleagues of mine in a neighboring city studied the case of a twenty-four-year-old fellow citizen whom no one had ever heard of until November, 1955. Then on one day he suddenly became known all over the world.

He was—it seems—a polite, friendly, courteous young fellow who had served in the Coast Guard but was, in November, 1955, working in a drive-in restaurant. So far as could be discovered he had always had a good record except for a few peculiar outbursts which came to light after the events shortly to be described. For example, when he was thirteen he seems to have become angry with his mother once and knocked her down. At another time he beat a cow to death, allegedly because it kicked him. Some years later he set fire to a garage in order to get revenge on a salesman who owned a car in the garage. None of this was known by the few acquaintances that he had, and he seemed to have been regarded by them as an average citizen, undistinguished, unremarkable, relatively inconsequential.

His mother, who had been staying with him and helping in the drive-in, decided to visit his half sister in Alaska. Without success he tried to persuade her to remain until Thanksgiving. She insisted upon leaving. Her stubbornness angered him, so he planned to punish her. He manufactured a time bomb composed of dynamite sticks and put it in a valise. It was so heavy that he had to pay $27 overweight charges when he dispatched it with his mother on the airplane in which she was departing.

Having seen her off, he took his wife and child to the restaurant in the airport for lunch, and then returned home and turned on the radio. While listening he was "very shocked" to hear the news that

a plane had just exploded in the air forty miles west. When he real-
ized it must have been the plane on which his mother embarked,
he wept bitterly for a long time.

When this case came to trial, the alleged motive for the crime
and the inhuman callousness to the tragic effects of the act presumably led the attorneys to request a psychiatric opinion of the
man's mental status. My colleagues were asked to examine this
man and did so very thoroughly. They found that in spite of his
superficially acceptable social adjustment he had always been psychologically abnormal and socially maladjusted. He possessed a low
tolerance for frustration and discipline, with egocentricity of a high
degree, severely impaired judgment capacity, and a poor work record. He had previously exhibited antisocial behavior of various
sorts, which had not led to treatment.

My colleagues drew the obvious conclusion from these symptoms—that this man was suffering from a mental illness of severe
degree at the time he blew up the airplane. But in their official
court report they then went on to say that although his was a mental illness in the sense that we psychiatrists understand it, it was
not exactly a mental illness in the sense that lawyers understand it!
He was undoubtedly irrational, illogical, psychopathic, sociopathic,
disorganized, and schizophrenic—these are the psychiatrists' words.
But, as they understood the stipulated legal terminology and construction, the offender was not "insane." He did not have the "it"
which the law recognized as necessary in order to make medical
"insanity" into legal "insanity." What is this "it"?

These doctors are acquaintances whom I respect and with whose
clinical findings I would expect to fully agree. They made a conscientious examination and they did their best to express their conclusions from their findings. Here was a crazy, irrational, dangerously disorganized fellow who moved about on the streets, un-
treated, until he calmly murdered a planeload of people to punish
his mother for leaving him. Does any intelligent person doubt that
he was mad? mentally ill? crazy? insane?

Then how could my intelligent and competent friends get themselves into such a fix by legal stipulation as to have to deny this?

At his trial, the issue of insanity was not raised! When the jury returned a verdict of guilty with a sentence of death, the defendant refused an additional sanity trial, which is permitted by state law. He was executed.

Now, I am just as terrified as everyone else to learn that a man no one much noticed or suspected would—and could—and did—dynamite an airplane full of innocent people. It was a peculiarly terrible crime, needless and heartbreaking for many people. I hope it never happens again.

But I want to do more than hope; I want to take steps toward preventing it. I know that *there is not a particle of preventive value in the wreaking of vengeance and anger in the quick elimination of this one wretch*. Putting him out of sight only puts the problem out of sight. Deterrence? Nonsense! Newspaper notices of what was done to an unknown, invisible malefactor somewhere out West is not going to have one iota of deterrent effect on another such twisted mind entertaining, God forbid, similar inclinations.

Then why this absurd, futile exhibition? If a violent passenger on an airplane seemed about to blow it up, I can see sense in someone's taking immediate desperate measures to prevent it, even to the point of killing. But after a terrible, shocking holocaust has been accomplished and everything destroyed, why pursue an animated corpse and solemnly destroy it, like some primitive people wreaking vengeance on a ritual victim? Do the courts not exist to prevent just such mob action?

But, you may ask—the man was dangerous, immoral, ruthless, unpredictable—why *not* eliminate him?

For the reasons that I have just stated. Eliminating one offender who happens to get caught *weakens* public security by creating a false sense of diminished danger through a definite remedial measure. Actually, it does not remedy anything, and it bypasses completely the real and unsolved problem of *how to identify, detect, and detain potentially dangerous citizens*.

What kind of creature was this anyway? And how did he get that way? What gave him the wild and fearful idea? What was he most afraid of? What was burning him inside? What *might* have deterred him? Why didn't any of his acquaintances—or even his mother—detect his madness and seek help? What danger signs did he give us—which we ignored? What kept out of his mind the terrible consequences to other people of what he planned to do? How do patterns of thought and action such as this get started, and how can the rest of us become alerted in time to prevent such tragedies?

We will never know the answers to these questions because we were in such a hurry to get this wretch disposed of, as if *he* were our only social menace, and the only one that ever would be born who would do such a ghastly thing! We can wish that, but we know better.

Peter Wyden [6] described a similar case that was dealt with differently:

The proprietor of a second-rate night club in an eastern city had problems. His wife and his business partner had become much too friendly, and no one likes to be cuckolded. After brooding about this for months, bitter but irresolute, the owner met a strange character who, for adequate compensation, agreed to shoot the business partner.

It worked out that way!

The hired killer was caught and charged with murder. He made a great spectacle of himself in court. He freely admitted his guilt although implicating his employer, but seemed to be inappropriately gleeful and frivolous.

Three well-known psychiatrists examined him and concurred unanimously in finding him to be actively hallucinated, "schizophrenic," and dominated by irrepressible irrational hostilities; further, that he had been *grossly mentally ill for some years!* They so testified.

Whereupon he was found guilty of murder in the first degree by the twelve-man jury and sentenced by the judge to be executed. Who cares what these psychiatrists say?

A minor case:

Offenders do not have to be irrational and violent to become the victims of vindictive elements in the established system. An illustration of this was reported to me by the chaplain of a penal institution which I do not want to identify. He was disturbed because of the frequency with which simple-minded, uneducated "common people" are mishandled in the name of justice and came to discuss it with me.

A farm boy who had been drafted into the army brought his wife and several children with him to his new job on a military base. Some months after arriving, his wife and children wished to return home to visit the grandparents, and the young soldier put them on the train, planning to follow in a few days when he had obtained a furlough.

Next door to him lived a married couple. The husband was away on detached duty. The morning after the soldier's family had left town, the neighbor woman's empty purse was found on his front lawn, and he was formally charged with forcible rape, she being the plaintiff.

While he was being held, the complaining witness returned to New York City from whence she had come. But the trial went on. The accused declared that the woman had been accustomed to entertaining men in her home but that he had never been one of them, nor had he ever talked with her or visited with her or propositioned her. A psychiatrist who examined the man said it was inconceivable that one of his temperament and disposition would molest anyone, let alone commit rape.

In spite of all this, however, the court-appointed attorney for the defense (!) urged this simple-minded, timid, frightened man of low intelligence to plead guilty, not to the charge of rape but to a lesser charge, that of molestation. Intimidated and badgered, he foolishly did so and was promptly sentenced to the penitentiary for one to five years. Probation wasn't even considered!

Obviously there was no cooperation between the legal and scientific professionals in this case to find the most expedient, the most economical, or the most humane thing to do. All the court was interested in, apparently, was the technicalities of justice—our old friend "justice" again.

I conclude this chapter seeming to have laid the heavier charges for the cold war at the door of the lawyers. Crime was, of course, within their domain for hundreds of years; we psychiatrists are johnny-come-latelies. But our attempt to join hands with the lawyers has not failed *only* because of *their* errors and resistances. In the next chapter, I shall make *our* confession.

CHAPTER 5

Right and Wrong Uses

of Psychiatry

As the cases and discussions in the previous chapter indicate, I believe heartily that psychiatry and psychiatrists must assume a considerable share of the blame for the impasse between the law and psychiatry in better solving the problem of preventing crime. A long and largely futile effort to communicate with one another and with the public has resulted in a failure for which psychiatry and psychiatrists must bear a large portion of the responsibility.

About seven hundred years ago Lord Bracton set forth the principle that some people, later to be called mentally ill, do not know what they are doing and seem to lack mind and reason "in such a way as to be not far removed from the brute."[1] Two ideas have persisted in the juridic view regarding *some* wrongdoers: First, that "insanity" is a lack of knowing what one does, and therefore of being unable to form the "intention" to do a wrong deed; secondly, that if there is a lack of intention there can be no technical guilt.[2]

Gradually these ideas took the more refined form of rules: that "insanity" negates criminal intent, that it impairs the knowing (understanding) of one's own conduct, that mental illness or defect (insanity) "causes" criminal behavior, and that the concepts and data of psychiatry can be transposed into moral judgments responsive and applicable to these tests.

All of this, of course, including the very word *insanity,* lacks any correspondence with modern psychiatry. But the courts have taken these rules seriously for several hundred years, and they are still current, with the same obsolete terminology. The law has tried, in recent years, to adapt this ancient language and viewpoint regarding misbehavior to a much less ancient scientific understanding of behavior. We have to go back to this old matter of punishment. The law, like a large part of the body politic, assumes that punishment is a proper thing for the proper persons. It is an axiom that one who breaks the rules must be punished. Whether this punishment does him any good or not, whether it actually deters him or others from further actions of the same sort, whether indeed it does not cost more than other forms of deterrence—all such questions are considered beside the point, in law as in public opinion. Scientific studies have shown that most punishment does not accomplish any of the purposes by which it is justified, but neither the law nor the public cares anything about that. The real justification for punishment is none of these rational "purposes," but an irrational zeal for inflicting pain upon one who has inflicted pain (or harm or loss).

But even the law began to have some qualms, as I have just said, about inflicting pain, even death, upon a sick person, a delirious person, a person totally unaware of his participation in the punishment. The law, in its evolution, began to look for an exceptions clause. Out of this grew the concepts of responsibility, intention, and *mens rea.* Psychiatry and psychology have *tried* to take these fictions seriously but they simply cannot. The whole cumbersome, confused, conflictual mummery about limited or nonexistent "responsibility" came about through this uneasiness regarding the propriety, the morality one might say, of *punishing* a sick human being.

The reader must remember that in earlier days punishment was carried out publicly and zealously and was intentionally shocking. A poor wretch staggering down the street roped by the neck to a horse cart while muscular yeomen lashed his naked back and blood dripped to the ground behind him was being punished, and this was righteous in the highest degree, and a most interesting public spectacle.

The concept of justice held that the victim, to receive the *maximum* official vengeance of the state, must be hale and hearty, at least physically. He must be mentally alert enough to fully appreciate the gravity of what the state was doing to him by beating or choking him to death. If merely getting rid of an undesirable was the sole object of capital punishment, the state should welcome physical or mental sickness as an assistant in its full purpose of extermination. But no; if the condemned prisoner begins to fail he must be propped up, medically treated, and nursed back to health before receiving the final, lethal blessing.*

Then public opinion finally began to sway the courts in what might be regarded as a direction of mercy and humanity. They began to look for face-saving devices. Are there some excuses that can be consistently invoked that would suspend the normal acts of retributory justice?

Thus, in 1843, there was enunciated the famous M'Naghten rule. Daniel M'Naghten had shot and killed Drummond, private secretary to Sir Robert Peel, believing him to be Sir Robert. M'Naghten was under the delusion that he was being hounded by enemies and that Sir Robert was one of them. The defense was insanity and the jury found him "Not guilty, on the ground of insanity." Substantially the rule held that a man was not a proper subject for hanging if he was unable to distinguish socially, i.e., acceptable, "right" from socially, i.e., unacceptable, "wrong" conduct. In practice this usually meant that because delirious and demented individuals were incapable of appreciating and profiting by the punishment of official vengeance, these cases might as well be taken out of the docket to save time and money.

---

* I blush to state that more than once I have been asked by the federal government or by an officer of my sovereign state to examine an offender who had been patiently waiting for his execution, pending an improvement in his health such that the ceremony could be carried out legally.

The psychiatrists of the day did not (sufficiently) dispute this pontifical "decision," and some have gone along with it ever since, despite its absurdity. It requires an incalculable degree of presumption to say whether *another* individual "knows" right from wrong, especially when few of us could truly say (except in utter naïveté or ignorance) what our own degree of expertise is in this distinction.

Trying to get around the absurdity of the M'Naghten criteria has invited the ingenuity of many lawyers, judges, and psychiatrists for a century.* No substantial progress was made until 1954 when the famous Durham decision rule was enunciated by Judge David Bazelon, Chief Justice of the United States Court of Appeals in the District of Columbia. It read:

> The rule we now hold . . . is simply that an accused is not criminally responsible if his unlawful act was the product of mental disease or mental defect. We use "disease" in the sense of a condition which is considered capable of improving or deteriorating. We use "defect" in the sense of a condition which is not considered capable of either improving or deteriorating and which may be congenital, or the result of injury, or the residual effect of a physical or mental disease.[3]

The Durham decision was a definite advance over the medievalism represented by the M'Naghten rule, and psychiatrists welcomed it for that reason. Many believe that the Currens decision of Chief Judge Biggs of the Third Court of Appeals made a few years later is somewhat more useful. The essence of it is that the jury must be satisfied that, at the time of committing the crime, the offender "as a result of mental disease or defect lacks substantial capacity" to resist doing what he did. The American Law Institute has proposed a rule very similar in intent, which six states have adopted, and the concept of "diminished responsibility" has been

* The Committee of the American Bar Foundation working on the problem of Mental Illness and the Law mentioned in the preface has devoted itself more recently to a report on this topic of impaired responsibility as a "defense."

used in England and California. The fact is that neither the Durham Rule nor the Currens Rule nor the American Law Institute Rule nor any other progressive rule has replaced the traditional practice in most American courts.

Modern Psychiatry

The descriptive psychiatry of forty years ago had emerged in medicine as a subdivision of neurology, a branch dealing with the clinical results of infection, injury, or other damage to the brain, spinal cord, and nerve trunks. Most neurological symptoms are of the nature of impairments of sensation and movement. Brain injuries sometimes produce confusion in psychological processes, and it was originally believed by the best scientists that any gross deviations in thinking, reasoning, and behaving were a reflection of these impairments in the tissues of the brain. A few psychiatrists still believe this.

After the experimental demonstrations of psychological illness in France and Vienna seventy-odd years ago, psychiatrists began to abandon the exclusively organic basis of illness and to describe various syndromes of inappropriate behavior and psychological deviations not referable to brain or spinal cord lesions.

The impulse to group or classify these syndromes led to thousands of them being described, classified, and named—often after their describer.* We still have many remnants of these efforts and no general agreement about designations or nosology. There are still a few "brain spot" psychiatrists, as they might be called, who believe that the only mental illness is one that reflects a brain lesion. We also have the "mind twist" psychiatrists, some of whom like to name the various twists and contortions of function and call them diseases. Others, like myself, think it is better to drop these names.

Behavior scientists today agree in the view that the individual attempts continuously to make an adaptation to the environment.

* Many of these are listed in the Appendix of my book *The Vital Balance* (New York: Viking Press, 1963).

Sometimes the individual seems to conquer his environment, at least in part; sometimes the environment seems to win. Most of the time one can speak of neither winning nor losing, but of co-operating with more or less satisfaction and minimal pain for both.

This cooperation has to reach a tolerable point for both parties so that a "vital balance," as I have called it, can be maintained. If the environment gets "kicked around" too much, it will react; and, if the individual becomes pressed upon too heavily, *he* will react. He will struggle, he will strive, he will make concessions, he will make little retreats.

These retreats and the other evidences of this struggle are called symptoms, if anyone notices them. Mr. X, we say, seems very nervous recently. His wife might tell us he is sleepless and distressed. Mr. Y is known to be using increased amounts of alcohol, and Mr. Z just gave up his job without any apparent reason. These symptoms can be more and more severe, because from this point of view delirium and delusions go right along with divorce and drunkenness. They all are signs of a losing struggle.

One can think of this as brain disease if one wishes to; one can call it mental illness, and give the illness a name; or one can view it in the broader perspective of demoralization or partial disorganization in a perennial adaptation struggle. This latter viewpoint seeks to find where the pressure is too great and where it can be lifted. What forces are driving adversely? Some men can be driven to drink, some to crime; some even to suicide. We are all driven to some extent, and we all have some resources to withstand the drives and take control of the situation. What happens to those who cannot? And, more important, what can be done to restore or strengthen their counteracting capacities? We seek these answers not out of sheer mercy but from a realization that what is happening to "him" affects us all.

The reader can see how utterly different this point of view is from the older notion that these retreats are, in some way or other, diseases that can be identified by name and defined as to form and course. The psychiatry that sticks to these old concepts can be of little help to a judge, and too many psychiatrists, I am afraid—at least those who testify in law courts—do stick to them.*

There is today an utterly new psychiatry, a new understanding of abnormal and normal behavior, as different from those held before Freud as the principles of modern physics differ from those in use before Einstein and even before Newton. For the first time in history we have a logical and systematic theory of personality, an explanation of what human nature is and how behavior is determined and modified. This enables psychiatry to graduate from a science dealing with the recognition and handling of crazy people to a science of understanding the behavior of *all* people, the so-called normal and the so-called abnormal ones, with increasingly less distinction between them. The dynamics of perceiving, thinking, willing, loving, hating, acting, not acting—these can and must all be seen in a setting of totality, the individual interacting with the environment.

This modern psychiatry in theory and practice remains largely unknown and unused in law courts today. Unconscious motivation for crime is as inconceivable there—officially—as eyeless vision. The most significant basic assumptions of modern psychiatry are actually in contradiction and opposition to many basic assumptions of the law! And this, I hasten to add, is not the fault of the courts or of the lawyers. It is the failure, in large measure, of psychiatrists and psychiatry.

* Sad to say, the American Psychiatric Association itself officially holds these eighteenth- and nineteenth-century notions. A committee of our worthy national body has just (1968) published a manual containing a full description of all the bewitchments to which human flesh is heir, with the proper names for each one, the minute suborders and subspecies listed, and a code number for the computer. The colleagues who prepared this Witch's Hammer manual are worthy fellows—earnest, honest, hard-working, simplistic; they were taught to believe that these horrible things exist, these things with Greek names and Arabic numerals. And if a patient shows the stigmata, should he not be given the label and the number? For me this is not only the revival of medieval nonsense and superstition; it is a piece of social immorality. And for all its officialness, I do not believe it is what most psychiatrists subscribe to or practice.

Psychiatrists' Failure

We psychiatrists have not succeeded in convincing the public of our true intentions, purposes, and usefulness. We have unwittingly, perhaps, but persistently—some of us—joined in a conspiracy with reactionary legal people so that the progressive members of the judiciary have been let down time after time, I blush to say, by my colleagues. The most dynamic leader of prison reform in one state has declared (off the record, so far as names are concerned) that his most persistent opposition came from local psychiatrists.*

What seems to happen is that some of my colleagues become involved in what Dr. Joseph Satten has called "a peculiar kind of conspirational relationship between at least four elements in the system: (1) the law enforcement people—police, prosecutors, and judges—who say they 'have no choice' about what they do when in fact there is much choice; (2) the correctional institutions who refuse to use the newer techniques because they say the public wants them to use the old techniques, when in fact there are many 'publics,' some of whom do want the new techniques used; (3) the 'public' which is either vindictive or apathetic; and (4) psychiatry which, except for a few isolated instances, is even more apathetic about the problem—with less excuse than the public—though perhaps for the same reasons. In any event, all of these groups, using devices of displacement and projection, create an equilibrium which is resistant to change." [4]

---

* Colonel Vincent J. Donahue declared in an address and later published in *The Police Yearbook* (1958):

"A specific characteristic of psychiatrists which causes mixed emotions of generally unflattering nature to be experienced by realistic observers in law enforcement is the . . . proclivity of the psychiatrists to be obfuscatory when expressing themselves. It can be readily noted in all their 'work-ups,' their contributions to the literature, their recondite treatises and their expressed opinions that psychiatrists are very adroit in the use of semantics. This is a trait very much in keeping with their deliberate cultivation of the esoteric.

"What the psychiatrists fail to realize, however, is that in the final analysis such verbal gymnastics serve little purpose other than to dismay perhaps even

The history of the attempted rapprochement of psychiatry and the courts should go a little further than the references made above to the M'Naghten Act. A rational explanation of irrational behavior was first offered * in the American courtroom, as far as I know, by William Alanson White in the trial of Leopold and Loeb in Chicago in 1924.† This case attracted great public attention, partly because the crime was strange and shocking, partly because the accused were prominent, wealthy, and of great promise, partly because many psychiatrists were called in to explain the paradox of misbehavior in the wellborn. Psychiatrists of the old school were kept waiting by the prosecution to refute and dispute these "radical" psychiatrists speaking for the defense. Reputable, scholarly, dignified, friendly colleagues were soon swept up in the same old courtroom spectacle previously described—calling one another liars and fools in public and apologizing to one another in private (not literally, of course, but quite definitely), swearing to the truth of answers to questions which they probably did not understand, and confusing the judges, the jury, and the public by interpretations of "facts" reported on the basis of utterly incongruous philosophies.

There was one difference in this trial. Without calling it insanity, without calling it a disease, without speculating about knowledge of right and wrong, Dr. White tried to explain the behavior of the

---

their protagonists. This verbal, fancy footwork only further alienates law enforcement in which direct thinking and equally direct action are the underlying criteria of efficient public service. Of the psychiatrists it can succinctly be said that the mobility of their words brings in its train the immobility of their reflection."

* I do not mean this as a literal declaration of priority. William Healy's book, *The Individual Delinquent*, came out in 1915, and he and many others in those days undoubtedly tried to present psychoanalytic principles informally in many cases.

† Colonel McCormick of the *Chicago Tribune* in 1924 offered Freud $25,000 or anything he would name to come to America to "psychoanalyze" Leopold and Loeb, and presumably demonstrate that they should not be executed. Hearst, hearing that Freud was ill, was prepared to charter a special line so that Freud could travel undisturbed by other company. Freud declined both offers. (Jones, Ernest: *The Life and Work of Sigmund Freud, Vol. 3: The Last Phase 1919–1939.* New York: Basic Books, 1957, p. 103.)

murderers as the product of impulses contrary to their conscious ideals but expressive of certain strange unconscious strivings that, for reasons not clear, overwhelmed their control. Neither the public nor the court quite understood this explanation, and most people were confirmed in the idea that psychiatrists could be found to say in court whatever they were paid to say. But it was a milestone.

That the veniality and corruptibility of psychiatrists seemed to be taken for granted was a grievous concern to many, and to no one more than to Dr. White. He himself was the author of several books urging a more enlightened view of behavior disorder on the basis of the new discoveries in psychology.[5] As president of the American Psychiatric Association, he seized the opportunity to appoint a committee to study these public exhibitions of legal ignorance and medical confusion.*

A carefully worded resolution prepared by this committee was offered to the American Psychiatric Association and unanimously

---

* I am proud to have been a member of that committee, along with numerous distinguished and experienced colleagues. They were: Dr. Herman M. Adler of Chicago, State Criminologist of Illinois and director of the Institute for Juvenile Research; Dr. L. Vernon Briggs of Boston, author of the celebrated Briggs Law of Massachusetts and of numerous books including *The Manner of Man That Kills;* Dr. Bernard Glueck of New York, first psychiatrist at Sing Sing Prison and author of *Studies in Forensic Psychiatry;* Dr. William Healy of Boston, pioneer in psychiatric juvenile court work and author of numerous books on psychiatric aspects of crime, particularly *The Individual Delinquent;* Dr. Smith Ely Jelliffe of New York, one of the deans of American psychoanalysis and author of numerous books on various aspects of psychiatry and editor of the internationally circulated *Journal of Nervous and Mental Disease;* Dr. Raymond F. C. Kieb, formerly superintendent of the Hospital for the Criminally Insane at Matteawan and now Commissioner of Corrections for the State of New York at Albany; Dr. Lawson G. Lowrey, director of the Child Guidance Institute in New York City and formerly chief medical officer of the Psychopathic Hospital in Boston; Dr. Thomas W. Salmon, Professor of Psychiatry in the Medical School at Columbia University and director of psychiatric work in the American Expeditionary Forces (replaced on the committee later by Dr. Winfred Overholser, director of the Division for the Examination of Prisoners in the Department of Mental Diseases of the State of Massachusetts); Dr. Frankwood E. Williams, director of the National Committee for Mental Hygiene; and later, Dr. William A. White, himself.

adopted by it in 1927, embracing several basic recommendations for effecting improvement in the functioning of psychiatrists in assisting the court in criminal cases. Because these recommendations involved cooperation with the legal profession, the committee chairman attended annual meetings of the American Bar Association for several years, speaking in the Criminal Law Section [6] in favor of a collaborative committee being appointed to draw up a corresponding statement of position on the part of the legal profession. Such a committee was appointed and conferred with the APA Committee; in August, 1929, the following recommendations were offered to the American Bar Association:

> The committee from the Section on Criminal Law of the American Bar Association, after a conference with the committee from the American Psychiatric Association, recommends to its own association that it advocate:
>
> 1. That there be available to every criminal and juvenile court a psychiatric service to assist the court in the disposition of offenders.
>
> 2. That no criminal be sentenced for any felony in any case in which the judge has any discretion as to the sentence until there be filed as a part of the record a psychiatric report.
>
> 3. That there be a psychiatric service available to each penal and correctional institution.
>
> 4. That there be a psychiatric report on every prisoner convicted of a felony before he is released.
>
> 5. That there be established in every state a complete system of administrative transfer and parole and that there be no decision for or against any parole or any transfer from one institution to another without a psychiatric report.

Thereafter, representatives of the American Psychiatric Association *and* of the American Bar Association met with representatives of the American Medical Association, and the same recommendations were then unanimously endorsed by the latter group. Thus the psychiatrists, physicians, and lawyers of America were *officially* in agreement on a few simple principles!

And what came of it?

The fact that the spokesmen of these national organizations had studied this problem and formulated principles did not mean that the rank and file of the membership either understood them or agreed with them. Most doctors, most lawyers, most psychiatrists had not had (and still do not have) anything to do with the problem, and this simple fact has to be kept in mind.

The patient, hopeful work of those committees was done over thirty years ago! Yet, aside from isolated demonstrations in a few progressive states and the leadership of a few outstanding judges and lawyers in making new proposals, there is little evidence of any change.

Court procedures have *not* been changed to permit the proper type of contribution from psychiatrists, and psychiatrists who did not grasp or concur with the foregoing list of principles, despite their official approval, continued to act beyond their competence and further the inept, inadequate kind of contribution which they thought was required of them.

Why This Failure to Communicate?

Is it not time that we psychiatrists ask ourselves most seriously what *our* failure has been in all this effort? Is it that too many of us cling to old and outworn concepts? Or is it that we are unable to put ideas into a credible and acceptable form which the legislatures and the courts could implement in the interests of public safety and economy? Are we unable to agree among ourselves to the extent of furnishing some assistance to the courts?

Have we psychiatrists ever systematically tried to help with the problem of public safety? Have we put ourselves at the disposal of the police, who are obliged to make so many split-second decisions about the handling of individuals who might be dangerous? Have we ever assisted at the booking desk to estimate the precariousness of a crime situation—externally an injury to society and internally an unstable equilibrium of impulse control in an individual now frightened and threatened? Have we consistently supported the upgrading of police standards? Have we really tried to give treatment to offenders? Are we best known to the public in this area for our occasional services as *amicus curiae* or for our confusing and ambiguous contributions to a rare sensational trial?

Have our predictions proved unreliable or have they been refuted by subsequent events? (Usually we are not even asked for a prediction.) Has our judgment been notoriously defective? A psychiatrist who prophesied that Oswald would be dangerous unless treated was ignored, but we are used to that. Most prisoners are released *without* psychiatric examination and without anyone's prediction.

Why are we, as public advisers, still suspect in the eyes of the very public from which individuals flock to us for help with personal problems and suffering? Are we suspected of trying chiefly to increase our "market," finding ourselves new jobs to do even though our efforts are known to be already overtaxed?

Do we pose a threat to the legal profession, a few members of which do not want to relinquish the control of the criminal trial? Does the public really believe that we psychiatrists look at criminals with a maudlin sympathy that ignores the viciousness of their acts? Are we considered sentimentalists who tend to identify ourselves with all underdogs and victims of circumstance? Does the public really think that psychiatric treatment of prisoners is a pampering process which permits them to live in luxury instead of working out their sins and salvation in penitence?

Yes! The public *does* indeed believe these things. It *does* have these simplistic childish views. Not all people, of course. But in spite of the spread of scientific knowledge, including modern psychiatry, large masses of the general public really remain ignorant of newer principles of behavior science and behavior control. Why?

People want to learn and they will learn if they are properly taught.

To properly teach we must use language that every intelligent person can understand. This is one place we have fallen down. We psychiatrists think it is lawyers who speak and write a quaint, contrived, redundant, obscure mishmash. We hear with glee such confessions as this one by Fred Rodell, a lawyer and a teacher in a law school:

> Legal language, wherever it happens to be used, is a hodgepodge of outlandish words and phrases because these words and phrases are what the principles of The Law are made of. . . . Written in ordinary English, everybody could see how silly, how irrelevant and inconclusive, they are. . . . [and then] The Law would lose its dignity and then its power—and so would the lawyers. So legal language, by obstructing instead of assisting the communication of ideas, is very useful—to the lawyers. It enables them to keep on saying nothing with an air of great importance—and getting away with it.
>
> Yet the lawyers, taken as a whole, cannot by any means be accused of *deliberately* hoodwinking the public with their devious dialectic and their precious principles and their longiloquent language. They, too, are blissfully unaware that the sounds they make are essentially empty of meaning. And this is not so strange. For self-deception, especially if it is self-serving, is one of the easiest of arts.[7]

Let us leave the lawyers' self-deception to them and face the fact that we psychiatrists deceive ourselves in exactly this way. We are ourselves immensely impressed by this legal jargon, and so we take our turn at impressing the public—*and* the lawyers—with polysyllabic Greek and Latin words.* We use words like *autistic, psychotic, schizophrenic, extrapyramidal, dysergasia, psychotropic anhedonia.* No educated man likes to admit that he does not understand words addressed to him by another educated man. The judge and jury do not understand many words used in the courtroom by

---

* "Followers and pupils of Freud found new Greek and Latin words in the dictionaries and enriched the psychoanalytic vocabulary. Later some of these technical terms not understood or misunderstood found their way into wider circles of educated or interested persons. A new language, *Psychoanalese,* was born. Firmly established by 1920, it has flourished for the past twenty-five years. . . . To speak *Psychoanalese* fluently does not mean to understand psychoanalysis, and a man who can use all of the technical terms correctly can be a very poor psychoanalyst." (Reik, Theodor: *Listening with the Third Ear.* New York: Farrar, Straus & Co., 1949, pp. 456-457.)

psychiatrists but hesitate to question us about them lest they seem naïve or ignorant (or receive an equally incomprehensible answer).

Only a little girl who had nothing to lose could say aloud, "Why, the emperor has on no clothes at all!" Only now and then, as Rodell says, "a lawyer comes along who has the stubborn skepticism necessary to see through the whole solemn sleight-of-hand . . . and who has the temerity to say so. . . . Time and again he [the late Justice Holmes] would demolish a fifty-page court opinion—written in sonorous legal sentences . . . with a few words of dissent, spoken in plain English: 'The Law as you lay it down . . . sounds impressive and impeccable. But of course it really has nothing to do with the facts of the case.' " [8]

Psychiatrists talk in public as if we all agreed about basic principles and about the meaning of our pompous fraternity jargon. Of course we don't. I think we ought to discard all of our obscurantist, pejorative designations, just as cultured people have discarded words that once had a specific meaning but which now connote an attitude rather than merely describe a fact. It used to be proper, at least in some circles, to refer to some of our fellow citizens as "niggers." And it used to be proper in psychiatric circles to refer to some individuals as "psychotics" and "schizophrenics." All such name calling should be abandoned. Judge David Bazelon was more than charitable when he said:

> Usually psychiatrists attached to public mental institutions are oriented in the use of what may be characterized as a dispositional diagnosis. In such quick work, labels . . . are employed to describe patients for the purpose of institutional classification—admissions, releases, types of ward assignment, shock treatment, and such. This special language, which may be worth something administratively —that is, *if people must be treated as merchandise*—is then applied to legal purposes; but is *considerably less than adequate as a means of conveying information to a jury.* [Italics mine.]

The big terms of a psychiatrist's discourse under any rule are large, ominous-sounding words which no one else in the courtroom really understands and which, as time goes on, clever lawyers are becoming quite adept at proving that the psychiatrist himself does not fully understand.[9]

Righto and bravo! say I.

Take this case as an illustration of obscurantic language:

On April 20, 1957, at 1:10 p.m., a twenty-three-year-old airplane mechanic walked into the hallway of an apartment house in Brookline, Massachusetts, where his former fiancée, Connie, lived with her parents on the second floor. He stopped in the hall and released the safety latch on the Belgian automatic 38 in his pocket. He then climbed the stairs and rang the bell. As Connie opened the door he took the gun out, but couldn't pull the trigger. When Connie slammed the door, Jim shut his eyes and shot nine times, killing her. He ran out of the house and encountered a policeman whom *he* finally *persuaded* to take him to the Brookline Police Station.

Jim had met Connie in 1949 when he was sixteen and she twelve. They became engaged in 1954 when Jim was in the Air Force. They exchanged wedding rings and made plans to be married, but as often as the plans were agreed on, Connie changed them, frequently at her mother's insistence. She always said, "Yes" and then "No." After Jim's discharge from the Air Force in 1956, he went to work in California and the Yes, No—Yes, No pattern continued. Finally in April, 1957, Jim came back to Boston determined to marry Connie or get his ring back. Connie and her mother were reluctant to return the ring.

Jim was later to describe his feelings at that moment thus:

> I became very upset . . . I had the idea that it was an utterly hopeless and solutionless and impossible situation which I had become entangled in . . . I fought this emotion down, kissed her goodbye, walked out of the house. I said, "You better get good and drunk, not just happy and sad, completely comatose." So I drove to a bar . . . and had two shots of bourbon . . . I remember I stared at some middle-aged woman sitting there, staring directly at me. I felt,

"She realizes what a big chump you are." And I thought of how Mrs. Gilman [Connie's mother] thought what a big chump I was, and how Connie either thought that or was using me. And I said, "This is the end." I went out to the car, I took my gun out of the glove compartment, put it in my jacket pocket, drove back to the house, parked the car. I got out of the car and started to cross the street and a number of ideas passed through my head. First, "I am going to kill her; I am going to put this gun right up against her forehead and pull the trigger and then I shall do the same for myself."

The second was, "Jim, this is foolish, there must be some kind of a solution." . . . I said, "Do you realize if you do this they will electrocute you?" And I said, "Yes." And then I thought of my father. I do not know why, it just shot through my head for a minute. And I came to the conclusion that that was exactly what I deserved, and that it fitted in with the idea that I have always had, that I would never live to be 30 years old and that I had adopted the attitude while in the service: live fast, die young, and have a good-looking corpse.[10]

In the next seventeen months Jim was seen by nine psychiatrists and three psychologists. The state used one set of psychiatrists to prove that he was "perfectly sane" and therefore "responsible," and the defense used other psychiatrists to show that Jim was sick and therefore "not responsible."

Jim's father had died from an accident when the boy was six. He had slipped on the ice, chasing his son, insisting he wear a warm cap on his way to school. Jim always felt he had killed his father. Thereafter, self-defeating and destructive acts were connected, in one way or another, with these feelings. As a twelve-year-old he swallowed iodine rather than go to school; at fifteen, he was badly bruised when he insisted on fighting five boys who attacked him. During his service in the Air Force, a buddy who saw him point a pistol at his head talked him out of the suicide attempt. As an Air Force mechanic, Jim felt guilty about the deaths of two pilots despite the fact that an official investigation determined their deaths to be due to pilot error rather than mechanical defect.

The jury, asked to correlate the testimony with the definition given in the instructions, found Jim guilty of murder in the first degree. It did not recommend leniency, so the judge was obliged to sentence him to be electrocuted.

After listening to the sentence, Jim said, "Thank you."

His conviction was affirmed by the Massachusetts Supreme Court, and when his counsel and his family petitioned the Governor to commute his sentence, Jim wrote the Governor:

> Now I do not ask for death in the form of punishment, but as mercy. Mercy in the guise of release from a life which is no longer honorable nor desirable. My wish is that you can put aside your moral regrets and do your duty, even as I have done mine.[11]

* * *

> If I could but feel that I honestly regretted my actions, I would welcome the prospect of imprisonment and rehabilitation. However, while I do not lack the qualities of pity or compassion, I do not feel one iota of remorse for the crime I have committed. It is not the enormity of the crime itself, but the ease with which I justify it to myself that precludes the possibility of my ever returning to society again. Under these conditions, execution is the only logical conclusion.[12]

The puzzled but conscientious Governor requested the Commission of Mental Health to start a study of the case to determine if Jim was too sick to be executed. Five psychiatrists and one psychologist were involved in this post-trial study. Jim was seen often by one or another of them in the following six months, and many reports were written to the Commissioners.

One psychiatrist wrote, "Mr. C is a pleasant, intelligent, and responsive young man who *shows no evidence of psychosis* [italics throughout are mine], nor does he show on first examination a sufficient degree of mental illness for me to recommend hospitalization (were he simply to walk into my office)."

And further, "It is quite probable that once it is definite that he will not be executed, the depression might deepen to the point of his making a suicide attempt . . . *I do not think he should be killed, but at the moment at least, I cannot say that he is too 'mentally ill' to be killed (whatever that means)."*

A state psychologist who administered the standard psychological tests concluded, "While on the surface this patient appears to be neurotic, his core problems and the defenses against them are psychotic in nature. His crime and his desire for destruction seem to be not a sudden eruption occurring in an otherwise normal person, but they seem to represent an attempted solution to a psychological conflict which had its beginnings in the early phases of childhood. *Given his personality* one might say that he had no choice but to act compulsively as he did."

The final report of this team to the Commissioners stated, "We find Mr. C an interesting *challenge* [!!!] in addition to [our] being *genuinely* interested in him as a human being. Our impression is that he is quite treatable and might some day be a useful member of society. I hope we have the opportunity to continue *working with* him."

Let us examine some of these phrases:

"Shows no evidence of psychosis." This familiar cliché is used by many colleagues in spite of the fact that leaders in the profession from coast to coast have urged that the word *psychosis* be abandoned. It has no clear meaning and no official or accepted definition. What does the reader think the psychiatrist meant by it? *

What *did* the word mean in this doctor's mind? He knew his patient was suffering from psychiatric symptoms considered to constitute illness. He said himself that the boy might become suicidal.

---

* About seventy-five years ago when the profession first took a stand against the legal word *insanity*, the word *psychosis* was coined to indicate a state of mental perturbation more severe in degree than what the neurologists had called *neurasthenia* or *neurosis*. The word *psychosis* rhymed with *neurosis* and a pair of poorly defined, quantitatively differentiated states of illness were thus christened. Anyone may call anyone else *neurotic* (or *psychotic*) because the words are so poorly defined that no definite slander or derogation is committed. (This is not true of the word *psychopath* and *schizophrenic;* judgments against defamatory users of these have been sustained.)

He knew the patient was *irrational*—perhaps not broadly delusional, but certainly not thinking straight. But this was still not
something the doctor thought ought to be called "psychotic" behavior! What *would* have been?

Nobody asked my colleague for his opinion about the morality
or propriety of killing the victim. They merely asked whether the
offender was or was not too crazy to appreciate the execution. This
is a harsh way of putting it, but an unequivocal way.

Note, then, the astonishing sentence that follows:

". . . *at the moment at least* [i.e., it may be different tomorrow]
I cannot say [as opposed to whatever he may think] *that he is 'too
mentally ill' to be killed."* Meaning what? What degree of mental
illness would properly disqualify execution?

If a tortured wretch can gain some relief from suffering by a retreat into delusions and hallucinations, why should the law insist
upon his restoration to full clarity of consciousness before dropping
the axe? If the state is to kill people, why not let nature spare them
what suffering it can? One is reminded of the medieval torture
dungeons where buckets of water were dashed on those who
fainted from the pain so that a proper appreciation of the torturing
could go on.

"Given his personality," wrote the psychologist, *"one might say
that he had no other choice but to act compulsively as he did."*

What on earth does this mean? Whose personality but "his own"
could the prisoner have or be "given"? And who gave it to him?
Does the ability to choose one's actions depend upon one's personality? Is there such a thing as free will and free choice or isn't
there? And if there is, who takes it away?

These scientists knew what they were doing when they were
examining the prisoner. But when it came to conveying that information to the judge, they did not possess the same degree of skill.

I believe that what these colleagues *meant* to convey was something like this: "This man is highly disorganized and maladjusted
to his environment. His way of life is incompatible with safety in
his community. His personality structure has continued to deter-

iorate since his murderous act to the point that he now has an overwhelming wish to be killed as the only conceivable goal. While grossly pathological, this wish is susceptible to treatment and possibly to cure. For the state to accede to the patient's wishes to be killed would be to yield to the irrational, antisocial demands of a very sick man. We, as citizens, in terms of our personal value preferences, do not concur in the desirability or morality of doing so."

As a matter of fact, the Commissioner of Mental Health and the Commissioner of Correction evidently came to very similar conclusions and both recommended commutation of sentence to life imprisonment with supportive therapy.

The prisoner was told of these recommendations. When he learned that the Governor was about to approve them, he eluded surveillance and hanged himself.

My point in all this—to recapitulate—is that psychiatrists have failed to achieve influence in reforming criminal procedure or in being helpful to their legal colleagues in large part because we do not make ourselves understood. We do not convey our real meaning by our language. Nor does the law ask us questions which we are particularly qualified to answer.

An Imaginary Courtroom Interrogation

To demonstrate how much depends on words differently understood by the participants in the legal dialogue, let me set up a courtroom scene in which I have been subpoenaed to testify in regard to a man accused of a crime. Let us suppose, for the purpose of illustration, that the judge rather than an attorney does the interrogating of the witness, so as to partially eliminate the adversarial element. He is an enlightened and conscientious judge who really wants to know what to do with a man who has got himself into trouble—perhaps forged a check, assaulted a neighbor, or even something worse. The judge thinks that a psychiatrist might contribute to the court's decision regarding an expedient disposal of the offender. And so here I am, sworn to tell the truth as I see it and trying to be helpful:

JUDGE: Do we understand, Doctor, that you have personally examined this man as to his mental condition?

ANSWER: Yes, Your Honor.

JUDGE: Has he waived privileged confidential communication rights so that you feel free to communicate any opinions that you may have formed?

ANSWER: He has, Your Honor.

JUDGE: Very well, then. Have you formed an opinion as to whether this man is properly in this court? I mean to ask, is this man competent in your opinion to stand trial?

ANSWER: No, Your Honor. I have not permitted myself to form such an opinion. I am not qualified to do so. I can tell you my *findings* in the examination of this man but to draw the conclusions you ask would be to assume a prerogative properly yours and the jury's. Whether or not these findings qualify him as being a proper prisoner at the bar is a legal and moral question, not a psychiatric one.

JUDGE: Well, in order for us to decide this, would you tell us your findings?

ANSWER: Yes, sir. At the time of my examination this man was conscious, fairly alert and intelligent, slightly confused but free from delusions so far as I could tell, emotionally stable although quite impulsive, and affected with a considerable loss of recent memory recall.

JUDGE: Are these symptoms of a mental disease?

ANSWER: Not of any named disease, but of a state of mental illness, yes.

JUDGE: One of your colleagues testified yesterday that the prisoner suffers from benign paralogia, of which, he testified—and I quote—"four subgroups are recognized: concept concatenation syndrome, intellect achievement discordance syndrome, incomplete escalation syndrome, and transcendental valuation syndrome." [13] Do you agree?

ANSWER: I cannot agree or disagree. I have heard those terms but I do not understand them.

JUDGE: Well, then what do *your* findings boil down to?

ANSWER: That he is moderately confused and disorganized, very forgetful, and becoming progressively more so.

JUDGE: Well, that's clear—and I think obvious enough—but does that make him steal?

ANSWER: I do not know what *makes* or made him steal. He probably does various inappropriate things.

JUDGE: You do consider him mentally ill?

ANSWER: Yes.

JUDGE: Insane, in other words?

ANSWER: No, Your Honor; the words are not synonymous. Whether this man's illness corresponds to the legal definition of "insanity" in the code of your state is a question for the jury.

JUDGE: All right, if insanity is a legal artifact, let me use *your* jargon. Is his illness severe enough to be psychosis? Would you be willing to say this man has a *psychosis?*

ANSWER: No, Your Honor, I would not be willing to say so.

JUDGE: Why not?

ANSWER: Because I do not understand the meaning of this word *psychosis* used in a categorical sense.

JUDGE: You don't! But your colleagues use this term! I read it in your scientific journals. I hear it used all the time.

ANSWER: So do I. But it is another word that leads to the confusion I am trying to eliminate. *Insanity* was invented and defined by lawyers, and the word *psychosis* was invented by doctors, but it was never defined. Rather, it has been defined in just as many ways by them as has insanity by the legislators of different states. Leading members of our profession [14] have repeatedly exhorted us to abandon the use of the word: I have heeded them.

JUDGE: Well, let me be more specific, then. Would you say that the prisoner suffers from the disease know as schizophrenia?

ANSWER: I do not know that such a disease exists.

JUDGE: Schizophrenia doesn't exist! Now you *are* being evasive.

Everyone has heard of schizophrenia—a progressive, malignant, incurable form of insanity.

ANSWER: Beg pardon, Your Honor, but I do not accept that statement as true, or that description as accurate.

JUDGE: But see here! Omitting that judgment about its alleged incurability, isn't schizophrenia an officially recognized disease—listed in your organization's *Diagnostic and Statistical Manual of Mental Disorders* which I hold here in my hand?

ANSWER: No, sir, it is *not*. No such disease name is listed there. The manual does describe (on pages 26 to 28) "schizophrenic *reactions*" of various types. But these are *not* diseases; anyone may experience them, and they are NOT "incurable." But, Your Honor, the word *does* imply "incurability" in the minds of many just as you, yourself, thought, and it cannot be stricken from the concept.

JUDGE: Well, Doctor, if you won't call this man crazy or insane, or lunatic or schizophrenic or psychotic, what *would* you call him?

ANSWER: I would not call him anything.

JUDGE: Why not? Hasn't he got something that has a name? You admit he is ill.

ANSWER: Yes, he is ill. But I think it is time for psychiatry to emerge from the name-calling state. Words such as *psychotic* and *schizophrenic* and *lunatic* have become pejorative terms; instead of calling someone a liar or a rascal, people now just call them by any of these psychiatric designations. These are damning words, and we psychiatrists should not use damning words; we should use helpful words, constructive words, words that do not imply a malignancy that is not necessarily present.

JUDGE: I see your point and I respect it, but I still want to know what is wrong with this fellow besides his forgetfulness and his propensity to steal. If you do not call such peculiar people anything, how do you refer to them?

ANSWER: I would refer to him just as you did, in the simplest possible descriptive terms. If the man is queer, or irrational, or disturbed, or violent—one could say just that. And you did.

JUDGE: But the question is, are forgetfulness and stealing part of the same disease? Should he be treated by doctors in an asylum for one thing or sent to jail for the other?

ANSWER: I agree that this is *the* question, and I will answer it. He is, in my opinion, severely ill, and he needs treatment. I call his condition an illness just because there is a medical treatment for it which experience has shown to be effective. Not in all cases, of course, but we doctors do treat these cases, and we do treat some of them successfully.

But may I take the liberty of reminding Your Honor that some people, even some of my colleagues, would not call this man's way of life an illness, chiefly because they do *not* think we doctors can do anything about it. They consider it merely a bad way of living, a social maladaptation. They think it is the product of society and the responsibility of society, not just of us doctors. In the last analysis, this is a question decided by universal public opinion, not by medical opinion.

Was Joan of Arc mentally ill? The public at that time did not think so. Does it now? The public did not think Lincoln's assassin was mentally ill at that time. Does it now?

If the public is angry at someone, it is not likely to call his symptoms, eccentricities, aggressions, and crimes indications of sickness. In our opinion, nevertheless, they often are.

JUDGE: Well, what about the question of whether or not this man is responsible under the law? He committed a crime; that we know. But there is still the question of his intentions and his capacity for knowing right from wrong, his capacity to refrain from the wrong if he knows what wrong is. If he is not responsible, then technically he is not guilty.

ANSWER: Your Honor, *responsible* is another one of these functionally undefined words. If he did the act, he was certainly in one sense responsible, whether he intended to do it or not. It was not an accident, it was not an "Act of God." If the prisoner was not responsible, who, indeed, was—or is?

JUDGE: But your colleagues have often testified in this court that in their opinion a certain prisoner *was* or was *not* responsible.

ANSWER: Yes, Your Honor, because the word *responsible* is in everyday use. But this use is different from the legal use, as you well know, and that fact is not always clear to your witnesses.

JUDGE: Yes, the legal point about responsibility is whether or not the accused had a certain *mens rea,* certain preconceived intentions, and was capable of making certain judgments. I do not suppose a man as forgetful as this one could hold a *mens rea,* but . . .

ANSWER: I am familiar with the official legal construction, but it is based on such obsolete concepts of human behavior that it no longer serves any purpose in describing the practical problems before us. It will not help you or the prisoner or anyone for me to say that this man is or is not responsible.

What you want to know, I suppose, is whether this man is capable of living with the rest of us and refraining from his propensity to injure us. You want to know whether he is dangerous, whether he can be deterred, whether he can be treated and cured—whether we must arrange to detain him in protective custody indefinitely.

JUDGE: Exactly. This is indeed what the court would like to know. But it seems we do not know how to communicate with one another, and our laws do not permit us to ask you. How, I beg of you, may I obtain direct, nonevasive answers to precisely these questions?

ANSWER: Your Honor, by asking for them. As you say yourself, you are not permitted by precedent and custom to do so.

And even if you were, and did, I am not in a position to answer them. Useful answers to these questions depend upon an examination of the total situation in which this offender did this act—and previous acts—and then of the offender himself. We have to know about the environment from which he comes, the training which he has had, the assets with which he is equipped, and the special handicaps from which he suffers. This has to be systematically inquired into. Obviously he has failed in his efforts to get along with and make the best of the environments and the events that have surrounded him—whatever they were. He has had to retreat; he is floundering and flapping like a fish out of water, trying to get back in and survive. He is a nuisance and a menace, but he is also a responsibility of our society. It is our responsibility to help him to better control himself. This we must do as economically as possible.

JUDGE: This is all very well. Your opinion is very convincing to me. But as a judge I bear in mind that this is only your opinion. Suppose I listen now to another psychiatrist—one of your colleagues—and then another and then another. Some are going to agree with you but some are not. You are going to have opinions that I am really not competent to decide between. What shall I do?

ANSWER: I have been waiting for this question, and now I would like to make my main point. Will Your Honor indulge me?

JUDGE: Proceed.

ANSWER: In my opinion, what you should do, what all courts should do, what society should do, is to *exclude all psychiatrists from the courtroom!* Put us all out and make us stay out. After you have tried the case, let us doctors and our assistants examine him and confer together outside the courtroom and render a report to you, which will express our view of the offender—his potentialities, his liabilities, and the possible remedies.

If we doctors cannot agree, let us disagree in private and submit majority and minority reports. That probably will not be necessary; our differences are going to be on minor points. We are not going to raise legal issues like "sanity" and "responsibility" because we are not going to talk legal jargon. Nor should we talk *our* jargon. We should try to say in simple English why we think this man has acted in this way so different from the rest of us, and what we think can be done to change his pattern.

You will then decide if we have been persuasive, and make possible by order what you think is the most promising recommendation.

Of course, this assumes that the medieval practice of capital punishment will soon be abandoned in theory as it has already been abandoned in fact, and that the absurd "insanity defense" will no longer be necessary or tolerated. "Why not?" ask two distinguished authorities.[15] Indeterminate sentence will be taken for granted, and preoccupation with punishment as the penalty of the law would have yielded to a concern for the best measures to insure public safety, with rehabilitation of the offender if possible, and as economically as possible.

The proposal that psychiatry and psychiatrists be excluded from the courtroom is by no means original with me. As early as 1936, Sheldon Glueck advocated this separation of guilt findings from disposition.[16] In his Isaac Ray Award Lecture for 1962, he declared that legislation and administration should substitute for the concept of responsibility and culpability the simple and "less emotion-arousing concept of *amenability to social control*." [17] The criminal court should cease with the findings of guilt and innocence, and the "procedure thereafter should be guided by a professional treatment tribunal to be composed, say, of a psychiatrist, a psychologist, a sociologist or cultural anthropologist, an educator, and a judge with long experience in criminal trials and with special interest in the protection of the legal rights of those charged with crime." [18]

The proposed elimination of the psychiatrist from the courtroom is not just because we do not like to be disputed by our colleagues, badgered by opposing attorneys, suspected of being purchasable and discredited as scientists. I oppose courtroom appearances because I consider guilt, competence, and responsibility to be moral questions, not medical ones. The judge and the jury are the community's representatives in this area. It is for them to make the judgment and apply the sanctions deemed appropriate, not us psychiatrists. Society decides—through them—what crime is and what proof it requires in any particular instance and what penalty applies.

Why should a psychiatrist be called to the stand in these cases? Why is he even summoned to the courtroom? Why not a clergyman or a philosopher? Or the mayor or the editor of the local newspaper? These are the people who can best represent the total community and express its sentiments on moral questions in general. Whether a prisoner's "symptoms" disqualify him from blameworthiness is for society or its representatives to say, and these people are actually more representative of the society that wants this question decided. But why the psychiatrist?

Remember—the psychiatrist is not self-invited to these parties. He is not a trespasser. He is called, then he is questioned, criticized, disputed, attacked, suspected, disregarded, and ridiculed. Legal commentators even complain that psychiatry is corrupting court procedure. (Slovenko [19])

Not long ago a friend put a great deal of work into the study of an obviously disorganized boy who had committed some strange, pointless, tragic murders. He tried to convey this concept of the prisoner's condition and the dynamics of his irrational behavior to the court. With what result is best expressed in a quotation from a local newspaper editorial written shortly after sentence was pronounced:

> [The prisoner] admitted killing all three. Late Friday night, ten men and two women ruled that he, in turn, must die. . . .
>
> One redeeming feature that might have come out of the . . . mess could have been a recognition of mental illness. For psychiatry, a relatively new science . . . *it could have been a moment of triumph* [Italics mine]. . . . Psychiatry might have come into its own. But instead . . . quite the reverse occurred. Instead of being portrayed as a competent, exacting science that could take its place once and for all in the field of medicine, and in the minds of men, psychiatry appeared as a catch-as-catch-can profession that depends less on who is examined than who is doing the examining.
>
> [The prisoner] is a schizoid, who could not control his actions, said psychiatric witnesses for the defense. [He] was not a schizoid, and he knew right from wrong, was the emphatic rebuttal from equally qualified representatives obtained by the opposite side. . . . [The jury] had the confusing job of choosing the testimony that best suited their opinions. Obviously they were not sufficiently impressed by testimony that his first 22 years were a model of abnormally con-

scientious behavior that suddenly exploded into actions of violence and death. . . .

Millions will continue to be served competently by psychiatry—many of them by the venerable doctors who appeared for both counsels at the . . . trial. But in the trial itself, with its conflicting, contradictory psychiatric testimony, what might have been one of psychiatry's finest hours succeeded only in making a mockery of an invaluable profession.[20]

Another reason for excluding psychiatrists from the courtroom is the growing tendency to use them to circumvent a speedy and public trial. This is a right guaranteed every citizen by the Sixth Amendment. But individuals are sent to jail, or to a psychiatric hospital frequently no better than a jail, pending the determination (by psychiatrists!) of the defendants' competency to assist in the preparation of the defense and to understand the nature of charges brought against them, and psychiatrists are ordered to determine and declare themselves on these matters.

In numerous public statements, Judge David Bazelon has made a point, with which I fully agree, that the competency of a man to stand trial cannot be properly determined or announced by psychiatrists. They may certainly examine an offender and submit a report of their findings, and these findings may assist a judge or a jury to come to some conclusions about the man's competence. But no psychiatrist should presume to accept the responsibility of deciding a highly technical legal question based on these findings. He can say that a man is distracted or deluded or hallucinated, but whether or not this state of mind is compatible with legal "competence" is something about which a psychiatrist has only common knowledge, and not scientific knowledge.

Thomas Szasz [21] has emphasized this point from the psychiatric standpoint, declaring that psychiatry is exploited to detain people unjustly, either because psychiatrists cannot make up their minds how to answer this competency inquiry or else because they have declared it to be their opinion that the accused is incompetent to stand trial and hence must remain locked up until competence is restored! Szasz cites several sad cases. All of us know that there are many unconvicted but *alleged* offenders waiting year after year after year for a fair trial which they may never get. Such facts provide some fanatics with ammunition to denounce all psychiatry and mental health efforts as tending toward illegal detention. But delusional as this position of the radical right obviously is, if a psychiatrist has blundered or has been pushed into the untenable position of using psychiatry as a legal weapon, and if psychiatrists are being coerced into confusing diagnostic conclusions (which we are qualified to make) with legal determinations (which we are not qualified to make), then we are all in Szasz's debt for publicizing the error and permitting us to extricate ourselves.

At the 1966 annual meeting of the American Psychiatric Association, professor of psychiatry John M. Suarez, lecturer at the School of Law of the University of California at Los Angeles, declared that once psychiatry became an established discipline, the legal system "gradually and subtly" unburdened itself of some of its responsibilities and placed them on the lap of psychiatry. "Particularly dangerous," said Dr. Suarez, "is the court practice of asking psychiatrists to make final decisions about a defendant's competence or responsibility." By this means a defendant may get the short end of justice. Dr. Suarez said that he knows of many people who have spent decades in mental institutions for minor crimes because testifying psychiatrists judged them "incompetent." (We all know of such persons.) As long as such practices prevail, psychiatrists will be "prevented from making their proper contribution [to law], whatever that may be." [22]

CHAPTER 6

The Apparent Indifference

of the Public to Its Safety

Consider these facts:

Our system for controlling crime is ineffective, unjust, expensive. Crime rates mount. Parks are unsafe at night. *Who cares?*

Our personal safety is threatened; our property is in jeopardy; our children and friends are daily exposed to danger. Yet no wave of public sentiment arises to end this. *Don't we care?*

Our city jails and inhuman reformatories and wretched prisons are jammed. They are known to be unhealthy, filthy, dangerous, immoral, indecent, crime-breeding dens of iniquity. Not everyone has smelled them, as some of us have. Not many have heard the groans and the curses. Not everyone has seen the hate and despair in a thousand blank, hollow faces. But, in a way, we all know how miserable prisons are. *We want them to be that way.* And they are. *Who cares?*

Professional and big-time criminals prosper as never before. Gambling syndicates flourish. White-collar crime may even exceed all others, but goes undetected in the majority of cases. We are all being robbed and we know who the robbers are. They live nearby. *Who cares?*

The public filches millions of dollars worth of food and clothing from stores, towels and sheets from hotels, jewelry and knick-knacks from shops. The public steals, and the same public pays it back in higher prices. *Who cares?*

"What has happened," asks J. Edgar Hoover, "to the civic pride, the righteous indignation of otherwise respectable citizens who turn their backs on helpless victims of beatings, robberies, and sex crimes? The incredibly indifferent attitude of these people . . . has helped to turn the streets and parks of many cities into virtual jungles of fear—where, according to a recent survey, nearly one-half of the residents are afraid to walk alone at night. Our crime rate is growing six times as fast as our population." [1]* There are, Hoover adds, five serious offenses recorded in this country every minute, a vicious crime of violence every two and one-half minutes, a robbery every five minutes, fifty-two automobiles stolen every hour.

What shall we say to Mr. Hoover? *Who cares?*

How *shall* we explain this apparent indifference? We all recognize it to be there—even in ourselves. Once the immediate reactions of anger, fear, and vengeance regarding a particular, recently reported crime have been verbally expressed, the average citizen washes his hands of all responsibility and leaves it (silently) to the official avengers. Few of us feel any responsibility for correcting the system or for preventing the recurrence of crime; maybe we think it is hopeless to attempt anything. In large part perhaps this reflects uncertainty as to what to do. Call it ignorance.

One motive for writing this book was my belief that if the public knew how bad things were, if it knew how we cheat ourselves, how we deceive ourselves, how we persuade ourselves that we are getting protection when we are steadily making matters worse by our ineffective methods, surely then we would do something about it. We would do more than merely gasp at the new horror story on the front page of the morning paper. We would act, and we would demand action. And, indeed, I think we will.

---

* On the other hand, Daniel Bell, professor of sociology at Columbia University, believes that crime statistics (by the F.B.I., for example) are overdrawn. Violence, thinks Bell, is less a factor in American life now than it was fifty or a hundred years ago, and I fully agree. (Reported by the press, March 1965.)

In 1948, when the wretched conditions of the state hospitals for the mentally ill were exposed to the public by the press and by such books as Mary Jane Ward's *The Snake Pit,*[2] it was striking to note how shocked the public was regarding many things that some of us thought everyone knew about. We—some of us—thought everyone knew that public psychiatric hospitals were crowded, dark, dirty, and unsanitary places where there was little hopefulness. It was customary at that time, indeed it was considered praiseworthy, for superintendents of state hospitals to return to the state treasury an unused portion of their appropriation. This token of efficiency and frugality was managed, of course, by just that much more starving and neglecting of the patients for whose care it had been appropriated. No one protested. The alumni associations of state hospitals have never had a strong lobby. If an occasional superintendent asked for more—rather than returning some of the appropriation—he was apt to get the treatment accorded Nicholas Nickleby at Dotheboys Hall.

When Kansas voters learned the facts about conditions in their state hospitals from the press and radio, they responded immediately. Contrary to the predictions of all the politicians, the people of Kansas approved a quadrupling of expenditures for state hospitals, putting at the head of the list nationally the state that had previously been in forty-seventh place. It has remained in first position ever since, but many other states have followed suit with respect to updating and upgrading their programs. State hospitals which were formerly crowded with chronic patients, most of whom were expected to remain there for life, today have empty beds despite the fact that there are many more admissions per year than three decades ago. The average stay in the better public psychiatric hospitals today is less than ninety days, whereas it used to be a matter of years. And, in the long run, this was a great economic saving to the state, because it made additional construction unnecessary and it greatly reduced the cost of curing (not merely detaining) each patient.

Why is it not equally obvious that we could save millions of dollars by a change in the penal system? * If individuals, who do not benefit from their confinement and are not given an opportunity to do constructive work, could be allowed to earn their way and contribute to the society that they have wronged, *everyone* would profit. Their enforced uselessness is no gain to anyone.

Is our failure to do something like this truly only a matter of ignorance? Time and time again somebody shouts about this state of affairs, just as I am shouting now. The magazines shout. The newspapers shout. The television and radio commentators shout (or at least they "deplore"). Psychologists, sociologists, leading jurists, wardens, and intelligent police chiefs join the chorus. Governors and mayors and congressmen are sometimes heard. They shout that the situation is bad, bad, bad, and getting worse. Some suggest that we immediately replace obsolete procedures with scientific methods. A few shout contrary sentiments. But the voices of progressive penologists have been loud and clear.

Associate Justice Brennan of the United States Supreme Court thinks improvement is about to begin. Recently he said, "We may be at the threshold of a major reexamination of the premises which underlie our system for the administration of criminal justice." [3]

I hope he is right. But *when* shall we look for these reexaminations? Do the clear indications derived from scientific discovery for appropriate changes continue to fall on deaf ears? Why is the public so long-suffering, so apathetic, and thereby so continuingly self-destructive? How many Presidents (and other citizens) do we have to lose before we do something?

The Sin of Apathy

Public apathy regarding serious common danger is an old whipping boy. Many of our great leaders beginning with Zoroaster and followed later by Isaiah and Jeremiah and Pericles and Socra-

---

* "Give me three to six months, two more psychiatrists, four psychologists, four psychiatric social workers, and adequate clerical staff, and I'll reduce the state's prison population by 50 per cent," said Dr. Karl Targownik of the Kansas Reception and Diagnostic Center.

tes and Plato and Jesus and St. John and St. Paul and hundreds of others have deplored public apathy. Long ago—about the fifth century—apathy was listed as one of the eight (not seven) deadly sins. It had a special name: *acedia.** Later it was dropped from the list of deadly sins and gradually evolved into a *psychiatric* (!) syndrome, along with depression and pessimism. The Fourth Lateran Council (1215) listed "the varieties and derivatives of disgust with life" (all sins, of course) as sorrow, laziness, weariness, spiritual negligence, lack of joy in general and particularly in prayer, despair in general and particularly in prayer, despair in general and particularly of one's own salvation, doubt, grief, tedium, and hatred of life. These were actually elaborations of Cassian's concept of acedia, a state of mind representing the need to avoid anxiety and not care!

Perhaps the medieval theologians began to wonder if the state of indifference to the world's troubles and to the soul's spirit, like sorrow and despair, might not be so irrational, so self-destructive, that it passed beyond mere sinfulness and indicated a kind of sickness. What the early Christian fathers recognized as evil and sinful in the various kinds of indifference was the aggressive element, which is *also* present in the symptoms of illness. Not caring is hurtful. Jesus put it well by saying that he who was not with Him was against Him. The practical consequence of apathy and withdrawal

* "Petrarch, who clearly suffered from acedia himself, gave it still another meaning. He himself manifested an important symptom that had never been mentioned in that connection: an almost voluptuous pleasure in one's own emotional sufferings. Another aspect of the syndrome that he unwittingly manifested was delight in exhibitionistic self-revelation, as shown in minutely-detailed accounts of his own spiritual sufferings. Furthermore, he defined the conditions as a disorder brought on by consideration of the miseries of human life rather than as a sin. Petrarch thus was the first to describe *Weltschmerz* in modern terms, and Goethe, Baudelaire, and others who later reveled in it were, knowingly or not, his followers. Moreover, Petrarch's unwitting additions to the list of manifestations of acedia removed the syndrome from the realm of theology to that of psychiatry. The psychiatric significance of acedia has been recognized by modern authors." (Altschule, Mark D.: "Acedia: Its Evolution from Deadly Sin to Psychiatric Syndrome." *Brit. J. Psychiat.*, 111:117–119, 1965.)

is inactive aid to the "enemy," and permission for the continuance of the evil.

George Bernard Shaw once said that it was necessary for the progress of society that people be shocked pretty often. But is the public becoming shock-proof?

In Chicago, Negro cab driver Lawrence Boyd tried to stop three Negro muggers from robbing two white youths. Boyd was shot twice, paralyzed in one arm, lost his job, and in 1965 was $9,000 in debt. In Upper Darby, Pennsylvania, George Senn fired a shotgun to prevent twenty thugs from attacking two girls and a boy outside his window. Senn was convicted of aggravated assault and battery and had to pay $491 in court costs, a $400 bail-bond fee, and $500 for legal and investigative expenses. He also faced a damage suit from his "victims."

Two medical students of my acquaintance were walking in a park in New Haven when they saw an elderly man stretched out on the ground. They successfully resuscitated him by mouth and with massage, called an ambulance, and took him to the hospital. The next day he died. The students found themselves in deep trouble over having tried to help.*

The Deputy, a play which has aroused worldwide attention, asked why *even the Pope* kept silent during the torture and slaughter of millions of innocent citizens. The Pope? Did the leader of *any* great religious body speak out at the continuance of that horror? Did the leader of any nation? Did England? Did America?

Some said it was "none of our business." Others said there was

---

* A Frenchman who fails to help another when he can do so without risk is liable for up to five years in prison and a $3,000 fine. The law's rationale, explained Sorbonne Law Professor André Tunc, is that a bystander "participates in the murder by his decision not to intervene." Similar laws are on the books in Britain, Germany, Italy, and Russia. Surveys do not show that citizens of these countries feel any more like helping, said Chicago sociologist Hans Zeisel. In a comparative study of U.S. and German students, Zeisel found that seventy-five per cent of the Americans and only forty-two per cent of the Germans opposed penalties for bad Samaritans—those who refuse help when it is obviously needed. (Wille, Lois: "Good Samaritans: Law and the Golden Rule." *The Nation,* April 26, 1965, pp. 447–449.)

nothing we could do. Many sighed and said, "Oh, it is probably just a newspaper story; greatly exaggerated. It can't be true." Later, much later, they beat their breasts and declared, "Who could believe. . . . We had no idea. . . . We didn't know."

Nonsense! We *did* know.*

The Public Is Not Really Apathetic

It is a daily, hourly struggle for each one of us to rise above primitive patterns of maintaining the internal balance of aggression and guilt, vengeance and mercy, self-defense and masochism, intolerance and compassion. But our intelligence does have its victories; it persists, and ultimately prevails—sometimes. And in spite of apparent public indifference about crime, and in spite of the public's secret satisfactions with crime (and hence with its present mismanagement), there are many who are very concerned and who continue to cry loudly and discordantly about the present situation.

There are some who accuse the public and its servants of *misplaced* concern. For example, listen to this broadside of the Honorable Senator Grady Hazelwood of Amarillo, addressed to the press of Texas:

> All legislative efforts are designed solely for the benefit of the criminal—to the end that many, many criminals are turned out of the penitentiary that should remain there, at least long enough for them to learn the lesson that crime doesn't pay.
>
> Brutal murders by ex-convicts continue on and on, and no one seems to consider the rights of the widows and orphans whose husbands and fathers they had a right to look to for companionship, love and affection, and financial support. What about the poor groceryman or businessman who is daily victimized by thieves and hot-check artists?

---

* See, for instance, "The Nazi Murder Plot" by Arthur Morse (*Look*, November 14, 1967). Even in July 1968, a political leader in West Germany declared that *he*, an acknowledged one-time member of the Nazi party, "did not know."

No thought whatever is being given to the right of the public to be protected from these criminals.[4]

No thought being given? No money spent? No efforts made?

Bishop Fulton J. Sheen has echoed these same fatuous emotional lies in a telecast carried by a number of U.S. stations.[5] The reader will have no trouble in adding samples of his own from the daily press. He can find them even in the comics:

Little Orphan Annie attended church with a reformed gunman who says, "Ah re'lize, Annie, you knows me as a killah! A 'fast gun'! Well, little David was no slouch with his slingshot; scriptures are full o' them as defended what they felt was right and just! So, I don't figger me believin' true, and goin to church reg'lar was evah meant to slow my draw ag'in any murderin' varmint turned loose on decent people."

Just then they pass an old crony of this pious killer. The old crony whispers that another ex-convict has been released.

"Slasher Weevil? Why, he kilt a whole little family jest for meanness! Soft haided circuit Jedge and twelve mixed-up he-biddies let him off with only life! Who let him out?"

"Parole Board! Jest thought y'should know!"

"Parole Board! That figgers! Ah heered they got a new expert on crime and cure headin' the board! Real book-trained penologless chap, fergit his name."

"Seems Slasher's seen th' error o' his ways! Figger he's now tamed down, fit t' return to society, as a shinin' example o' true reformation."

"Yeah! Most lawmen has heered that gobbledygook 'til it jest makes 'em sick t' their stummicks!"[6]

The illustrative samples just cited clearly contradict the thesis that people are apathetic about crime and about its present management. Some are secretly or overtly pleased with the present system; some are angry! Some are disgusted; some alarmed. Part of the contradiction arises from the fact that most citizens are either too close to crime and criminals to be objective or else too far from them to be aroused. One close to an offense is either angry on be-

half of himself or the injured victims, *or else* he is aware of the
special reasons actuating the offense and hence sympathetic or at
least tolerant toward the offender. If one is *far* from the crime, as
are the people in the other part of town or in the next state, he is
unlikely to care much what happens about the particular case.

Hence there seems to be both a great stagnation of movement in
regard to an obsolete, inefficient, unjust, unsafe system but, at the
same time, a ferment of dissatisfaction and criticism. The public as
a whole may *seem* to be apathetic about this lack of improvement
or change by denying the evil ("We didn't know how bad it
was") or withdrawing from involvement ("It really is none of
my business"), or avoiding from genuine fear ("It is dangerous to meddle with these people"). The public listens to many
voices, some stridently attacking the police, some the courts, some
the lawyers, some the psychiatrists and criminologists.

Criminology, penology, sociology, psychology, and psychiatry
have never had the public respect which the physical sciences
command. Millions get into airplanes and ride everywhere on earth
with only the vaguest knowledge of what physical discoveries and
mechanisms they are putting reliance upon, whereas the very suggestion of comparable innovations in social action would cause a
panic. The proposals of psychiatrists and other social scientists
might work, but, on the other hand, they might disturb the time-
honored techniques for dealing with dangerous citizens so that the
situation might become worse than it is now. So thinks the public.

A respected law enforcement man, Donald Tulloch, recently declared:

> In recent years there has been a tendency to permit the psychiatrist,
> the psychologist and the social worker, not to mention organized
> minorities of lay people with a fancied mission to cure the ills of the
> world, to assume a position of direction of the course of criminology,
> and particularly penology. Both fields have a certain appeal to the
> imagination, and the author, the script writer and the scenarist have
> taken full advantage of this. The resulting rash of novels, television
> programs and movies concerning the activities of the criminal ele-

ment has given the average person a feeling of confidence in his status as an expert in solving the crime problem. Furthermore, since Sigmund Freud introduced his stimulating theories of human behavior, psychiatry and psychoanalysis have become the catch words.

The American public loves gimmicks, and when a new drug or a new scientific discovery comes along it immediately becomes a panacea. When psychiatry entered the picture, the public latched onto it as the cure for all the problems involving abnormal behavior. Because of its popularity, it became a lucrative field for the practitioners. Consequently, there has been a tendency to oversell and overpublicize psychiatry in many areas, penology among them.[7]

For all his cracks about my profession and colleagues, I do not consider Sheriff Tulloch altogether wrong. I too think that the piecemeal, unsystematized introduction of pyschiatry into the present system is of little value. The point of my citing this is to show how the public has legitimate doubts as to whether all this psychiatry business is going to effect any real improvement. What proof is there? What assurance is there that a psychiatrist will not just "mess things up" worse?

Resistance to Change

A large community of prison officials and others has a vested interest in the present power structure and would be opposed to reform of any kind from any source. But the public is not so involved. Why should it be indifferent to the possibility of improving the system with some scientific assistance? The public behaves as a sick patient does when a dreaded treatment is proposed for his ailment. We all know how the aching tooth may suddenly quiet down in the dentist's office, or the abdominal pain disappear in the surgeon's examining room. Why should a sufferer seek relief and shun it? Is it merely the fear of pain of the treatment? Is it the fear of unknown complications? Is it distrust of the doctor's ability? All of these, no doubt.

But, as Freud made so incontestably clear, the sufferer is always somewhat deterred by a kind of subversive, internal opposition to the work of cure. He suffers on the one hand from the pains of his affliction and yearns to get well. But he suffers at the same time from traitorous impulses that fight against the accomplishment of any change in himself, even recovery! Like Hamlet, he wonders whether it may be better after all to suffer the familiar pains and aches associated with the old method than to face the complications of a new and strange, even though possibly better way of handling things.

Once Freud had called our attention to this, we could all see it. We psychiatrists see it daily in our patients. Psychoanalytic treatment consists in considerable part in calling his resistance to the attention of the patient and bringing him to face the reasons for this self-betrayal.

Could we do something like that in the case of the ailing social organization, the body politic? Might one, in some figurative way at least, listen like a psychoanalyst to what people say about the problem of crime and crime control and deduce the roots of the resistance to change in this field? What *is* the secret satisfaction of the present system? What is the secret fear? And back of these secrets, what is the guilty wish? Why don't we care, or act as if we did?

Does the Public Need Crime?

The inescapable conclusion is that society secretly *wants* crime, *needs* crime, and gains definite satisfactions from the present mishandling of it! We condemn crime; we punish offenders for it; but we need it. The crime and punishment ritual is a part of our lives. We need crimes to wonder at, to enjoy vicariously, to discuss and speculate about, and to publicly deplore. We need criminals to identify ourselves with, to secretly envy, and to stoutly punish. Criminals represent our alter egos—our "bad" selves—rejected and projected. They do for us the forbidden, illegal things we *wish* to do and, like scapegoats of old, they bear the burdens of our displaced guilt and punishment—"the iniquities of us all."

Them we can punish! At them we can all cry "stone her" or

"crucify him." We can throw mud at the fellow in the stocks; he has been caught; he has been identified; he has been labeled, and he has been proven guilty of the dreadful thing. Now he is eligible for punishment and will be getting only what he deserves.

The vicarious use of the criminal for relieving the guilt feelings of "innocent" individuals by displacement is no recent theory, but it constantly eludes public acceptance. The internal economics of our own morality, our submerged hates and suppressed aggressions, our fantasied crimes, our feeling of need for punishment—all these can be managed in part by the scapegoat device. To do so requires this little maneuver of displacement, but displacement and projection are easier to manage than confession or sublimation.

Hence, crowds of people will always join in the cry for punishment. Often their only interest in the particular victim is the fact that he is a labeled villain, and the extermination of villains is a "righteous act." The definition of villainy does not have to be a matter of common agreement or scientific investigation. It is enough that someone has been "fingered," accused, arraigned, sentenced. "He, not I, is the purveyor of evil, the agent of violence. Crucify him! Burn him! Hang him! Punish him!"

Crime in the news is often a kind of sermon; it is a warning, a reminder of the existence of evil and the necessity for good to conquer it. And are not the forces of good gradually overwhelming the forces of evil? We want to think so. It is the perennial hope of and for our civilization. Hence the wretched handling of the offender, from beginning to end, is part of a daily morality play—a publicly supported, moralistic ritual enactment, without benefit of clergy.

Because he has summarized this public need of the crime-punishment ritual so eloquently and comprehensively, I would like to quote Dr. Hans W. Mattick, associate director of the Center for Studies in Criminal Justice at the University of Chicago:

> While the general public has some interest in the subject of imprisonment, their knowledge of it is selective and very limited. By and large, they view the representation of crime, criminals and treatment

methods as a contest between good and evil. The mass media report the crime and its immediate consequences and the public participates, vicariously, as the forces of law and order go about their business of bringing the offender to justice. There is high interest in the details of the crime, there is suspense while the criminal is being sought, and interest extends to police procedure, trial and conviction. At that point, as far as the public is concerned, the drama is over and, presumably, justice is done. . . .

Generally speaking, there is very little appreciation on the part of the public that this "contest between good and evil," and the whole "drama of crime," is taking place within the larger arena of our political system and this, in part, helps to determine public opinion about the nature of crime, criminals and how they are dealt with. The mayors of our towns and cities, and the town assemblies or city councils, through the police chiefs they appoint and the policemen they employ, are tied directly to the lowliest criminal who offends against society, for the public interest is involved in how these public actors will respond. Similarly, the public prosecutors and the judges who are elected or appointed have their roles to play. Again, the governors of our states, through the correctional division heads and parole boards they appoint, and the prison wardens and guards they employ, may find their fortunes tied directly to the conduct of the lowliest of inmates in the prison furthest removed from the state capitol. All of these functionaries, and many others, also have a great stake in how the crime problem is perceived by the general public.

If a sensational crime is committed, if there is a prison riot or an escape, if an ex-convict on parole commits a new offense, that is news and the mass media bring it to the public. Public interest is aroused and, naturally, there are questions and demands for action. No one in such a situation, least of all public officials and functionaries, is a disinterested observer who views the scene with scientific detachment and leisurely selects the most rational method for dealing with the problem at hand. Great pressures are built up and the demand to "do something" is overriding. . . .

As long as the public continues to view crime as a simple moral problem, that is, "a contest between good and evil," their interest extends only to the point of public resolution, if there is one. And the point of public resolution is the conviction which brings the public drama of a trial to an end. The judge pronounces sentence and the public feels that justice has been done. They seem to forget, altogether, that life goes on in prison and beyond.

Such a morally simplistic view of the crime problem results in a seeming paradox. The most securely imprisoned population that exists is the general public that is uninformed about the nature and consequences of imprisonment as practiced in America today. They are imprisoned in a mass delusion which, in the long run, punishes society far more severely than society can ever punish a convicted criminal.[8]

This is precisely what I mean by declaring that the prevalent punitive attitude of the public toward criminals is self-destructive, and hence itself a crime.

CHAPTER 7

Innate Violence

We have to confess that there is something fascinating for us all about violence. That most crime is not violent we know but we forget, because crime is a breaking, a rupturing, a tearing—even when it is quietly done. To all of us crime seems like violence.

The very word *violence* has a disturbing, menacing quality, enhanced by the contrast of such gentle words as *violin* and *violet,* and hinting in a partial pun at something *vile*. In meaning it implies something dreaded, powerful, destructive, or eruptive. It is something we abhor—or do we? Its first effect is to startle, frighten, even to horrify us. But we do not always run away from it. For violence also intrigues us. It is exciting. It is dramatic. Observing it and sometimes even participating in it gives us acute pleasure.

The newspapers constantly supply us with tidbits of violence going on in the world. They exploit its dramatic essence often to the neglect of conservative reporting of more extensive but less violent damage, the flood disaster in Florence, Italy, for example. Such words as crash, explosion, wreck, assault, raid, murder, avalanche, rape, and seizure evoke pictures of eruptive devastation from which we cannot turn away. The headlines often impute violence metaphorically even to peaceful activities. Relations are "ruptured," a tie is "broken," arbitration "collapses," a proposal is "killed." A football team is "mauled," "smashed," "routed," "smothered," "gouged," "hammered," "toppled," "trounced," "blitzed," "crushed."

Meanwhile on the television and movie screens there constantly appear for our amusement scenes of fighting, slugging, beating, torturing, clubbing, shooting, and the like, which surpass in effect anything that the newspapers can describe.* Much of this violence is portrayed dishonestly; the scenes are only semirealistic; they are "faked" and romanticized. The train robber of the American West and the Chicago gangster of the 1930s are folk heroes. Jesse James, Billy the Kid, and Al Capone are remembered with admiration, whereas the men who tried to apprehend them are forgotten. The present folk hero is Ian Fleming's James Bond, a machine-like man who is licensed to kill and destroy. He is more violent, more callous, and more aggressive than the old-style criminal hero.

Pain cannot be photographed; grimaces indicate but do not convey its intensity. And wounds—unlike violence—are rarely shown. Bloodstained bandages are almost a stylized symbol. We like to watch violence from a safe, clean distance.

This phony quality of television violence in its mentally unhealthy aspect encourages irrationality by giving the impression to the observer that being beaten, kicked, cut, and stomped, while very unpleasant, are not very painful or serious. Such experiences may incapacitate a weakling but do not hurt a "he-man." For after being slugged and beaten the hero rolls over, opens his eyes, hops up, rubs his cheek, grins, and staggers on. The *suffering* of violence is a part which we all tend to repress, in present scenes and in historical records.

"Consider it not so deeply," said Lady Macbeth to her husband, stricken by the thought of red-handed murder. And "Consider it not so deeply," we say to those who remind us of the pain of violence. The unglorious, unthrilling, unexciting misery and agony *behind* much of which, especially that of war, we might all do well to consider more deeply, and more often, in the interests of securing a war-free world.

Allan Nevins, Pulitzer Prize historian and long a professor of

---

* "Violence seems to have been consecrated in many parts of the world," declared Secretary U Thant of the United Nations. He was referring to its use in television programs, movies, and popular literature. (*Topeka State Journal*, April 22, 1968.)

American history at Columbia University, turns to some scenes long forgotten—indeed never seen by any of us today—to serve this purpose:

> Take two contrasting scenes later in the war, of the same day—the day of Malvern Hill, July 1, 1862. That battle of Lee and McClellan reached its climax in the gathering dusk of a lustrous summer evening, no breath of wind stirring the air. The Union army had placed its ranks and its artillery on the slope of a great hill, a natural amphitheatre, which the Southerners assaulted. Participants never forgot the magnificence of the spectacle. . . . But the sequel! The troops on both sides sank exhausted on their arms. From the field the shrieking and moaning of the wounded were heart-rending, yet nothing could be done to succor them. . . .
>
> Night descended on a field ringing with cries of agony: Water! Water! Help!—if in winter, Blankets! Cover! All too frequently no help whatever was forthcoming. After some great conflicts the wounded lay for days, and sometimes a week, without rescue. Shiloh was fought on a Sunday and Monday. Rain set in on Sunday night, and the cold April drizzle continued through Tuesday night. On Tuesday morning nine-tenths of the wounded still lay where they fell; many had been there forty-eight hours without attention; numbers had died of shock or exhaustion; some had even drowned as the rain filled the depressions from which they could not crawl. Every house in the area was converted into a hospital, where the floors were covered with wretches heavily wounded, sometimes with arms or legs torn off, who after the first bandages, got no nursing, medical care or even nourishment. "The first day or two," wrote a newspaper reporter, "the air was filled with groans, sobs, and frenzied curses, but now the sufferers are quiet; not from cessation of pain, but mere exhaustion." Yet at this time the war was a year old.[1]

These gruesome scenes of war we dread to think about—indeed we do not let ourselves think about them. The cost in continuing pain, suffering, and disability is excluded from our contemplations of violence—glorious or otherwise—on the stage and screen. Not only these ugly consequences but the ugly motives producing them are quickly eliminated from our thinking. Man cannot be so fiendishly cruel to his fellow man; he cannot be so wicked, so destructive.

Pointless vandalism, destruction of beauty for the fun of destroying, always infuriates us. "Why?" we ask. The extent of the urge to commit ruthless, pointless damage was indelibly impressed upon me during World War II by the sights I saw where our troops, in passing through evacuated towns, had in many instances destroyed right and left for the very sake of destroying. Bombs had been thrown into abandoned dwellings, churches, stores, and other structures along the line of march without objective purposes. And more recently in Vietnam and this in Africa:

> We arrived at the village before nightfall. The women were coming and going unsuspectingly, carrying water. The children played in the dust, laughing and calling to each other. We stopped a moment in the brush, watching. Then came the order to open fire. The machine guns and our new Belgian rifles opened up. The women shrieked, they fell. The kids stopped, flipped over like rabbits by the bullets. We charged, continuing to fire. A few of us put cans of gasoline against the huts and set them afire with matches. Others threw phosphorous grenades which turned the victims into human torches impossible to extinguish. The moans, shrieks and cries of the blacks begged for mercy. Amidst all of that the unbelievable yells of the commandos: obviously, they loved it. At last, away from the village, the silence. Far off the cries of the wounded and those of the tropical birds, hardly discernible, settled in the warm, humid night. . . . "We had done nothing else since our departure farther south; destroying innocent villages of small farmers who didn't give a damn for the war." The orders of mercenary leader Major Michael Hoare were to shoot all the blacks on the spot. "Even if you see men, women and children running toward you, even if they beg you on their knees, don't hesitate, shoot. Not to wound, to kill." [2]

These terrible scenes seem far away. So do the debacles of Nero's day, when the general public clamored for public exhibitions of strangling, crushing, disemboweling, stabbing, and laceration by claw and teeth. And we raise our eyebrows at our Spanish neighbors who still so thoroughly enjoy seeing horses disemboweled and bulls teased and tortured.

And here in America, we do a little peeking at such orgies when we get a chance. We operate our own bloody sport spectacles such as boxing—"of all forms of so-called sport the only one which has as its prime and direct object, now that we no longer have available the sport of hunting and butchering 'the noble redskin,' the physical injury of the contestants," to quote the courageous Father Kenneth Murphy. "People . . . pay to see a man hurt. . . . The time the crowd comes alive is when a man is hit hard over the heart or the head, when his mouthpiece flies out, when blood squirts out of his nose or eyes, when he wobbles under the attack and his pursuer continues to smash at him with pole-axe impact." [3] *

"An exercise in brutality," "a study in cruelty," "disgusting," "almost bestial"—so went the morning-after judgments of Cassius Clay's eighth successful defense of the heavyweight boxing championship, this time against Ernie Terrell in Houston. . . .

What was odd was that sportswriters should feign such innocent surprise at the lack of sportsmanship in what is, after all, a brutal, cruel, disgusting and relatively bestial business enterprise. . . .

A champion prizefighter is supposed to be a hero—strong, manly, humble, honest if possible, and full of kind words about the unfortunate fellow he has just bruised, bloodied and, if possible, knocked unconscious. He is, in a sense, supposed to apologize for his sport, and for our adrenal fascination with it. If he is a Negro, he is (or was) supposed to be gratefully aware of the opportunity for Negroes that professional boxing, until recently almost alone among sports, provided for fame and fortune. [4]

---

* Let's go to the prize fight, buddy
Where the punches whistle and sing;
Let's sit where it's smelly and bloody,
Close up, with our knees on the ring.
Maybe we'll see a jaw shattered,
Or a pug lose the sight of an eye,
Or an amateur brutally battered—
Maybe we'll see a boy die.

(Tribune Publishing Co., Oakland, California, 1962)

"Why do you suppose some people say baseball is a dull spectacle?" asks a recent newspaper advertisement (by Rheingold beer
and others!). "No shoot-'em-up, no stabbing, no sex, no sock-thud,
no robbery (except stolen bases)."

When Truman Capote published a book describing dispassionately the sensational but pointless murder of a farm family in Kansas,[5] some reviewers reacted violently to his coldness—not merely
regarding the meaning and motives of the murders, but to the certain public satisfaction in reading about bloody, human slaughter,
for which, of course, the public is willing to pay money.* "It
seems to me," wrote Kenneth Tynan of *The Observer*, "that the
blood in which the [Capote] book is written is as cold as any in
recent literature."

They Clasp Destruction with the Laughter of Desire

The reader may feel that by now he has waded through
pools of blood and horror and is becoming a little resentful at having been offered such unpalatable fare. "I am not one of these sa-
dists," he will say. "I don't enjoy these things. I don't even like to
acknowledge their existence. Certainly I don't want to pore over
the details. Why do you spread them before us?"

I do so to make the point that although most of us *say* we do
not like such scenes and deplore such cruelty and destructiveness,
we are partially deceiving ourselves. We disown violence, ascribing
the love of it to other people. But the facts speak for themselves. We
do love violence, all of us, and we all feel secretly guilty for it,
which is another clue to public resistance to crime control reform.

What is it about violence that so intrigues us? Is it man's true

* The moving picture version of *In Cold Blood* directed by Richard Brooks
is infinitely more moving. The pointless murder is not shown, but the pointless execution of the two offenders is shown in vivid detail. There is no fun
in it, no relieved feelings of one killing to match another. As movie critic
Bosley Crowther put it: "The ironic playing out of society's ritualistic compensation of damage already done . . . leaves one helplessly, hopelessly,
chilled." (*New York Times,* December 15, 1967.)

nature? Are we all so violent, so destructive, so criminal at heart? Is it an "instinct"?

Yes! There can be no doubt of this fact in spite of the occasional waves of pollyannaism and denial. Twenty-five centuries ago Empedocles recognized this violent side of human nature and told the civilized world about it, as did Zoroaster before him. All the religions of the world have presented various versions of how man may save himself from it.

Zeus, the great God of the Greek Scriptures, had a violent father whom he fought and finally destroyed. But when Prometheus, who was, in a way, the Greek Jesus Christ, sought to benefit the human race, his rebellious doctrine antagonized Zeus. So Prometheus was punished in that famous terrible way: chained to a rock, forever subject to the continuous lacerating attacks of a liver-loving eagle.

Even then the vengeful Zeus was not satisfied. He punished mankind for its passive sin of having enjoyed Prometheus' gift of fire. Roared he: "I shall give men an evil as the price of [that] fire. *They will clasp destruction with the laughter of desire!"*

Mark these fateful words! They show us that the Greeks knew about this lust for aggression and self-destruction twenty-five hundred years before Sigmund Freud reformulated it. Man the destroyer is man the self-destroyer. The Romans knew that "man is the wolf of mankind." The early Hebrews knew it and cried out all through their history, "What shall I do to be saved?"

And in the twentieth century, Sigmund Freud confirmed, from the standpoint of science, that man "is driven by an instinct for destructiveness, an instinct which would be self-destructive if it were not possible to turn it upon objects other than the self. The individual sometimes saves his own life by destroying something external to himself."

The discoveries of Freud made clear what ethical religions have taught mystically and empirically for over two thousand years, that the control of our constitutional destructive aggressiveness is the key to successful human living. The great sin by which we all are tempted is the wish to hurt others, and this sin must be avoided if we are to live and let live. If our destructive energies can be mastered, directed, and sublimated, we can survive. If we can love, we can live. Our destructive energies, if they cannot be controlled, may destroy our best friends, as in the case of Alexander the Great, or they may destroy supposed "enemies" or innocent strangers. Worst of all—from the standpoint of the individual—they may destroy us, ourselves.

Destroy ourselves? Surely this is a strange objective. Do we not all endeavor to save our skins and better our living? How can one hold the view that our aggressive nature, which is necessary for self-protection (and in small amounts for amusement!)—how can anyone say that this same aggressive, destructive energy will be turned inward upon ourselves? Are we our own enemies?

The facts are before us and he who runs may read. Dreadful as are the violent murders and criminal assaults reported in the morning papers, the unreported suicides occurring over the world every day are *far greater in number*. But suicides happen quickly and are over. Most externally directed violence is not murder and most internally directed violence is not suicide. There is such a thing as chronic, long-drawn-out suicide. One can invite cancer by persistent cigarette smoking in the face of many warnings. One can drink oneself into a fatal cirrhosis of the liver. Many medical conditions represent a compromise between self-preservative and self-destructive wishes. Or one can do it in a hurry with a rope, a gun, or a sports car.

"Why, the instinct of self-preservation is the normal law of humanity."

"Who told you that?" cried Yevgeny Pavlovitch suddenly. "It's a law, that's true; but it's no more normal than the law of destruction, or even self-destruction. . . ."

Lebedyev greedily caught up [the] paradox. . . . "Yes, sir, the law of self-destruction and the law of self-preservation are equally strong in humanity! The devil has equal dominion over humanity til the limit of time which we know not. You laugh? You don't believe in the devil? Disbelief in the devil is a French idea, a frivolous idea. Do

you know who the devil is? Do you know his name? Without even
knowing his name, you laugh at the form of him, following Vol-
taire's example, at his hoofs, at his tail, at his horns, which you have
invented; for the evil spirit is a mighty menacing spirit, but he has
not the hoofs and horns you've invented for him." (Dostoevski in
The Idiot.[6])

The Control of Innate Aggression

Over the centuries of man's existence, many devices have
been employed in the effort to control these innate suicidal and
criminal propensities. The earliest of these undoubtedly depended
upon fear—fear of the unknown, fear of magical retribution, fear
of social retaliation. These external devices were replaced gradually
with the law and all its machinery, religion and its rituals, and the
conventions of the social order.

But some *internal* psychological devices of restraint have gradually become built-in mechanisms of the human personality. These
reflect man's religion and his laws and his culture. The aggressive
drives are to be harnessed and deployed in productive work, or
they are modified in nature to permit play and art to take the place
of war and mayhem.

The routine of life formerly required every individual to direct
much of his aggressive energy against the environment. There were
trees to cut down, wild animals to fend off, heavy obstacles to remove, great burdens to lift. But the machine has gradually changed
all of this. Today the routines of life, for most people, require no
violence, no fighting, no killing, no life-risking, no sudden supreme
exertion; occasionally, perhaps, a hard pull or a strong push, but no
tearing, crushing, breaking, forcing.

And because violence no longer has legitimate and useful vents
or purposes, it must *all* be controlled today. In earlier times its expression was often a virtue; today its control is the virtue. The control involves symbolic, vicarious expressions of our violence—violence modified; "sublimated," as Freud called it; "neutralized," as
Hartmann described it. Civilized substitutes for direct violence are

the objects of daily search by all of us. The common law and the Ten Commandments, traffic signals and property deeds, fences and front doors, sermons and concerts, Christmas trees and jazz bands—these and a thousand other things exist today to help in the control of violence.

John Fischer has written most charmingly as to these "Substitutes for Violence" in *Harper's,* January, 1966, reviewing the fact that primitive man led a life of incessant battle and awarded praise and prizes to the most aggressive, and sketching the progressive decline in the prestige of destructiveness. Instead of requiring our young men to kill a lion or a human enemy, we expect them to demonstrate professionally, if not in superiority, in strenuous and risky activities such as skiing, surfing, drag racing, football playing, and reckless driving. Mr. Fischer suggests some more useful forms.

The old value of vicarious discharge has been questioned by William Honan of *The New Yorker,* who wrote in answer to colleagues who had defended stage violence by citing precedents in Shakespeare and the Greek dramatists:

> Not a single murder takes place on stage in all of the thirty-two extant Greek tragedies. There is a "partially concealed" suicide in Sophocles' *Ajax,* and freshly-severed heads are produced on stage in the *Bacchae* and the *Electra* of Euripides, but without further exception acts of violence, including not only murder but also such deeds as the blinding of Oedipus and the torture of Antigone are never seen by the audience. The Greeks invented a special character, usually called the Messenger, to report all such happenings to the other characters on stage as well as to inform the audience. As the Attic scholar H. W. Smyth has explained, "Murder in the sight of the spectators in the Greek theatre was forbidden by a sense of artistic propriety cooperating with, or induced by, the fact of the physical difficulties." (*Aeschylean Tragedy,* Berkeley, 1924, p. 193.)
>
> Shakespeare, of course, is the dramatist with the worst reputation for leaving the stage strewn with corpses. Altogether, he portrayed fifty-two murders and suicides in the thirty-five plays which are presumed to have been written by him, and there are nine more in *Titus*

Andronicus for which Shakespeare is believed to have written some verse. Many apologists have argued that Shakespeare's plots were not of his own choosing; that they were dictated to him by history, or by the earlier writers who invented the stories which he adapted. A better defense might be that compared to the fifty-two violent deaths which Shakespeare does show his audience, he placed an even greater number—sixty-four—behind the scenes. This latter figure includes by far the most lurid killings, such as the tearing apart of Cinna in *Julius Caesar,* as well as those which very possibly "gentle" Shakespeare himself could not bear to see, such as the murder of Cordelia in *King Lear,* or even the death of Falstaff in *Henry V* so affectionately described by Mistress Quickly:

". . . after I saw him fumble with the sheets and play
with flowers and smile up his fingers' ends . . . ."

One might also observe that the same gloomy bard who concludes *Hamlet* with no less than four corpses sprawled about the "Wooden O" also wrote *Henry V,* a dazzling tidy play about war, in which traitors are caught and executed, thieves sentenced and hung, and battle casualties reported to be over ten thousand, yet not a single one of these deaths is shown to the audience; in fact, in none of the scenes representing the Battle of Agincourt does Shakespeare require French and English soldiers actually fighting on stage.[7]

But does the contemplation of such mock violence relieve our own pent up emotions and impulses? Do bullfight and prizefight patrons (or participants) go home refreshed, reconstituted, calmer, kinder, and more self-controlled? Perhaps some do; others may react in a contrary way. Is there a vicarious satisfaction of our buried but turbulent criminal strivings? Is the viewer of television violence relieved or the more aroused? A scientific study recently made suggestions that instead of helping by vicarious discharge, television programs portraying violence increase the temptation to imitation, i.e., to enact crime.[8] Television defenders seem to be ready to "put the blame on Mame," i.e., on movies,* which are fill-

* "The public is thirsting for more," said film-maker Russ Meyer—and he is hastening to provide it. "The violence is there just to lend excitement, action. The way to succeed in this business is to get that audience whipped up, so

ing the home screens. In a special issue of *The Journal of the Producers Guild of America,* Dr. Frederic Wertham stated his opinion of violence in films:

> A standard excuse is the claim that showing a lot of violence is a deterrent to violence. War movies are an example. They are promoted under the pretext that they teach us to deplore war, when in reality they make war look adventurous and exciting. . . . Sometimes laughter and comedy are introduced . . . but I do not think that under any circumstances violent death is something to laugh about. In general, it is a great fallacy to believe that in order to combat violence you have to show it as gorily as possible.
>
> The idea that has done the greatest harm to American audiences, especially to youths, is the notion that film violence provides a safe outlet for hostility and pent-up aggression; that it functions as a safety valve; that it provides a vicarious satisfaction, thus preventing violent acts; that it has a cathartic effect by relieving tensions that might otherwise explode into real action. It is interesting how many intelligent and educated people have fallen for this belief that the representation of sadistic scenes prevents the execution of sadistic acts. This whole conception is completely unsubstantiated clinically and experimentally. On the contrary, research shows that mass media violence, including movies, acts not as a substitute but as a stimulus.[9]

Play as a Replacement of Violence

One theory of the value of play as a method of discharging or absorbing violence is that it preserves the vital balance of mental health. Nearly all games serve such a function to some extent. But because I and various psychoanalytic colleagues have given more thought to chess than to other games, I would like to digress for a few paragraphs and discuss the symbolic meaning of chess playing.

Chess is a miniature war in which the aggressive patterns characteristic of different personalities are clearly discernible in the nature

---

they'll walk out of that theater saying, 'Good God, did you see *that?*' When you can do that, you know a full house will be walking in the next day." (*The Wall Street Journal,* April 24, 1968.)

of style of play adopted. There are the strong attackers, the strong defenders, the provocative players, the cautious players, and the attack-from-behind players. Some individuals are particularly skillful in the use of the Queen, an individually powerful piece; others are especially fond of the Pawns (the underdogs); others like the Bishops (oblique attack) or the Knights (ingeniously indirect).

There are many legends regarding the origin of chess which suggest its value as a method of safely discharging or absorbing violence. According to one story, it was invented by the Buddhists in India as a substitute for war because they felt that actual war and the necessary slaying of one's fellowmen, no matter for what purpose, was immoral. A Burmese story has it that chess was invented by a queen who hoped by this distraction to keep her king out of war. According to another legend, the game was invented by the wife of a king of Ceylon in order to amuse him with an image of war while his metropolis was closely besieged.

Of various Chinese stories, this one is typical: A certain general who was a genius as well as a good soldier was attempting to conquer Shensi province. Winter came on and his soldiers, "finding the weather much colder than what they had been accustomed to, and also being deprived of their wives and families, became clamorous to return home." To keep them amused and at the same time "inflame their military ardor" the general invented the game of chess, with which the soldiers became so delighted that they not only passed the winter without further discontent but in the spring conquered the rich country of Shensi.

Although chess has a literature greater than that of any other game, it cannot be said to be a popular form of recreation. It is not difficult to learn, much less so, for example, than bridge; it is very inexpensive (in contrast to poker, golf, and backgammon); it requires less time than many games, and it is not the slow, dull game some believe. The picture of two individuals sitting peacefully regarding a piece-studded board is misleading. Silently these men are plotting and attempting to execute murderous campaigns of patricide, matricide, fratricide, regicide, and mayhem. Certainly one and perhaps both are worrying intensely about something of absolutely no importance.

Chess playing has been a favorite recreation of some of the world's military leaders, including William the Conqueror and Napoleon. Ernest Jones points out that the motive actuating chess players is not only the conscious one of pugnacity (which characterizes all competitive games) but also "the grimmer one of father-murder," inasmuch as the goal of the game is the capture (immobilization) of the King, a familiar symbolic father figure.[10] But I believe Jones errs in equating capture and murder. There is a legend about the origin of the game which deals with this very point: There were two brothers, a good one and a bad one. The bad brother declared war on the good brother but was routed, and as he was escaping on his white elephant, the good brother ordered him pursued and captured without a hair of his head being harmed. This was done; the bad brother was surrounded and sat still on his white elephant. His captors went to assist him to dismount, only to find him dead from heart failure or shame or some other obscure cause, but not through any aggressive act of the victorious brother and his warriors.

Many years ago when I played chess occasionally with the Topeka Chess Club, one snowy-haired player, an author and historian, intrigued me. In ordinary life he was the meekest, kindest, gentlest man imaginable, but over the chessboard he would become rampant and belligerent. He moved his pieces with lightning speed, crashing his moved piece to the board with a clatter that occasionally jarred all the other pieces from their places. Incidentally the violent sweep of his gestures extended to the glass of root beer nearby, and a painful delay ensued while the spilled fluid was mopped up. This accomplished, however, stillness reigned again in the room except for the clicking of the old gentleman's emphatically placed men of war.

I mention my old friend to illustrate how aggressions may be released in so apparently peaceful a game as chess. Whatever else it

is, playing chess is not relaxing. It is a very intense and exciting experience which is fully appreciated only by one who has gotten
well into it. Some people find it exhausting, others obsessively absorbing. I was very much surprised once to hear a gentle, urbane
friend of mine say, "Perhaps you are not mean enough; you know
you have to have a mean streak in you to play this game successfully." The fact that chess appears to be such a pacific "old man's"
game belies its underlying fierceness.

The way in which games serve to dissipate aggression is beautifully illustrated in the analysis of the psychology of many sports
and games, such as skiing, boxing, hunting, tennis playing, and
others, by a panel of experts in Slovenko and Knight's recent book
Motivations in Play, Games and Sports. The writers referred in
particular to the psychological studies of football by Alan Stone
and of hunting by Stonewall Stickney. From the latter I quote:

> The beauty of that moment was marred a few instants later. Mov-
> ing over toward an irregular, noisy thrashing, up the hill from me, I
> saw a wounded spike buck crawling through a barbed wire fence.
> One snap shot at his neck and he went down, seemingly, but disap-
> peared over the edge of the rise. When I arrived at the fence I saw a
> strange and ugly sight. The stricken animal, breathing and moaning
> desperately, was pushing itself across the muddy oat patch. Both its
> forelegs were broken. My friend Gideon, who had broken the first
> foreleg with a bad shot, came panting up just then, and we each
> urged the other to go put the animal out of his misery. I recall firing
> two barrels at close range at the buck's neck, and missing him clean.
> My friend, torn between laughter and revulsion, had to finish him off
> with birdshot at a range of inches because he and I had run out of
> buckshot. The aftermath for me was something close to nausea, but
> not in the stomach. All over.
>
> Later, when another hunter arrived with a station wagon to haul
> the carcass to camp, he got stuck in the soft patch and it took hours
> of work to get the vehicle out. Meanwhile, we recalled that the week-
> end's whiskey supply was in this wagon, and by the time we had
> torn down a board fence and an old shed to build a causeway out of

the mud, all of us were obviously drunk and hilarious. Somehow, since that time I've had little zest for deer hunting, and haven't killed another one. They do look at you. . . .

Anyway, I'd much rather shoot doves, geese, ducks; something that flies by swiftly, beautifully and impersonally. It doesn't look at you, and you never hear it breathe or moan, or see it bleed. When it falls, it is usually dead. The fall itself is a beautiful thing, a sudden and artless surrender to death and gravity, as if without regrets. From my earliest days with the slingshot I recall the sheer joy of killing in this fashion, and the thrill of pleasure when I picked up the fallen bird.[11]

Many of the new games show little concealment of how aggressive play may be. A recent campus craze called "The Hunt" was described in *Time:*

> Players are divided into "hunters," who are given the names of their prey, and "victims," who are simply notified that they are on someone's assassination list. One session of the hunt goes on for four days; then the directors assay the kills, award one point if the kill was technically feasible and actually was carried out, two points if the kill was technically brilliant. However, if the hunter is killed by his victim, he loses one point; if he kills a bystander, he loses two points. The first to win ten points is named a "decathlon" (as in the movie) and gets a party thrown in his honor.[12]

The game is considered to have originated at Oberlin College and spread to many universities. "What makes the game fun?" asked *Time.* "A means of letting off aggression."

An incident in Redl and Wineman's book, *Children Who Hate,* adds an interesting comment to the idea that aggression is dissipated through sports and work.

> On the way home from school, in the station wagon there was some incipient scapegoating of Larry and also a good deal of aggressive throwing. This forced us to stop the wagon several times. After treats, following our arrival home, the counselors suggested a game of dodge ball in the backyard. The group is quite keen about this game, only they call it "murder ball." The game went well. Larry was forgotten and they did not select him unnecessarily as a target.

The few rules which this game has—such as waiting until the "tar-get" knows you are going to throw and admitting when you are hit, etc.—were well kept. There was obvious keen enjoyment of all the throwing. Their ability to stick to the rules was especially amazing in view of the ugly mood they were in before the game. Just before dinner we stopped, and, as though by magic, the offensive pre-game disposition returned and Larry again became a target for group at-tack. He was accused of doing things wrong in the game which while it was going on were completely ignored—if they were not even being manufactured now. Even his "baby" behavior at school was hauled out as an issue; they started calling him "pisswillie" though he is one of the few who do not wet. Mike climbed up on the garage roof and started heaving debris at him and then fanned out to a more generalized "bombing," and Danny began lumbering to chase Larry around, calling him "Larry, the berry," a phrase which for some reason infuriates him and by this token is relished by the group as an insult.[13]

Oft-times it is considered that a person has a fixed amount of aggression and that all that is necessary is some outlet for it. Through work or sports, an individual may become physically tired, but he is soon ready to have another go at it. Destructiveness is more a matter of quality than quantity. Some individuals need "outside controls" all the time. Thus, whenever a game ends or a teacher leaves the room—whenever outside controls drop out— some individuals again resort to delinquent behavior.

My colleague, Bruno Bettelheim, thinks we do not properly edu-cate our youth to deal with their violent urges. He reminds us that nothing fascinated our forefathers more. The *Iliad* is a poem of violence. Much of the Bible is a record of violence. Our penal sys-tem and many methods of child-rearing express violence—"violence to suppress violence." And, he concludes, "We shall not be able to deal intelligently with violence unless we are first ready to see it as a part of human nature and then we shall come to realize the chances of discharging violent tendencies are now so severely cur-tailed that their regular and safe draining-off is not possible anymore."[14]

And so wrote Sigmund Freud in his greatest essay, which ends with the words, "The fateful question for the human species seems to me to be whether and to what extent their cultural development will succeed in mastering the disturbance of their communal life by the human instinct of aggression and self-destruction." [15]

The Psychology of Violence Control

Where in the control of emergent violence do we put the role of conscience? Surely the reader has wondered if we had forgotten it. Until the twentieth century the internal control of violence was ascribed to an independent psychological faculty called *will power*. Will power aided by intelligence, or at least by common sense, and guided by conscience was supposed to be trainable by proper discipline, i.e., to respond properly to pleasure-pain conditioning of the "right sort." Thus habits of reaction could be established that would—like an automatic pilot—keep the individual always on the safe course.

The discoveries of Sigmund Freud completely changed that model and made us realize the fallacies upon which we had been relying for conforming behavior. The ego (will power) can indeed suppress, divert, sublimate, or otherwise handle the dangerous impulses. It does so on the basis of a policy determined partly by experience and partly by the "advice" of the conscience.

The theological and philosophical libraries of the world contain hundreds, if not thousands, of volumes on the nature of the conscience. But Freud threw an entirely new light on the matter when he pointed out the existence of an *unconscious part* of the conscience, which is often rigid, prejudiced, corruptible, and cruel. It is formed before the child has any understanding of the reasons for the prohibitions and commands he receives from his parents and teachers (who may be playmates).

Noël Mailloux, a Catholic priest and also a psychoanalytic authority who has done much research with delinquent youths, has described this "archaic conscience," which is normally replaced by a cogent, usefully differentiating conscience. Mailloux believes that many delinquents do not achieve this maturation.[16] He thinks that most offenders are "perfectly capable of distinguishing good from evil and recognizing the illegality of the activities in which they are involved" but are too deeply rooted in the immature, narcissistic attitudes toward the environment to form any positive attachments to anyone. They come to feel that there is no distinction between themselves and their actions, and because their deeds are bad, they—the offenders—are bad. Each one thus "sees himself as the very incarnation of badness or, if we wish, as wicked by nature." What often gives the impression of barefaced boldness is a kind of frenzied aggression which the victim—villain—himself hopes will in some way be cut short but which he cannot stop. Unable simply to give himself up to the police, he leaves clues everywhere he goes, "tantamount to writing his name on the walls [or wandering] about openly with his burglar tools under his arm."

The late Franz Alexander in his book, *The Criminal, The Judge, and The Public*,[17] made the point that many offenders committed serious crimes in order to be punished for minor offenses or even acts that might not be crimes at all, but about which they felt—because of childhood misapprehensions—extremely guilty.*

Seymour Halleck says that the pattern of delinquency is frequently an expression of just what the child—at a certain age—thinks the parents want. What the parents did, the grownup child does. Later the child is abused for anything he does and a period of confusion sets in: You can't please anybody; why try? The only way to get attention is to hurt people.[18]

Frederick Proelss, a Protestant clergyman and lawyer who has also studied offenders with great perceptiveness, emphasizes this

---

* Alexander labeled the syndrome "Criminality Out of a Sense of Guilt." This can be simply stated thus: I feel guilt which only punishment can assuage, not for Crime A of which they accuse me, but for Crime B. So I accept the "unjust punishment" as just.

Prosecuting attorneys are approached after every sensational crime by persons who insist without any substantiation that they committed the act. They are possibly guilty of something, usually quite minor, but not the crime for which they are pleading guilty.

immature, insecure, confused aspect of their personalities. Not only are most of them from a low socio-economic level, but they are apt to be of an especially low cultural level. Consequently it is not surprising that "the impulse control of such individuals is crude, indeed. They are rough and aggressive. Their minds are underdeveloped, twisted, and hostile; their interests are limited and primitive; their tastes, loud and vulgar. Life-goals and life-values are badly distorted, and the inner control mechanisms which permit or prohibit the acting out of this whole warped world are deficient and feeble." [19]

Proelss continues that because in conscience "we find that seat of all cultural values and decisions of an ethical quality. . . . this most precious capacity of man which allows him to share the knowledge of such manifold values with himself . . . must become the outstanding concern of the prison chaplain." The prison is a replica of the childhood state; the prisoner is clothed, housed, fed, cared for, told what to do and what not to do, where to go and where to stay. As in childhood, he has a good deal of free time, what a child would call play time. But prisons are usually pervaded with great hostility. Prisoners are cut off from the possibility of normal sexual outlets; they are constantly threatened by homosexuality; they feel that they have been steamrollered by the police detectives and attorneys, cheated by their own lawyers, misunderstood by the judge, and let down by so-called friends, even by family. Already immature, they tend to regress to still earlier phases of development.

This is not a chapter on the psychology of the criminal, but rather on the psychology of the average citizen who is not a criminal in terms of conventional definition. We are concerned with how people control *some* aggression at least *some* of the time. Why aren't we all criminals? We all have the impulses; we all have the provocations. But becoming civilized, which is repeated ontologically in the process of social education, teaches us what we may do with impunity. What then evokes or permits the breakthrough?

Why is it necessary for some to bribe their consciences and do what they do not approve of doing? Why does all sublimation sometimes fail and overt breakdown occur in the controlling and managing machinery of the personality?

These questions can be translated into common terms: Why do we sometimes lose self-control? Why do we "go to pieces"? Why do we explode? Why do these explosions carry some of us across the line of legality?

These questions point up a central problem in psychiatry. Why do some people do things they do not want to do? Or things we do not want them to do? Crime is merely one dramatic aspect. Sometimes crimes are motivated by a desperate need to act, to do *something* to break out of a state of passivity, frustration, and helplessness too long endured, like a child who shoots a parent or a teacher after some apparently reasonable act. Granting the universal presence of violence within us all, controlled by will power, conscience, fear of punishment, and other devices, granting the tensions and the temptations that are also common to us all, why do the mechanisms of self-control fail so completely in some individuals? Why do self-perceptive, self-protective, self-regulating functions of the ego not rise to the occasion in case of crisis and keep the individual from the final break? Is there not some pre-existing defect, some moral or cerebral weakness, some gross deficiency of common sense that lets some people stumble or kick or strike or explode, while the rest of us just stagger or sway?

"I am a congenital believer in laws and punishment," H. L. Mencken once said, and he believed in scientists who will continue to improve the methods of handling of men because they are "happily devoid of that proud ignorance which is one of the boasts of the average judge, and they lack the unpleasant zeal of district attorneys, jail wardens and other such professional blood-letters. They need only show us the proofs that this or that punishment is ineffective to see it abandoned for something better, or, at all events, less obviously bad. But when they begin to talk of criminals in terms of pathology, even of social pathology, they speak a language that the plain man cannot understand and doesn't want to hear." [20]

Mencken is a bit old fashioned now and his strictures were often poses. But he discerned something here which everyone feels some way or other. The reader thinks, "I could be a criminal with a little hard luck, or a great frustration, or utter despair. I subscribe to all you have been saying about the viciousness of us all. But what is it that pushes some of us over the critical brink?"

Halleck, with whose philosophy and theories about crime and criminals I completely agree, has answered this in simple English that Mencken would have greatly enjoyed. The criminal, Dr. Halleck holds, is a person who for all sorts of reasons is chronically and basically more uncomfortable than most of us.[21] Like us he has his internal tensions, but these are heightened by special circumstances relating to his situation in life. His personal freedom is restricted in a way that is particularly painful to him, and his way of regaining some measure of that freedom is not ours. The persuasive word, the new proposal, the reasoned argument—for these he has no skill. His constitutional method of dealing with his discomfort is by direct actions.

Halleck develops the point that *criminality* is one of four types of adaptation available for the relief of the sense of helplessness—*conformity, activism,* and *mental illness* being the others. His thought is that blockage of any one of the four increases the probability that one or several of the other three modes will be used more conspicuously. Whether one decides that crime is a more healthy-minded state of existence than mental illness will depend a little upon one's value system, but there can be no doubt that for some individuals the unwillingness to surrender to passivity, to suffering, to dependence upon others—all of which are implied by illness—obliges the individual to activism, even to the extent of criminal behavior. In other words, many individuals perform criminal acts in order not to "go crazy," or not to become neurotically inhibited or highly disorganized. This fits into my adaptation of "general system theory" to psychological functioning, the maintaining under stress of a vital fluid equilibrium through the use of various maneuvers.[22]

When a psychiatrist examines many prisoners, writes Halleck, he soon discovers how important in the genesis of the criminal outbreak is the offender's previous *sense of helplessness or hopelessness*. All of us suffer more or less from infringement of our personal freedom. We fuss about it all the time; we strive to correct it, extend it, and free ourselves from various oppressive or retentive forces. We do not want others to push us around, to control us, to dominate us. We realize this is bound to happen to some extent in an interlocking, interrelated society such as ours. No one truly has complete freedom. But restriction irks us.

The offender feels this way, too. He does not want to be pushed around, controlled, or dominated. And because he often feels that he is thus oppressed (and actually is) and because he does lack facility in improving his situation without violence, he suffers more intensely from feelings of helplessness.

The offender often puts it, "There was nothing else to do" or "I had to do it." His actions "can be viewed as a direct effort either to combat the painful effect of helplessness" or to prevent its emergence. When a person is engaged in energetic behavior intended to alter a situation, he feels less helpless even though his actions aggravate rather than relieve his actual state of helplessness. Furthermore, the committing of a crime increases a man's sense of freedom through providing him both mental and physical preoccupation that eludes restriction. "During the planning and execution of a criminal act, he is a free man. He is immune from the oppressive dictates of others since he has temporarily broken out of their control."

Another conscious determinant to which we cannot shut our eyes is the fact that some forms of crime are exciting. They offer possibilities for great excitement in a life that may otherwise be dull, monotonous, dreary, and despairing. Crime is a game played for high stakes. The offender may or may not fully comprehend the risks and the stakes, but it is fun. It is always fun to outwit or deceive others; we *all* love it. The dangers involved in crime call for considerable use of faculties and talents of various kinds that might otherwise lie dormant.

> The future criminal is usually a person who has had little opportunity to use his creative abilities [in a socially acceptable manner], and planning an illegal act provides an outlet for this potentiality. . . .
>
> It must be admitted that each criminal act has its own distinctive motivations and pleasures. Obviously some crime holds out the possibility of financial rewards. If you can avoid detection, crime can pay very well indeed. Certain types of crime offer substantial sexual gratification [particularly to individuals who cannot find their sexual gratification in the ordinary ways]. But these are all fringe benefits which tend to encourage [not cause] antisocial violence. (Halleck) [23]

Unconscious Determinants of the Criminal Break

Penetrating scientific studies by many competent workers of the lives of criminals have shown that the end obtained in the violent act is *rarely* and exceptionally what the offender wanted or set out for! (No prosecuting attorney believes this.) The effect of a violent act—the death of a victim, the acquisition of money, the gratification of sexual excitement—these are rarely the determining factors in any crime! The offender himself may insist that they are, but the truth is he does not know, as a rule, what pathological factors in his personality eroded his self-control and perverted his conscience in such a way as to eventuate in his self-destructive methods of living. The best he can say (as he usually does) is that "it seemed like a good thing at the time."

What seems to be an elective act of behavior is always a choice of alternatives. If things are going well, one chooses the greater or more promising good. If things are going badly, one chooses the lesser evil. Any criminal act is just such a choice made by the offender under pressure. The outside world usually assumes that the pressure is the desire or need for the thing stolen, or for the elimination of the person killed. The real pressures are of a very different order. What the offender does at the time seems to him like a good thing, as he says, because it *actually is* a good thing in the sense of seeming to be the lesser of several evils that confronted him.

Violence and crime are often attempts to escape from madness; and there can be no doubt that some mental illness is a flight from the wish to do the violence or commit the act. Is it hard for the reader to believe that suicides are sometimes committed to forestall the committing of murder? There is no doubt of it. Nor is there any doubt that murder is sometimes committed to avert suicide. It is a choice of the lesser evil, *as it seemed to him.*

Dr. William R. Boniface of Cincinnati has put the point cleverly in a short poem he wrote about my book *The Vital Balance*. His own title was "Apology for Murder," but others have suggested the titles: "Righting Reflex"; "Pardon Me"; "Balance Restored"; and "Murder and Remorse." Whatever its title, it neatly epitomizes the economic principle of psychological functioning:

> You came near as I was falling
> And—I threw you down to right
> Myself. I threw too hard. Now,
> I have you on my conscience.
> As a counterweight.

Strange as it may sound, many murderers do not realize whom they are killing, or to put it another way, that they are killing the wrong people. To be sure, killing anybody is reprehensible enough, but the worst of it is that the person who the killer thinks should die (and he has reasons) is not the person he attacks. Sometimes the victim himself is partly responsible for the crime that is committed against him. It is this unconscious (perhaps sometimes conscious) participation in the crime by the victim that has long held up the very humanitarian and progressive sounding program of giving compensation to victims. The public often judges the victim as well as the attacker.*

* See Michael Fooner's article, "Victim-Induced Criminality," in *Science,* September, 1966.

The discoveries made by a patient of mine in psychoanalysis many years ago are relevant here. He was a great hunter, but only of one species of animal. He became extremely proficient at killing these animals. Although they were edible, he killed far more than he could eat or dispose of. He often told me what great lust he had for killing swiftly and continually. "I have often wondered why I had it in for them so," he used to tell me, "but I just like to see them die and know that I caused it." In the course of his psychoanalytic reflections it suddenly occurred to him one day that his father's given name coincided—in another language—with the name of the animals that he so ruthlessly slaughtered. More than that, his father had once borne a nickname that referred to this same species, and confirming this he had a dream in which the target at which he was aiming with a deadly weapon turned into his father's face. He could no longer doubt whom he had been so eager to kill, over and over again, all his life.

Here is a presumptive example: A California newspaper carried the story of a man who stormed out of his home, climbed behind the wheel of his station wagon, and began what the newspaper called an "Odyssey." Psychiatrists would call it a series of attempted displacements of escaping violent impulses. The following description is abstracted from the newspaper account:

> With a defiant roar, he ripped back out of his driveway, across the street, and up onto a neighbor's lawn. Then . . . in forward gear not a block away he side-swiped a car. About a half hour later police picked up his trail. When another car appeared in front of him he rammed the car in the rear, but instead of stopping, he just kept ramming. The driver in the front car jammed on his brakes but the angry man shoved him 125 feet out into the southbound traffic of the main highway, then backed off and proceeded south on the same highway. A policeman who had seen him ram and shove the car sped after him. When the pursued car and the patrol officer whipped through a red light at an intersection, another traffic police officer joined in the chase. A car that appeared in front of the pursued driver was rammed, the nearly demolished station wagon bouncing

off the rammed car onto the shoulder of the highway for 500 feet before it ran into a fence and finally stopped.

After being treated for a cut lip at a nearby hospital [the offender] was taken to the County Jail where he was booked for hit-run driving. He told the highway patrolman he left home because he was arguing [*sic*] with his wife.[24]

Rape and other sexual offenses are forms of violence so repellent to our sense of decency and order that it is easy to think of rapists in general as raging, oversexed, ruthless brutes (unless they are conquering heroes). Some rapists are. But most sex crimes are committed by undersexed rather than oversexed individuals, often undersized rather than oversized, and impelled less by lust than by a need for reassurance regarding an impaired masculinity. The unconscious fear of women goads some men with a compulsive urge to conquer, humiliate, hurt, or render powerless some available sample of womanhood. Men who are violently afraid of their repressed but nearly emergent homosexual desires, and men who are afraid of the humiliation of impotence, often try to overcome these fears by violent demonstrations. Sometimes they attack children as being less dangerous than grown women.

The need to deny something in oneself is frequently an underlying motive for certain odd behavior—even up to and including crime. Bravado crimes, often done with particular brutality and ruthlessness, seem to prove *to the doer* that "I am no weakling! I am no sissy! I am no coward! I am no homosexual! I am a tough man who fears nothing." The Nazi storm troopers, many of them mere boys, were systematically trained to stifle all tender emotions and force themselves to be heartlessly brutal and ruthless.

"Ah," the reader will say, "perhaps that may be true in those violent rape and murder cases, but take everyday bank robbing and check forging and stealing—you cannot tell me these people are not out for the money!"

I would not deny that money is desired and obtained, but I would also say that the *taking* of money from the victim by these devices means something special, and something quite different from what you think it does. There are much easier ways to get money than by robbing. Anyone (unfortunately) can borrow these days. Why go after it the hard way?

Man perennially seeks to recover the magic of his childhood days—the control of the mighty by the meek. The flick of an electric light switch, the response of an automobile throttle, the click of a camera, the touch of a match to a skyrocket—these are keys to a sudden and magical display of great power induced by the merest gesture.

Is anyone already so blasé that he is no longer thrilled at the opening of a door specially for him by a magic-eye signal? Yet for a few pennies one can purchase a far more deadly piece of magic—a stored explosive and missile encased within a shell which can be ejected from a machine at the touch of a finger so swiftly that no eye can follow. A thousand yards away something falls dead—a rabbit, a deer, a beautiful mountain sheep, a sleeping child, or the President of the United States. Magic! Magnified, projected power. "Look what I can do. I am the greatest! "

One recalls the words of the Grand Inquisitor in *The Brothers Karamazov* reproaching the returned Christ for having resisted that greatest of all temptations, that magnificent opportunity to use magic to win power. Said the Inquisitor, "What you so foolishly and criminally rejected, the Church will take and use. We will *use* that magic; and we shall win but you we shall burn."

It must have come to every thoughtful person, at one time or another, in looking at the revolvers on the policemen's hips, or the guns soldiers and hunters carry so proudly, that these are instruments made for the express purpose of delivering death to someone. The easy availability of these engines of destruction, even to children, mentally disturbed people, professional criminals, gangsters, and even high school girls is something to give one pause. The National Rifle Association and its allies have been able to kill scores of bills that have been introduced into Congress and state legislatures for corrective gun control since the death of President Kennedy. Americans still spend about two billion dollars on guns each year; in addition the federal government disposes of about one hundred thousand guns annually at bargain prices.[25] This is a heavy burden on the control of instinctual restrictiveness.

On November 13, 1966, the papers announced the murder of four women and a little girl in Mesa, Arizona, by one Robert Smith, aged eighteen. I quote two excerpts from the news story that appeared in the *Chicago Tribune:*

" 'I just wanted to get myself a name. I wanted to be known.' He said he had been planning a mass murder *ever since his parents gave him a gun three months ago* for target practice." (Italics mine.)

On August 8, 1966, on the campus of the University of Texas, a twenty-five-year-old student climbed onto the campus tower and began shooting everyone in sight—killing twelve and injuring others. His father, who was described as "an authoritarian, a perfectionist, and an unyielding disciplinarian" was quoted thus: *"I raised my boys to know how to handle guns."* (Italics mine.)

Secret grudges that have been nursed from childhood, and the feeling of the impossibility of ever achieving the parent's stature often motivate big crimes. Petty, backbiting crimes such as check forging are notoriously frequent in children of financially upright and outstanding citizens. I have known numerous women who humiliated and chagrined their Back Bay or Main Line mothers by shocking social and sexual misconduct for much the same reason.

A fifty-year-old bachelor in Wisconsin murdered two middle-aged women, dissected and mutilated their bodies, and then began desecrating recent graves of middle-aged women. These crimes provoked widespread indignation. He was the son of a grocery-man, and had been forbidden as a child to enter the butchershop department. But he used to watch, surreptitiously, the forbidden bloody procedure there with great fascination. He was very much attached to his mother and was never interested in any other women. Twelve years after his mother's death, he more or less accidentally shot and killed a middle-aged woman. He took her body home to his house and kept it, not quite certain how to dispose of it. After that he began to rob graves, always selecting female corpses and always taking them home to *keep them with him in the house!*

One does not have to be a psychoanalyst to see some of the deep unconscious meanings of this strange behavior. His mother, whom he strove to "keep," was originally a very powerful, dominant woman, all of whose sons were inordinately devoted to her. When she had a stroke and was partially paralyzed, this particular son took care of her personally and attended her until her death, which depressed him terribly. Afterward he kept thinking he heard her voice calling him. The mixture of his love of her and his need for her, and his buried hate and fear of her, was clearly shown in his fantastic, irrational reconstruction of the earlier home situation.*

These reflections about violence are, it seems to me, now illustrated daily in our newspapers. Dealing with individual criminals is one thing; coming face to face with thousands and even tens of thousands of angry, desperate people is another and more convincing thing; and the danger is that, instead of understanding, we only seek to quell.

In a letter to Sarah Patton Boyle, author of *The Desegregated Heart* and *For Human Beings Only,* John Griffin, author of *Black Like Me,* wrote:

> It is all a great and tragic mess—a satanic one. In Wichita . . . the white men were caught, the Negroes (unarmed except for sticks and stones) were caught; the young Negroes were brutalized on the way to the jail. The next morning the white offenders were released

---

* The reaction of the community to the paradox was studied by some of my colleagues in Wisconsin, particularly Milton Miller, Peter Eichman, and Edward Burns ("The Sanity Hearing." *Bull. Menninger Clin.,* 23:97–105, 1959) and George Arndt ("Community Reactions to a Horrifying Event." *Bull. Menninger Clin.,* 23:106–111, 1959). The latter recorded the curious popularity of grim "sick jokes" among people in the community as a device for dealing with their horror and anger over the discovery. It "became the most discussed topic in the state with pseudo-horrorists trying to outdo each other with the latest." Many of these jokes had to do with cannibalism: e.g., when

under a $1,000 bond, the Negroes under a $5,000 bond; and no church group, no white raised a voice in that community.

I need not tell you how maddening this is to the Negro communities; how finally there comes the decision simply to destroy, to wreck, to take down as many whites as they can before the end. . . . Negroes have now issued orders to the snipers to shoot to kill anywhere that local white officials . . . give police and guard orders to shoot to kill. The new oath is to take ten whites before death. "Take ten," the young Negroes shout to one another jovially in the streets and supermarkets, and the whites think they mean "take a ten-minute break."

I have had young men tell me with tears in their eyes, "A year ago I knew right from wrong. Now I don't care. They broke my wrist, they sprayed insect repellent in my eyes, they treated me like a mad dog. . . . You drive us crazy and then you call it sedition when we act crazy." These are not only young: there are middle-class, middle-aged men in these meetings. Many of them are college students.[26]

Mrs. Menninger and I were on the streets ourselves watching the parade-demonstration and its obstruction referred to in this news story by Joseph Sander:

One youth, identifiable because of his long hair, was spotted by a policeman whom he had earlier eluded and suddenly, though things had long since quieted down, the boy saw the policeman rushing at him. He began to run and the officer ran after him, beating him on the head with his night stick, and finally brought in his prey. . . . One young man who couldn't obey a police order to move because of the crush of people behind him, was arrested and dragged away by two officers, to whom he offered no resistance, while a third sprayed him with Mace en route. Mace could be used even more wantonly, as those arrested discovered. The door of a locked paddy wagon would be opened and an arm would enter, spray Mace inside the wagon,

---

asked how his folks were, he replied, "Delicious." To a late-arriving guest he said, "Sorry you weren't here a little earlier—everybody's eaten." He may not have been very popular with girls, but the joke had it that "There were always a lot of women hanging around his place."

withdraw, and then the door would be shut again on the unventilated space.

Wedged between two policemen near the fountain at the edge of the plaza, Mark DiSuvero, a sculptor who is working temporarily on a major project in Chicago, was wrestled off balance and thrown into the fountain, where he was beaten with clubs and sprayed with Mace before being arrested. More than half of those arrested report that they were subjected to Mace *after* arrest. One person said that Mace was used on him as he lay strapped to a stretcher inside a Fire Department ambulance that was taking him to the hospital.

After the immediate area had been cleared, the police hunted in posses through the Loop, beating and arresting many whose buttons identified them as march participants. . . . A photographer from the Chicago *Sun-Times* was beaten and had his clothes torn when he tried to take a picture of a woman who had been knocked to the sidewalk, and a reporter on assignment from the City News Bureau likewise suffered a policeman's night stick.[27]

All this the Kerner Report *—which ought to be on every living-room table in the land—deals with in documentary detail. The plain facts in the matter are: Sow the wind and reap the whirlwind. Meet violence by violence, and you will have more violence.

What can we psychiatrists say when we see the mounting, persistent rage of masses of desperate and embittered people? What shall we say when college students denied counsel and the right of participation can find no better way of expressing their rage and disappointment than by vandalism? What is the explanation of smug and affluent "success" which looks upon such behavior in fellow man as merely incomprehensible and negligible because they "never had it so good"?

A St. Louis *Globe Democrat* reporter telephoned me recently, saying: "We have had ten murders in five days in this city and we are almost hysterical. Is it an epidemic? Is everyone going mad? Or only we newspaper people? What do you psychiatrists say?"

And what indeed do we say? What is the diagnosis of such ob-

* *Report of the National Advisory Commission on Civil Disorders.*

vious disorganizations of personality and society? And what is the treatment?

I do not think we can answer these questions in terms of the old-fashioned individualistic, psychotherapy-oriented, talking-cure psychiatry. But neither do I think we psychiatrists can remain dumb or put on blinders and concentrate upon long, drawn-out studies of single affluent individuals, protected as we are in our ivory towers. We have to reshape some of our basic assumptions and models. We have to turn again to our colleagues in sociology and economics and cooperate with them in planning programs to prevent the spread of a psychological epidemic and find ways to treat not hundreds but millions of patients. We must find ways to prevent personality and social disorganization in hundreds of thousands of patients for whom we do not even have a good diagnostic description, let alone an adequate therapeutic prescription at the present time.

We have gone a long route to prove that violence is a part of life, a component of the personality of every one of us, and only more conspicuous in criminals because it has—for many interesting reasons—escaped control in a way that hurts or frightens us. I have tried to show that violence properly modified has its purposes and its uses. I have suggested some of the conscious and unconscious determinants of particular levels of violence, because—as a psychiatrist—I have had occasion to observe these, and have an interest in correlating them with better methods of crime control.

But I have left out of consideration entirely what may be the most powerful dynamic motivating force, both in the commission of crimes by criminals and in the crimes committed by us against criminals in the present obsolete inhuman system of "due process." This factor will be dealt with in the next chapter.

CHAPTER 8

Vengeance Is Mine, Saith the Lord

The great secret, the deeply buried mystery of the apparent public apathy to crime and to proposals for better controlling crime, lies in the persistent, intrusive wish for vengeance.

We are ashamed of it; we deny to ourselves and to others that we are influenced by it. Our morals, our religious teachings, even our laws repudiate it. But behind what we do to the offender is the desire for revenge on someone—and the unknown villain proved guilty of wrongdoing is a good scapegoat. We call it a wish to see justice done, i.e., to have him "punished." But in the last analysis this turns out to be a thin cloak for vengeful feelings directed against a legitimized object.

It is natural to resent a hurt, and all of us have many unfulfilled wishes to hurt back. But in our civilization that just is not done—openly. Personal revenge we have renounced, but official legalized revenge we can still enjoy. Once someone has been labeled an offender and proved guilty of an offense he is fair game, and our feelings come out in the form of a conviction that a hurt to society should be "repaid."

This sentiment of retaliation is, of course, exactly what impels most offenders to do what they do. Except for racketeers, robbers, and professional criminals, the men who are arrested, convicted, and sentenced are usually out to avenge a wrong, assuage a sense of injury, or correct an injustice as they see it. Their victims are individuals whom they believe to be assailants, false friends, rivals, unfaithful spouses, cruel parents—or symbolic figures representing these individuals.

In the old days no one apologized for feelings of vengeance. Poets, playwrights, and other artists have been preoccupied with it for centuries. One goes to the opera and listens to beautiful music that was inspired by such sordid vengeance-dominated plots as those of *Tosca, Il Trovatore, La Forza del Destino,* and a hundred others. Or one thinks of the fascination that *The Count of Monte Cristo, Hamlet, Othello,* and many other revenge stories have had for millions of people for hundreds of years. What has changed in our modern thinking or feeling that this noble urge to repay, at all costs, the wrong done to me and mine is no longer so highly esteemed? Has Christianity actually had some effect? Or is it merely a surface repudiation of our pre-civilization character in the interests of a decent social façade?

"Vengeance is mine," God is quoted as declaring. But vengeance by the individual worked its way back in, somehow. Various scriptural citations imply that God expects some human assistance in dealing out vengeance. His spokesmen and His agents have always laid about them with zealous vigor and great self-assurance to do what the Lord wanted done, and to whom. "Thou shalt not suffer a sorceress to live." [Ex.22:18] "Ye shall tread down the wicked; for they shall be ashes under the soles of your feet." [Mal.4:3] "Happy shall he be, that taketh and dasheth thy little ones against the rock." [Ps.137:9] (Or see King David's last words to his son.)

Angry at the poor rebellious peasants in 1525, Martin Luther wrote:

> For a prince and lord must remember in this case that he is God's minister and the servant of His wrath (Romans XIII), to whom the sword is committed for use upon such fellows. . . . If he can punish and does not—even though the punishment consists in the taking of life and the shedding of blood—then he is guilty of all the murder and all the evil which these fellows commit, because by willful neglect of the divine command, he permits them to practice their wickedness, though he can prevent it and is in duty bound to do so.

Here then, there is no time for sleeping; no place for patience or mercy. It is the time of the sword, not the day of grace. . . . Stab, smite, slay, whoever can. If you die in doing it, well for you.[1]

The initiation of official retaliation for crime is sometimes inaccurately ascribed to the Anglo-Saxons, to Calvin, to the Romans, and to the children of Israel. Clear demands for legal tit-for-tat appear in much more ancient documents. Typical citations from the Babylonian code of Hammurabi, four thousand years ago, are these:

196. If a man destroy the eye of another man, they shall destroy his eye.
200. If a man knock out a tooth of a man of his own rank, they shall knock out his tooth.
195. If a son strike his father, they shall cut off his fingers.

The Hammurabi Code (1750 B.C.) and the Lipit-Ishtar Code (1900 B.C.) were harsh, but they were meant to limit the revenge. *No more than this penalty may ye take!*—that was the essence of it. Hammurabi apparently instituted the law to control practices of family and tribal revenge that went further than the offenses being repaid and which were perpetuated in feuds. Revenge has a tendency to do this.

But three hundred and fifty years before Hammurabi, a more civilized people than the Babylonians had a criminal code imbued with a far more humane philosophy. King Ur-Nammu of Sumeria was a most enlightened monarch who instituted many social and moral reforms. He ruled against the "chiselers and grafters" of the kingdom, described in the code as "the grabbers of the citizens' oxen and sheep and donkeys." He established a method for "honest and unchangeable weights and measures." He saw to it "that the orphan did not fall prey to the wealthy" and that the "widow did not fall prey to the man of one mina (sixty shekels)." The crowning, dramatic feature of Ur-Nammu's law code was the elimination of vengeance from criminal procedures. Restitution and monetary fines rather than the infliction of pain were the official consequence of wrongdoing.[2]

This was over forty centuries ago. Jesus of Nazareth came about midway between then and now and recommended that we turn the other cheek. The early Christians did so and were martyred; the German Jews did so and were cremated. Isn't it natural to defend oneself and one's home and one's honor?

Eighteen hundred and twenty-six years after the advent of Jesus, a great and really very humane statesman, Edward Livingston, proposed in his "System of Penal Law for the State of Louisiana" that the following be inscribed on every murderer's cell:

> In this cell is confined, to pass his life in solitude and sorrow, A. B., convicted of the murder of C. D.; his food is bread of the coarsest kind, his drink is water, mingled with his tears; he is dead to the world; this cell is his grave; his existence is prolonged, that he may remember his crime and repent it, and that the continuance of his punishment may deter others from the indulgence of hatred, avarice, sensuality, and the passions which led to the crime he has committed. When the Almighty in his due time shall exercise toward him that dispensation which he himself arrogantly and wickedly usurped toward another, his body is to be dissected, and his soul will abide that judgment which Divine Justice shall decree.[3]

What is behind such vindictiveness? Certainly not Christianity, not Judaism, nor indeed any religion! And yet certainly not specific hatred! And surely not an expectation of eliminating crime!

Today criminals rather than witches and peasants have become the official wrongdoers, eligible for punitive repayment. Prosecuting attorneys have become *our* agents, if not God's, and often seem to embody the very spirit of revenge and punition. They are expected to be tough, and to strike hard.

Pierre Berton, traveling through the town of Goderich in southern Ontario in 1959, was horrified to learn that a fourteen-year-old boy had been sentenced to hang for murder. He wrote this poem:

Requiem for a Fourteen-Year-Old

In Goderich town
The sun abates
December is coming
And everyone waits:
In a small, stark room
On a small, hard bed
Lies a small, pale boy
Who is not quite dead.
The cell is lonely
The cell is cold
October is young
But the boy is old;
Too old to cringe
And too old to cry
Though young—
But never too young to die.
It's true enough
That we cannot brag
Of a national anthem
Or a national flag
And though our vision
Is still in doubt
At last we've something
To boast about;
We've a national law
In the name of the Queen
To hang a child
Who is just fourteen.

The law is clear
It says we must
And in this country
The law is just.
Sing heigh! Sing ho!
For justice blind
Makes no distinction
Of any kind;
Makes no allowance for sex or years,
A judge's feelings, a mother's tears;
Just eye for eye and tooth for tooth—
Tooth for tooth and eye for eye:
If a child does murder
The child must die.
Don't fret—don't worry . . .
No need to cry
We'll only pretend he's going to die;
We're going to reprieve him
By and by.

We're going to reprieve him
(We always do),
But it wouldn't be fair
If we told him too.
So we'll keep the secret
As long as we can
And hope that he'll take it
Like a man.[4]

No less an authority than Chief Justice William Howard Taft wrote in 1928 that the "chief purpose of the prosecution of crime is to punish the criminal and to deter others tempted to do the same thing from doing it because of the penal consequences. . . . It is a mistake of huge proportion to lead criminals by pampering them, and by relaxing discipline of them and the harshness of prison life, to think that they are wards of the state for their comfort, entertainment, and support." [5]

One attorney says: "Despite attempts to curb the vengeful urges of district attorneys, however—and despite Constitutional restrictions upon 'cruel and unusual punishments' and other methods of venting sadistic feelings—modern American law goes to considerable lengths to help *express* vengeful strivings." [6]

"I think," said the distinguished jurist Sir James Stephen as late as 1883, "it is highly desirable that criminals should be hated, that the punishments inflicted upon them should be so contrived as to give expression to that hatred, and to justify it so far as the public provision of means for expressing and gratifying a healthy natural sentiment can justify and encourage it." [7]

The prison sentence, determined by law, intended to prevent both the abuses of tyrants and the bloody orgies of mob vengeance. We no longer inflame the public with such scenes as these:

> The sheriffs, attended by two marshals and an immense number of constables, accompanied the procession of the prisoners from Newgate, where they set out in the transport caravan, and proceeded through Fleet Street, and the Strand; and the prisoners were hooted and pelted the whole way by the populace. At one o'clock, four of the culprits were fixed in the pillory. . . . Immediately a new torrent of popular vengeance poured upon them from all sides—blood, garbage, and ordure from the slaughter house, diversified with dead cats, turnips, potatoes, addled eggs and other missiles, to the last moment. . . . The vengeance of the crowd pursued them back to Newgate, and the caravan was filled with mud and ordure. No interference from sheriffs and police officers could restrain the popular rage. . . .
>
> Then—it was June, 1594—the three men, bound to hurdles, were dragged up Holborn, past the doctor's house, to Tyburn. A vast crowd was assembled to enjoy the spectacle. The doctor, standing on the scaffold, attempted in vain to make a dying speech; the mob was too angry and too delighted to be quiet; it howled with laughter . . . and the old man was hurried to the gallows. He was strung up and—such was the routine of the law—cut down while life was still

in him. Then the rest of the time-honored punishment—castration, disembowelling, and quartering—was carried out. Ferriera was the next to suffer. After that, it was the turn of Tinoco. He had seen what was to be his fate, twice repeated, and close enough. His ears were filled with the shrieks and moans of his companions, and his eyes with every detail of the contortions and the blood. . . . Tinoco, cut down too soon, recovered his feet after the hanging. He was lusty and desperate; and he fell upon his executioners. The crowd, wild with excitement, and cheering on the plucky foreigner, broke through the guards, and made a ring to watch the fight. But, before long, the instincts of law and order reasserted themselves. Two stalwart fellows seeing that the executioner was giving ground, rushed forward to his rescue. Tinoco was felled by a blow on the head; he was held firmly down on the scaffold; and like the others, castrated, disembowelled, and quartered.[8]

What was "socially acceptable" behavior toward criminals in 1594 is not so today. The avid curiosity and brutality of the public toward the miscreant who is caught must find less revolting expression. But the savagery is still there.

"Distrust," said Nietzsche, "all in whom the impulse to punish is strong." No one is more ferocious in demanding that the murderer or the rapist "pay" for his crime than the man who has felt strong impulses in the same direction. No one is more bitter in condemning the "loose" woman than the "good" women who have on occasion guiltily enjoyed some purple dreams themselves. It is never he who is without sin who casts the first stone.

Along with the stone, we cast our own sins onto the criminal. In this way we relieve our own sense of guilt without actually having to suffer the punishment—a convenient and even pleasant device for it not only relieves us of sin, but makes us feel actually virtuous. A criminal trial, like a prizefight, is a public performance in which the spectators work off in a socially acceptable way aggressive impulses of much the same kind that the man on trial worked off in a socially unacceptable way.[9]

The man who wrote these eloquent lines was a former winner of the Isaac Ray Award, Professor Henry Weihofen. In his book, *The*

Urge to Punish, he shows how clearly and piously this phenomenon replaces an unavowed wish for vengeance. We all have it, but
some people deceive themselves more than they deceive others.

The man on the street knows so little about the total situation
that it is not surprising that he explodes in rage at the news of
some horrendous crime. He is merely saying loudly that he is
against evil. He wants to believe that "things are being taken care
of," that the brave, tough "cops," the "good guys," deal "adequately" with the tough "bad guys," and so all is well—or as well
as things can be in our rough-and-tumble world. So he is not too
much disturbed to hear it alleged that (some) police have
usurped the power to punish and believe that the use of "legitimate
violence" is their occupational prerogative and monopoly. If the
police thereby obtain "results," the community is satisfied. And
since "those who suffer are most often the poor, the ignorant and
the friendless, no one complains (except to the American Civil
Liberties Union or to some minority organization) and the
police can congratulate themselves on the improvement of their
public relations."[10] Most policemen would deny any feelings of
vengeance toward offenders—just necessary and legitimate counter-
violence.*

But there are a few political leaders, writers, and even psychiatrists and other scientists who are heard from now and then in
terms that leave no doubt about their vengefulness. And here, to top
the list, is what a man of God, committed to teaching the gentle-
ness of Jesus and the forgiveness of Christian love, recently published in a syndicated column:[11]

> Modern literature . . . has now gone to the . . . extreme where
> pity is for the rapist and not for the raped, for the criminal and
> not the victim. This false compassion started with novelists like
> William Saroyan and John Steinbeck who presented the "lovable

---

* I work constantly with police officers and have a strong identification with
them and a concern about their public image. I belong, as an associate member, to the National Fraternal Order of Police. Yet I myself have been
roughly dealt with by policemen for no more serious offense than asking a
question about a gathering crowd in New York's Central Park. Such gratu-

bums," the shiftless, the drunks, as "beautiful little people." The next stage was to excite pity for the genial rapist, the jolly slasher, the dope pusher, the adulteress playing musical beds, the rich kid who sells "goofballs," knifers, sluggers, muggers, and the homosexuals.

But today, thanks to a few social workers, a few incompetent judges, and woolly-minded thinkers, and many "sob sisters," compassion is extended not to the one who was mugged, but to the mugger, not to the policeman, but to the dope pusher, not to the girl killed by a dope fiend, but to the rich boy from an interesting family. [Could this be an appeal to class distinction?] No blame may be laid at the door of the criminal or the degraded. The new saviors of a perverted society say: "Neither do I condemn thee. Go, and sin some more."

With what *result*? [Italics mine.] Crime increases about nineteen per cent a year in the United States. [!!]

Contrast this with the following letter by Professor Anatol Hold,[12] father of a three-and-one-half-year-old girl slain by an honor student, which was written early in the morning a few hours after the confession had been obtained:

Dear People of Philadelphia:

I write to you this morning, at the rise of dawn, still in the midst of a tormented wake, the most terrible grief which has ever seared my soul.

Yesterday afternoon, on June 4, I lost the most precious thing that life ever gave to me—a three-and-a-half-year-old girl child of surpassing purity and joy; a being profoundly close to the secret wellsprings of life itself—a closeness from which she derived great unconscious strength which made her irresistibly attractive to human beings with whom she came in contact.

She was murdered at three in the afternoon, in the basement of a house only a few doors away from ours, by a fifteen-year-old boy. . . .

The boy himself has also always given an excellent formal account of himself—honor student, gentle in manner, handsome and all the rest. . . .

---

itous rudeness and bullying is, of course, to be balanced against the courtesy, dignity, and genuine helpfulness of many other policemen; but with more belligerent, embittered subjects, an experience such as mine is enough to start trouble for which all of us have to pay—including the police.

I am sure that his parents have been God-fearing, upright citizens, too uneducated in matters of the human soul to have recognized the plight of their child during the years of his growth.

They undoubtedly took naïve pride in his constant good behavior, neat appearance, and good performance at church and school, never suspecting that this very goodness was a serious cause of worry in the light of what must have been left unaccounted for.

It is, of course, worrisome, from the social point of view, that there are parents with such lack of understanding. It is, I submit, much more profoundly worrisome that it should have been possible for this boy to go through his whole fifteen years without anyone who was responsible for his upbringing—such as his school and his church —having taken note (out of uncaring or lack of understanding) of the danger signals before the tragedy.

Beware, citizens. The human animal cannot be cheated forever. It will have love, or kill.

You will understand that I am not lecturing to you for the pure joy of sounding wise. I am hurt to the depths of my being, and I cry out to you to take better care of your children.

My final word has to do with the operation of the machinery of justice. Had I caught the boy in the act, I would have wished to kill him. Now that there is no undoing of what is done, I only wish to help him.

Let no feelings of cave-man vengeance influence us. Let us rather help him who did so human a thing.

[Signed] A Sick Father

The final sentence of this letter deserves immortality.*

In sharp contrast is the following case, which has also been in my files a long time:

---

* Still another instance of the repudiation of vengeance is this historical vignette: Perhaps nothing in President McKinley's life was equal in greatness to his last moments. Standing in a reception line at the Buffalo Exposition, he patted a little girl on the head and, as she passed on, he turned and smilingly extended his hand to the next in line. This was his assassin. Knocking aside the proffered hand of the President, the assassin lunged forward

Last week a man was tried in New York State for the shooting of his son-in-law, who had seduced his daughter. He was acquitted of murder or manslaughter on some unintelligible point of unwritten law. The trial was brief but exceedingly painful. At great cost to herself, the widow of the murdered man came to give evidence. Resisting her father's embraces in the courtroom, she still testified in order to save him, though she made it clear to everyone that she loved the man who had been killed. Her father confessed he was drunk when he killed the youth, but he said the youth was of evil life, and this allegation, tending to give horror to the seduction, probably weighed greatly with the jury. At any rate, they acquitted him, amid the cheers of a friendly crowd.

So long as one could assume ordinary human comprehensions on the part of the acquitted man, this verdict need not seem dead loss. In some ways it approximates the ideal of many people, leaving the culprit to his own conscience. But even if this is pure romanticism, the acquittal could be condoned if the trial had made some effect. Hear, however, some reflections of the exonerated citizen, imparted to a reporter of the *World:*

"This is without doubt the merriest and happiest Christmas of my life. True, my daughter is not herself, but I guess she will be all right in a few days. . . . Do I think she saved my life? Why, no! I am sure that even without her help I would have been acquitted. You see, I did not know what I was doing; so how could I have been guilty? Anna knew she had disgraced us and so she wished to do all that lay in her power to atone.

"While I certainly would undo my act if it lay in my power, I feel sure Anna will be happier with us than if she were the wife of Eugene Newman. Marriages of that kind always end in misery, whereas now she will just take up the threads of her former life and be happy. She intends to resume her music. She is a splendid pianist. When she recovers her health all will be as before.

---

and shot McKinley through the abdomen. A security officer leaped forward and knocked the assassin to the floor. As McKinley slumped back into a chair, his eyes followed his killer and McKinley was heard to say, "Don't let them hurt him." And then, in a whisper, "My wife! Be careful how you tell her. Oh, be careful." (Courtney, John F.: "Doctors and the McKinley Assassination." *The Resident Physician,* 14:72–80, March 1968.)

"I never said I was going to sign a pledge never to drink again. I always have drunk like a gentleman.

"Has my daughter forgiven me? What do you mean? What has she to forgive? Our relations are most loving. She was always a most obedient child—quiet, unexpressive, but with a sweet disposition. I could not understand her disobeying us the way she did by going with this boy and marrying him in view of our expressed objections. But now that is all over, and she is again our sweet loving daughter."

The daughter, according to the reporter, is completely crushed. She loved her husband, but she guesses her parents knew best, for "see what her disobedience has done." [13]

Angry as it makes us to see a father so indifferent to his great guiltiness—guilt for a heartless murder, guilt for brutal sadism to his crushed daughter—what would *we* like to do with him? What would appease our aroused sense of injustice? We want him to be sorry, but he is not, and we cannot make him feel sorry for what he has done. Even if we could, it will not comfort his daughter or return her husband to her, and it may even deprive her of a meal ticket. We might tie him to the public whipping post, as they have long done in Delaware, and *hurt* him. He would suffer, and be very sorry about *that,* and also very angry. He then, as well as we, would feel the sense of injustice. But we would carry an additional burden of having done a cruel thing pointlessly, trying to make ourselves feel better and not succeeding. In kind, if not in degree, we then line up with the Marquis de Sade, who believed in pleasure, especially pleasure derived from making someone else feel displeasure.

We cannot expect the public to be objective, either in judging the criminal or in judging us psychiatrists. Especially we cannot expect them to understand our repudiation of punishment, if not as an actual "treatment" device, then at least as a matter of (Kantian) principle. It is a part of the common folk-ways, a standard value judgment. Robert Waelder[14] has written of this, urging us to "go easy" in denouncing punishment and pushing the principle to its extreme form. For the public believes in punishment deeply, although it is willing to make many exceptions to the rule if these are properly stipulated. Gradually the public will come to realize that not *some* cases, but *all* cases are exceptions. But in the meantime, we should perhaps give lip service to the possible merits of punishment in some instances.

Price, Penalty, and Punishment

It is time for me to speak unequivocally about the inference of the title of this book. Is it true, I am asked, that you oppose *all* punishment for *everyone?* Think of some of the fiendish crimes that we all hear about from time to time. Do you think such persons should go unpunished? You seem to favor penalties; how do they differ from punishments?

Certainly the abolition of punishment does not mean the omission or curtailment of penalties; quite the contrary. Penalties should be greater and surer and quicker in coming. I favor stricter penalties for many offenses, and more swift and certain assessment of them.

But these are not *punishments* in the sense of long-continued torture—pain inflicted over years for the sake of inflicting pain. If I drive through a red light, I will be and should be penalized. If a bridge player overbids, he is promptly and surely penalized, and his opponents can even double the penalty. If he cheats, he may be excluded from the game, but no one beats him or locks him up.

If a man strikes a rock in anger, his suffering from a bleeding hand is a penalty, not a punishment. If another man over-smokes and develops lung cancer, the affliction is a penalty, not a punishment. If we disregard traffic signals we are penalized, not punished. If our offense was a calculated "necessity" in an emergency, then the fine is the "price" of the exception.

Price is an agreed-upon, predetermined value, voluntarily tendered in exchange for a desired goal or gain. Penalty is a predetermined price levied automatically, invariably, and categorically in direct relation to a violation or infraction of a pre-set rule or "law."

In a sense it, too, is voluntary; the payer of the penalty knew from the outset what it would be if he incurred it.

All legal sanctions involve penalties for infraction. But the element of punishment is an adventitious and indefensible *additional* penalty; it corrupts the legal principle of *quid pro quo* with a "moral" surcharge. Punishment is in part an attitude, a philosophy. It is the deliberate infliction of pain in addition to or in lieu of penalty. It is the prolonged and excessive infliction of penalty, or penalty out of all proportion to the offense. Detention in prison was supposed to be a mollification of pain infliction, but it is often more cruel and destructive than beating. What is gained for anybody when a man who has forged a check for sixty dollars is sentenced to the penitentiary for *thirty years* (at public expense, of course)? I saw such a case in 1967. The judge's rationalization was that the man had offended in this way *twice before* (!) and had served shorter sentences without reforming!

This is not penalization. This is not correction. This is not public protection. (Is any check forger so dangerous as to require such expensive precautions?) This is not reformation. It is sadistic persecution of the helpless at public expense, justified by the "punishment" principle.*

When a seventy-seven-year-old woman driving her car in heavy traffic struck and killed an eight-year-old child, everyone concerned, including the parents of the child, the judge, and the woman herself, agreed that she should renounce automobile driving forever; this was her penalty. No "punishment" was imposed.[15]

If a burglar takes my property, I would like to have it returned or paid for by him if possible, and the state ought to be reimbursed for its costs, too. This could be forcibly required to come from the burglar. This would be equitable; it would be just, and it would

---

* A particularly eloquent statement on the justification of punishment is quoted from Sir Edward Fry by Mercier: "Punishment, in short, is an effort of man to find a more exact relation between sin and suffering than the world affords us. . . . It seems to me that men have a sense of the fitness of suffering to sin, of a fitness both in the gross and in proportion; that so far as the world is arranged we realize this fitness in thought, it is right; and

not be "punitive." Just *what* the penalties should be in the case of many offenses is a big question, I realize, but it could be answered if all the public vengeance and lust for seeing people hurt by punishment could be ignored.

I do not think this means that we psychiatrists are too sentimental. Being against punishment is not a sentimental conviction. It is a logical conclusion drawn from scientific experience. It is also a professional principle; we doctors try to relieve pain, not cause it. It is the unthinking public who is sentimental—sentimental in the sense of reacting emotionally to the first impact of unpleasant, grievous "news," i.e., a few of the bare facts of a case. A wave of emotion sweeps over them; they are shocked, horrified, alarmed. Instinctively, they want quick, eliminative action which they think of as punitive. Let some time elapse, and a little more of the facts become known, and the swift resolution about dispatching the offender becomes altered. It may even swing to the opposite pole so that the public is moved to pity or even shame by the revealed circumstances. Then it wants instant restitution and release.

So far as prisoners are concerned, there is an uncomfortable hypocrisy about our professed repudiation of vengeance. The conviction, the punishment, is in some way or other implicit in the concept of justice. We have to keep things even, or equal. I do not think anyone really believes this, but they feel it. They express it. What they feel is a wish for vengeance.

Most of the great philosophers, beginning with the Greeks and repeated later by Hobbs, Locke, Spinoza, and others, had this idea. For example, Protagoras said, "No one punishes the evildoer for the reason that he has done wrong—only the unreasonable fury of a beast acts in that manner. But he who desires to inflict rational punishment does not retaliate for a past wrong which cannot be

---

that so far as it fails of such arrangement, it is wrong . . . and consequently that a duty is layed upon us to make this relationship of sin to suffering as real and actual and as exact in proportion as it is possible to be made. This is the moral root of the whole doctrine of punishment." (Mercier, Charles: *Criminal Responsibility*. New York: Physicians and Surgeons Book Co., 1926, pp. 37–38.)

undone. He has regard for the future, and is desirous that the man who is punished, and he who sees him punished, may be deterred from doing wrong again. He punishes for the sake of prevention, thus clearly implying that virtue is capable of being taught."

And Plato said that no man is to be punished "because he did wrong, for that which is done can never be undone, but in order that, in the future times, he, and those who see him corrected, may utterly hate injustice, or at any rate abate much of their evil-doing." Yet he also goes on to say that the law "should aim at the right measure of punishment." This qualification seems, in turn, to be balanced by his remarks on the death penalty, which he thinks should be imposed only on the incurable who cannot profit from punishment and whose execution "would be an example to other men not to offend." [16] *

Immanuel Kant declared that the offender *must* be made to suffer, not to deter him—Kant knew this was nonsense—but to balance his evildoing. He insisted that the purpose of punishment is *not* the deterrence of others from doing the forbidden deed, not the reformation of the criminal, not the welfare of society, not even that tricky business about official violence holding down the urge for public violence (mob law). Kant did not even concede the need for vengeance as a proper factor. "Juridical punishment," he said, "can never be administered merely as a means for promoting another good, either with regard to the Criminal himself, or to Civil Society, but must in all cases be imposed only because the individual on whom it is inflicted *has committed a Crime*. [Italics mine.] . . . The Penal Law is a Categorical Imperative; and woe to him who creeps through the serpent-windings of Utilitarianism to discover some advantage that may discharge him from the Justice of Punishment, or even from the due measure of it." [17] Kant gave the illustration of an "abandoned island." Suppose, he said, that a

* Plato also said, "The right of retaliation . . . properly understood . . . is the only principle which . . . can definitely guide a public tribunal as to both the quality and quantity of a just punishment." (As quoted in *Eighteenth Century Penal Theory* by James Heath. New York: Oxford University Press, 1963, p. 272.)

society living on an island plans to leave that island because it is going to disintegrate. Before doing so, those condemned to death must be executed. This punishment is not done for the benefit of the inhabitants, inasmuch as they will soon be leaving; the executions must be accomplished simply because there exists a superior moral law that requires punishment.

But to renounce vengeance as a motive for punishing offenders leaves us with the equivocal justification of deterrence. This is a weak and vulnerable argument indeed, for the effects of punishment in this direction cannot be demonstrated by sound evidence or research. Furthermore, to make an example of an offender so as to discourage others from criminal acts is to make him suffer not for what he has done alone but because of *other* people's tendencies. Nevertheless the deterrence theory is used widely as a cloak for vengeance. As Bittner and Platt comment, in discussing this point:

> The idea that punishment simply executes some norms implied in the ideal of justice did not disappear from penological polemics, but it carried relatively little weight. . . . Punishment has grown progressively milder and milder. It is important to emphasize that the decline in the severity of punishment is not a development accompanying the growth of civilization in general, rather, it belongs peculiarly to the 19th and 20th century.[18]

I, myself, find it difficult to restrain my own feelings of vengeance in connection with the parents of what have come to be called "battered children." There is no question now that many parents are fiendishly, but covertly cruel in their home treatment of children—breaking their bones, lacerating their flesh, and often killing them. Some of these parents are brought for psychiatric examination, and it is hard to be objective in performing one's professional duty.

Nevertheless, I once examined the father of a child whose terrible beating was observed by the horrified neighbors who had him arrested. I had read about it in the newspaper and felt almost obliged to disqualify myself as an examiner. When I interviewed him, and learned all the details of the case, I felt very penitent for having been so righteously indignant, so just plain vengeful in my thoughts. The essence of the case was that this man really loved his child; he was perhaps the only person who did. He was usually most kind and gentle with his son who, however, had bitterly disappointed him on this occasion. But there were many other factors that brought his rage to the boiling point at the particular moment when the beating occurred. It was not excusable, but it was really understandable. No one was more penitent than this father, and I am glad to be able to report that he was immensely helpful subsequently in obtaining for the child much-needed opportunities of growth and development.

I must confess, too, that sometimes after reading about some particularly shocking crime, like everyone else I let myself wonder if it would not be simpler and cheaper and more "satisfactory" all around if such an individual could just be quietly exterminated. He has done irreparable and horrible damage; he can never recover; he can never be any good to the world; he will always remind us of terrible sorrow; his continued existence is a burden to himself and a burden for us.* But then I reflect that I myself am becoming unobjectively and inconsistently sentimental. The principle of *no* punishment cannot allow of any exception; it must apply in every case, even the worst case, the most horrible case, the most dreadful case—not merely in the accidental, sympathy-arousing case.

Let us return for a moment to the question as to whether the spectacle, the threat, or the experience of punishment actually does deter repetition of the offense by the offender. Scientific research regarding the effectiveness of punishment as a controller of individual behavior shows that it varies with a wide variety of "param-

---

* Eichmann is a case in point. He might have been kept alive but in confinement, to brood over his evil past. He might have been minutely studied as a specimen of human depravity, or he might have been spared the torture of his conscience by being quietly executed. Perhaps the last was the most merciful of the three. But was that the intention of the judges?

eters," as psychologists call them. Dr. Richard L. Solomon of the University of Pennsylvania, editor of *The Psychological Review,* summarized some of the factors affecting punishment as a controller of instrumental behavior in a recent study:

> [The] (a) intensity of the punishment stimulus, (b) whether the response being punished is an instrumental one or a consummatory one, (c) whether the response is instinctive or reflexive, (d) whether it was established originally by reward or by punishment, (e) whether or not the punishment is closely associated in time with the punished response, (f) the temporal arrangements of reward and punishment, (g) the strength of the response to be punished, (h) the familiarity of the subject with the punishment being used, (i) whether or not a reward alternative is offered during the behavior-suppression period induced by punishment, (j) whether a distinctive, incompatible avoidance response is strengthened by omission of punishment, (k) the age of the subject, and (l) the strain and species of the subject.[19]

What all this says in plain English is that common sense is correct in thinking that the swift, on-the-spot infliction of sufficiently painful stimulation to sufficiently influence animals—dogs or human beings—will tend to dissuade them from certain types of behavior of which we do not approve and which we wish to teach them not to do. But it does not deter *others* not so treated.

It is facile and fallacious to assume from this fact that human beings in general can be conditioned by threats of punishment or by the delayed infliction of penalties of attenuated painfulness from yielding to the temptation of impulsive crimes. If society were able to catch most offenders, and then if it were willing to punish them promptly without any discrimination, inflicting the penalties fairly but ruthlessly, as it were, most crime could be prevented. But society is neither able nor willing to do this. Almost no crime is punished promptly. Many crimes are punished unfairly. And some crimes are punished so severely that the whole world reacts against the action.*

* See the case involving Stephen Dennison cited in Chapter 2, page 24.

It is a curious thing, first called to my attention by my colleague, Dr. Sydney Smith, that in juvenile cases where the question of punishment comes up there seems to be a tacit assumption that the child who has gotten into trouble has somehow miraculously escaped previous experiences of punishment. One hears some vengeful judges declaiming against the wickedness of youth and the waywardness of adolescents and the need for stern punishment as if the child had never had any. Dr. Smith has said eloquently:

> Granted there are instances in which children have been reared in an atmosphere of inconsistency where value training of any kind was entirely missing; but even in these cases it is the lack of loving guidance and structure rather than the lack of punitive retribution that has triggered the behavioral manifestations of delinquency. *In a high percentage of court cases, there is evidence that the child has met with punishment that has not only been frequent but in many cases excessive.* [Italics mine.] In fact, one of the sources of the child's own inadequate development is the model of open violence provided by the parent who has resorted repeatedly to corporal punishment, usually because of his own limited imagination. This indoctrination into a world where only might makes right and where all strength is invested in the authority of the mother or of the father not only makes it easy for the child to develop aggressive patterns of behavior but makes him emotionally distant and distrustful.[20]

Drunken driving is almost nonexistent in Scandinavia, where the sureness, swiftness, and severity of the penalty is well known. But the legislators of many states in this nation have repeatedly rejected proposed bills entailing severe punishment for drunken drivers. Do we need to ask why?

Legislators are much less frequently inclined to rob banks or commit burglaries than to drive while intoxicated. Hence it is much easier to legislate severe penalties for these much less dangerous offenses, and the rest of us approve. We approve severe penalties for those offenses which most of us feel little temptation to commit.

Occasionally something goes wrong with the system and the usual exemptions do not work. An example of this is the sentencing of seven executives from leading manufacturing companies in 1961. Although found guilty of sizeable crimes, these men were sentenced for very short terms. Twenty of them drew suspended sentences.

All were prominent citizens; many were officers in their churches; one was president of his local chamber of commerce; one was a bank director. Each one was described by his lawyer as an "honorable man." The crimes were described by the Attorney General as being "so willful and flagrant that . . . more severe sentences would have been appropriate." One of the attorneys declared that the company in question "abhors, sought to prevent, and punished this conduct." The judge disagreed with this statement, declaring that the company's rule "was honored in its breach rather than its observance."

"No further punishment is needed to keep these men from doing what they have done, again," one of the attorneys said. "These men are not grasping, greedy, cut-throat competitors. They devote much of their time and substance to their communities." Another attorney made a general attack on the government's demand for jail terms. He said government lawyers were "cold-blooded" and did not understand what it would do to a man like Mr. —— to "put him behind bars" with "common criminals who have been convicted of embezzlement and other serious [*sic*] crimes." [21]

It is true that even a short jail sentence was a terrible thing for these men. It is a terrible thing for *any* man. The real meaning of such protests is that we have a gentleman's agreement that people with money and good names and highly placed friends, when caught in derelictions, are not supposed to be dealt with like poor people who are not well known and who do not have highly placed friends.

One value of this sad episode may be to bring home to the public the fact that there is a difference between a penalty (which I advocate) and punishment which the law prescribes. It would have been far more equitable in this case to have allowed the company to assess the penalty on the men involved—which their attorneys say it did—and then let the court assess a penalty on the company, which it also did. The penalty on the company ought to be something other than the mere expense item of a fine. No fine is going to be of any value unless it is large enough to wipe out the profits made by illegal activity. But *who* deserves the "punishment"?

Violence to Children Repaid

For many years the essence of vengeance against the offender has been implicit in the upbringing of the child. Perhaps it is too far-fetched an illustration, but is there possibly some connection between the thesis of the popular German nursery rhyme by Hoffman, *Der Struwelpeter,* and the ethics and the social philosophy of Nazi Germany in the 1930s and 40s? Take this verse from the version of the nursery rhyme by Maxine Kumin:

> Now look at Konrad the little thumb-sucker.
> *Ach!* but his poor mama cries when she warns him
> The tailor will come for his thumbs if he sucks them.
> Quick he can cut them off, easy as paper.
> Out goes the mother and *wupp!* goes the thumbkin in.
> Then the door opens. Enter the tailor.
> See in the picture the terrible tongue in
> His grinning red mouth! In his hands the great shears.
> Just as she told him, the tailor goes *klipp und klapp.*
> Eight-fingered Konrad has learned a sad lesson.
>   Therefore, says Fräulein, shaking her chignon,
>   Suck you must not or the tailor will chop! [22]

This quaint nursery (!) rhyme seems funny to some. It has been considered *good* for children by millions of intelligent, civilized people. But its sadistic, vengeful essence is obvious. And surely we are all aware of the unjustified, unexcused, unadvertised cruelty to children that abounds in some levels of society.

The late Dr. Adelaide Johnson and some of her colleagues in the Mayo Clinic were especially impressed with the way in which the violent destructiveness of the criminal is so often a reflection of the cruel and violent way in which he was treated as a child. I cite two of her many cases to show again that the fruit of violence is violence, vengeance for vengeance, hate for hate. It is a vicious circle.

Case 1.—In a jealous rage, a thirty-year-old man found an ax and, in the presence of neighbors, killed his former sweetheart. Originally, he had seduced her away from his brother when the latter went to Europe on military duty.

This man, the second of six children, had been the target for the most violent uncontrolled brutality on the part of the father, who, although he had a good job as a shop foreman, was a philandering alcoholic and a physical and mental sadist in his relationships with the prisoner's mother. The father's wild beatings of the boy were so frightening that neighbor men often interceded. The mother said she continued to live with the father only "to be sure he did not kill one of the boys," while at the same time her husband doted on the older daughter, of whom the prisoner was violently jealous. The father often beat and choked the mother in the children's presence. He shouted that she was a whore and that he would kill her some day. From the time the boy was three years old, the mother said, he recurrently ran away from home because he was so terrified of the father. From the time the boy was fourteen years old, his father accused him of vicious sexual practices with girls, a charge which was not true at the time. The mother said that the father constantly "spoke evilly about other people's sex lives" in the presence of the children. At no time did the father ever accept any responsibility for his brutal acts, and he never expressed any remorse. The boy never dared to bring a young friend into the home.

The mother offered no protection to the child against the father's attacks, but she did console him afterward. She never called the police to protect the boy. She and the prisoner leaned on each other emotionally, and apparently he was always tender with her. At no time did the mother express any guilt or responsibility for having kept the boy in such a savage environment, and at the time we saw her the next oldest son was experiencing a similar life with the father. The prisoner said that without her warmth and comfort he would have killed himself long ago. He cried and moaned about his love for her for fifteen minutes when she was first mentioned in the interview. He could not recall any conscious hostility toward his mother.

Case 2.—The prisoner was twenty-seven years old when he strangled his sweetheart. When we saw him he was unable to account for his killing her. "Those twelve months with her—I wouldn't trade them even to being in this prison for life." He murdered her when she refused to marry him.

He said he wondered if he had not "misidentified" his victim with her interfering mother, of whom he said in all seriousness he would "gladly wring her neck." He also remarked, "If it hadn't been Rosie I killed, it would have been someone else—it was inevitable."

He was exceedingly bitter toward his own mother. "Mom hated me since the day I was conceived. I was an unfortunate burden on her. It wasn't my fault I was born. She has punished me ever since, though, for it. I can remember all the unmerciful beatings she gave me. She is happy now that she has completely destroyed my life."

He said she was vicious; she would choke him and beat him so hard with a barrel stave that he became bruised and bleeding. She used to say to him: "What did I ever do that God thinks I deserved to have you wished on me!"

The mother told us of how her father "ran out" on the family when she was five years old, and she said he never supported them. . . . It is clear how this hostility toward her father had carried over toward the son. . . .

"His whole childhood was filled with anger," said the mother. She said she always thought he would get into trouble. "He grew up thinking the same way. He felt everyone was against him." At the time we saw her, she said she was glad the son was in prison and she hoped the authorities would never release him.[23]

More recently, Nevitt Sanford has described this principle clearly. We all know that in most cases of vicious acts there is a harsh, brutal father or mother in the childhood background. Sanford says that this is frequently an immigrant father who struggled against odds to adapt himself to a strange environment and saw his authority undermined and flouted. He quotes from the autobiography of the son of a Greek immigrant serving a sentence for armed robbery:

> My first memory has to do with Dad beating Mother. It seems that Mother and Aunt Catherine, who in the meantime had arrived from Greece, were having an argument. I do not recall its exact nature. However, Dad entered the room cursing Mother. He called her a son of a bitch and an old whore, and kicked her in the stomach. I began to cry and felt extremely sorry for Mother, who with her hands pressed to her abdomen had fallen into one of the dining room chairs. . . .
>
> Dad came home angry one night. Business had fallen off; he was discouraged and was thinking of closing the store. Mother said that it was too bad. If she said anything else, I cannot remember it. Dad swore at her. She ran from the table. Dad kicked back his chair and started for her. She ran out in the hall toward the piazza. Dad ran and kicked her. She cried, "Don't." He stood there and cursed. . . . I ran and put my hand on his leg and between sobs asked him not to hit Mother. He told me to get away from him and struck at me. I ran up the hall. Poor Mother, heavy with child, stayed on the piazza until he had become quiet and then with a red nose and a drawn, haggard face crept into bed, afraid to speak, afraid to open her mouth for fear that her husband would kick her. Years later, when he would begin to curse, this scene would unfold itself, and I would rise and for every vile epithet he used, call him one in return, while four young children sat and listened.[24]

In our book, *Love Against Hate*,[25] my wife and I tried to suggest how this vicious circle of vengeance evokes vengeance, and evoked vengeance tends to be perpetuated not only in and out of the courtroom and jails but within the family. Clinical experience has indicated that where a child has been exposed early in his life to episodes of physical violence, whether he himself is the victim or, as in the case just described, the witness, he will often later demonstrate similar outbursts of uncontrollable rage and violence of his own. Aggression becomes an easy outlet through which the child's frustrations and tensions flow, not just because of a simple matter of learning that can be just as simply unlearned, not just because he is imitating a bad behavior model and can be taught to imitate something more constructive, but because these traumatic experiences have overwhelmed him. His own emotional development is too immature to withstand the crippling inner effects of outer violence. Something happens to the child's character, to his sense of reality, to the development of his controls against impulses that may not later be changed easily but which may lead to reactions that in turn provoke more reactions—one or more of which may be "criminal." Then society reacts against him for what he did, but more for what all of us have done—unpleasantly—to one another. Upon him is laid the iniquity of us all, *unless* he can be shown to have been touched (punished) by God—absolved from guilt by a *previous* affliction. This is the philosophy of the irresponsibility doctrine.

The whole question of reading the nature of the malignant (or otherwise) intent in the offender's mind is one which the public is loath to refer to psychiatrists. Psychiatrists applaud this, because they have even greater doubts about the ability of *anyone* to determine accurately anyone's *intent*. If the criminal lacks a special self-evident excuse, a King's X of some kind, the vengeance of the people will often rise like a windstorm and sweep away all humanity, intelligence, Christianity, and common sense.

The scientists, and penologists and sociologists I know, take it for granted that rehabilitation—not punishment, not vengeance in disguise—is the modern principle of control. But in practice it is not. In the law it is not. Somebody is being "kidded."

Self-Control Is Mental Hetlth

For a long time it was popular in psychiatry to declare the mental healthiness of getting rid of one's aggressions. Inhibition and remorse seemed to be our most dreadful enemies and we encouraged patients to turn their hairshirts wrong side out and feel better. We never meant to say, as we have been interpreted as having said, that everyone should be as belligerent and aggressive as the spirit moved him to be. We never advocated that society return to the primitive days when "every man did that which was right in his own eyes" (Judges 21:25).

At any rate, the *new* psychiatry, faced with scenes of mounting and persistent rage of desperate and embittered people, must reemphasize the equal necessity for plain self-control. We must scotch the impression that it is always mentally healthy to get rid of one's anger promptly and directly. The present danger is upon us, and we are all suddenly realizing that vengeance is a two-edged sword, and that we cannot cure ourselves by stabbing one another. Nor can we justify our stabbings by calling our offenders dangerous or communistic or members of a gang. "Shoot to kill," cries an excited mayor to his policemen, thereby urging them to commit crime to stop crime, and start a new chain of revenge.

For an effective program of making the offender suffer by beating him to his knees, there must be unassailable power ranged against him, otherwise he will rise up in *his* vengeance and pay us back. *He* will do a little punishing according to *his* lights. "They that live by the sword shall die by the sword" is what we were taught. But we never have believed it.

Portugal has beaten two colonies into submission. It takes no great political prescience to predict that Portugal is on the way out, following the same route that far more powerful nations have taken. But whether this flight into historical prophecy has any basis, it is no secret that in all the great cities of the world today we are experiencing the phenomenon of revenge for dissatisfactions being turned against those nearest at hand and least prepared for the onslaught. We have always said that there were many people less than sane, but we have never really expected to see this "insanity" rise in great masses and turn in bitterness against *our* "sanity."

When a young lawyer, Governor William H. Seward, later Abraham Lincoln's Secretary of State, learned of a man in the Auburn State Prison who had apparently been driven mad by the flogging and other tortures that had been given him there, Seward went to see the man. Later he defended him in court—unsuccessfully. But this experience so aroused his interest in such problems that at the risk of professional, political, and personal ruin, he undertook the defense of an obviously demented old Negro accused of murder. In Seward's own words:

> I sat here two weeks during the preliminary trial. I stood here between the prisoner and the jury nine hours, and pleaded for the wretch that he was insane and did not even know he was on trial: and when all was done, the jury thought, at least eleven of them thought, that I had been deceiving them, or was self-deceived. They read signs of intelligence in his idiotic smile, and of cunning and malice in his stolid insensibility. They rendered a verdict that he was sane enough to be tried—a contemptible compromise verdict in a capital case; and then they looked on, with what emotions God and they only know, upon his arraignment. . . . Gentlemen, you may think of this evidence what you please, bring in what verdict you can, but I asseverate before Heaven and you, that, to the best of my knowledge and belief, the prisoner at the bar does not at this moment know why it is that my shadow falls on you instead of his own! . . .
>
> I speak with all sincerity and earnestness; not because I expect my opinion to have weight, but I would disarm the injurious impression that I am speaking merely as a lawyer for his client. I am not the prisoner's lawyer. I am indeed a volunteer in his behalf; but Society and Mankind have the deepest interest at stake. I am the lawyer for Society, for Mankind; shocked, beyond the power of expression, at the scene I have witnessed here of trying a maniac as a malefactor![26]

Seward lost his case, of course (until the appeal). He was politically persecuted, reviled in the press, and denounced from the pulpit. Why? Because he suggested that punishment of an offender be suspended. And mark well that he suggested this *not* because he opposed punishment for criminals, but because the man they were bent on punishing was sick! (And, of course, sick men cannot appreciate punishment.)

Cases like this dramatize how much the attitude of society has changed in a hundred years. But the punitive attitude persists. And just so long as the spirit of vengeance has the slightest vestige of respectability, so long as it pervades the public mind and infuses its evil upon the statute books of the law, we will make no headway toward the control of crime. We cannot assess the most appropriate and effective penalties so long as we seek to inflict retaliatory pain.

CHAPTER 9

Have There Been

No Improvements?

Just about a century ago (1870) some American prison administrators assembled to discuss their common problems and founded what is now the American Correctional Association. At the very first meeting these remarkable men set down a justly famous "Statement of Twenty-two Principles."

Among the twenty-two were these:

—*Reformation, not vindictive suffering, should be the purpose of the penal treatment of prisoners.*

—*The prisoner should be made to realize that his destiny is in his own hands.*

—*Prison discipline should be such as to gain the will of the prisoner and conserve his self-respect.*

—*The aim of the prison should be to make industrious free men rather than orderly and obedient prisoners.*

Can anyone read these amazingly intelligent, high-minded, far-visioned "principles" without a surge of admiration for the humanity and the intelligence of our long dead predecessors, and a sigh of regret for the dismal contrast of present practice with these noble ideals?

Remember, please, that these men had none of the modern inventions or conveniences. They knew nothing of depth psychology, dynamic psychiatry, behavioral sciences, or social case work. Given no decent "facilities" or equipment for reforming men, they kept their charges in the gloomy dungeons and bleak castles considered appropriate at the time, and employed untrained, illiterate help to "guard" their wards.

But they had their ideals and their "principles" and they had come to envision better things. They were men and women who had been hired by the state to treat rough men rough, to make them sorry, and to keep them miserable. Nonetheless, they erected and proclaimed a higher conception of their job. Untrammeled by the wretchedness of their appointments and the vindictiveness and unenlightenment of their tax-paying supporters, they met and formulated their purposes and their methods at a level that would be ultramodern in any institution today—one hundred years later.

The American Correctional Association is still a thriving, energetic, idealistic organization. In an address delivered at its annual meeting in 1961, the president, the distinguished Sanger Powers, declared *that a large part of the far-sighted program of a century ago still remains to be applied, and many of the evils of the system indicated there are still with us.*

Reformation of the individual is *still* not the purpose of our system. The infliction of vindictive suffering has *still* not been repudiated. The prisoner *still* has little to do with his destiny, and can scarcely imagine that he does have. Prison discipline, far from gaining anyone's good will or conserving anyone's self-respect, *still* tends to do just the opposite. And a prison whose primary aim is to make offenders into "industrious, free men rather than orderly and obedient prisoners" is yet to be born!

Can the reader think of any other human discipline—any science, any art, any industry, any department of our civilized life—which, in this past hundred years of turbulent expansion, has made so little progress in bringing practice up to ideal and vision?

Local, state, and national correctional associations have exercised a strong influence in bringing about improvements in correctional institutions and services, in addition to performing such functions as assisting prisoners and ex-prisoners to make a new start in life.* Some of these organizations make recommendations to the state legislatures. The Correctional Association of New York, founded in 1846, is required by its charter to make legislative recommendations. The scope of its interest and effort is indicated by the fourteen recommendations it made to the New York State Legislature in 1965 on the following subjects: a "new penal law"; narcotic addiction programs; nonresidential programs for youth in trouble; an identification and intelligence system; a modification of procedure for the selection of judges; qualifications of personnel in county correctional institutions; pre-parole camps; the treatment of elderly offenders; the problem of police court alcoholics; need of additional personnel trained in educational and behavioral sciences for state and correctional institutions; the handling of lesser offenders by work furloughs and by installment payment of fines; the expansion of camp programs for offenders; the grievous problem of bail bonds, and the abuses and limitations of the present procedure; and a proposal to establish an academy of correctional training in the New York State Department of Correction.

If ten per cent of these recommendations were followed, we might indeed have cause to rejoice.†

---

* Among the oldest of these associations are the Pennsylvania Prison Society, the Correctional Association of New York, the Connecticut Prison Association, and the John Howard Association of Chicago. Younger agencies such as the Osborne Association, a nationwide program with headquarters in New York City, have also stimulated and guided correctional progress. More than a score of organizations were combined to form the National Prisoner's Aid Association, which became the Correctional Service Federation–U.S.A. in 1962.

† In part through the activities of this organization, a temporary commission on the revision of the penal law and criminal code in New York was created, with a mandate to prepare for submission to the legislature a revised, simplified body of the substantive laws relating to crime and offenses, to revise "in a thorough-going fashion" both the penal law and the code of criminal procedure. Also stimulated in part by this association was the reorganization of the courts in New York State in 1962.

Historical Notes on Prisons

"Improvements" in our penal system were begun two hundred years ago. A small band of Quakers and Free Thinkers met in Philadelphia at the home of Benjamin Franklin to listen to a paper by a psychiatrist, Dr. Benjamin Rush (1787). The paper was about a new program for the treatment of prisoners. He proposed the establishment of a prison that would include (a) the classification of prisoners for housing, (b) a rational system of prison labor, (c) indeterminate periods of punishment, and (d) individualized treatment of convicts according to whether crimes arose from passion, habit, or temptation. (Two hundred years ago!)

But it was Quaker belief that a man who had done wrong, and had been convicted of it, must be brought to realize that he had done wrong, and desire to do better; he must become penitent before he could be helped. To accomplish this the Quakers established solitary cells in the Walnut Street jail of Philadelphia (1790) where the evildoers were confined alone to meditate over their sins and wrongdoing. This jail has been called the "birthplace" of the prison system, in its present meaning, not only in the United States but throughout the world.*

About the same time, New York State established a prison at Auburn where solitary cells were built for the oldest and most hardened criminals, as a test of the Pennsylvania system. Some Frenchmen, including the famous de Tocqueville, observing this test at first hand, condemned it outright as conducive to depression and insanity, and endangering life.[1] Prison architecture and policies were later modified so that inmates, although still confined in solitary cells at night, were allowed to work together and eat together in the daytime. They were not allowed to talk to one an-

---

* It is often said that this is the first institution called a *penitentiary,* but there was an earlier one in Massachusetts. (See Edwin Powers' *Crime and Punishment in Early Massachusetts, 1620–1692.* Boston: Beacon Press, 1966.)

other. This general pattern prevailed throughout the United States for the next one hundred and fifty years!

The Italian, Cesare Beccaria, denounced in 1764 the cruel penal codes and arbitrary judges of his day so effectively as to start a wave of humanitarian reform reflected by the "twenty-two principles" promulgated a little over a hundred years later. He and his proposals were vigorously opposed then just as they are today by "commonsense" penologists. Declared the British economist Sydney Smith in 1922: "I would banish all the looms in the [jails] and substitute nothing but the treadmill of capstan [engines of drudgery that accomplished nothing] or some species of labour where the labourer could not see the results of his toil—where it is as monotonous, irksome, and dull as possible—pulling and pushing instead of reading and writing—no share in the profits—not a shilling." [2]

It was an attempted compromise between these two positions that produced the monstrosity known as a penitentiary, for combined punishment and reformation. This attempt to combine the incompatible philosophies of punishment and reformation still divides penologists and confuses the public.

Something of the non-progress achieved may be judged from a brief consideration of what was called the Livingston Code, developed in the 1820s. Although printed in England, France, and Germany and studied and acclaimed all over the world, it was never adopted by any state in the United States, where it originated. Nonetheless it was influential. Sir Henry Maine spoke of its author as "the first legal genius of modern times." [3]

Edward Livingston * clung to the classical Quaker doctrine that if a prisoner were secluded initially, he would have time to reflect upon his transgressions and begin his own reformation. For this reason Livingston advocated that each prisoner have a cell of his

---

* Livingston's works include: *Reports of the Plan of the Penal Code* (1822); *System of the Penal Law of the State of Louisiana* (1826); *System of Penal Law for the United States* (1828); *Complete Works on Criminal Jurisprudence* (1873).

own. But he emphasized the importance of work and educational opportunity for the exemplary prisoner.

> [The prisoner's] own reflections must be his only companions for a preliminary period, during which he is closely confined to his cell. . . . [He] must suffer the tedium arising from want of society and of occupation, and when he begins to feel that labour would be an indulgence, it is offered to him as such; it is not threatened as an evil, nor urged upon his acceptance as an advantage to any but to himself; and when he is employed, no stripes, no punishments whatever, are inflicted, for want of diligence; if not properly used, the indulgence is withdrawn, and he returns to his solitude and other privations, not to punish him for not labouring, but merely because his conduct shows that he prefers that state to the enjoyment with which employment must always be associated in his mind in order to produce reformation. . . . Experience shows that employment, even under the lash, is in most cases preferred to solitude.[4]

Livingston's views, although not adopted in statutes, gave impetus to the spread of new ideas in the United States as well as abroad. His advocacy of a return to solitary confinement was partly a reaction against the miseries and degradation of the congregate prison, with its promiscuity and complete lack of privacy, which had replaced the original Philadelphia and Auburn plan.

It should also be remembered that at this time almost every form of corporal punishment was employed in prisons to "enforce discipline." Livingston was seeking to change this brutal regime without challenging the vengeance motive. He contended that physical punishment was not necessary and that it was sufficient to let the prisoner suffer the remorse of idleness and loneliness. He wanted to send prisoners back to the outside world convinced that work is a privilege and something pleasant. Little did he visualize how this ideal would one day become distorted and corrupted by the chain-gang and other forms of prisoner slave-labor.

A half century after Livingston developed his penal code, the American Correctional Association was organized and made its famous statement of principles. Then another half century passed, and a far-visioned governor, Alfred E. Smith, appointed a State Prison Survey Committee in New York whose famous Wickersham Report (1922) * was revolutionary in its recommendations of sweeping reforms. Its introductory statement called attention to the fact that Governor DeWitt Clinton had denounced the evils of the prison system over a hundred years earlier, that Governor Throop had done so in 1830, Governor Marcy in 1834, Governor Seward in 1840, Governor Clark in 1856, Governor Robinson in 1879, and Governor Cornell in 1882. All had stressed the evils of the system in messages to the legislature. In 1919 Governor Hughes had recommended the reorganization of the system.

The Wickersham Report recommended (as had the Prison Association of New York in 1846 and again thereafter) that county jails be abandoned as places of punishment, that prisoners be sent to clearing houses for a diagnosis, that sentences be made "truly" indeterminate, and that paroles be issued only after a prisoner's problems had been sufficiently well met to warrant a belief that, supervised by a psychiatric social worker, he could adapt himself to the community.

These were indeed intelligent and sensible recommendations! But uttered and publicized with what effect?

A few years later another commission appointed by Governor Smith came up with another set of excellent proposals including, among others, these:

—That the jury should determine only the guilt or innocence of the person on trial.

—That after a jury has returned a verdict of guilty the power of imposing sentences should be taken from the judge who presided at the trial and given to a special board to be created by a constitutional amendment.

—That the members of the board should include legal experts, psychiatrists, and penologists devoting their entire time to this work.

* One section of the report was entitled "A Plan for the Custody and Training of Prisoners Serving a Sentence in the County Jails," but it is usually referred to as the Wickersham Report.

—That this board should determine whether a convicted felon should go to a state prison or to an insane asylum; and that it should determine the length of punishment and the extent to which he may be subject to parole.

Again, this would have been great progress. But where was it ever done?

Meanwhile in St. Louis, Guy A. Thompson, president of the city and state bar associations, was urging upon his colleagues the need for a similar study, and in 1924 the Missouri Association for Criminal Justice was organized to implement and conduct a survey. It examined successively and intensively the functions of the police, sheriffs, coroners, prosecution, and defense; it studied the selection of the juries, the role of judges, and the trial process; it examined the record systems, pardons, paroles and commutation, releases and recidivism. Subcommittees of experts, both scientists and jurists, assisted with special reports submitted to and studied by the committee as a whole.

Another magnificent report [5] emerged, this one over six hundred printed pages in length. One of its most startling conclusions (repeated in the President's Crime Commission's Report of 1967!) was that what we know about the perpetrators of crimes is largely inferential and presumptive since most offenders are never even caught, let alone studied! The people we call criminals constitute a small minority of offenders characterized by stupidity, clumsiness, inefficiency, poverty, and other characteristics not in and of themselves criminal. Concerning the management of these captured offenders, and also concerning the control of the larger number who escape capture, the Missouri Crime Survey submitted farseeing proposals.

I should like to be able to say that the city of St. Louis and the state of Missouri soared to the heights of intelligent social control and set models for the rest of the nation in law enforcement, criminal detection, and the reconstructive management of those arrested, detained, convicted, and sentenced. Unhappily, I must record that Missouri continued the same disconsolate record of fail-

ure and ineptitude as before, little different from that of most
states.

A loyal New Yorker—a judge—who heard me speak on this subject, wrote to remind me that "in our state we have improved
things this much: we no longer use county jails in which prisoners
serve sentences of punishment. We only detain them in these
county jails pending trial."

Very well; let us credit New York with *this* improvement. But
my kindly critic may not have known that at the moment he was
writing there were over five thousand people being detained in the
jails of his city who had *not been sentenced* to jail; they were not
officially enjoying punishment, but merely awaiting a decision as to
whether they *should* be given the punishment they were already
getting. Besides these there were the usual petty thieves, narcotic
peddlers, drunks, and homosexual offenders.

"But, Really, No Improvements at All?"

Yes, of course there have been some improvements in facilities and methods here and there, and in some respects generally
and widely. Yet, as every one of us knows, the crime situation
grows worse. The public is no safer; offenders are more numerous; recidivism increases; violence is a national scandal. Professor
Francis A. Allen, now Dean of the University of Michigan Law
School, thinks that:

> Although one is sometimes inclined to despair of any constructive
> changes in the administration of criminal justice . . . the history of
> the past half-century reveals . . . the widespread acceptance of three
> legal inventions of great importance: the juvenile court, systems of
> probation and of parole. During the same period, under the inspira-
> tion of continental research and writing, scientific criminology be-
> came an established field of instruction and inquiry in American uni-
> versities and in other research agencies. At the same time, psychiatry
> made its remarkable contributions to the theory of human behavior
> and, more specifically, of that form of human behavior described as
> criminal.

But then Allen goes on to say:

> These developments have been accompanied by nothing less than a
> revolution in public conceptions of the nature of crime and the
> criminal, and in public attitudes toward the proper treatment of the
> convicted offender.[6]

With this conclusion I cannot concur. I cannot perceive this revolution in the public conception of the nature of crime, nor do I believe, the country over, that there is a basic change in the attitude
toward or the treatment of the convicted offender.

The American Correctional Association, whose noble principles
declared so many years ago are still dependable guideposts, is still
trying to achieve the goals of improvement. Its *Manual of Correctional Standards* is the best available. In the opinion of able leaders
such as Peter P. Lejins,[7] President of the Association in 1963, a
concerted emphasis on clear-cut formulation of these standards is
the most important improvement immediately available to close the
gap between the best and the worst in correction. With this development of standards, he thinks, must go the development of effective methods of evaluation not only of the prisoners but of the institutions. This, of course, leads to the question of preparing, selecting, training, and elevating the personnel, which is of paramount
importance. We learned long ago—and forgot and relearned many
times—that the recovery and discharge of patients in our psychiatric hospital was directly and intimately connected with the *quality* as well as the quantity of personal attention. The prison administrators of the country know this but they have not been able to
sell it to their state budgeteers.

The Diagnostic Center

In my opinion, the most promising improvement in recent
years is the diagnostic center. Perhaps I am influenced in my views
by my close personal association with its development in the state
of Kansas. Most prisons have reception wings or units where a certain amount of diagnosis is carried on, but there are only a few

reception centers operated as separate and distinct facilities, and not all of these serve the courts as the Kansas Reception and Diagnostic Center does.

Facilities of this type combine personality evaluation, social investigation, psychological testing, industrial and vocational appraisal and guidance or assignment, and many other functions. In other words, a group of social scientists including psychiatrists, psychologists, social workers, and others are permitted to make an unpressured examination of the offender and of the situation in which his offense was generated and executed. His personality assets and liabilities are carefully appraised and compared with the assets and liabilities of the social environment in which he has lived.

In Kansas, a tentative sentence has already been pronounced when the prisoner is referred to the Diagnostic Center for study, but the sentence can be and frequently is changed by the judge where there are indications that a better disposition might be made —one which would offer more toward the prisoner's rehabilitation and society's safety.

It is only fair to say, however, that the concept of the diagnostic center is still undergoing evolution. In actual practice, some suffer from a disastrous unclarity of relationship and authority between the professional psychiatric staff (identified with their roles as mental health workers) and the correctional staff (identified with the need for security). In the Kansas example the clinical director, Dr. Karl Targownik, and the superintendent, J. B. Noble, cooperate to achieve results which have been very pleasing to most of the judges. But this is not always the case.

An even more critical problem is that in many states the diagnostic center is equipped to do a sophisticated job of personality assessment, but places for differential modes of treatment or rehabilitation do not exist elsewhere in the state. Fitting the man to the right rehabilitative program may be largely wasted effort when the only available placement is the state prison.

A report, detailing the background of the offender, the circumstances of the offense, the psychiatric and psychological findings, and the conclusions to be derived from the foregoing, has become a potent tool for making judges much more aware of the psychological intricacies of the offender who comes before them. The report may recommend probation or assignment to the reformatory, the penitentiary, an honor camp, a prison farm, or a state mental hospital. The report may suggest the type of supervision or special treatment needed and propose academic or vocational training.*

Treatment for Juveniles

I am aware of the scores of thriving efforts over the nation to improve the methods and programs of institutions for juvenile delinquents. I am aware, too, of the strenuous efforts made by many conscientious juvenile court judges and youth commissions to prevent the necessity of institutionalization for thousands of cases that come before them. But I am also aware of the general admission from all quarters that all our efforts and all our institutions are far below the number and quality needed for proper rehabilitation of wayward and alienated youth.†

* It was a psychoanalyst, a very wise one whose recent death has saddened us all, who suggested the following clear, if oversimplified, table as a general guide to disposition (Waelder, Robert: "Psychiatry and the Problem of Criminal Responsibility." *U. Pa. Law Rev.,* 101:378, 390, 1952):

Diagnostic Characterization	Disposition
Dangerous, Deterrable, Treatable	Punishment and Treatment
Dangerous, Deterrable, Not treatable	Punishment
Dangerous, Not deterrable, Treatable	Preventive custody and Treatment
Dangerous, Not deterrable, Not treatable	Preventive custody
Not dangerous, Deterrable, Treatable	Punishment with Probationary period and treatment
Not dangerous, Deterrable, Not treatable	Punishment, perhaps with Probationary period
Not dangerous, Not deterrable, Treatable	Treatment
Not dangerous, Not deterrable, Not treatable	Release

† See Seymour L. Halleck's paper, "Psychiatric Treatment of the Alienated College Student," presented at the 123rd Annual Meeting of the American Psychiatric Association, Detroit, May 11, 1967.

In my own state of Kansas the institution for the treatment of young boys was long ago turned over to the State Division of Institutional Management, which is also responsible for our hospitals for the mentally ill and the mentally retarded. The result has been that the Boys Industrial School, as it is now known, has become famous throughout the United States, under the direction of superintendent Jack C. Pulliam and clinical director Stuart Averill. The staff consists of psychiatrists, clinical psychologists, psychiatric social workers, and psychiatric residents from the Menninger School of Psychiatry. The School's treatment-oriented milieu program has become widely known for its success in the reduction of juvenile crime. Its rate of recidivism is between four and nine per cent compared, for example, with that of Massachusetts' juvenile institutions, reported in a recent issue of *Federal Probation,* of between forty-three and seventy-three per cent. The Division of Law and Psychiatry of The Menninger Foundation is now conducting an extensive follow-up study on boys released from the Industrial School in the hopes of isolating those factors that contribute to this remarkable success story.

Prisons

The California correctional system, under the brilliant leadership of Richard McGee, has been far out in the lead among the states, with excellent programs of work, education, vocational training, medical services, group counseling, and other rehabilitative activities.* A notable feature is the combination of diagnosis, eval-

---

* Moral or milieu treatment is an expression applied to that combination of assigned work plus recreation, education, and orderly living in a kindly atmosphere. It has been tried by exceptional prison wardens fortunate enough to have the necessary backing from their governing boards. By 1960, the program had acquired an additional designation: the "therapeutic community approach," a term used particularly by Dr. Maxwell Jones. This is well reported by Ernest Reimer of the California Department of Corrections and Glynn B. Smith of the California Rehabilitation Center for narcotic addicts at Corona. (Reimer, Ernest, and Smith, Glynn B.: "A Treatment Experience in Prison Community Living." *Amer. J. Correction,* 26:4–10, January–February 1964.)

uation, treatment, and classification at its hospital-clinic-prison center, the combined Medical Facility and Reception Center at Vacaville. This constitutes a systematic effort along scientific principles, to ascertain from collected case history data and from first-hand examinations just what the assets and liabilities of the floundering individual are. At Vacaville, and at the Southern California Reception Center at Chino, educational, vocational, medical, social, and psychological evaluations are made, and the conclusions from the case studies are presented to the disposition board. Group psychotherapy is available and is participated in by nearly all of the prisoners at the Facility. The superintendent is customarily a psychiatrist.

In California, nearly thirty years ago a group of idealists—Kenyon J. Scudder, John Joe Clark, Isaac Pacht, August Vollmer, George Briggs, and others—became convinced that the methods of dealing with offenders "were archaic, inefficient, antisocial and, in many instances, brutal." There was no adequate system of procedure for segregation or dealing with inmates on the basis of their past history, mentality, and family relationships, or facilities for their early rehabilitation.

These men persuaded the California legislature to back them in establishing a model prison at Chino. Kenyon J. Scudder, who inaugurated and shaped its progressive policies, was its first superintendent. From the very beginning the prison-for-punishment theory was discarded. All of the dehumanizing aspects of the old penology went with it. Listen to this description in the words of one of the prisoners:

> The days of men in penal institutions like Chino are filled with creative work, the evenings with study and diversion. Each man is assigned to a job for which he is best fitted, or he is trained in vocational work for which he shows an aptitude. He is assigned to an industry where he learns good work habits and for which he is paid.
>
> Men in prison are addressed and referred to as inmates instead of convicts; the guards are correctional officers. A well staffed and equipped hospital is provided.

An athletic coach will help him choose his games. The library has all the current books and magazines. Volumes of fine books are available to the men. His living quarters are equipped with a two-channel radio receiving headset. The television programs are the best. The latest movies are screened and members of his family and friends are urged to visit regularly.[8]

Another interesting experiment is that of warden John C. Watkins of the Draper Correctional Center in Elmore, Alabama—"a maximum security state prison for youthful offenders, mostly between the ages of sixteen and twenty-seven, who are serving sentences ranging from a few years for theft to life imprisonment for murder." Wardin Watkins, a sociologist, assisted by Dr. John McKee, a psychologist, set up a program designed to break up the convict structure and establish a different kind of atmosphere in which the emphasis was placed on reconstructing the individual's personality, and on education to fit the prisoner for a better life. Instead of blaming the prisoner for his failure, they tried to enlist his cooperation in making a scientific study of what went wrong in his life and what was needed to change it.

They have reported that in five years seventy-five inmates obtained high school diplomas; thirteen paroled inmates have entered college on scholarships for ex-prisoners and one of them is eligible for Phi Beta Kappa. Twenty-five per cent of the students voluntarily postponed their parole to finish their education program, and only seven per cent of the prison school enrollment became dropouts. About sixty-five per cent of the students have been given early parole dates. The education program received grants of nearly half a million dollars from the National Institute of Mental Health and the Manpower Development and Training Act.

The educational techniques used at Draper have already been adopted in penal institutions in Florida, Georgia, Indiana, Nevada, New York, Oklahoma, South Carolina, Tennessee, and Hawaii.[9]

The stated purpose of another project, in Oregon, is to develop a cooperative system of education within the prison setting run by an outside agency such as a college or university. The method calls for setting up seminar-type groups for the purpose of focusing upon some substantive area of learning, but the expectation is that these seminars will become group-dynamics sessions ultimately having some beneficial effect on the inmate's self-concept and sense of personal effectiveness. Inasmuch as ninety per cent of the inmates are school dropouts, this program is seen as one method of bringing about a reengagement with the educational process. It is one way of increasing self-esteem and taking advantage of whatever motivation the inmates may have. Some follow-up is provided in that inmates who have demonstrated their abilities in the program will have access to revolving funds to continue their higher education after release from prison. Some efforts will also be made by the university to reduce the sense of isolation that many released inmates experience.

As long ago as 1913, one progressive state, Wisconsin, saw the possible value of permitting qualified prisoners to leave the prison during the daytime hours and accept paid employment or receive technological training in various places in the nearby community. The prisoners would then return to their institutions at night and on Sundays. A man could thus earn money to pay his "expenses" inside and outside the jail and support his dependents as ordered by the court. (Upon discharge any balance in the prisoner's account was turned over to him.) This was known as the Huber Act,[10] enacted in Wisconsin half a century ago, and more recently in North Carolina, California, Idaho, Missouri, Montana, North Dakota, New York, Oregon, Virginia, Washington, and Wyoming.

South Carolina has in recent years developed a complex of progressive features in its state correctional program. There are training programs in computer programming, bricklaying, welding, car driving, as well as an intensive elementary educational program for illiterates. There are required courses in property rental, money borrowing, and budgeting. The last ninety days of each prisoner's sentence are spent in one of seven state correctional centers, during the latter part of which stay they are permitted to work at an outside job during the daytime. All of this reflects the leadership of Ellis C. MacDougall, a trained criminologist who has been the department director since 1962 and is president of the American Correctional Association for 1968. The state also has a private nonprofit society of sizeable membership—the Alston Wilkes Society—which actively assists prisoners and ex-prisoners and their families.[11]

Another important step forward in recent years was the establishment by Congress of the Joint Commission on Correctional Manpower and Training, with a grant of $1,100,000 to be administered by the Vocational Rehabilitation Administration. The function of the Joint Commission is to help expand the number of qualified personnel, especially in the professionally and technically trained categories, available to the nation's correctional institutions and agencies. In order to provide rehabilitation services to prisoners and other public offenders, manpower and personnel problems have to be solved. New approaches to training, in order to help obtain a larger professional work force, are being studied by the Joint Commission.

The Federal Prison System has had the advantage of centralization and the good fortune of highly enlightened leadership. Reports made to Congress regarding persistently bad conditions in the Federal Prison System prior to 1929 led to the creation of the Bureau of Prisons. Sanford Bates, now the dean of the American correctional field, became its first director and served until 1937. His successor was James V. Bennett, another progressive and capable administrator.

These two distinguished leaders brought the Federal Prison System to a position of preeminence in the correctional field. They improved the morale, self-respect, and responsibility of prison personnel, brought in specialists with professional and technical training, took the prisons and the parole system out of politics, built new institutions with emphasis on medium and minimum security, and developed programs of rehabilitative training and treatment suited to the great variety of prisoners found in the federal institutions. One of Bennett's significant accomplishments was securing passage of the 1958 Omnibus Sentencing Act, which allows greater parole flexibility and permits a judge to commit a man for three to six months for observation before a final sentencing, thus encouraging courts to tailor the sentence to the man.[12, 13]

On his retirement in 1964, after twenty-seven years of service as director, Bennett was succeeded by another dedicated man, Myrl Alexander. Alexander had entered the Federal Prison System in 1930 and had served as assistant director under Bennett. When he was recalled to head the Bureau, he was serving as director of the Center for the Study of Crime, Delinquency and Corrections at Southern Illinois University. His appointment gave renewed encouragement to well-wishers for further improvement in the Federal System. One of the significant achievements under his administration, during the period when Nicholas Katzenbach was Attorney General, was the passage by Congress of the Prisoner Rehabilitation Act of 1965. This permits the establishment of community residential treatment centers, granting home leave for carefully selected prisoners in emergencies, development of a work-release program under which qualified prisoners work or take training in the community during the daytime and return to their institutions at night, and the extension of the federal pre-release guidance centers for young offenders, which were already in operation in six large cities.

The 1930 legislation also gave responsibility to the United States Public Health Service for the provision of medical and psychiatric care to persons confined in federal institutions. As a result there occurred during the 1930s a cooperative development of programs between the Bureau of Prisons and the United States Public Health Service that resulted in the construction of new hospitals, the modernization of equipment, and the assignment of medical officers, psychiatrists, psychologists, nurses, and technicians to the institutions of the federal penal system.

Quite early during this relationship the need for a hospital-type institution within the system was recognized, and by 1933 the United States Medical Center for Federal Prisoners at Springfield, Missouri, had been constructed and opened. It has functioned throughout the past thirty years as a general medical and surgical hospital for technically difficult cases, as well as for psychiatrically-ill prisoners from the far-flung institutions of the federal system. It has a four-hundred-and-fifty-bed psychiatric division, staffed with psychiatrists, social workers, nurses, and specially trained correctional officers, who function as a team to apply prompt and effective treatment directed toward returning the prisoner to his original institution as quickly as possible. Since 1949 the psychiatric division of the Medical Center has also performed a service for the federal courts throughout the United States. Persons charged with federal offenses may be sent to Springfield for a period of psychiatric evaluation and observation, which is reported back to the court. Those adjudicated incompetent by the court may be accepted at the Medical Center for treatment for a limited period of time in hopes of restoring their competency.*

Numerous other social experiments are being conducted throughout the world. An outstanding example is the unique institution for apparently incorrigible offenders at Herstedvester, Denmark, long directed by Dr. G. K. Stürup. The philosophy there is that imprisonment is for social protection and that the lawbreaker

---

* I had the privilege of serving as consultant to this institution during the years when my good friend, Dr. Russell O. Settle, presently on the staff of The Menninger Foundation, was in charge of the institution. Through the years the Medical Center has served as something of an example for other systems that have moved toward developing psychiatric treatment institutions for convicted offenders. The California Medical Facility at Vacaville, for example, was in part at least pioneered by physicians who had served at the Springfield institution, notably Dr. Marion King and Dr. Justin K. Fuller.

who wishes to live in society must prove his fitness for release. The court that placed him in the institution has the responsibility for determining how long he shall stay there and also when he should be released. It must first be satisfied that he is not likely to return to crime.

This reality position is explained to the offender, and treatment is offered to help him change his life pattern if he wishes to earn his freedom. Doctor Stürup says that the institution receives mostly chronic offenders and that although it may hold them for an indefinite period, in practice the time is surprisingly short. Of the approximately fifteen hundred sentenced to this institution in the past twenty-five years, about a thousand are now making a social adjustment, one hundred are dead, and four hundred are in custody at the present time. In the past eighteen years, nine hundred severe criminals have been admitted and all were discharged. While some of these returned, their crimes were less severe the second time, and they made shorter stays, so that less than ten per cent remained in detention at the time of his report.[14]

Pre- and Post-Release Programs

In a number of prisons throughout the country, a program of pre-release preparation is conducted with the aid of inside and outside personnel, the objective of which is to assist prisoners about to be discharged in making the transition to the outside world.* This is vigorously supported in some places by an organization, the 7th Step Foundation, originally called Freedom House. When a prisoner has completed his pre-release course and been helped to make sure of employment outside, he leaves the prison and becomes a member of an alumni association, which has headquarters in the nearest city for rendezvous and social contacts. Preceding graduates lend their help and friendship during the early difficult

---

* A Pre-Release Guidance Center program inaugurated by the Federal Bureau of Prisons for the Treatment of Youth Offenders is the subject of a research study edited by John J. Galvin and published by Correctional Research Associates under a grant by the Ford Foundation.

days of readaptation. This sense of belonging is most important in reestablishing ego identity and ego strength, so necessary to complete independence from the "old life." Officials of the Kansas program of the 7th Step Foundation report that as of April 1, 1967, it had helped 880 graduates; and of this number, 132 have been obliged to return to prison or are in violation of parole. These figures represent an eighty-five-per-cent show of success.

Dr. Sydney Smith describes his experience with a pre-release group thus: "There must have been fifty ex-convicts in the room and one by one the chairman would call on each man to stand before the group and describe for the others the pitfalls in his past life that had finally caused him to stumble into a prison term. The thing that impressed me most was the need to confess, not only about previous misdeeds but about current temptations. The similarity between this meeting and that of an Alcoholics Anonymous group came readily to mind as member after member recited his success in painfully turning his back on an open cash register, or forcibly taking himself in hand to pass up a parked car with a key still in the ignition, or resisting the idea of pocketing some momentarily unguarded object of value. These 'confessions' did not sound too different from those of the problem drinker who recounts the inner struggle he experiences in trying to walk by a bar or refuse a 'social' drink. Listening to these troubled accounts of convicts grappling with inner urges they don't understand, one could become convinced of the 'addictive' nature of crime. And, interestingly, some of the same techniques that help the members of an AA group seem also to be effective with the 'ex-cons'—an organizational structure that supports their internal battle, an availability of interested peers, and an opportunity to 'talk out' their urgencies rather than act them out." [15]

Post-release assistance is also offered in a small way by many struggling private agencies over the country. For example, over a period of twelve years, St. Leonard's House in Chicago placed over twelve hundred ex-prisoners who stayed under its temporary shelter for a few days to a few months while employment, friends, and homes were found. But in the meantime over a million prisoners have been discharged from prisons over the country, most of whom do not have access to such helpful programs.

These things are being done—improvements of many sorts and kinds—all across our land. There is a ferment of discontent and desire for finding better ways. But I am obliged to say, regretfully, that the flame is still a feeble one.

I must speak with caution here because I am, after all, only an amateur. My professional work has been mostly outside prisons where, God knows, there are also troubled people. But not infrequently it has taken me inside prisons, and what I saw there, over and over, saddened and disturbed me. My observations led me to make recommendations to various branches of the state and federal government (usually not followed). They led me to become acquainted with wonderful people like Austin MacCormick, once assistant director of the Federal Bureau of Prisons and once Commissioner of Corrections of New York City. For over twenty-five years, he has been executive director of The Osborne Association and a dominant figure in American penal reform. For the most part, The Osborne Association has been Austin MacCormick: * year after year, it has issued the *Handbook of American Prisons,* which attempts to say what progress has been made in the various prisons in the various states, taken one by one.

As far back as 1942, MacCormick could declare in his *Handbook of American Prisons:*

> Among the tenets now generally accepted as fundamental are the following: that, whatever may be true of criminals in general, prisoners come predominantly from the lower economic and social strata of

---

* John Bartlow Martin, the crime journalist, wrote in 1953, "about all that is left of The Osborne Association is Austin MacCormick, a sort of one-man supervisor of the 19th century prison societies. . . . Despite public apathy, Austin MacCormick has continued to write, teach, and organize in the interests of penal reform." (Martin, John B.: *Break Down the Walls.* New York: Ballantine Books, 1953.)

society; that they do not differ greatly from free persons on those levels of society; that they present marked individual differences and cannot be treated effectively on a mass basis; that the ultimate aim of the institutional and parole system, to cause the offender to become a law-abiding citizen, can best be accomplished by training and treatment on an individualized basis; that the institution's first task is to learn everything possible about each prisoner, and to assemble the essential data in usable form; that a program should then be planned for each prisoner on the basis of the full data in his case and his probable future; that the program should involve every form of training and treatment that may remove handicaps and disabilities, increase desirable and useful knowledge and skills, correct individual and social maladjustments, change undesirable attitudes, and in general prepare the prisoner for free life; that the length of stay in the institution should depend primarily, within reasonable limits, on the fitness of the prisoner for release; that a release from an institution, in most cases, should be followed by a period under the type of supervision and control that a good parole system provides; and that the success of the released prisoner in free life depends not only on his own attitude and effort but also on the degree to which society gives him the opportunity and the encouragement necessary to success.[16]

And, after this magnificent portrait of the ideal prison, MacCormick admitted that:

No individual institution or prison system in the United States has been able as yet to establish such a program in its entirety, especially in the all-important essential of trained personnel. In several federal and state institutions most of the program outlined above has been put in operation, but even in those where it has been possible to keep the population down to a reasonable limit, and where constructive efforts are not defeated by the twin evils of over-crowding and idleness, the officials would be slow to claim that they had achieved the elusive goal of individualized treatment. Experienced workers in the correctional field know that there is something inherent in institutions that tends to defeat their purpose. The measurable progress which can be made by superior personnel operating a well rounded program in an adequate plant is always retarded and impaired in some degree by the intangible effects on the prisoners of what is called institutionalization, effects which are felt increasingly in institutions operating on a mass treatment basis.

MacCormick, like a handful of exceptional leaders, has managed to maintain a perennially hopeful and positive attitude. He assures me that he has seen much change and improvement in the prison system of this country.

But my own experience and observations, while incomparably less than his, tend to make me sympathize with the viewpoint of Robert Lindner, expressed some twenty years ago. Here and there, he said, the long, sad, silent shuffles may have been replaced with a new spirit, but we have nothing to feel good about. Even the so-called "new prison," he says, with its well-ventilated cells and rehabilitation-minded warden is not the improvement it seems to be.

"No, it is not the structure, brick upon brick, of detentional and rehabilitative places which needs to be examined or criticized . . . nor is it the way in which prisoners are handled today, despite the . . . countless other hellish vestiges that persist here and there that need exposure and examination; it is, rather, the self-delusion of modern penology, its sham, and its complete failure. . . ." [17]

"What does the man want?" you may inquire. "What would satisfy him? What delusion is he talking about? We have just built a fine new minimum security prison in our state, and such accusations make us downhearted and discouraged."

Lindner was making the same point that James Russell Lowell did in *The Vision of Sir Launfal:* "The gift without the giver is bare." We cast larger alms to the beggar; we put a new coat of paint on the slave quarters. We shine up the tools. But our heart is not in it. We don't really care. Keep 'em out of our sight; keep 'em quiet. Let up on the brutality; feed 'em. Keep 'em busy, but watch 'em. Don't let 'em escape.

We don't love criminals. We hate them. We despise them. We regard them as disagreeable, dangerous failures. And we do not really believe, most of us, that they can be rehabilitated, that they *can* change for the better, or that it is worthwhile making the effort.

Now and then, a saint or a prophet or a dedicated humanitarian and public servant arises who does love the least of these, his brethren, and who raises his voice and invests his life in refuting our pessimism. But William Penn and Benjamin Rush are forgotten today for their efforts; the wonderful words and deeds of George Kirchwey—who remembers them? There was Thomas Mott Osborne, the businessman who voluntarily served a sentence in his own state's prison in order to discover its defects, and who worked out a system of self-government by the prisoners; his programs have been long abandoned. There was warden Lewis Lawes, who died before he ever saw the acceptance of his main recommendation—the abolition of the absurd death sentence.[18] There were Kenyon Scudder, Grace Abbott, Clinton Duffy, Miriam Allen de Ford, Richard McGee, Howard Gill, Sanger Powers, Norman Fenton, Sol Rubin, Dean Pound, Vernon Briggs, Irving Ben Cooper, Bolitha J. Law, Anna Kross, Lloyd McCorkle, Harry Elmer Barnes, William Cox, G. Howland Shaw, James Bennett, and others I have mentioned earlier.

But do the people of this country even know these names? Do the people know their accomplishments or their messages?

Do the people of Massachusetts appreciate the benefits of their Vernon Briggs Law? Do the citizens of California give the moral support that it deserves to Richard McGee's progressive system? Do the people of the middle west know what a unique federal institution is located in Springfield, Missouri? Are the citizens of Baltimore and Maryland as proud of their remarkable Patuxent as they are of their Johns Hopkins? (I do not blush to make the comparison; both are great experiments; the world knows about the one, whereas about the other not even Maryland people know, as I discovered when I testified recently as *amicus curiae* in a case brought *against* the institution.)

Is it any wonder the professionals in the field are discouraged? "We stand alone between society and crime," cried most wistfully a recent police department house organ.[19] And in a large sense they *are* alone. We do not help much. We do not even know what troubles they have.

The cold statistical summary supplied by the President's Crime Commission reinforces this opinion:

> Two and a half million offenders were involved in the system last year. Of that total, one-third were in institutions, "often fortress-like constructions where security is the predominant goal and where rehabilitative programs are absent."
>
> The other two-thirds were in the community, "under the supervision of overworked, underpaid and poorly trained probation and parole officers."
>
> Only two of fifty states claim they do not put children in jails. Last year a quarter of the 400,000 children detained were locked up with hardened criminals.
>
> Only five states have "halfway houses" to aid offenders in making the leap from prison back into society.
>
> Eleven states have no probation service for adults convicted of misdemeanors and most offer it on a "spotty basis." As for felonies, half of the nation's parole officers carry caseloads exceeding 100 persons, far above the recognized standard. Thirty per cent of all the state prisons have no vocational training.

Can we call that improvement?

The following news item quotes a famous expert, not a psychiatrist, not a sociologist, not a sentimentalist—but a highly intelligent lawyer and former judge and a "jailer" of vast experience:

> More than ninety per cent of the girls and women in the Women's House of Detention, the notorious landmark of [Greenwich] Village Square, are "social deviates," not criminals, and shouldn't have been arrested in the first place. Mrs. Anna M. Kross, as [New York] City Correction Commissioner . . . was asked, "Why do you arrest these women?"
>
> "I laughed," Mrs. Kross said. "I said, I've been asking that question for over forty years. I don't believe most of the women—over ninety per cent of the women that are in the Women's House—

should be arrested. They're social deviates. . . . Whatever the court sends, we have to take."

The Women's House of Detention, built for four hundred and often housing more than six hundred, was once called a "fortress of despair" by Mrs. Kross. It has been denounced as outmoded, inhuman, inadequate almost since the cornerstone was laid in 1930. . . . [Commissioner Kross said it was about time that someone admitted that "We don't know why we send (people) to jail."]

"There is this feeling," she added, "that all we have to have is more policemen and arrest them and give them a taste of jail, and we'll solve the problem. But . . . we've been doing that for years and years and we haven't solved the problem." [20]

I have said several times in this book that the deplorable conditions that exist in this country *cannot be laid at the feet of prison directors* in any general way, but I would prefer that more wardens and correction division heads would speak out as bravely as Commissioner Kross. Certainly there are some sadistic and reactionary wardens. However, most of them want to improve things but are baffled and frustrated by their inability to obtain public support for the measures they feel to be so important. As her consultant, I personally witnessed the anguish of Commissioner Kross when her recommendations and proposals were from time to time rejected or diminished.

The excuse is always that it costs too much or is risky, or that the public will cry "pampering"; all of which is penny wise and pound foolish, as the prison officials well know, but usually they are the last department or agency to be heard by ways-and-means committees. This is no accusation, either, of a lack of humanity in legislators. It is only intended as a reproach to their misinterpretation and underestimate of the benevolent potentialities of the public they represent and serve.

If a warden gets a new vision of what might be done and manages to get it past the cautious state director of corrections, the moment he tries to get the necessary additional appropriation he will be asked about reducing the daily costs, warned that he had better think more about "greater security," forget these fancy fur-belows, and settle back in the old rut. Understaffed parole depart-ments, like the prison wardens, are up against the solid brick wall of the legislature, and the legislators do not read criminological or sociological journals; they read annual reports and budget hearings and county newspapers.

Legislators listen to the public, but the public certainly knows very little about the world of the captured offender, either before or after the offense, except what it reads about an occasional case in the news. Seemingly, it couldn't care less.

If a judge wants to institute any procedures that would enable him to dispose of his charges more intelligently, he runs the risk of unpleasant newspaper notoriety, if not the death of his political life, for doing so. Even then he may not get any cooperation from the people he needs. And even then he will still have an overloaded docket of unresolved cases.

"During my fourteen years on the bench of the country's busiest criminal court, I have sentenced more than fifteen thousand young people for their first serious offenses against the law," wrote the then Chief Justice of the Court of Special Sessions of the City of New York, Irving Ben Cooper. "Three out of five of these, after serving the prison terms I was compelled to impose, went on from crime to more vicious crime. . . . Had my court possessed the proper tools of correction and rehabilitation, I believe we could have saved eighty per cent. . . . And this is true of similar tribu-nals throughout the nation." [21]

Judge Cooper left the bench because, as he told me in the pres-ence of numerous colleagues of the judiciary, "I couldn't bear it any longer. The very best I could do was nowhere nearly good enough. Many a time I have passed judgment on a hundred boys in a day, not a dozen of whom I could possibly ascertain the whole truth about. I found myself committed to a task not only inhuman but, as I came to feel it, more and more immoral. That is not the way to do it."

Hope

What then *is* "the way to do it"? We have heard about all the wrong ways; what is the right way? Who should *say* what it is? And who should put it into effect? What can *we* do?

The President's Commission on Law Enforcement and the Administration of Justice in February, 1967, issued a report of its two-year study. Entitled *The Challenge of Crime in a Free Society*,[22] it tells what nineteen commissioners think you *might* do to help matters. These commissioners had the assistance of eighteen jurists (no scientists), supported by a technical staff of two score, and consultants and advisers by the hundreds, the present writer among them. My personal experience was to be summoned to Washington for a hasty, disorganized, one-day conference in a crowded room on a topic concerning which some usable research was presented but which only a few persons in the room had the time or opportunity to discuss. Whatever conclusions the clerical staff was able to draw from the scattered comments were never submitted in writing to the participants; indeed, I never heard from the commission again after this one hectic session.

Certainly *someone* kept at it assiduously. For within two years an elaborate report appeared making two hundred specific recommendations; this, after an initial acknowledgement that things "could hardly be worse" and that no one knew exactly how bad they were. "Its [the report's] major intellectual contribution," commented a British writer, "seems to be an admission of almost total ignorance—about the extent of the crime problem in the United States (perhaps only a tenth of all crimes are reported), or the causes of crime, or the prevention, or the correction, or even the *definition* of crime." [23] The summary of the summary alone fills eight pages of fine print. Statistics have been collected, juvenile delinquency especially studied, police functioning examined, the operation of the courts reviewed, the general principles of corrections analyzed, at least descriptively, correctional institutions examined (briefly), organized crime, narcotics, and drunkenness considered separately. It was all done in a hurry, understandably, and too much in the old legal, rather than the modern scientific spirit. Social scientists were rather generally ignored. The words *science, behavior, psychiatry, psychology,* and *personality* are absent even from the index.

This is not entirely fair, I grant. The report does ask wistfully for research. It describes imprisonment as "segregation" and hopes for some better ways of dealing with offenders once they are caught. It favors the elimination of unfairness and injustices "so that the system of criminal justice can win the respect and cooperation of all citizens."

The sad thing about this report is that most people will never see it. Some of the recommendations will be quoted by the papers. The comments on sex crimes will be headlined. The hard-boiled, let's-have-no-coddling boys will be quoted as taking issue with the report's conclusions as not tough enough. The various task force reports will be requested by agencies or individuals to whom they appeal or apply.

The public will learn that the government has done something, but I am afraid it won't ever read or appreciate the report's wise and true declaration that "individual citizens, social-service agencies, universities, religious institutions, civic and business groups, and all kinds of governmental agencies at all levels must become involved in planning and executing changes in the criminal justice system." In my opinion this is the only solution, and it *could be done.*

Postscript, July 1968: I recently had a talk with Nathan Leopold, who had just come from a visit to his "alma mater"—the Illinois state prison at Statesville (Joliet). He was enthusiastic about the marvelous metamorphosis that it had undergone since his long stay there. When I expressed some skepticism he reminded me that he had more reason to doubt such a change for the better than had I, but the miracle really had happened. A committee of us went to see, and were immensely impressed with what we found that Warden Pate and his staff are doing. It is one of the most progressive prisons I have visited.

CHAPTER 10

Love against Hate

Nor to Avenge Any Wrong

Now am I veined by an eroding doubt,
Insidious as decay, with poison rife.
Is love indeed the end and law of life,
When lush, grimacing hates so quickly sprout?
I thought in ignorance I had cast out
The sneaking devils of continuing strife,
But as the cancer thwarts the surgeon's knife,
So does revenge my sword of reason flout.
    But though hate rises in enfolding flame
    At each renewed oppression, soon it dies;
    It sinks as quickly as we saw it rise,
    While love's small constant light burns still the same.
    Know this: though love is weak and hate is strong,
    Yet hate is short, and love is very long.

(Kenneth Boulding [1])

We come to a final chapter and, in keeping with the classic formula, the reader no doubt expects a happy ending. The minor chords which have filled so many of the pages of the long score must dissolve into cheery and conclusive tonic majors, so that the reader may close the book with a sigh of relief and a feeling that, in spite of blunder and turmoil, all's right with the world, or getting to be so.

But all is *not* right with the world in respect to crime and criminals—not yet. And if the reader closes this book with a sense of relief, I have failed. He must close it rather with a disturbed feeling of shared guilt and responsibility, perhaps even a sense of mission. I will have succeeded if he has begun to feel that it may be *up to him* whether or not crime is to be better controlled and public safety insured. Only through such a sense of disturbed concern on the part of intelligent readers and leaders are these results likely to be achieved.

Fifty years ago, Winston Churchill declared that the mood and temper of the public in regard to crime and criminals is one of the unfailing tests of the civilization of any country. Judged by this standard, how civilized are we?

The chairman of the President's National Crime Commission, Nicholas Katzenbach, declared recently that organized crime flourishes in America because enough of the public wants its services, and most citizens are apathetic about its impact. It will continue uncurbed as long as Americans accept it as inevitable and, in some instances, desirable. Do we *believe* crime is an inescapable part of our civilization, the eradication of which would require the surrender of our "freedom," our personal liberty, to a painful degree? Were we to limit the range of individuality, would we sacrifice the courage of innovation, the spark of initiative which delights in taking risks and courting dangers?

The famous simile of the shivering porcupines applies today more accurately than ever. We human porcupines multiply in numbers but remain confined within a limited life area, surrounded by the intense cold of outer space. But the more we seek to huddle together for warmth and comfort and communication, the more we wound and are wounded. What shall we do?

Human beings have one advantage over porcupines: we can see what the problem is. Are there steps that we can take which will reduce the aggressive stabs and self-destructive lurches of our less well-managing fellow men? Are there ways to prevent and control the grosser violations, other than the clumsy traditional maneuvers which we have inherited? These depend basically upon intimidation and slow-motion torture. We call it punishment, and justify it with our "feeling." We know it doesn't work.

Yes, there *are* better ways. There are steps that could be taken; some *are* taken. But we move too slowly.

The reader knows by now some things which I think would hasten the improvement. I have suggested various changes which seem to me to recommend themselves during the discussion of the obvious faults in the system. Much better use, it seems to me, could be made of the members of my profession and other behavioral scientists than having them deliver courtroom pronunciamentos. The consistent use of a diagnostic clinic would enable trained workers to lay what they can learn about an offender before the judge who would know best how to implement the recommendation.

This would no doubt lead to a transformation of prisons, if not to their total disappearance in their present form and function. Temporary and permanent detention will perhaps always be necessary for a few, especially the professionals, but this could be more effectively and economically performed with new types of "facility" (that strange, awkward word for institution). I also favor enabling and expecting offenders to make restitution to the state and to the injured parties, if feasible, although I recognize the complications of framing this requirement legally.*

I assume it to be a matter of common and general agreement that our object in all this is to protect the community from a repetition of the offense by the most economical method consonant with our other purposes. Our "other purposes" include the desire to prevent these offenses from occurring, to reclaim offenders for social usefulness, if possible, and to detain them in protective custody, if reclamation is *not* possible. But how?

The Preface of this book made reference to the famous trial of two disturbed young men who had pointlessly killed a younger friend. Their sentence to life imprisonment was a compromise be-

---

* See for example the study of Ellen Bersheid of the University of Minnesota and Elaine Walster of the University of Rochester, "When Does a Harm-Doer Compensate a Victim?" (*Journal of Personality and Social Psychology*, 6:435, 1967.)

tween acquittal and "punishment" by execution. One of the offenders was killed by a fellow prisoner; the other spent many years in prison. Application was then made for his parole to work in the laboratory of a mission hospital in Puerto Rico. Petitions were filed, endorsements were obtained, and a psychiatric examination was made which reported him to be free from antisocial attitudes and impulses. I furnished a letter of opinion on the eve of his release and received the following acknowledgment from him:

> It continues to amaze me, Dr. Menninger, that [busy men] are willing to take the time and trouble to come to the aid of a man situated as I am. It shouldn't amaze me, for my experience has been all in this one direction: Professor Einstein, for example, found time to be kind to me—and to hearten me.

His petition was granted and he went to Puerto Rico where in the space of one decade he served first as laboratory and X-ray technician and later as social worker for Castañer Hospital. At fifty-five he returned to school and earned a Master of Social Work degree at the University of Puerto Rico. After graduation, he served four years as research associate and project director in the Department of Health. He spent a year as consulting sociologist to the Urban Renewal and Housing Administration and then became research associate in the Medical School of the University, where he made a survey of leprosy in Puerto Rico.

Now for the question: Were we right in recommending that this man be permitted to leave the prison and try to remake his life? In doing so he has made some restitution to society; he has relieved suffering; he has supplied comfort and hope to many miserable and needy people, and perhaps he has inspired some errant and mistaken men to believe they might remake *their* lives, even after catastrophe and desolation.

Should we have done this?

Or should we have held to the ancient, savage ritual of confinement and punishment, and continued his slow suffocation at public expense?

Treatment

The word *treatment* has many meanings. Applied to human beings, it may mean kindness or it may mean cruelty. "Alcoholics should be treated like sick people, not like criminals," someone exclaimed in my hearing recently; two different meanings of treatment were obviously implied.

The medical use of the word *treatment* implies a program of presumably beneficial action prescribed for and administered to one who seeks it. The purpose of treatment is to relieve pain, correct disability, or combat an illness. Treatment may be painful or disagreeable but, if so, these qualities are incidental, not purposive. Once upon a time, we must admit, we doctors with the best of intentions did treat some patients with torture. That, thank God, was long ago.*

But the treatment of human failure or dereliction by the infliction of pain is still used and believed in by many non-medical people. "Spare the rod and spoil the child" is still considered wise warning by many.

Whipping is still used by many secondary schoolmasters in England, I am informed, to stimulate study, attention, and the love of learning. Whipping was long a traditional treatment for the "crime" of disobedience on the part of children, pupils, servants, apprentices, employees. And slaves were treated for centuries by flogging for such offenses as weariness, confusion, stupidity, exhaustion, fear, grief, and even overcheerfulness. It was assumed and stoutly defended that these "treatments" cured conditions for which they were administered.

Meanwhile, scientific medicine was acquiring many new healing methods and devices. Doctors can now transplant organs and

---

* The intentional infliction of pain for the treatment of any physical illness or disability is rare today except in the most ignorant circles. A persistent exception is the treatment of bed-wetting in children by whipping and various humiliations. I discovered recently that convulsions in children are treated with beatings in some families in certain communities.

limbs; they can remove brain tumors and cure incipient cancers; they can halt pneumonia, meningitis, and other infections; they can correct deformities and repair breaks and tears and scars. But these wonderful achievements are accomplished on *willing* subjects, people who voluntarily ask for help by even heroic measures. And the reader will be wondering, no doubt, whether doctors can do anything with or for people who *do not want* to be treated at all, in any way! Can doctors cure willful aberrant behavior? Are we to believe that crime is a *disease* that can be reached by scientific measures? Isn't it merely "natural meanness" that makes all of us do wrong things at times even when we "know better"? And are not self-control, moral stamina, and will power the things needed? Surely there is no medical treatment for the lack of those!

Let me answer this carefully, for much misunderstanding accumulates here. I would say that according to the prevalent understanding of the words, crime is *not* a disease. Neither is it an illness, although I think it *should* be! It *should* be treated, and it could be; but it mostly isn't.

These enigmatic statements are simply explained. Diseases are undesired states of being which have been described and defined by doctors, usually given Greek or Latin appellations, and treated by long-established physical and pharmacological formulae. Illness, on the other hand, is best defined as a state of impaired functioning of such a nature that the public expects the sufferer to repair to the physician for help. The illness may prove to be a disease; more often it is only vague and nameless misery, but something which doctors, not lawyers, teachers, or preachers, are supposed to be able and willing to help.

Only a few centuries ago, many conditions recognized today as illness were considered either sin or possession by the Evil One. The sufferers were not regarded as ill, nor taken to doctors for relief, but were disposed of in cruel ways in order to thoroughly intimidate the demons and witches (and the general populace). There were trials and tests and ordeals and tortured confessions; many thousands of our forebears were destroyed in this way.

Finally, about four hundred years ago a courageous and influential doctor, John Weyer, spoke out publicly against this church-endorsed practice. He denounced and ridiculed the witch theory, declaring that these peculiarly acting people were ill and needed a doctor, not an incinerator. He was joined (not very rapidly) by others.*

Peculiar and erratic and bemused individuals were then put in a legally defined category of illness called "insanity." This saved them from the death penalty for their acts, but it did not spare them confinement, punishment, whippings, starving, dunking, and other abuses which, however, were done in the name of medical "treatment" and were considered appropriate and helpful in these forms of illness. Public dislike and suspicion of irrational behavior persisted, but it was increasingly regarded as the expression of a queer form of illness and one that the *doctors* rather than the priests and judges should be expected to deal with.

While the doctors repudiated the superstitious belief that a witch or a devil had to be gotten out of the patient, they kept alive the elimination theory and a little of the punishment theory. The "bad-

---

* Reginald Scot, a county squire in Kent, a member of Parliament, and a justice of the peace, also became convinced (from considering the cases brought before him and their accusers) that it was not witches that afflicted these people but mental illness. "My greatest adversaries," he wrote, "are young ignorance and old customs." (Hunter, Richard, and Macalpine, Ida: *Three Hundred Years of Psychiatry, 1535–1860,* p. 32. London: Oxford University Press, 1963.) What a wonderful statement of a perennial truth!

King James VI of Scotland exemplified the "young ignorance." In *Demonologie,* he spoke "against the damnable opinions of two principally in our age, whereof the one called Scot an Englishman, is not ashamed in public print to deny, that there can be such a thing as Witch-craft. . . . The other called Wierus, a German Phisitian . . ." James was the only reigning monarch, say medical historians Richard Hunter and Ida Macalpine, who wrote a book which gave impetus (although negatively) to the development of psychiatry.

King James began in 1603 to enforce a new witchcraft act more severe than the Elizabethan one of 1563. He ordered Scot's book seized and burned, so that few copies have survived. (The library of The Menninger Foundation is proud to possess one.) But Scot's ideas prevailed in spite of the frightening penalties of the law which made judges wary.

ness" to be gotten rid of—as they saw it—was black bile, or blood poisons, or stones, or accumulated body wastes, or malignant growths. Patients were cupped and leeched and sweated and clystered and physicked unmercifully. They were given emetics to make them vomit and diuretics to make them pass more urine. All these draining and drenching treatments were efforts to eliminate from the patient's otherwise normal body the noxious substances "causing" the illness.*

Today medicine has swung generally to the opposite modality; rather than drawing something out of the patient, the treatment of illness is apt to involve putting something into him—pills, capsules, hypodermics, transfusions, infusions, implants, transplants, injections. (A witty psychiatric colleague added to this list: "And insight.") These puttings in and takings out do have reasonable scientific justification, but they also have and have always had an *irrational* basis which is usually overlooked. They reflect unconsciously held concepts of illness. But similar irrational, unconscious motivations determine our present-day notion of the proper "treatment" of offenders: Drive the evil out of them or pump some goodness into them.

Illness is what we call those unpleasant states of being for the relief and alteration of which the medical profession exists and is consulted. We have admitted that most criminal behavior is not a disease, nor even—for the most part—a commonly recognized illness. Crime is still a willful and avowed breaking of the rules, a flagrant disobedience, a flaunted infraction. The pain experienced by the subject is negligible compared to the pain suffered by society. Most recognized illnesses, however disagreeable for society, involve some conspicuous suffering or disability for the subject. The propensity for committing crime does not *look* like suffering; nor does it cause any obvious disability. It rarely arouses pity except in

---

* The discovery of pathogenic bacteria, a century or two later, seemed to afford scientific support to this old metaphysical notion of illness as evil invasion.

those very close to the offender. It doesn't correspond to the commonly held notion or general course of illness or sickness or disease.

Nevertheless, many a parent today *secretly* takes his son to doctors for just exactly this kind of illness—insufficiently controlled aggression. To the parent the son's behavior is not normal, not comprehensible, not consonant with health. It *must* be a symptom of illness. He wants to believe it is something the doctor can cure. It is a horrid, alien thing afflicting and deforming his otherwise lovable and promising child. His neighbors and friends may not concur in this view. With the aid of a lawyer he might persuade a judge to agree with it. But even his family physician may give the theory little support. For there is no such disease described in the textbooks of medicine and surgery.

When the community begins to look upon the expression of aggressive violence as the symptom of an illness or as indicative of illness, it will be because it believes doctors can do something to correct such a condition. At present, some better-informed individuals do believe and expect this. However angry at or sorry for the offender, they want him "treated" in an effective way so that he will cease to be a danger to them. And they know that the traditional punishment, "treatment-punishment," will not effect this.

What *will?* What effective treatment is there for such violence? It will surely have to begin with motivating or stimulating or arousing in a cornered individual the wish and hope and intention to change his methods of dealing with the realities of life. Can this be done by education, medication, counseling, training? I would answer *yes.* It can be done successfully in a majority of cases, if undertaken in time.

The present penal system and the existing legal philosophy do not stimulate or even expect such a change to take place in the criminal. Yet change is what medical science always aims for. The prisoner, like the doctor's other patients, should emerge from his treatment experience a different person, differently equipped, differently functioning, and headed in a different direction from when he began the treatment.

It is natural for the public to doubt that this can be accomplished with criminals. But remember that the public *used* to doubt that change could be effected in the mentally ill. Like criminals, the mentally ill were only a few decades ago regarded as definitely unchangeable—"incurable." No one a hundred years ago * believed mental illness to be curable. Today *all* people know (or should know) that *mental illness is curable* in the great majority of instances and that the prospects and rapidity of cure are directly related to the availability and intensity of proper treatment.

In the city in which I live there had been for many years a gloomy, overcrowded, understaffed place of horror called "the insane asylum." In its dark wards and bar-windowed halls, as late as 1948, one psychiatrist and one nurse were on duty for nearly two thousand sick people. There was no treatment for them worthy of the name. There was no hope. There were few recoveries.†

Today this old asylum is a beautiful medical complex of forty one- and two-story buildings, with clinics and laboratories and

* The curability of mental illness was statistically demonstrated *over* a hundred years ago at the Worcester State Hospital in Massachusetts, and in a number of other hospitals in New England and New York. But this magnificent demonstration was forgotten in the confusion of Irish immigration and the Civil War and Reconstruction in our country (and comparable upheavals in other lands). For one hundred years there was no progress in the treatment of the mentally ill. Despair, waste, neglect, and public scandal obscured the whole scene of psychiatry, and few doctors concerned themselves with the gloomy and unsavory mental-illness problem. It was left to politicians. (See Norman Dain, *Concepts of Insanity in the United States: 1789–1865*. New Brunswick, N.J.: Rutgers University Press, 1964; and Gerald N. Grob, *The States and the Mentally Ill*. Chapel Hill: University of North Carolina Press, 1966.)

† Some years previously the staffing was much better! The year 1948 was a low point which really triggered the "revolution." Unhappily, however, many such asylums still exist in the United States for lack of legislative action. In twenty-one of them there is not a single psychiatrist on duty today! (See "What Are the Facts About Mental Illness?" compiled in 1966 by the National Committee on Mental Illness, Inc., Washington, D.C.)

workshops and lecture halls surrounded by parks and trees and recreational areas. Some patients are under intensive treatment; others are convalescent; many are engaged in various activities in the buildings or about the grounds. Some leave their quiet rooms each morning to go to work in the city for the entire day, returning for the evening and their night's rest at the hospital. The average length of time required for restoring a mentally ill patient to health in this hospital has been reduced from years, to months, to weeks. Four-fifths of the patients living there today will be back in their homes by the end of the year. There are many empty beds, and the daily census is continually dropping.

What Is This Effective Treatment?

If these "incurable" patients are now being returned to their homes and their work in such numbers and with such celerity, why not something similar for offenders? Just what are the treatments used to effect these rapid changes? Are they available for use with offenders?

The forms and techniques of psychiatric treatment used today number in the hundreds. Psychoanalysis; electroshock therapy; psychotherapy; occupational and industrial therapy; family group therapy; milieu therapy; the use of music, art, and horticultural activities; and various drug therapies—these are some of the techniques and modalities of treatment used to stimulate or assist the restoration of a vital balance of impulse control and life satisfaction. No one patient requires or receives all forms, but each patient is studied with respect to his particular needs, his basic assets, his interests, and his special difficulties. In addition to the treatment modalities mentioned, there are many facilitations and events which contribute to total treatment effect: a new job opportunity (perhaps located by a social worker) or a vacation trip, a course of reducing exercises, a cosmetic surgical operation or a herniotomy, some night school courses, a wedding in the family (even one for the patient!), an inspiring sermon. Some of these require merely prescription or suggestion; others require guidance, tutelage, or assistance by trained therapists or by willing volunteers. A therapeutic team may embrace a dozen workers—as in a hospital setting—or it may narrow down to the doctor and the spouse. Clergymen, teachers, relatives, friends, and even fellow patients often participate informally but helpfully in the process of readaptation.

All of the participants in this effort to bring about a favorable change in the patient, i.e., in his vital balance and life program, are imbued with what we may call a *therapeutic attitude*. This is one in direct antithesis to attitudes of avoidance, ridicule, scorn, or punitiveness. Hostile feelings toward the subject, however justified by his unpleasant and even destructive behavior, are not in the curriculum of therapy or in the therapist. This does not mean that therapists approve of the offensive and obnoxious behavior of the patient; they distinctly disapprove of it. But they recognize it as symptomatic of continued imbalance and disorganization, which is what they are seeking to change. They distinguish between disapproval, penalty, price, and punishment. (See page 205.)

Doctors charge fees; they impose certain "penalties" or prices, but they have long since put aside primitive attitudes of retaliation toward offensive patients. A patient may cough in the doctor's face or may vomit on the office rug; a patient may curse or scream or even struggle in the extremity of his pain. But these acts are not "punished." Doctors and nurses have no time or thought for inflicting unnecessary pain even upon patients who may be difficult, disagreeable, provocative, and even dangerous. It is their duty to care for them, to try to make them well, and to prevent them from doing themselves or others harm. This requires love, not hate.

This is the deepest meaning of the therapeutic attitude. Every doctor knows this; every worker in a hospital or clinic knows it (or should). I once put this principle in a paragraph of directions for the workers in our psychiatric hospital:

> If we can love: this is the touchstone. This is the key to all the therapeutic programs of the modern psychiatric hospital; it dominates the behavior of its staff from director down to gardener. To our patient who cannot love, we must say by our actions that we do love him.

"You can be angry here if you must be; we know you have had cause. We know you have been wronged. We know you are afraid of your own anger, your own self-punishment—afraid, too, that your anger will arouse our anger and that you will be wronged again and disappointed again and rejected again and driven mad once more. But we are not angry—and you won't be either, after a while. We are your friends; those about you are all friends; you can relax your defenses and your tensions. As you—and we—come to understand your life better, the warmth of love will begin to replace your present anguish—and you will find yourself getting well." [2]

Right You Are If You Think You Are

There is another element in the therapeutic attitude not explicitly mentioned by me in that paragraph. It is the quality of hopefulness. If no one believes that the patient can get well, if no one—not even the doctor—has any hope, there probably won't be any recovery. Hope is just as important as love in the therapeutic attitude.

"But you were talking about the mentally ill," readers may interject, "those poor, confused, bereft, frightened individuals who yearn for help from you doctors and nurses. Do you mean to imply that willfully perverse individuals, our criminals, can be similarly reached and rehabilitated? Do you really believe that effective treatment of the sort you visualize can be applied to people *who do not want any help,* who are so willfully vicious, so well aware of the wrongs they are doing, so lacking in penitence or even common decency that punishment seems to be the only thing left?"

Do I believe there is effective treatment for offenders, and that they *can* be changed? *Most certainly and definitely I do.* Not all cases, to be sure; there are also some physical afflictions which we cannot cure at the moment. Some provision has to be made for incurables—pending new knowledge—and these will include some offenders. But I believe the majority of them would prove to be curable. The willfulness and the viciousness of offenders are part of the thing for which they have to be treated. These must not thwart the therapeutic attitude.

It is simply not true that most of them are "fully aware" of what they are doing, nor is it true that they want no help from anyone, although some of them say so. Prisoners are individuals: some want treatment, some do not. Some don't know what treatment is. Many are utterly despairing and hopeless. Where treatment is made available in institutions, many prisoners seek it even with the full knowledge that doing so will not lessen their sentences. In some prisons, seeking treatment by prisoners is frowned upon by the officials.

Various forms of treatment are even now being tried in some progressive courts and prisons over the country—educational, social, industrial, religious, recreational, and psychological treatments. Socially acceptable behavior, new work-play opportunities, new identity and companion patterns all help toward community reacceptance. Some parole officers and some wardens have been extremely ingenious in developing these modalities of rehabilitation and reconstruction—more than I could list here even if I knew them all. But some are trying. The secret of success in all programs, however, is the replacement of the punitive attitude with a therapeutic attitude.

A therapeutic attitude is essential regardless of the particular form of treatment or help. Howard Gill of the American University's Institute of Correctional Administration believes that thirty per cent of offenders are overwhelmed with situational difficulties, and for such individuals crisis intervention often works wonders. Case work, economic relief, or other social assistance often will induce a favorable behavior pattern change in these offenders. In another thirty per cent, he estimates, personal psychological problems exist in the offender which require technical treatment efforts. For these the help of psychiatrists, physicians, and psychologists are needed. Still another thirty per cent of prisoners are essentially immature individuals whose antisocial tendencies have never found the proper paths of distribution and transformation in socially acceptable ways. These men are usually amenable to redirection, education, and guidance. They can achieve development of self-control and social conformity by the various programs which we call milieu treatment. In other words, one can think of the categories of treatment as falling largely into the three modalities of sociological, psychological (medical), and educational.

The reflective reader, recalling the history of our mental hospital reformation, may now feel prompted to ask, "Could not sufficient diagnosis and treatment be provided for offenders who need it in our presently existing psychiatric hospitals? We read that the population in these hospitals is diminishing rapidly; could not this empty space be used to treat offenders who might be transferred there?"

Unfortunately, the answer is not clearly in the affirmative at present. In the first place, the victims of our penal system are usually so embittered and, indeed, so outright aggressive that a degree of security is necessary for them, especially in the beginning, which the average psychiatric hospital is not physically prepared to insure. Even more significantly, our psychiatric hospitals are not psychologically prepared at the present time to be assigned the task of detaining and treating patients who have been labeled prisoners. We have had a long, painful experience with this in my own State of Kansas.

Please remember that psychiatric hospitals have themselves only recently emerged from a state of public obloquy which was nearly as bad as that now affecting prisons. Those hospitals which have raised their standards are proud of their achievement, proud of their respectability and good name, proud of being known as places where people come to be made well by the best of scientific medical effort. Ailing, faltering, erring, or even dimly conscious patients brought to them are soon surrounded by new-found friends who take in the newcomer and minister to him as companions, aides, fellow sufferers, amateur repairmen.

But if, into such an environment, there is introduced an individual who is not only angry and unsocial and generally hostile but who has a public record of having been caught and convicted for something heinous, the atmosphere immediately changes. No matter how obvious his suffering, sympathy and therapeutic idealism will not always be sufficient to neutralize the suspicion and negative feelings aroused in patients and staff members alike.*

Treatment for the Many

In thinking of ways to provide truly corrective therapy for large numbers of offenders at minimal expense, penologists might take a leaf from the book of modern psychiatry. It was long assumed that only under detention, i.e., *in the hospital,* was it possible to effectively control and treat and change severely disturbed individuals. Early in the twentieth century an experiment of "outpatient" psychiatric treatment was made in Boston by Ernest Southard of Harvard. Today, half a century later, the *majority* of all psychiatric patients are in outpatient status! Furthermore, there is a steadily rising preponderance of outpatients over inpatients. "Day hospitals," where patients spend some daylight hours in scheduled activities with other patients but go home in the evening

---

* Dr. Linda Hilles has described this phenomenon vividly in a case which was really most pitiful. A fifty-four-year-old grocer, after several futile attempts to get psychiatric treatment in a small university town, suddenly turned a shotgun on his wife and then ran from the house to his store, where he cut off both his own hands by laying his arms before an electric meat-cutting saw. He was found guilty of murder but was sent to one of our best state hospitals for treatment of both his handlessness and his disturbed mental state. I was a party to this recommendation.

As can well be imagined, he was deeply melancholic and, of course, almost utterly helpless, and required much personal attention. In spite of his obvious demoralization, his presence in the hospital seemed to be resented by all members of the nursing staff, by the other patients, and even by one doctor. This continued even after his helplessness was reduced by equipping him with artificial hands. The failure to deal effectively with him did not stem from indifference or lack of interest and effort; an inordinate amount of time and energy was invested by the staff members in meetings, discussions, and reviews of the problem. These produced no gratifying results.

Dr. Hilles analyzed these unscientific attitudes and feelings as well as she could and concluded that in dealing with a patient who is also a murderer, the prime asset of the psychotherapist trained to work with the mentally ill, his empathy, may prove a liability and he may become disturbed by an awareness of the murderous impulses within himself. (Hilles, Linda: "Problems in the Hospital Treatment of a Disturbed Criminal." *Bull. Menninger Clin.,* 30:141–149, 1966.)

for sleep, privacy, and family adaptation, have also proved useful. Similarly, "night hospitals" came into use for patients who could adapt themselves well enough to a work situation or a school setting but who did better by spending their nights under the protective care of the friendly hospital.

Thus there has developed the outpatient principle, which holds that it is optimal for the patient to continue living and working in his ordinary, everyday-life ways as much as possible, seeing his psychiatrist, psychologist, social worker, therapist, teacher, or clergyman in successive sessions at intervals *in their offices.* Obviously this is a great saving of time and money for everyone. And, curiously, it has proved to be just as effective, statistically measured, in nurturing favorable change in patients as were our carefully planned and elaborated inpatient hospital programs. Not the least advantage was the diminished stigmatization of the non-confined patient.

All this the correctional system might emulate—and in some progressive jurisdictions it does. Some individuals have to be protected against themselves, some have to be protected from other prisoners, some even from the community. Some mental patients must be detained for a time even against their wishes, and the same is true of offenders. Offenders with propensities for impulsive and predatory aggression should not be permitted to live among us unrestrained by some kind of social control. *But the great majority of offenders, even "criminals," should never become prisoners if we want to "cure" them.*

What we want to accomplish is the reintegration of the temporarily suspended individual back into the main stream of social life, preferably a life at a higher level than before, just as soon as possible. Many, many precariously constituted individuals are trying to make it on the outside right now, with little help from us. We all have to keep reminding ourselves that *most offenders are never even apprehended.* Most of those who are caught and convicted, we must remember, are released either free or on probation. But they rarely have the benefit of treatment.

Parole and probation officers are thus indispensable, and the profession should be vastly elevated in numbers, in prestige, and in salary. Its responsibility is great and should be greater. By their counsel, encouragement, warning, and befriending, many one-time offenders, with whom they keep in touch, are supported in new life efforts by these skilled and experienced guides and friends.*

It is a curious thing that, important as we all recognize probation and parole to be, it rarely gets very much discussion. The President's Commission on Law Enforcement and Administration of Justice has many Task Force Reports, but not one on probation or parole, which are discussed in two chapters of the small volume on Corrections. There are numerous books on the subject, however, but not enough.†

A New Trend

A recent development in psychiatry is referred to by some as our "Third Revolution." After the cruelties of witchcraft trials, even the dreariness of custodial asylums in remote places reflected a revolutionary progress. Then came the modern concept of psychiatric hospitals, described earlier, which latterly included the day hospital, the night hospital, the half-way house, supervised foster home placement, and affiliated outpatient diagnostic and treatment departments. All this was the "Second Revolution."

The "Third Revolution" occurred when the therapeutic success

---

* "Denver courts have gained nation-wide attention through their pioneer work rehabilitating probationers and have made probation services and presentence investigation possible to misdemeanants. This program . . . was started in July of 1966 through the interest and efforts of Denver County's Chief Judge William Burnett even before such a recommendation was made by the President's Crime Commission. . . . Two features of the program are of paramount importance. These are the use of volunteers as probation supervisors, and the rapid evaluation of, and reporting on, the misdemeanant." (Afton, W. E.: "Denver Courts Blaze Trail with New Probation Services." *Bethesda Bulletin,* 43:4–6, Summer 1967.)

† See for example *Probation and Parole* by R. K. Clegg (Thomas, 1964) and the bibliography therein; and *A Guide to Psychiatric Books* by Karl Menninger (Grune & Stratton, 1956), pages 93–96.

and the economic advantages of outpatient treatment led to a general and widespread demand for more of it, more easily accessible. Psychiatric hospitals had nearly always been located in widely separated and far-removed places, often difficult of access for the majority of people. Psychiatrists in private practice were few, and located only in the larger cities. Consequently, psychiatric outpatient clinics began to develop in association with general hospitals and medical clinics.

These clinics often lacked provision for emergency care, temporary hospitalization for critically severe cases, and the special requirements for the treatment of children and young adults with psychiatric problems. They generally lacked, also, facilities for supervised work and recreation programs.

Thus, there arose the idea of *comprehensive mental-health centers* in various parts of every state (and in various locations within the big cities), heavily subsidized by the federal government, to make certain that no citizen would be more than a few hours from such a refuge, and could go there for any kind of psychiatric emergency at any time, and at a cost he could meet. The ideal staffing is a team of one or more psychiatrists, plus psychologists, social workers, therapists, secretaries, and others trained in the programs of scientific therapy described in earlier pages. To these clinics may come anyone in trouble or crisis: the depressed woman, the alcoholic man, the excited youth, the delinquent boy, the school failure, the discordant couple, the bewildered parent.

This description omits one essential feature. The mental-health center seeks to be in direct communication and in a working relationship with all the people of the area—not just the sick ones. Hence it will be in touch with all the institutions of the community which it serves—the schools, the hospitals, the police court, the prison, the industries, the churches—indeed with *every* form of organized human activity. The counsel of the clinic staff is available to the management of all these sister institutions.

It is the hope that a continuing improvement in the public attitude toward mental illness will follow and that instead of a dreaded affliction which strikes down some poor victims who must then be isolated in a state asylum somewhere, mental ill health will be seen as something which, in varying degrees, affects all citizens and which, in most instances, can be helped before reaching such extremities of manifestation or treatment requirement. Only the most severely disabled persons will have to be removed from the community for treatment, and they will be returned as swiftly as possible, not as tabooed objects, but as objects of the concern of local citizens.

A Proposal for Crime Prevention

Now for a flight of fancy regarding crime control and crime prevention. I submit it for the reader's contemplation:

Why couldn't something similar to what is being done for the insurance of public mental health be created for the insurance of public safety?

Why not a large number of *community safety centers* or crime prevention centers? A new and very different kind of glorified and dignified police substation *near* the people, known to the people and used by the people might be visualized. There would be many of these in larger cities—one for each neighborhood. They would contain records, laboratories, public safety materials, and offices for the police and parole officers. Each would have a defined authority for the protective surveillance and peace maintenance in a designated area.*

Such a center would be concerned far more with the preservation of peace and the prevention of crime than with the arrest and the mop-up. There would be free and intimate communication with the people and the group activities of that community—the schools, the churches, the parks, the beaches, the parades, the funerals. It

---

* I am not by any means the first to suggest decentralized police authority. There are many advantages in centralization, especially in finance and general control, but there are also well-known disadvantages, and I am proposing that these be taken seriously, or at least a trial of decentralization. (See also the article by Dr. Dae Hong Chang of Northern Illinois University in *Police*, March 1968, entitled "Police Reorganization as a Deterrent to Crime.")

would be the staff's function to assist the citizens in any kind of social difficulties which they encounter, up to and including such a difficulty as being molested or assaulted. Their concern would be for both the offender and more especially for those who *might be* offended.

The inhabitants of the area would also have their responsibility in assisting the officers of the center by consultation, by notification of plans, absences and arrivals, and by the taking of planned steps to correct known dangers. The field force would continually act to prevent vandalism, theft, assault, and similar offenses. However, if and when a crime occurs, as it undoubtedly will, the offenders or supposed offenders upon capture would be conveyed immediately to the proper center for identification and examination, and then, if indicated, transferred to a central court and/or diagnostic center. Later—if the judge so desires—a program for continuing correction and/or parole could be assigned, again to the officers of the local center.

These centers would inevitably elevate the prestige and importance of the police, upon whose improved functioning their success would hinge. The public would come to know them in a new and better way. Throughout history, police have gone from positions of ruthless, sadistic power to positions of mortified and frustrated impotence, and back again. In our culture, they are for the most part rather lonely individuals, pretty much restricted to the fellowship of their profession, and pretty sure that their efforts are not appreciated. They are subject to an incredible amount of uncertainty, anxiety, reproach, misunderstanding, misgivings, and temptations, as was brought out in the Report of the President's Commission on Law Enforcement.[3]

The reader may think of these neighborhood public safety centers as tending to give the police too much power, running the risk of the always-to-be-feared police state. The public wants the help of the police when danger threatens but it is reluctant to put them in a position to be protective, lest they become tyrannical. Right now the police are confused because they have been forbidden some of the old illegal and improper techniques which had been customary in many places for many years. This disconcerts and frustrates them; it gives them a sense of insecurity, because they have not all learned their new and proper roles and tools. To make matters worse, they are encouraged to entertain delusional thinking about the problem by some Senators and law professors who seriously suggest that even members of the Supreme Court are *conspiring* to impede their righteous and zealous efforts to "stop the criminal" at any cost!

August Vollmer, the great pioneer of modern American police science, made a remarkable report entitled "Policemen as Social Workers" to the International Association of Chiefs of Police as far back as 1919. In it he urged all police to take an active interest, and even assume leadership wherever possible, in general movements to improve their communities. It was an essential part of crime prevention and control, he said, for the policeman to help get better housing in slum areas, better schools, more health clinics for children, improved welfare services for indigents, more adequate aid for the physically and mentally handicapped.*

It seems to me obvious that the police of the city should all be superior individuals if we expect to identify and curb transgressions. They should all have a good basic education plus a thorough preparation in technical training and theoretical substructure which would include an orientation in behavioral science. The training

* "Few professional urban police agencies would accept Vollmer's thesis as their functional responsibility. The probable police response to Vollmer's report today would be: Whose side are you on? . . . [This question] is part of a scare process. The exhortation, 'Support Your Local Police' may really mean, according to Joseph D. Lohman, Dean of the School of Criminology of the University of California, a defensive posture by the police to further polarize the public in reference to such questions as the celebrated Supreme Court decisions." (Webster, John A.: "Whose Side Are You On?" *Issues in Criminology*, 3:1–6, 1967.)

Nevertheless, there is a new spirit and social philosophy in the police profession which is most heartening. See, for example, the account of one young intelligent leader in Detroit: Mlecyko, L.: "A Humane Cop (Donald Stevens) Urges Change by and for Police." (*Police Times*, 5:5, 1968.)

emphasis should be on prevention rather than upon detective actions. Granted that there is no school like that of experience, a preparation for the best use of that experience as it involves the policemen should go far beyond training in the use of a revolver and filling out a notification of arrest and court summons.

What is much needed and almost completely neglected in police training is child and adolescent psychology. The importance of such understanding takes on new meaning when one realizes that in almost every case the child's initial contact with the law is with a policeman. Any child engaged in a delinquent act will see a policeman before he sees a social worker or a psychiatrist or a court officer, and the skill with which that initial contact is managed can have a great deal to do with that child's developing attitudes about authority.

One group has recently included a public relations training program for their police schooling. It consists of both lecture materials and role-playing situations. The program topics indicate the nature of the coverage:

1. The development in police officers of an appreciation of the civil rights of others.

2. The development in police officers of the ability to meet without undue militance, aggressiveness, hostility, or injustice, police situations involving minority groups.

3. The development in police officers of an adequate social perspective.

4. The development in police officers of an awareness of individual and group difference.

5. The development of understanding by police officers of how their words and actions may be perceived by the public.

6. The development in police officers of an acceptance of integrated situations.

7. To develop in police officers the knowledge of the fact that their behavior will infuse similar intergroup behaviors and attitudes in other members of the police force.

8. The development in police officers of a recognition and awareness of the role of associated community human relations agencies.

9. The development in police officers of the skills requisite for antici-pating and meeting the police-human relations aspects of: (a) their work; (b) incidents rooted in factors of race, religion, and national origin; (c) juvenile offenses; (d) civil rights complaints; and (e) community tensions.[4]

Few police officers receive training in these critical areas. Those who have studied this matter intensively can say more specifically what the training should include, but it is indisputable that there should be more of it, higher standards, and much higher pay. Only in this way can police corruption and police brutality and police bullying be eliminated and replaced by the dignity, public respect, and public cooperation which this function of our government de-serves.*

The police officer is expected to do a superman's job. He is ex-pected to be more brave, more upright, more self-controlled, more resistant to bribery and other temptations, more courteous, more discriminating, more shrewd, more unruffled by humiliation and frustration than all other citizens. He has to make rapid decisions many times a day in difficult situations. The average policeman renders far more judgments of guilty and not guilty than does the average judge. He has to call upon extraordinary resources of tact, experience, knowledge, and training to deal correctly at the needed moment with threatening or suspicious behavior.

To this paragon of virtue, courage, and responsibility, the com-munity pays almost its lowest civic wage, but even so it is generally higher than that received by parole and probation officers and by prison "guards."

* Having visited or entertained or listened to or counseled with the police in his community, the average citizen might pay a visit to his local jail. Groups of citizens could go together. Most jail personnel will welcome such a show of interest in what they are trying to do. They may even confess some of their misgivings about present practices, or air their needs. It is sur-prising how few citizens have ever visited a jail or attended a criminal trial or even a police court session. Why not include such visits as a part of both public school and adult education?

"Policeman as Philosopher, Guide and Friend" is the wonderful title given to a recent report by a mental-health research unit. Is he that? Could he become that? Is this not something the public must help accomplish? These workers kept track of eight hundred and one incoming telephone calls at the complaint desk of a metropolitan police department over a period of three or four days. One hundred and forty-nine (18.6 per cent) of these were excluded from analysis for good reasons. The remaining six hundred and fifty-two calls were requests for service. About one-third of these were for service in connection with things or possessions, traffic violations, losses or theft, unlocked doors, fallen power wires, and so on. About one-half of the calls were for requests for support or assistance with regard to problems of health, safety, or interpersonal relationships.

What interests us more, however, are several impressions which the workers reported:

First: poor, uneducated people appear to use the police in the way that middle-class people use family doctors and clergymen—that is, as the first port of call in time of trouble.

Second: the policeman must often enforce unpopular laws among these poor people at the same time that he sees these laws being flouted by those in positions of power.

Third: many policemen are themselves recruited from and are sympathetic to the class of people from whom most of the "interpersonal" calls for assistance come.

Fourth: the police have little knowledge of or liaison with social agencies or even medical agencies, and seem to feel that these agencies' activities are irrelevant to the problems they, themselves, face.

Fifth: the police appear to have a genuine concern for children and for those they regard as disturbed and ill. They are tolerant, for example, about many crank calls, and will, if a car is available, help a paranoid old lady search her house for the malignant intruder she feels sure is hiding there. Nevertheless, it is possible to see clearly in various revealing episodes how their own values transcend the rights of the individual.

Sixth: many policemen are bitter about their low pay, the label "punitive" applied to them in a world that values "warmth," the conflicting demands of their jobs, and the ingratitude of the public.[5]

Police science is gradually changing for the better but it needs encouragement from a more understanding public. The police can't be shouted at by one faction to "treat 'em rough and keep 'em out of our sight" and exhorted by another faction to be the friendly monitors of public safety.

Citizen Responsibility

There are throughout the country many citizen action groups and programs for the prevention and control of crime and delinquency. The National Council on Crime and Delinquency, founded in 1907 as the National Probation Association, since 1955 has established state citizen action councils in nineteen states and the District of Columbia, and over one hundred and fifty local citizen action committees. Its aim is eventually to establish state and local councils in all states.

In the state of Washington a strong public information and citizen involvement program was brought into being in about a five-year period. One newspaper wrote an editorial to the effect that "more had been accomplished during the past five years than the previous ninety-five from the standpoint of prison and correctional reform." A great many major reform pieces of legislation were passed. When the program was started, over half of the daily newspapers in the state wrote extremely negative news stories and editorials. However, after the involvement of several news-media people on the Washington Citizen's Council and the release of many reports to the public on problems and needs in the correctional field, every one of the daily newspapers in the state began to write approvingly of the program.

A significant change in public thinking was brought about. The state, which in 1955 was cited by United Press International as having the "worst prison system in the country," was, five years later, considered to have one of the nation's better correctional systems.

Correction has been completely removed from partisan politics, and a merit system effected. Labor, for the first time in history, supported the first state prison industries program. The office of sheriff was removed from politics. A twenty-five-million-dollar bond issue, including several million dollars for correctional facilities, was voted by the people.[6]

A group of concerned women formed an anti-crime crusade in Indianapolis in 1962, demanding of city officials safe streets for themselves and their children. Tired of the "We're doing our best" clichés, they acted on their own! They exerted their energies and efforts in many ways, including evaluation of the law enforcement agencies and their needs, and analyzing the operation of the courts. In 1965, the crime rate in Indianapolis dropped for the first time since 1959, while the national rate rose six per cent.[7]

With such attitudes of inquiry and concern, the public could acquire information (and incentive) leading to a change of feeling about crime and criminals. It will discover how unjust is much so-called "justice," how baffled and frustrated many judges are by the ossified rigidity of old-fashioned, obsolete laws and state constitutions which effectively prevent the introduction of sensible procedures to replace useless, harmful ones. It will learn of the sentencing schools which some judges attend to try to make the best of a bad situation, and of the Model Penal Code evolved by so much painstaking effort by representatives of the American Bar Association and Bar Institute.*

* Many opportunities exist today for the citizen to learn something about crime from sources more reliable than television skits, murder mysteries, and newspaper stories. Many civic and literary clubs pay some attention to crime problems, and the conferences, institutes, and courses available in university towns and in the larger cities are very numerous. They are listed and described briefly each month in *News Bulletin* of the National Council on Crime and Delinquency. A new book in the field appears almost daily—some of which are superb, such as Seymour Halleck's *Psychiatry and the Dilemmas of Crime* (New York: Harper & Row, 1967). There are several scores of journals in the field, and many periodicals now contain well-written scientific essays on aspects of crime and crime prevention. A few of the journals

Will the public listen?

If the public does become interested, it will realize that we must have more facts, more trial projects, more checked results. It will share the dismay of the President's Commission in finding that no one knows much about even the incidence of crime with any definiteness or statistical accuracy. We are told that of two thousand *known* crimes the police are only notified in about fifty per cent of the cases; when notified they come about three-fourths of the time; and in four out of five times no arrest is made. Of the twenty per cent of offenders who are arrested, more than one-half are dismissed without a trial; of the forty per cent who are tried, about one-half are convicted, and *some* of these serve some kind of a sentence. Usually it is for the second or third or tenth time.[8]

About all this, we need more information, more research, more experimental data. That research is the basis for scientific progress, no one any more disputes. Industry knows it; the military establishment knows it; all scientists know it. The public gives tacit approval to it, and in many instances pays the bills generously without being sure what the research is, where it is needed, or what is or should be done.

The average citizen finds it difficult to see how any research would in any way change his mind about a man who brutally murders his children. But just such inconceivably awful acts most dramatically point up the need for research. Why should—how can—a man become so dreadful as that in our culture? How is such a man made? Is it comprehensible that he can be born to become so depraved?

With so many different proposals of new programs and experiments in rehabilitation, there should be a way to check on how successful each of these actually is. Almost any program will get *some* results and is apt to be praised indiscriminately. But it is not so

---

I see regularly are: *The British Journal of Criminology, Crime and Delinquency, Crime and Delinquency Abstracts, Federal Probation, Excerpta Criminologica, Issues in Criminology, Key Issues, The Journal of Criminal Law, Criminology and Police Science.*

easy as it might appear to check accurately on the effectiveness of a rehabilitative program. Social research is a particularly difficult field and requires careful planning and control. Even our present prisons, bad as many of them are, could be extensively used as laboratories for the study of many of the unsolved problems.

There are thousands of questions regarding crime and public protection which deserve scientific study. What makes some individuals maintain their interior equilibrium by one kind of disturbance of the social structure rather than by another kind, one that would have landed him in a hospital? Why do some individuals specialize in certain types of crime? Why do so many young people reared in areas of delinquency and poverty and bad example never become habitual delinquents? (Perhaps this is a more important question than why some of them do.) Why is there so little delinquency and crime in Greece * and in China?

These and a great many other questions remain to be solved by the patient methods of scientific investigation. But, in the meantime, we need not wait for results of the new research findings. *For we have at hand great quantities of research findings which clearly indicate what we should be doing. Much indeed we don't know, but we are not doing one-tenth of what we should about what we already do know.*

Consuming Justice

What I am proposing here is simply that the public take seriously the difficulties and complexities of insuring the peace, and take a hand in the matter rather than dumping all the responsibility onto the police. They must help the police. They must help

---

* I inquired of several colleagues about the crime situation in Greece when I was in Athens and elsewhere in that beautiful country. They suggested that Greek men do have many vices, some of which would cause arrest in this country. They beat their wives and fight with their friends—then all is forgiven. But holdups, robberies, assaults, rapes, and murders are less frequent. Why is this? What has Greece that we do not have? What do the Greek mothers do that we fail to do?

the judges. They must help the parole and probation officers. It is *our* safety and welfare which is involved.

The public, in short, could be and should be what Edmond Cahn called *consumers of justice,* instead of merely providers of it, supplying it, endorsing it, paying for it, and deploring its poor distribution. How does one become a consumer of justice? In these ways, answers Professor Cahn:

> He consumes justice by being safeguarded and regulated from day to day as one fills his place in society . . . [one consumes] public justice whenever one talks or writes, works or sleeps, buys or sells. One may also consume it in a more dramatic way, as by engaging in a lawsuit or being charged with a crime.
>
> In a democracy, a citizen consumes justice still more extensively when he influences the shape of policy and legislation, casts his vote, and asserts the interests of a special group or of the whole community.
>
> Finally, there is a third way to consume justice. It consists of the people's examining and assuming responsibility for what officials do in their name and by their authority—the unjust and evil acts as well as the beneficent and good.[9]

Charles D. McAtee, director of Penal Institutions for the State of Kansas, recently declared:

> If we really intend to combat the problem, let's start at the grass-roots level with community action committees who can best pool and coordinate the local resources available to combat crime. I believe that an informed, concerned, and aroused citizenry can have a tremendous impact on the causative factors of crime and delinquency, and that local community committees, dedicated to this effort and utilizing local community resources, can not only prevent crime, but can more adequately provide reasonable alternatives to imprisonment, for some of those who are involved in criminal offenses.[10]

I agree completely. Public education and involvement are the first steps in any permanent, constructive change in our wretchedly inadequate, self-destroying, self-injuring, crime-encouraging system. Not that the public will straightaway rise up and ask for the radical changes that ought to be made. But once it knows, once it really perceives that the present pretentious procedure is falling on its face and endangering us all, once it discovers that better methods are well known and available but ignored and unused by those in authority—once the public becomes informed, it will become correspondingly aroused. It will let its demands be known to legislatures and officials, and the situation will change.

I have seen it happen. I saw the reaction of the people of Kansas to the discovery of the facts about their wretched state hospitals as exposed by the newspapers in 1948, and I saw the legislators' reactions to the people's reaction. They promptly hired a director of state institutions at twice the Governor's salary and told him to do what was necessary to modernize Kansas mental hospitals. Furthermore, they voted him the money to do it, and he did it. And I saw the people of Kansas confound the legislature and the political leaders two years later by voting two to one in favor of a constitutional amendment for a permanent mill tax for hospital construction, an amendment which was "sure to be defeated."

What had happened? Simply a change of attitude based on adequate information. The public learned that their relatives were not getting effective treatment and that with such treatment these patients could return (or could have returned) home. True, effective treatment would cost some money, far more per day than the state had been spending, but since the number of days would be reduced from thousands to scores, the people would save money and the patients would be saved suffering.

The people believed what we said, and their legislators voted the additional money. The cost *per day* went up five times. But the cost *for each discharged patient* went down *more* than five times. The state mental hospital budget has never since then been an item of political controversy, and not once in nineteen years has it been seriously curtailed.

Today there are forty times as many psychiatrists and graduate nurses in the Kansas state hospitals as in 1948. More than forty times as much therapy is given—and there are forty times as many recoveries. And there are forty times forty more private citizens helping with the state mental-health programs as volunteers, companions, foster parents, or staff employees.

Some day, somewhere, the same thing will happen with respect to transgressors and offenders. It will be harder to bring about, for reasons we have given: the public has a fascination for violence, and clings tenaciously to its yen for vengeance, blind and deaf to the expense, futility, and dangerousness of the resulting penal system. But we are bound to hope that this will yield in time to the persistent, penetrating light of intelligence and accumulating scientific knowledge. The public will grow increasingly ashamed of its cry for retaliation, its persistent demand to punish. This is its crime, *our* crime against criminals—and incidentally our crime against ourselves. For before we can diminish our sufferings from the ill-controlled aggressive assaults of fellow citizens, we must renounce the philosophy of punishment, the obsolete, vengeful penal attitude. In its place we would seek a comprehensive, constructive social attitude—therapeutic in some instances, restraining in some instances, but preventive in its total social impact.

In the last analysis this becomes a question of personal morals and values. No matter how glorified or how piously disguised, vengeance as a human motive must be personally repudiated by each and every one of us. This is the message of old religions and new psychiatries. Unless this message is heard, unless we, the people— the man on the street, the housewife in the home—can give up our delicious satisfactions in opportunities for vengeful retaliation on scapegoats, we cannot expect to preserve our peace, our public safety, or our mental health.

Can we? Will we?

I must stop here, leaving this unfinished. The whole subject is an area of accelerated change. This in itself is heartening. There is hope, too, in the news that . . .

Reference Notes

1. The Injustice of Justice

1. *Time,* September 9, 1966, pp. 26–27.
2. Carpenter, Don: Review of *In Cold Blood* by Truman Capote. *Ramparts,* April 1966, pp. 51–52.
3. Nietzsche, F. W.: *Beyond Good and Evil,* Vol. 15 of *Complete Works of F. W. Nietzsche,* Helen Zimmern, tr. New York: Macmillan, 1910.
4. Schafer, William J., III: "How About a Constitution for the Victim?" *Police,* March-April 1967, pp. 82–84.
5. Cahn, Lenore L., ed.: *Confronting Injustice: The Edmond Cahn Reader.* Boston: Little, Brown and Co., 1966, p. 385.
6. *Ibid.,* p. 239.

2. Who Is to Blame?

1. Holmes, Oliver Wendell: "The Path of the Law," 10 *Harvard Law Review,* 457, 469 (1897).
2. *Time,* March 25, 1966.
3. Eliot, T. S.: *The Cocktail Party.* New York: Harcourt, Brace and Co., 1950.

3. Crimes against Criminals

1. Emrick, Robert L.: Quoted in *Science News,* 90:305, October 15, 1966.
2. Vorenberg, James: *Ibid.*
3. LaFave, W. R.: *Arrest.* Boston: Little, Brown and Co., 1966.
4. Westley, William A.: "Violence and the Police." *Amer. J. Sociol.,* 59:34–41, 1953–54.

5. *The One Hundred and Twentieth Annual Report of The Correctional Association of New York.* State of New York Legislative Document (1965), No. 97, p. 31.

6. *Time,* June 12, 1964, pp. 67–68.

7. Goldfarb, Ronald: *Ransom: A Critique of the American Bail System.* New York: Harper & Row, 1965.

8. See also the series in *Indianapolis Star,* 1959–1960.

9. *The New York Times,* February 24, 1964.

10. Goldfarb, Ronald: "No Room in the Jail." *The New Republic,* 154: 12–14, March 5, 1966.

11. *Chicago Sun-Times,* December 6, 1967, p. 1.

12. *Ibid.*

13. Some other books are: Barnes, Harry E., and Teeters, N. K.: *New Horizons in Criminology,* 3rd Edition. New York: Prentice-Hall, 1959. Barnes, Harry E.: *The Repression of Crime.* New York: Doran, 1926. Beaumont, Gustave de, and Tocqueville, Alexis de: *On the Penitentiary System in the United States and Its Application in France.* Philadelphia: Carey, 1833 (Reprinted by Southern Illinois University Press, Carbondale, Ill., 1964). Deutsch, Albert: *The Trouble With Cops.* New York: Crown Publishers, 1955. Gillin, John L.: *Taming the Criminal.* New York: Macmillan, 1931. Martin, John Bartlow: *Break Down the Walls.* New York: Ballantine, 1954. Osborne, Thomas Mott: *Prisons and Common Sense.* Philadelphia: Lippincott, 1924. Sutherland, Edwin H.: *Principles of Criminology,* 5th Edition. Philadelphia: Lippincott, 1955. Tannenbaum, Frank: *Wall Shadows: A Study in American Prisons.* New York: Putnam, 1922.

14. Howard, John: *The State of the Prisons, in England and Wales.* Printed by William Eyres, 1777. Abridged edition published by Dent in 1929.

15. *Time,* April 29, 1966, p. 53.

16. Newman, Donald J.: "Pleading Guilty for Considerations: A Study of Bargain Justice." *J. Crim. Law, Criminol. & Police Sci.,* 46: 780–790, 1956.

17. Kalven, Harry, Jr., and Zeisel, Hans: *The American Jury.* Boston: Little, Brown and Co., 1966, p. 361.

18. *Miami Herald,* March 16, 1967—Jeff Antevil, staff writer.

19. Frank, Jerome: *Courts on Trial.* Princeton: Princeton University Press, 1949, pp. 91–93.

20. Berne, Eric: *Games People Play.* New York: Grove Press, Inc., 1964.

21. Rapoport, Anatol: *Fights, Games, and Debates.* Ann Arbor: University of Michigan Press, 1960.

22. *Time,* May 13, 1966, p. 81.

23. Marshall, James: *Law and Psychology in Conflict.* New York: Bobbs-Merrill Co., 1966.

24. Stafford, Ellen: "The Ordeal of Steven Truscott." *The Nation,* 202: 614–617, 1966. Williams, Robert S., Jr.: "I Was Accused of a Sex Crime." *Saturday Evening Post,* August 9, 1952, pp. 17 ff. Phelan, James R.: "Innocent's Grim Ordeal." *Saturday Evening Post,* February 2, 1963, pp. 63–67. Radin, Edward J.: *The Innocents.* New York: William Morrow & Co., 1964. Borchard, Edwin M.: *Convicting the Innocent.* New Haven, Conn.: Yale University Press, 1932. Hale, Leslie: *Hanged in Error.* Baltimore: Penguin Books, 1961.

25. Zeisel, Hans: Personal communication.

26. Appleman, John A.: *Cross-Examination.* Fairfax, Va.: Coiner Publications, 1963.

27. Kalven and Zeisel: *op. cit.,* p. 4.

28. *Ibid.,* pp. 5–6.

29. Lindner, Robert M.: *Stone Walls and Men.* New York: Odyssey Press, 1946.

30. Kalven and Zeisel: *op. cit.,* pp. 498–499.

31. Cited in "Why Judges Can't Sleep" by Ruth and Edward Brecher. *Saturday Evening Post,* 230:25, 96–98, July 13, 1957.

32. *Ibid.*

33. Wootton, Barbara: *Crime and the Criminal Law.* London: Stevens & Sons, 1963, pp. 91–92.

34. *Wichita Eagle,* November 18, 1965, p. 1.

35. The Model Sentencing Act appears in the October 1963 issue of *Crime and Delinquency,* with interpretative articles by Gerald F. Flood, Manfred S. Guttmacher, George Edwards, and Sanger B. Powers. It is also published as a separate pamphlet by the National Council on Crime and Delinquency. See also Sol Rubin's article "The Model Sentencing Act" in the *New York University Law Rev.* (39:251–262, April 1964).

36. Ulmer, Walter F.: "History of Maine Correctional Institutions." *Amer. J. Correction,* 27:33, July-August 1965.
37. Bennett, James V.: "In the Can as Men or Sardines." *Atlantian,* 24: 2–3, Fall, 1965.
38. Barnes, Harry Elmer: "The Contemporary Prison: A Menace to Inmate Rehabilitation and the Repression of Crime." *Key Issues,* 2:11–23, 1965.
39. Clemmer, Donald: Cited in "Barriers to Progress in Corrections: The High Cost of Taking Science Seriously" by Joseph Satten. *Amer. Corr. Assn. Proceedings of the 93rd Annual Congress,* 1963, pp. 23–31.
40. Lindner, *op. cit.*
41. Sykes, Gresham M.: *The Society of Captives.* Princeton: Princeton University Press, 1958.
42. Sands, Bill: *My Shadow Ran Fast.* Englewood Cliffs, N.J.: Prentice-Hall, 1964, pp. 52–54.
43. Barnes: "The Contemporary Prison," pp. 14–15.
44. Gillin, John L.: *Taming the Criminal.* New York: Macmillan, 1931.
45. *Chicago Daily News,* April 17, 1967.
46. Rubin, Sol: *The Law of Criminal Correction.* St. Paul, Minn.: West Publishing Co., 1963.
47. Gollwitzer, Helmut; Scheider, Reinhold; and Huhn, Käthe, eds.: *Dying We Live.* New York: Pantheon Books, 1956.
48. Settle, Russell: Personal communication.
49. Smith, Sydney: "Delinquency and the Panacea of Punishment." *Fed. Probat.,* 29:18–23, 1965.
50. Goldstein, Joseph: "Police Discretion Not to Invoke the Criminal Process: Low-Visibility Decisions in the Administration of Justice." *Yale Law J.,* 69:543 ff., November-March, 1959-1960.

4. The Cold War between Lawyers and Psychiatrists

1. Gould, Donald: "Doctors in the Witness Box." *New Statesman,* October 14, 1966, p. 548.
2. *Saturday Review,* July 2, 1966, p. 49.
3. Ross, Neil W.: "Some Philosophical Considerations of the Legal-Psychiatric Debate of Criminal Responsibility." *Issues in Criminology,* 1:34 ff., 1965.

4. Rodell, Fred: *Woe Unto You, Lawyers!* New York: Pageant Press, 1939, 1957.
5. Ross, *op. cit.*
6. Wyden, Peter: *The Hired Killers.* New York: William Morrow & Co., 1963.

5. Right and Wrong Uses of Psychiatry

1. Roche, Philip Q.: "A Plea for the Abandonment of the Defense of Insanity." In *Crime, Law and Corrections,* Ralph Slovenko, ed. Springfield, Ill.: Charles C Thomas, 1966, p. 406.
2. Roche, Philip Q.: *The Criminal Mind.* New York: Farrar, Straus and Cudahy, 1958.
3. *Durham v. United States,* 214 F.2d 862.
4. Satten, Joseph: Personal communication.
5. White, William Alanson: *Insanity and The Criminal Law.* New York: Macmillan, 1923. *Crimes and Criminals.* New York: Farrar & Rinehart, 1933.
6. Menninger, Karl: "The Psychiatrist in Relation to Crime." In *Proceedings of the American Bar Association, Criminal Law Section,* Denver, Colo., July 13, 1926.
7. Rodell, *op. cit.,* pp. 130–131.
8. *Ibid.,* p. 131.
9. Bazelon, David L.: *Equal Justice for the Unequal* (Isaac Ray Lectureship Award Series of The American Psychiatric Association, University of Chicago, 1961.) Unpublished.
10. Wiseman, Frederick: "Psychiatry and Law: Use and Abuse of Psychiatry in a Murder Case." *Amer. J. Psychiat.,* 118:289–299, 1961.
11. *Ibid.,* p. 297.
12. *Ibid.,* p. 297.
13. Glasner, Saul: "Benign Parological Thinking." *Arch. Gen. Psychiat.,* 14:94–99, 1966.
14. Bowman, Karl, and Rose, Milton: "A Criticism of the Terms 'Psychosis,' 'Psychoneurosis,' and 'Neurosis.'" *Amer. J. Psychiat.,* 108:161–166, 1951.
15. A scholarly article on this subject is that of Joseph Goldstein and Jay Katz: "Abolish the 'Insanity Defense'—Why Not?" *Yale Law J.,* 72:853–876, 1963.

16. Glueck, Sheldon: *Crime and Justice.* Boston: Little, Brown and Co., 1936.
17. Glueck, Sheldon: *Law and Psychiatry: Cold War or Entente Cordiale?* Baltimore: Johns Hopkins Press, 1962, p. 145.
18. *Ibid.,* p. 152.
19. See the excellent essay of my associate, Ralph Slovenko: "Psychiatry, Criminal Law, and the Role of the Psychiatrist." *Duke Law J.,* 1963, pp. 395–496.
20. *Hutchinson* (Kansas) *News,* December 11, 1965.
21. Szasz, Thomas: *Psychiatric Justice.* New York: Macmillan, 1965.
22. Suarez, John M.: "The Law Psychiatry Conspiracy." Unpublished manuscript reviewed by Patricia McBroom in *Science News,* 89:385, 1966.

6. *The Apparent Indifference of the Public to Its Safety*

1. Hoover, J. Edgar: "The Fortress of Free Men." *The New Age Magazine,* December 1965.
2. Ward, Mary Jane: *The Snake Pit.* New York: Random House, 1946.
3. Brennan, William J., Jr.: "Law and Psychiatry Must Join in Defending Mentally Ill Criminals." *Amer. Bar Assn. J.,* 49:239–253, 1963.
4. *Amarillo Daily News,* March 11, 1965.
5. *U.S. News & World Report,* January 23, 1967.
6. *Topeka Daily Capital* and other newspapers, November 7, 1965.
7. Tulloch, Donald P.: "The Sheriff and the County Jail." In *Program of the 28th Annual Convention of The National Jail Association,* August 28–September 1, 1966, p. 13.
8. Mattick, Hans W.: Foreword to "The Future of Imprisonment in a Free Society." *Key Issues,* 2:4–10, 1965.

7. *Innate Violence*

1. Nevins, Allan: "The Glorious and the Terrible." *Saturday Review,* September 2, 1961, pp. 9–11.
2. Munn, Geoff: Quoted in "Books and the Arts" by Paul F. Semonin. *The Nation,* January 31, 1966.
3. Cousins, Norman: *Saturday Review,* May 6, 1962, p. 15.
4. Fremont-Smith, Eliot: Book review of *Black Is Best* by Jack Olsen. *The New York Times,* February 10, 1967.

5. Capote, Truman: *In Cold Blood.* New York: Random House, 1965.

6. Dostoevski, Feodor: *The Idiot,* Constance Garnett, tr. New York: Modern Library, 1935, p. 356.

7. Honan, William H.: "TV and the 'Bloody' Classics." *Quart. J. Speech,* 51:147–151, April 1965.

8. Menninger, Karl: "Toward the Understanding of Violence." *J. Human Relations,* 13:418–426, 1965.

9. Wertham, Fredric: "Is So Much Violence in Films Necessary?" *The Journal of the Producers Guild of America,* 9:4–5, December 1967.

10. Jones, Ernest: "The Problem of Paul Morphy: A Contribution to the Psychoanalysis of Chess." *Int. J. Psychoanal.,* 12:1–23, 1931.

11. Slovenko, Ralph, and Knight, James A., eds.: *Motivations in Play, Games and Sports.* Springfield, Ill.: Charles C Thomas, 1967.

12. *Time,* May 13, 1966.

13. Redl, Fritz, and Wineman, David: *Children Who Hate.* New York: Free Press, 1951.

14. Bettelheim, Bruno: "Violence: A Neglected Mode of Behavior." *Ann. Amer. Acad. Polit. Soc. Sci.,* 364:50–59, March 1966.

15. Freud, Sigmund: "Civilization and Its Discontents." In *The Complete Works of Sigmund Freud,* Vol. 21, James Strachey, tr. London: Hogarth Press, 1961, p. 145.

16. Mailloux, Noël: "Functioning of the Superego in Delinquents." *Int. Psychiat. Clinics,* 2:61–81, 1965.

17. Alexander, Franz: *The Criminal, The Judge, and The Public.* New York: Macmillan, 1931.

18. Halleck, Seymour: "Psychopathy, Freedom and Criminal Behavior." *Bull. Menninger Clin.,* 30:127–140, 1966.

19. Proelss, E. Frederick: *Reflections on the Social, Moral, Cultural, and Spiritual Aspects of the Prison Chaplain's Ministry.* Riker's Island, New York: New York City Correctional Institution for Men, n.d.

20. Mencken, H. L.: "Criminology." *Baltimore Evening Sun,* July 12, 1926.

21. Halleck, Seymour: *Psychiatry and the Dilemmas of Crime.* New York: Harper & Row, 1967.

22. Menninger, Karl: *The Vital Balance.* New York: The Viking Press, 1963.

23. Halleck: *Psychiatry and the Dilemmas of Crime,* pp. 77–80.

24. Redwood City, Calif., *Tribune,* November 9, 1963.
25. Sherrill, Robert G.: "The Big Shoot." *The Nation,* 202:260–264, 1966.
26. Boyle, Sarah Patton, and Griffin, John Howard: "The Racial Crisis: An Exchange of Letters." *The Christian Century,* 85:679–683, May 22, 1968.
27. Sander, Joseph L.: "A Study in Law and Order." *The Nation,* 206:655–657, May 20, 1968.

8. *Vengeance Is Mine, Saith the Lord*

1. Luther, Martin: *Works of Martin Luther,* Vol. IV. Philadelphia: A. J. Holman Co., with the Castle Press, 1931.
2. Kramer, Samuel Noah: *History Begins at Sumer.* New York: Doubleday, 1959.
3. Livingston, Edward: *Complete Works on Criminal Jurisprudence,* 2 Vols. New York: National Prison Association of the United States of America, 1873.
4. *The Atlantian,* Fall 1965, pp. 24, 26.
5. Taft, William Howard: "Toward a Reform of the Criminal Law." In *The Drift of Civilization.* New York: Simon & Schuster, 1929.
6. Shoenfeld, C. G.: "In Defense of Retribution in the Law." *Psychoanal. Quart.,* 35:108–121, 1966.
7. Stephen, Sir James: *A History of the Criminal Law of England,* Vol. II. London: Macmillan, 1883, p. 81.
8. Rubin, *op. cit.*
9. Weihofen, Henry: *The Urge to Punish.* New York: Farrar, Straus & Cudahy, 1956, p. 138.
10. Dodd, David J.: "Police Mentality and Behavior." *Issues in Criminology,* 3:54, 1967.
11. *Kansas City Star,* June 4, 1966.
12. Copyright 1959, *Philadelphia Evening Bulletin.*
13. *The New Republic,* December 26, 1914, pp. 9–10.
14. Waelder, Robert, and Morris, Clarence: "The Concept of Justice and the Quest for a Perfectly Just Society—A Dialogue." *U. Pa. Law Rev.,* Vol. 115, No. 1, November 1966.
15. "Woman Vows Not to Drive." *Topeka Daily Capital,* June 7, 1956.
16. Encyclopaedia Britannica: *The Great Ideas: A Syntopicon of Great*

Books of the Western World, Vol. II. Chicago: Encyclopaedia Britannica, 1952, pp. 488–495.

17. *Ibid.*

18. Bittner, Egon, and Platt, A. M.: "The Meaning of Punishment." *Issues in Criminology,* 2:79–99, 1966.

19. Solomon, Richard L.: "Punishment." *Amer. Psychologist,* 19:239–253, 1964.

20. Smith, Sydney: "Delinquency and the Panacea of Punishment." *Fed. Prob.,* 29:18–23, 1965.

21. Lewis, Anthony: "7 Electrical Officials Get Jail Terms in Trust Case." *The New York Times,* February 7, 1961.

22. *The New Yorker,* January 14, 1961.

23. Duncan, Glen M.; Frazier, Shervert H.; Litin, Edward M.; Johnson, Adelaide M.; and Barron, Alfred J.: "Etiological Factors in First-Degree Murder." *JAMA,* 168:1755–1758, 1958.

24. Sanford, Nevitt: *Self and Society.* New York: Atherton Press, 1966, p. 123.

25. Menninger, Karl: *Love Against Hate.* New York: Harcourt, Brace and Co., 1942.

26. Conrad, Earl: *Mr. Seward for the Defense.* New York: Rinehart & Co., 1956, pp. 258–259.

9. Have There Been No Improvements?

1. Weeks, H. Ashley: "Treatment: Past, Present and Possible." *Key Issues,* 2:57–62, 1965.

2. Teeters, Negley K.: "The Dilemma in the Field of Modern Corrections." *Criminologica,* 2:11, February 1965.

3. *Cambridge Essays,* 1956, p. 17.

4. Livingston, Edward: *Complete Works on Criminal Jurisprudence.* New York: National Prison Association of the United States of America, 1873.

5. Missouri Association for Criminal Justice: *Missouri Crime Survey,* Raymond Moley, ed. New York: Macmillan, 1926.

6. Allen, Francis A.: "Criminal Justice, Legal Values and the Rehabilitative Ideal." *J. Crim. Law, Criminol. & Police Sci.,* 50:226–232, 1959.

7. Lejins, Peter P.: "Agenda for Corrections." *Amer. J. Correction,* Vol. 25, No. 5, September-October 1963.

8. "A Lesson from Chino." *Pioneer News*, 25:31, June 1966.
9. Wolfe, Burton H.: "Reshaping Convict Behavior." *Think*, 32:25–29, September-October 1966.
10. Rubin, *op. cit.*, p. 290.
11. Sadler, Ray: "How One State Helps Former Convicts Stay Free." *The National Observer*, December 18, 1967, p. 6.
12. *Time*, September 4, 1964.
13. Bennett, James V.: *Of Prisons and Justice*. Washington, D.C.: U.S. Government Printing Office, 1964.
14. Stürup, G. K.: "The Treatment of Chronic Criminals." *Bull. Menninger Clin.*, 28:229–243, 1964.
15. Smith, Sydney: Personal communication.
16. MacCormick, Austin H., ed.: *Handbook of American Prisons and Reformatories*, 5th edition, Vol. II. New York: The Osborne Association, 1942.
17. Lindner, *op. cit.*, p. 401.
18. de Ford, Miriam: *Stone Walls*. New York: Chilton Co., 1962.
19. *The Bench Warrant* (Topeka Police Department house organ), April 11, 1967.
20. *New York Herald Tribune*, February 22, 1965.
21. Cooper, Irving Ben: "To Make the First Step in Crime the Last." *Reader's Digest*, 63:35–39, 1953.
22. *The Challenge of Crime in a Free Society: A Report by the President's Commission on Law Enforcement and the Administration of Justice*. Washington, D.C.: U.S. Government Printing Office, 1967.
23. Kopkind, Andrew: "And Now the Safe Society." *New Statesman*, March 3, 1967, p. 281.

10. Love against Hate

1. Boulding, Kenneth: *There is a Spirit: The Nayler Sonnets*. New York: Fellowship Publications, 1945.
2. Menninger, Karl: "The War Against Fear and Hate." *Bull. Menninger Clin.*, 8:101–106, 1944.
3. *The Challenge of Crime in a Free Society, op. cit.*
4. Siegel, Arthur I., and Baker, Roy C.: *Police-Human Relations Training*, pp. 79–84. Wayne, Pa.: Applied Psychological Services, 1960. See also Siegel, Arthur I.; Tederman, Philip; and Schultz,

Douglas: *Professional Police Human Relations Training.* Springfield, Ill., Charles C Thomas, 1963.

5. Cumming, Elaine; Cumming, Ian; and Edell, Laura: "Policeman as Philosopher, Guide and Friend." *Social Problems,* 12:276–286, Winter 1965.

6. Rowan, Joseph R.: Personal communication.

7. Varner, Van: "We Want Safe Streets Now!" *Guideposts,* September 1966, pp. 24–27.

8. Ennis, Phillip H.: "Crime Victims, and the Police." *Trans-Action,* June 1967, pp. 39–40.

9. Cahn, Edmond: "The Meaning of Justice." In *Confronting Injustice: The Edmond Cahn Reader.* Boston: Little, Brown and Co., 1966.

10. McAtee, Charles D.: "An Overview of the Administration of Criminal Justice in Kansas." Report to Chairman of the Charitable, Benevolent, and Penal Institutions Committee of the Legislative Research Council, State of Kansas, September 20, 1966, p. 8.

ADDITIONAL PUBLICATIONS

OF MERIT AND RELEVANCE

RECOMMENDED BY THE AUTHOR

Allen, Richard C.; Ferster, Elyce Zenoff; and Rubin, Jesse G., eds. *Readings in Law and Psychiatry*. Baltimore, Md.: Johns Hopkins Press, 1968.

American Correctional Association. *Proceedings of the 97th Congress of Correction*. Washington, D.C.: American Correctional Association, 1967. (Also previous volumes.)

Amos, William E.; Manella, Raymond; and Southwell, Marilyn A. *Action Programs for Delinquency Prevention*. Springfield, Ill.: Charles C Thomas, 1965.

Amos, William E., and Manell, R. L., eds. *Readings in the Administration of Institutions for Delinquent Youth*. Springfield, Ill.: Charles C Thomas, 1965.

Arendt, Hannah. *Eichmann in Jerusalem*. New York: The Viking Press, 1963.

Barth, Karl. *Deliverance to the Captives*. New York: Harper & Row, 1961.

Bird, Otto A. *The Idea of Justice*. New York: Frederick A. Praeger, 1967.

Blumberg, Abraham S. *Criminal Justice*. Chicago: Quadrangle Books, 1967.

Bond, Raymond T. *Handbook for Poisoners*. New York: Collier Books, 1962.

Bromberg, Walter. *Crime and the Mind*. New York: Funk & Wagnalls, 1968.

Brown, Wenzell. *Women Who Died in the Chair*. New York: Collier Books, 1963.

Cardozo, Benjamin N. *The Nature of the Judicial Process*. New Haven, Conn.: Yale University Press, 1921.

293

Christiansen, K. O., *et al.*, eds. *Scandinavian Studies in Criminology*, Vol. 1. London: Tavistock Publications, 1965.

Clegg, Reed K. *Probation and Parole*. Springfield, Ill.: Charles C Thomas, 1964.

Committee on Homosexual Offenses and Prostitution. *The Wolfenden Report*. New York: Stein & Day, 1963.

Cook, Fred J. *The Secret Rulers*. New York: Duell, Sloan & Pearce, 1966.

Cross, James. *To Hell for Half-a-Crown*. New York: Random House, 1967.

Curran, William J. *Law and Medicine*. Boston: Little, Brown, 1960.

Dearman, H. B. *Not the Critic*. Kingsport, Tenn.: House of Wingate, 1965.

Duffy, Gladys. *Warden's Wife*. New York: Appleton-Century-Crofts, 1959.

Edwards, George. *The Police on the Urban Frontier*. New York: Institute of Human Relations Press, 1968.

Fontana, Vincent J. *The Maltreated Child*. Springfield, Ill.: Charles C Thomas, 1964.

Ford, Gerald R., and Stiles, John R. *Portrait of the Assassin*. New York: Simon and Schuster, 1965.

Gellhorn, Walter. *Ombudsmen and Others: Citizen Protectors in Nine Countries*. Cambridge, Mass.: Harvard University Press, 1966.

Grant, Bruce; Demos, George C.; and Edwards, Willard, eds. *Guidance for Youth*. Springfield, Ill.: Charles C Thomas, 1967.

Hacker, Fredrick. *Versagt der Mensche oder die Gesellschaft? Probleme der modernen Kriminalpsychologie*. Vienna: Europa Verlag, 1964.

Harris, Richard. "Annals of Legislation: If You Love Your Guns." *The New Yorker*, April 20, 1968.

Hart, H. L. A. *Punishment and Responsibility: Essays in the Philosophy of Law*. London: Oxford University Press, 1968.

Henry, Andrew F., and Short, James F., Jr. *Suicide and Homicide*. New York: Free Press, 1964.

Hersey, John. *The Algiers Motel Incident*. New York: Alfred A. Knopf, 1968.

Hibbert, Christopher. *The Roots of Evil*. Boston: Little, Brown, 1963.

Kafka, Franz. *The Penal Colony*, Willa and Edwin Muir, tr. New York: Schocken Books, 1948.

Kenney, John P., and Pursuit, Dan G. *Police Work with Juveniles,* Ed. 3. Springfield, Ill.: Charles C Thomas, 1965.

Leopold, Nathan F. *Life Plus 99 Years.* New York: Doubleday, 1958.

Levi, Primo. *Survival in Auschwitz.* New York: Collier Books, 1961.

Lorenz, Konrad. *On Aggression,* Marjorie Wilson, tr. New York: Harcourt, Brace & World, 1966.

Lunden, Walter A. *The Prison Warden and the Custodial Staff.* Springfield, Ill.: Charles C Thomas, 1965.

Marshall, James. *Intention in Law and Society.* New York: Funk & Wagnalls, 1968.

Marshall, James. *Law and Psychology in Conflict.* New York: Bobbs-Merrill, 1966.

Masur, Harold Q. *The Legacy Lenders.* New York: Random House, 1967.

Men in Jail: A Study of the Minor Offender in Cook County Jail. Chicago, Ill.: Loyola University, 1965.

Norman, Charles. *The Genteel Murderer.* New York: Collier Books, 1962.

Oberholzer, Emil, Jr. *Delinquent Saints.* New York: Columbia University Press, 1956.

Ostermann, Robert. *A Report in Depth on Crime in America.* Silver Spring, Md.: The National Observer, 1966.

Phillips, George Lewis. *American Chimney Sweeps.* Trenton, N.J.: Past Times Press, 1957.

President's Commission on Law Enforcement and Administration of Justice. Task Force Reports: *The Police; The Courts; Corrections; Juvenile Delinquency and Youth Crime; Organized Crime; Science and Technology; Assessment of Crime; Narcotics and Drugs; Drunkenness.* Washington, D.C.: U.S. Government Printing Office, 1967.

———. Research Studies: Field Surveys I: *Report on a Pilot Study in the District of Columbia on Victimization and Attitudes Toward Law Enforcement;* Field Surveys II: *Criminal Victimization in the United States;* Field Surveys III: *Studies in Crime and Law Enforcement in Major Metropolitan Areas,* 2 Vols.; Field Survey IV: *The Police and the Community,* Vol. 1; Field Survey V: *National Survey of Police and Community Relations.* Washington, D.C.: U.S. Government Printing Office, 1967.

———. *National Symposium on Science and Criminal Justice.* Washington, D.C.: U.S. Government Printing Office, 1967.

Radin, Edward D. *The Innocents.* New York: William Morrow, 1964.

Ray, Isaac. *A Treatise on the Medical Jurisprudence of Insanity,* Winfred Overholser, ed. Cambridge, Mass.: Harvard University Press, 1962.

Shoolbred, C. F. *The Administration of Criminal Justice in England and Wales.* New York: Pergamon Press, 1966.

Slavson, S. R. *Reclaiming the Delinquent by Para-Analytic Group Psychotherapy and the Inversion Technique.* New York: Free Press, 1965.

Tait, C. Downing, Jr., and Hodges, Emory F., Jr. *Delinquents, Their Families and the Community.* Springfield, Ill.: Charles C Thomas, 1962.

Tompkins, Dorothy C. *Bail in the United States: A Bibliography.* Berkeley, Calif.: Institute of Governmental Studies, 1964.

———. *The Confession Issue—From McNabb to Miranda: A Bibliography.* Berkeley, Calif.: Institute of Government Studies, 1968.

———. *Juvenile Gangs and Street Groups: A Bibliography.* Berkeley, Calif.: Institute of Governmental Studies, 1966.

———. *The Offender—a Bibliography.* Berkeley, Calif.: Institute of Governmental Studies, 1963.

———. *White Collar Crime: A Bibliography.* Berkeley, Calif.: Institute of Governmental Studies, 1967.

U.S. National Advisory Commission on Civil Disorders. *Report.* New York: Bantam Books, 1968.

University of Chicago Law Review, The, Vol. 22, No. 2, Winter 1955.

Vedder, Clyde B. *Juvenile Offenders.* Springfield, Ill.: Charles C Thomas, 1963.

Wertham, Frederic. *A Sign for Cain.* New York: Macmillan, 1966.

Index